TIMBER
FIRE IN THE PINES

A.L. SANDERSON

Design by: Vince Pannullo
Print by: RJ Communication.

Printed in the United States of America

ISBN:978-0-9884253-0-9

PROLOGUE

THE NORTH ATLANTIC
MARCH 1883

EYES narrowed, he looked up at the sky. He could not tell what time it was because the sun was hidden behind layers of thick, roiling black clouds. It had to be barely past noon, but the growing darkness made it appear that night was fast approaching. He looked out at the heaving of the green-black ocean, no longer gently rolling. The dips were deepening and the rises were beginning to form crests that rolled over and fell, gaining steadily in intensity. The waves began to grow larger and larger, feeding upon their own force. The water, which had earlier lapped gently at the sides of the wooden ship, was now crashing against it, sending a cold, salty spray into his face and sheets of water and small fish up and over his feet.

"I am frightened." The girl standing beside him looked up at him, her eyes pleading, her hands clinging desperately to the rail.

He pulled his eyes away from the menacing sea and glanced down at her. Just then a wave washed onto the ship and knocked him off balance. He grabbed her, not so much to save her as to do what he did instinctively—the right thing. It took all of his strength to keep them both upright. "Go below," he ordered angrily.

His eyes traveled over the ominous black of sky and water, wanting only for the girl to leave him alone. She had attached herself to him the day they left port. At first her parents kept calling her back to them, but they had become seasick and were barely able to care for themselves, much less ride herd on a stubborn sixteen-year-old.

"Go below with the others!" He was losing patience with her.

"Are you coming?" she asked stubbornly, eyes darting from him to the hatch leading below and then back again.

"No. I will not, but you must." He put his hand on her shoulder and said, somewhat more gently, "Go to your parents. They will be worried about you."

She reached up and touched the spot where his hand had been, but then quickly grabbed the rail again. "They are too sick to worry about me. Come with me. We can sit together."

He didn't bother to answer, but instead looked out across the angry water, his brow furrowed. At home, they had always gone to the root cellar during a bad storm. Here, on this ship, he would not go to the cellar.

"They will come and make you go below with the rest of us," she called to him over the wind as she reluctantly backed unsteadily away from him.

"Go!" he ordered harshly, jabbing a finger toward the hatch.

He couldn't blame her for not wanting to go below. He remembered all too well the first night at sea. He had gone down there with the rest of the passengers, and the hatch had been bolted down tight so no one could go on deck during the night. "For your own safety," the second mate had told him when he protested. He had lain awake on his narrow berth throughout the night, listening to the groans of sick women and children. There was no light and little air, and he heard the retching and smelled the vomit until he nearly vomited himself from the stench.

The next night when the second mate began herding people into the hold, he hid in a dinghy. Far better, he thought, to drown in the ocean than to die in the fetid bowels of a ship with far too little space for its human cargo. He spent that night curled up in the dinghy, breathing the fresh salt air and looking up in awe at the vast, star-filled sky. At home the sky stretched only as far as the next patch of forestland, and he became aware for the first time of the immensity of the world outside of Dalarna.

The second mate had seen him climb out of the dinghy the next morning and had immediately gone to report it to the ship's captain. "That one over there," he said, pointing to the tall youth who leaned casually against the rail watching the crew with narrowed eyes and suspicious curiosity, "slept in one of the dinghies. He thinks he doesn't have to go below with the rest of them. Thinks he can do as he damn pleases."

The captain looked at the tall Nordic youth for a long time, and their eyes finally met and challenged each other across the distance of half the length of the ship. Something about the boy struck him. The captain had been carrying emigrants from Sweden to North America for nearly ten years, and in all that time he had not met one who projected such a sense of repressed power. Despite the boy's obvious youth, something dangerous smoldered just beneath the surface of his startlingly handsome face.

"Let him be," the captain ordered, waving the first mate away with an impatient toss of his hand. He watched his rebellious passenger, who was no longer paying any attention to the captain, but was watching several of the other passengers hanging over the rail, their faces greenish-white, spewing vomit alongside the ship. The captain could see that the boy was clearly untroubled by the ship's motion.

The captain was right. He was not bothered by it. Neither the gentle roll of the waves nor the robust heaving of the swells affected him. He stood, legs spread like a seasoned sailor, unperturbed by the sea but curious about the men in charge of the vessel that bore him across it. His eyes followed the sailors into the rigging, and when the captain stopped watching him, his eyes turned back to the captain. He watched the captain as he paced along the gangway, his eyes turning back to Thor every now and again, as curious about the boy as the boy was about him.

This one's different, the captain thought to himself. *He's not like the rest of them. They're nothing but land worshiping, stupid fools, content only when they're anchored to the land by a plow. Brainless. Spineless. Tell them to go below and they go. Like sheep. Mud and manure is all they know. But this boy is no sheep.*

Again the captain was right about him. Thor Nilsson was neither awed nor frightened by the strange world of the ship, nor the captain and crew who ruled that world, as were most of the other passengers. The Swedish emigrants aboard Captain Lorenzo Smyth's ship had known hunger and deprivation enough to drive them from their homeland; but they had never experienced anything like the agonizing misery the ocean brought them. They were made sick as much from the motion as from the fear they felt of surroundings about which they knew nothing.

Ever since that second night, Thor had spent his nights sleeping under the canvas in one of the dinghies or curled up in a coil of rigging. It did not occur to him to wonder why the captain and crew acquiesced to his comings and goings aboard ship; he only knew they'd have to put him in chains to get him into the hell below deck.

He glanced behind him to make certain the girl had gone below, then turned his attention to riding out the storm.

"Bring 'er up!" he heard the captain shout through the wind. He squinted toward the bridge, the rain obscuring his sight, barely able to make out the shape of the captain. He inched sideways along the rail until he was close enough to see and hear what was going on. The captain's feet were spread wide on the slippery quarterdeck, and his craggy weathered face was lifted upward toward the sails, oblivious to everything but the safety of his ship.

"Enough! Enough! Bear off! She's too high to windward!"

"Aye, Captain!" The helmsman shouted as he struggled with the wheel, he and the ship locked in a wild watery dance as the now gale-force winds shifted erratically.

For the next hour, Thor clung to the rail and watched the crew struggle to keep the ship headed into the fifteen-foot waves. The furious salt spray stung his face and he raised an elbow and lowered his face to it, swiping it against the coarse wool of his jacket, the taste of salt strong on his lips. He barely heard the voice of the second mate, inching toward him along the slippery, slimy deck, clinging to the rail and fighting the wind that whipped his rain-slicked oilskins.

"Get below, you fool!" the mate shouted, his voice carried off by the roar of wind and ocean.

Thor gripped the rail tighter and glared at him without moving, his ear tuned to the wooden sounds of the old ship creaking and groaning in protest to the storm that engulfed it.

"Drown if you want to, you dumb bastard," the mate mumbled as he fought his way back toward the forward hatch. "If you won't go below with the rest of 'em then be damned!" He had done all he could; now he was done with it. If the fool went to a watery grave it would be on the captain's shoulders. Remembering his captain's orders to leave this one alone, the second mate focused on getting himself safely below, heedless now to the danger to his stubborn passenger.

Just then the ship lurched and changed the downward slope of the deck to an upward slope. Thor lost hold of the rail and slid crazily backward until his back slammed against the wooden hatch, knocking the wind out of him. He tried to get to his knees, but the ship heaved again and he was thrown against the rail as a wave rolled over the ship and threatened to take him with it over the side and into the raging water. Somehow he groped his way along the rail until he managed to grab hold of the mizzen shrouds and hoist himself into a dinghy. He felt around in the dark for the coil of rope he had hidden beneath one of the seats and tied himself in.

He looked up suspiciously at the tall mizzenmast, wondering if it could withstand the violent pounding that it was taking. He had been told by one of the crew that the masts were made of white pine; pine taken from the forests of North America. This same pine would either drag him into the depths of the ocean or would carry him safely to America; and if he got to America, the white pine would make him a rich man.

Thor Nilsson was only sixteen years old, but he had grown strong and sinewy from laboring in the fir forests of his homeland. His parents had indentured him to one of the wealthy villagers who owned a large tract of forestland. Because she soon saw that he was no ordinary boy, the man's wife took to him. His cheerful willingness to work and to learn, and the way he never complained—no matter how long the days or how hard the labor—greatly impressed her. The woman thought him beautiful with his white-blonde hair and his pure, clear blue eyes. She had never had children of her own, and he filled the void that had so long hollowed her soul.

Every night when her husband fell asleep in his chair after supper she and Thor would sit together at the table in the glow of the lamplight. She taught him to read and to write and how to do sums. She read to him, and after a time he was able to read to her.

It was from her that he learned about the land toward which he now voyaged. She had shared letters from her brother, who had gone to America and now lived in a place called Michigan. He told of the stands of white pine that made the forests of Dalarna look puny by comparison, and of the money to be made by a hard-working woodsman.

Now, as he tested his lashings to be certain they were secure, he paradoxically sensed his freedom. He was helpless against the storm that raged all around him; but he was free. No one could force him to stay in Dalarna, and no one could force him to go below deck to gasp and to gag. If he was going to die this night he would remain free, in the open air, until the water took him. He curled up, rested his cheek against the rough planking of the dinghy, listened to the canvas beating against his makeshift bed, and after many hours, slept.

Toward morning he was startled awake by the shouts of sailors climbing overhead in the rigging. The storm was over. He swung himself out of the dinghy, springing to the deck like a lion from a tree. It was still dark. He reached into the dinghy and pulled out his rucksack and made his way aft. He took a long drink from his ration of fresh water, ate some dry, hard bread, some dried fish,

and one of the shriveled apples he had taken from the root cellar on his grandfather's farm. Then he stood watching the night die and the rim of the sun emerge
golden against the clear, steel-blue sky.

Suddenly he was filled with the memory of a young girl's face, ringed with a
halo of golden braids. Annika. He felt a knot forming in his throat. He inhaled
the smell of the ocean and then let out a rush of air from his lungs, as if to purge
himself. He closed his eyes tight and shook his head, shaking her image loose
from his vision; trying to dispel the hurt that had enveloped him so often since
she told him she was going to marry Olaf Hanson.

Annika wanted land on which to raise many sons, and Olaf Hanson would
inherit much land from his father. He would be the one who would father her
sons. She would not marry Thor because he would inherit little. His grandfather
was still in control of the family farm; too stubborn to admit it was time to let
go. When he was gone, Thor's father and his father's five siblings would share
the land. When it was finally left to Thor and his own siblings and his cousins,
the parcels would be so small as to be virtually non-existent.

He had loved Annika since they were children playing along the edge of the
forest as they tended their family's cattle in the high pastures. They were together
every summer until he was old enough to be sent to the forests; but even then
he found a way to see her often. It was in the high pastures that they had lain
together amid the wild flowers and shared their first love.

He felt the pain well up inside, pain that sometimes gnawed at him and
sometimes tore at him. The pain had seldom left him since that awful day; the
day Annika could no longer look into his eyes. Instead, she had looked away
from him and down at the deep grass, flattened by their bodies where they had
lain only moments before. She told him it was over between them forever, and
that it would be Olaf Hanson who would share her marriage bed.

Remembering, he turned and slammed his fist into the rough boards of the
bulkhead, barely feeling the pain in the torn skin of his knuckles. "No more!"
He raised his arm toward the east, making a fist that turned his knuckles white
beneath the red blood trickling from them. "No more! I am done with this
hurting!"

Then, his face set in steely determination, he made a solemn oath to
Annika—and to himself. "I will be back. I will be back and I will no longer be
the poor wretch you spurned so easily. I will be very rich. Rich enough to buy
land and take a wife. Someone younger and more beautiful even than you! You

will be sorry, my once beloved, and it is *your* heart that will be empty of everything except pain. Make no mistake; you will pay for what you have done to me!"

Revenge! The thought of it filled him. He leaned back against the rough boards of the bulkhead, wrapped his bleeding knuckles with a handkerchief from his pocket and looked one last time in the direction of his homeland. He vowed he would never love again; never open himself up to the suffering he had endured because he loved Annika. Oh yes, he would marry. But for revenge—not for love. Never again *anything* for love.

Now he felt no pain, either physical or emotional; he felt instead a new thing. It was the satisfying, succoring promise of sweet revenge. He turned and walked to the lee side of the ship, placed his hands on the rail and turned toward the strange land called America.

His eyes had always been soft and gentle, like the blue Swedish sky on a summer's day. But as he stared now toward the western horizon they grew deep and dark and cold; as deep and dark and cold as the black frozen waters of an arctic fjord.

CHAPTER 1

Late Winter 1893

SARAH pulled the lap robe closer around her, trying with little success to shut out the cold dampness that penetrated through to her skin. It was not raining, but the air was heavy enough with moisture to make even the warmest clothing uncomfortable.

"Why did Uncle send you to bring me home?" It was the third time she had asked the old man the same question. Just as before, he grunted but did not answer.

She gave an impatient sigh and leaned forward to look out at a small house nestled in a clump of trees beside the road. The windows were dark and unseeing, and she had the desolate, lonely feeling that comes of being abroad in the black night while most people lie sleeping contentedly in their warm beds. A dim light approached them and a carriage passed from the other direction and she turned her head and watched it as it drove off into the night. She was sure they at least knew the purpose of their nocturnal journey, and she wished she knew the purpose of hers.

When they finally entered the outskirts of Boston an hour later, a lighted window relieved the darkness now and then but did nothing to lift her spirits. She remained silent, listening to the horses' hoof beats on the cobblestones. Finally she looked again at the old man, this time determined to get an answer from him.

"You must know why Uncle has sent for me. I insist that you tell me." She struggled to keep the anger from her voice.

He glanced sideways at her and spoke in his halting, stuttering manner. "I...I'm sorry, Miss Sarah. I ain't heard much." He paused for a moment, and then continued. "All I...the only thing I know is that...that Mr. Stewart told Mrs. Stewart to let the servants go—except me and Katie. Guess they still...still got to eat and still need somebody to see they get where they're going and such...

such as that." He sat more erect, as though being one of the last two remaining servants in the Stewart household lent him some stature. "That's all...all I know," he added, in a tone that told Sarah she'd get nothing more out of him.

It didn't surprise her. The servants treated her no better than the family did—as though she didn't deserve their attention. The only exception was Katie, the Stewart's cook. It was from Katie that she had gotten the only affection she ever received in William Stewart's household.

She sat back and closed her eyes, trying not to think; but she was unable to keep the dread thought of being once again in her uncle's house from intruding upon her. She dreaded it even more knowing that something must be terribly wrong or her uncle wouldn't have dispatched Toby to bring her home so near the end of the school year.

The carriage finally pulled up in front of her uncle's house and Toby climbed down and walked around the carriage to help her down. He moved slowly, his bones stiff from the long ride and the damp night air. She ignored his offer of help and climbed down unassisted.

"Don't be angry with old Toby, Miss Sarah," he begged, fearful she might tell her uncle he wasn't doing his job.

Even in the darkness, she could see the fear in his rheumy eyes. It seemed everyone was afraid of her uncle's wrath. "I'm not angry with you Toby," she said sincerely, sorry that she had upset the poor old man. None of this was his fault, and there was no need for her to take out her anger on a helpless old man who should not be required to drive through the night doing her uncle's bidding. The poor old fellow deserved to be asleep next to his wife. She reached out and put her hand on his arm. "Good night, Toby. Go home and get some rest. I'll tell Uncle you won't be in until late tomorrow."

"Oh...oh no!" he said quickly, shaking his head violently back and forth. "That would n...never do. Mister Stewart wouldn't like that. I'll b...be back f...first thing in the morning in case...in case somebody needs me."

She waved her hand at him wearily. "Oh alright, Toby. Go along and get some rest."

He climbed back up onto the carriage with a great effort and she reached out a hand to help him but quickly drew it back. He flicked the reins wearily and she watched him drive around toward the carriage house to take care of the horses. She knew it would be a long time before he put her luggage inside the back door and then walked the long mile to his own little house to sleep.

She turned, sighed deeply, and reluctantly faced the tall black iron gate and stared up the long walkway. She reached up and pulled the gate open, its hinges creaking eerily into the darkness. She wrinkled her forehead, puzzled that no one had oiled the gate hinges.

Her uncle was fanatic about such things. After all, what would people think when they came to call? Uncle was always greatly concerned about appearances; about the image he presented to the world. Both he and his gate hinges always operated smoothly. Then she remembered that Toby had said most of the servants had been let go. For the first time she began to feel concerned rather than annoyed.

There were no lights on in the house to soften its dreary facade. She hated the house, with its tall turret on the northeast corner reaching toward the heavens like an accusing finger. Her aunt and uncle had the house designed and built in a style they spoke of as "majestic." Sarah saw nothing majestic about it; to her it was just plain big and ugly. She vowed that when she was old enough to leave her uncle's house for good she would never again live in a place she hated.

As she climbed the front steps she felt a cold shudder. *Home.* It was the only home she had ever known. Boarding school was not home either. It was simply somewhere to pass the time while she waited for her eighteenth birthday, now less than a year away. She wished with all her heart that she was still back there and not here in this awful place. She knew that in less than a year she would receive her inheritance and would then be free to marry her fiancé, Steven. But a year seemed a very long time to her just then—especially a year spent in this house. An intense loathing clutched at her as she reached for the door latch, and she hoped she could find the strength to remain in her uncle's house until she was free to leave once and for all and forever.

As she expected, no one was there to greet her, or to explain why her uncle had dispatched the carriage to bring her home from school. She stood for a moment, letting her eyes grow accustomed to the darkness of the entrance hall. It, and the rest of the house, was furnished with heavy carved mahogany and plush furniture. The gleaming polished floors were adorned with lavish oriental rugs. Every flat surface was carefully arranged to show off expensive pieces of porcelain, silver or crystal. She hated it all. She hated every last piece of bric-a-brac in her uncle's house. She did not see beauty in any of it.

Appearances. The way he furnished his home and dressed his wife and daughter were part of a lavish show, carefully designed to keep up appearances so he would someday be accepted into Boston society, along with his money. Sarah knew that underneath his smooth and proper exterior lay a cold indifference to everything and everyone except his desire to achieve status and wealth.

She took a deep breath, trying to steel herself. Then, with a grimace, she climbed the wide winding stairway to her room and went inside, closing the door behind her.

The room smelled of dampness, little more pleasant than the carriage had been. She knew no one had bothered to freshen up her room before her return. Not even Katie, who Sarah imagined now had far too much to do. She felt her way across the still-familiar room to the fireplace and groped along the mantle for matches. There were none. Her fingers were stiff from the cold, and she longed for the warmth of a fire to take the damp chill from the room. All at once she was overcome by a dull, aching fatigue. She quickly undressed and crawled into bed, pulling the clammy covers up around her shoulders, shivering so hard her teeth chattered.

Then, as she had done for as many years as she could remember whenever she was falling asleep, she thought of her parents. She pictured her mother's face, a picture formed in the imagination of a lonely child who had actually never seen the faces of either of her parents. She imagined her mother's soft hand on her forehead, soothing her gently, lulling her to sleep. In the picture, too, she saw her father, handsome and distinguished looking, smelling of tweed and expensive cigars and of bay rum. In her imagination he always stood next to and slightly behind her mother, watching lovingly as his wife tucked their daughter into bed. Her imaginings about her parents comforted her again, as they had for all the lonely nights of her childhood.

She thought of Steven and smiled to herself. Steven was real, not someone she had only imagined to fill her emptiness. Sometimes she was convinced her parents had a hand in sending him to her. But Sarah had a practical side, too, and whenever such thoughts entered her head a voice inside of her asked her to explain why that same parental—or divine—providence had left her orphaned to spend her childhood with an aunt and uncle who so obviously cared little for her. Soon, her head filled with a mixture of contentment, confusion and contradictions, she began to grow warm, and she finally fell into a deep, dreamless sleep.

She awoke suddenly while it was not yet light. Something had startled her and she sat bolt upright in bed, listening. The faint drone of voices somewhere far below her in the house broke the stillness. She slipped from her bed, fumbled her way to the wardrobe and put on her wrapper and slippers and then noiselessly found her way into the hall. Gripping the handrail, she followed along the upper hall, peering over the railing to the anteroom below. As she passed her Cousin Amelia's room she stopped a moment at the closed door and listened. She turned the knob and slowly opened it. She could hear her cousin's soft breathing and knew that she was asleep and she quietly closed the door again. The door to the library below was slightly ajar and the flicker of lamplight escaped through the narrow crack. She crept down the stairs and was nearly at the bottom when she could finally make out words. She crouched down on the steps and listened.

"Why don't you come to bed, William," she heard her aunt ask in her usual whining, slightly nasal voice. "Don't you want to sleep? Don't you think you could do something about this awful business if you were rested? *Please?*"

"Rest? Sleep? My God, you stupid woman! Don't you understand? I'm ruined! We're penniless. What in hell is *rest* going to do for me?"

"Please don't shout, William. You'll wake everyone in the house. Surely it's not as bad as all that. We only have to cut down expenses a bit, or we could sell some things, maybe some of the furniture and...."

Silence, then her aunt continued, "And there's always Sarah's money. I'm sure Lorna would want us to borrow some of it if we needed it badly enough. When you're on your feet again, we can pay it back."

"Sarah's money? Hah! That money's been gone for months. You don't think I'd let the money from her whore of a mother lie around when we needed it, do you?"

Even from her position on the stairs, Sarah could hear her aunt gasp, "Gone? What do you mean, *gone?*"

"We earned every penny of that money, letting that miserable brat live here all these years. Treating her like our own, giving her our name, keeping your sister's secret. She was a filthy whore and her money was as dirty as she was!" Then, after another moment of silence, "Don't look at me like that!"

Sarah had never heard her aunt disagree with her uncle in all the years she had lived in their house. Her aunt had never dared his wrath by defending herself, and certainly had never extended herself to spare Sarah his wrath. And now she was defending Sarah's mother; a mother who Sarah never had the slightest idea needed to be defended, much less defended against something so awful that the reality of it did not immediately penetrate her consciousness. All she could think of were the raised voices, and how the thought of being penniless seemed to have made something snap in her aunt's head.

Her aunt's voice had grown very loud but she did not sound in the least hysterical. It was as if a dam had broken and the words were forced out of her, filled with the pent-up power of being held back for such a long time.

"I have endured your insults about my sister for seventeen years. That *filthy* woman's *dirty* money was plenty good enough for you, wasn't it? You had absolutely no right! How could you! You're nothing but a thief!"

"How dare you speak to me like that!" her uncle shouted back at his wife. Sarah could imagine her Uncle's face growing red, as it always did when he was angry. Sometimes it got so red it looked like he was going to explode. "How dare you suggest I had no right to use that slut's money when we needed it!"

Sarah glanced up toward Amelia's door, wondering why the noise didn't wake her. There was silence for a long moment and then above the sudden ringing in her ears Sarah heard her Aunt Lettie's voice, firm and angry. It was the voice of a woman Sarah had lived with all her life but had never really known; a woman as strange as her very existence had suddenly become.

"You know as well as I do that Lorna sent us more than enough money to care for Sarah. And when she died, she left enough for Sarah to make her a wealthy woman. Now you're telling me it's gone? All of it?" She let out a groan of disgust and then said, her voice even more harsh and biting, "You're nothing but a thief. You're the filthy one! My sister took care of her child in the only way she knew how. And you've gone and ruined my poor niece's life."

Silence once more, then, "And you...you pig! You've ruined *your* child as well! She hasn't even a dowry! What is she supposed to do? What are *any* of us supposed to do?"

Her aunt's words rang in her ears, and the truth of what she was hearing began finally to penetrate. Her head reeling and her heart pounding, Sarah turned and ran up the stairs to her room, slammed the door behind her and leaned against it, the back of her hand pressed against her mouth to stifle the scream in her throat. Then, through the awfulness that threatened to engulf her, she heard the loud crack of a gunshot.

CHAPTER 2

WILLIAM Stewart was buried two days later; the wooden coffin closed to hide the remains of what had been his face. The library door was not opened again until William's older brother arrived, leaving the ugly mess drying on the carpet and the drapes behind the desk. No one had had the stomach to go into the library after the body had been removed.

John Stewart grimaced when he saw part of his brother splattered around the room, but he felt a grim kind of satisfaction that it was the last mess his younger brother would ever make.

William was born when John was eleven years old, and he seemed to always get into scrapes that his older brother had to get him out of. As a result, John had grown to thoroughly dislike his younger brother. What he felt now was annoyance at having to tidy up after him one more time; he felt no grief.

Lettie Stewart had somehow continued to manage the household after her husband shot himself, but she had grown silent and withdrawn. She spoke only when necessary and carried herself stiffly through her duties. When John arrived she slumped into helplessness and turned control of her life over to him. She had defied her husband only one time. He had then reached into his desk drawer, taken out a revolver, put it into his mouth and pulled the trigger. She vowed she would never again unleash the awesome power of her tongue. She would instead let her husband's brother take care of her however he would.

Amelia had grown silent, too. She considered sulking but realized it would do no good. No one seemed to care if she sulked—or to even notice—now that her doting father was gone. She went through the motions of being grieved, when in truth her strongest emotion was fury at what her father had done to her. Her one hope was that she could get her uncle into a position where he would indulge her as her father had done.

Her uncle, however, was merely annoyed with her. He and his wife had three sons and he knew nothing about girls. He admitted to himself, however, that she was pretty enough. He knew he could quickly arrange a suitable marriage and be rid of her. He thought in particular of a recently widowed friend of his. He was growing a paunch and his hair was thinning, but he had so much money that he wouldn't care if his pretty young bride was without means. Her ripe young body would easily make up for her being spoiled and petulant.

As far as his sister-in-law was concerned, in the back of his mind he expected that Lettie might be useful to his wife. After all, she had managed to run the household before the recent unfortunate events, hadn't she? And from the look of it, it had been an elegant and efficient household. His wife was good at ordering the servants about. He was convinced she would make good use of Lettie and her skills.

He had already decided he would not be responsible for Sarah. He felt no obligation to her whatever. He knew she had no recourse against the estate because he quickly learned that there was no legal documentation regarding Sarah's money. While going through his brother's papers, he had found the only evidence that existed; a personal letter from Sarah's mother saying she trusted William to take care of Sarah's inheritance until she was eighteen. She wanted him to put it into his bank and let it draw interest. John shook his head as he read the letter, amazed that a woman who had been able to amass a fortune using women to get money from men had been so naive about people. But it was she who made the mistake of trusting William; it wasn't John's problem. As soon as he read the letter he destroyed it. That was the end of the Stewarts' obligation to the girl. Besides, she was engaged. Let her fiancée take care of her.

Sarah was too numb to notice or to care what John Stewart was doing—or intended to do—about their lives. She felt nothing. She moved about mechanically doing what was expected of her, wearing the dark mourning clothes that appeared in her wardrobe and standing mute whenever any one of a string of mourning visitors spoke words of comfort to her. "Poor child," everyone who attended the funeral said of her. "She must have loved her uncle very much. She looks completely lost."

Sarah's fiancée arrived the day of the funeral. Steven Caldwell was training with his father, planning to one day take over the family medical practice. The Caldwells were not wealthy, but their family was one of the oldest in Boston's Back Bay.

William Stewart had hoped for just such a marriage for his daughter, Amelia, but Steven had chosen Sarah. It had given the Stewart's one more reason to resent Sarah. They were, however, too concerned about making an impression with Steven's family to risk letting him know their true feelings. Appearances. Being related to the Caldwells would be very good for business and for their social position. They tried hard to ignore the fact that the relationship was through their niece and not through their pampered and adored daughter.

After the funeral, when the guests had gone from the Stewart house, except Steven and John, they all sat together in the darkened parlor. The room smelled of dampness and roses and death, but no one seemed to feel the need for light and air. Amelia and Lettie were sitting quietly listening to John Stewart, in his tedious and pedantic manner, giving instructions about packing up and coming to New York to live with him and his family. He seemed to deliberately exclude Sarah from his plans, but no one—even Sarah—seemed to notice or to care.

When he began to talk about how the house and all of its contents were to be sold and the money used to pay creditors, Steven Caldwell grew uncomfortable. He felt it most inappropriate for him to hear of the family's misfortune. He had heard the rumors, as everyone had. He knew that up to several months ago William Stewart had been a respected banker. However, the recent hard times had caused many of his best clients to lose money. He was forced to call loans on men who couldn't pay them and in a rapid series of bad events, his bank failed. Rumor had it that it was his own wife who placed the last straw upon his unfortunate back. But no one spoke of what that straw had been.

Listening to John Stewart now, Steven knew he would probably be able to marry Sarah sooner than he had expected. He knew, however, that it would be improper to broach the subject to Lettie Stewart or her brother-in-law at such a delicate time.

He turned to Sarah. Her eyes seemed clouded over, blind and unaware even of him. He rose from his chair and walked over to her and leaned down, speaking quietly into her ear. "Walk with me. We must talk."

She stared vacantly at him without speaking.

"Come along, Sarah," he said softly, taking her hand and pulling her from the chair. No one paid any attention to them, engrossed as they were in John's lecture about preparations to leave Boston. That is except Amelia, whose eyes narrowed as she watched the couple leave the room.

He put on his coat and placed her black cloak gently around her shoulders. She seemed slightly dazed, willing to let him guide her through the movements he required of her. He led her through the kitchen and out the back door to the path leading to the rose arbor.

Katie watched them as they passed through her kitchen, and then continued with her supper preparations. "Poor child," she muttered under her breath, shaking her head slowly from side to side. "Poor child. Thank God for Steven." She raised her eyes heavenward and crossed herself.

The late-winter garden looked cold and bleak, filled only with the dead remains of a summer long past. There was still no sign of spring; no sign that summer would ever come again. When they reached the rose arbor and stood with dead branches climbing all around them, Sarah reached up numbly to touch a dead, dried rose. She stared blankly as a drop of bright red blood appeared on the tip of her finger. Her eyes registered neither pain nor surprise, and Steven put her finger to his mouth and sucked the blood from it. Then he pulled her against him and wrapped his arms gently around her as he made soothing noises against her hair. She felt as limp as a rag doll in his arms; not soft and yielding as she had been at Christmas time when he proposed to her and they had made furtive love in an attic room in his parents' house.

Sarah had emerged from that room vowing never to let it happen again until after they were married. She had felt somehow soiled, and now the mildly unpleasant and physically painful event had taken on an even more unpleasant meaning for her.

"Sarah, please don't turn away from me. I'm here to help. I know how much you're hurting, but...."

She pulled slightly away and looked up at him as if realizing for the first time where she was. Her face suddenly took on a pained expression. How was she going to tell him? What would she do if he didn't understand? But surely he would understand. Hadn't they vowed to love each other forever? Hadn't they promised each other that as soon as she was eighteen they would marry? Hadn't she given herself to him based upon that promise? She had to trust him and his love for her. It was all she had left.

"Steven," she said, "there's something...something I must tell you...."

He seemed not to be listening. He pulled her back against him, his cheek against the top of her head, her breath warm against his neck. "Let's get married right away. My parents were hoping for a long engagement, but they'll understand. I'll make them understand. Please, Sarah. There's nothing to make you stay with your aunt and your cousin. John Stewart will see to them, and I can't bear having him tell you what to do with...." He stopped speaking, knowing it would be tactless to discuss her inheritance at a time like this.

Just then they heard a footfall on the paving stones and they turned and saw Amelia coming toward them. When she was within a few feet she stopped short and stood, her eyes contemptuous of their embrace, her pretty face distorted, her mouth twisted into a sneer.

"My oh my, isn't this cozy?" she spat at Sarah. "You'd think you could at least let my poor father cool in his grave before you started behaving like your whore of a mother!"

Steven looked at Amelia in horror. "Don't take it out on Sarah just because you're suffering over the loss of your father!" He wondered if Sarah had told her cousin about their lovemaking.

"Suffering? Yes. I'm suffering. And so is Mummy. And it's all Sarah's fault."

"Your father shot himself!" Steven protested. "How on earth can you blame Sarah for that?"

She glared at Sarah and said, "You haven't told him, have you?"

Sarah was silent, but Steven said, "Told me what? What are you talking about, Amelia?" He looked at Sarah, his eyes filled with apprehension. "What is it you have to tell me, Sarah? What is she talking about?"

"I...." Sarah seemed unable to speak, and her silence seemed to goad Amelia into speaking with even more venom.

"I'll tell you what I'm talking about," Amelia spat.

Sarah stood in dumb silence, not wanting to listen but unable to stop her cousin's words. In some awful, incomprehensible way she was fascinated by the story she had never heard; a story so far from what she had been led to believe that she almost felt as if she was dreaming. But she soon knew she wasn't dreaming. It was all becoming far too real.

"I've waited a long time to tell you this, Sarah," Amelia said through clenched teeth, her eyes blazing with cruel satisfaction, "but father made me swear to keep it to myself. Now it doesn't matter anymore. It's time you knew the truth."

Sarah looked at her cousin, not able even to feel the hatred she usually felt toward her. She began to feel light-headed and wondered vaguely if she was going to faint.

"Your whore of a mother got herself pregnant and your father wouldn't marry her."

Sarah stared dumbly at Amelia, wishing she could block out the sound of her cousin's voice, thinking dimly that if she fainted she wouldn't have to listen anymore.

"So she ran off with a man who was twenty years older than she was. He owned a saloon that catered to a certain kind of men. Your mother, whore that she was, took to it like a duck to water. She liked sleeping with a different stranger every night more than she liked taking care of her own child, so she sent you to us. The man died and she stayed where she was. She turned the saloon into a full-fledged bawdyhouse, and she sold it just before she died of some...some disgusting disease. That's where your so-called inheritance came from! That story about your parents being killed in a fire, and being so loving and caring and providing so well for you is nothing but balderdash! The only parent you had was a whore just like you!" Her chin was raised, her eyes glowing with cruel, triumphant satisfaction.

Steven was staring hard at Amelia, as if waiting for her to say something more. When she didn't, he asked, "So? So what? What has any of that got to do with your father shooting himself?"

Amelia appeared surprised by his question, and a mixture of emotions began to contort her features. Then her expression cleared and she said, calmly, "When Daddy's bank failed, Sarah's inheritance went with it and...."

"Are you saying he shot himself because Sarah's money was....?" He stopped speaking and stared at her, unable to say the word "gone." Then he continued, "I heard that it was because your mother...."

"My mother couldn't bear it when she heard Sarah's money was gone, too," Amelia said, half in truth, "and Daddy's heart was broken when he saw her like that so...so he...he did it."

Sarah's head was swimming, both from the awful truth of what she was hearing about her parents, the painful memory of her loose behavior with Steven, and from the way Amelia was twisting what had happened so that Sarah was a perpetrator instead of a victim. She looked at Steven, trying to figure out what to say to him to defend herself. But the look on his face stunned her and she couldn't find any words. She looked again at her cousin, wondering how Amelia had managed such an effective speech. Usually she merely chattered; but this time she had been convincing and sure of herself—like a prosecutor arguing that Sarah should be hanged for her crimes.

She looked back at Steven, stung further by the look in his eyes as he stared back at her. She opened her mouth to again try to speak, but no words came. She knew she had to explain, but how could she? The story about her parents must be true; her mother must indeed have been a whore, her father had been a scoundrel and had simply run away, and her uncle had shot himself because Lettie had accused him of stealing Sarah's money. Now her inheritance was gone, and she, herself, was soiled—just as her mother had been. It didn't occur to her that this was the man who had soiled her. All she knew was that the whole sordid mess was true. She no longer had the sweet imaginings about her parents to sustain her, her virginity was gone, and she was penniless.

Somehow, she was able to rouse herself enough to understand that the last fact—her inheritance being gone—was what mattered most to Steven. Now he would never marry her. She could see it on his face and she could feel it in the searing pain in her chest. She lifted the hem of her dress and turned and ran toward the house, her heart pounding. She stopped only once to look back, vaguely wondering if maybe none of it was true—or if somehow it had all been a bad dream.

But it was no dream. Amelia was looking innocently up at Steven, her hand resting on his arm. He seemed very interested in what she was saying.

"You fool!" Sarah said bitterly to herself, hating him. "*She* has no inheritance, either."

Then she turned and ran toward the house, leaving her cousin and her former fiancé standing together under the dead remains of last year's roses.

CHAPTER 3

S UNLIGHT poured through the stained-glass windows behind him as he ran his hands over the rich mahogany of the desk at which he sat. He felt content, satisfied with himself and with his station in life. Not proud, mind you, because "pride goeth before a fall;" but not quite humble, either. He was sure God would expect him to enjoy the fruits of his labors, and to be comfortable as he went about answering his divine calling.

The Reverend Duncan MacKenna was a wealthy man, and had done nothing so foolish as to make a vow of poverty when he answered his calling to serve God. Instead, he used his wealth for certain appurtenances of his status, such as the extra servants and the lavishness of his table and his wine cellar. But that, too, he knew God would approve. Those comforts did, after all, make him all the more able to be effective with his lambs.

On this particular Sunday morning he was feeling more than his usual appreciation of himself. He brushed a hand over his hair, satisfied with its rich fullness. He envisioned himself earlier that morning in the pulpit, his words filling the church with their power, his hand raised in admonition against those sinners who failed to seek salvation through him by their offerings to the church. In fact his sermon had so moved many of his parishioners that morning that many of them had been reduced to tears and the collection plates had overflowed.

He was absolutely certain that the pale and lovely young woman who had asked to see him after the service was eager to join his church and become one of his lambs. He had asked the housekeeper, a tall bony woman with a stern face and a pointed beak of a nose, to usher her to his office after the service. He sat waiting for her, hands folded on the desk, the light shining through the stained glass from behind and streaking the gray of his hair with rainbow colors. He did not rise to his feet when she entered, but only nodded as she nervously sat down across from him. Whenever he was in this kind of particularly pleasing mood, he preferred not to move around too much; movement always broke the spell.

The girl looked around the room without speaking. She seemed to be trying to get her bearings. It disappointed him that she looked more agitated than awed, and his fine mood began to dissipate. He cleared his throat and spoke. "What can I do for you, young lady?"

"I...." she began, then stopped, her eyes on him briefly, then again scanning the room.

"Yes? What is it?" She seemed unsure of herself, and he wondered what could be troubling her. He thought she was beautiful with her rich auburn hair and her dark eyes framed with thick black lashes. Her skin was fair for someone with such dark hair and eyes, but it suited her. It occurred to him that she was unaware of how beautiful she was. For the first time, he noticed that she was dressed in mourning. He decided not to speak to her about it; at least not until she had agreed to become a member of his congregation.

"I hoped...." She hesitated again.

He reached up and ran a finger inside the front of his collar and lifted his jaw and moved it back and forth several times. Something about her was making him uneasy, but he couldn't put his finger on what it was. His eyes fell to her throat, to the brooch she was wearing. "Please go on," he said, suddenly visibly agitated. He took a heavy gold watch from his pocket and looked at it, his brow furrowed as he looked back at her. "I do not have much time."

She leaned slightly toward him and began to speak. "I'm sorry to bother you, Sir. Reverend. Sir. It's just that...." She seemed to again lose her confidence, and she grew silent.

"Oh for Heaven's sake, girl, out with it." He stood up and began to pace the floor behind his desk. Maybe she seemed familiar to him because she reminded him of all the other sniveling females who were forever getting themselves into trouble and coming to him for answers. He much preferred the ones who were still innocent. He was becoming altogether sick of the ones who had been sleeping around. He made up his mind right then to allow the elders of the church to get an assistant pastor to take on some of the less-pleasant duties.

He would do the more rewarding tasks, such as preaching the word of God from the pulpit. Oh, he would still minister to the pretty young women who needed his advice and guidance to save them from the lecherous young males who were so prevalent in these decadent times; but he would choose the still-innocent ones. If they were used and with child, the new assistant pastor could deal with them.

Sarah watched him as he paced, feeling an immediate dislike for him. She wanted to get up and leave this pompous man; but she had come this far and she dared not leave until she had done what she came to do. "Do...do you have a brother? A brother named Doyle?"

It startled him and he stopped pacing. A muscle in his jaw began to twitch and he seemed to be struggling, as if his face was a clay mask and he feared it might crack. He turned quickly away from her so she couldn't see his face.

"Do you?" she asked again. "I must find him. Please. Can you help me?"

Her voice had grown very soft, pleading, and he turned back to look at her, composed once again. "What would you be wanting with my brother?" he asked coldly.

She leaned back in her chair and sighed with relief. "Then he *is* your brother. I feared it might not be true."

"It's true, but I don't see what it has to do with me. I haven't seen my brother in...in I can't even remember how long." He was staring at her as he spoke, studying her features.

"Do you know where he is?" She asked hopefully.

"I don't see that it's any of your business where my brother is," he answered, turning away from her again and staring up at the stained glass window. He rubbed one hand on the back of his neck and turned his head slowly from side to side, trying to work out the soreness that was settling there.

She was silent for a long moment and when she spoke, she spoke so softly he could barely hear her words. "But it *is* my business. You see, Doyle MacKenna is my father."

He was still turned away from her and his back stiffened. She waited, determined not to let him intimidate her just because he was an important man in the church. To her he was nothing but her father's brother and all she wanted from him was information. Having met him, she knew she'd be lucky to get that. If some small part of her had expected anything more from him—such as perhaps shelter or financial help—she now knew better.

"What are you talking about?" he said aloud, finally turning back to look down at her. "My brother had no children."

"*Had? Had* no children?" She stood up suddenly, "Is he...." She dared not even say the word.

"Dead? I have no idea whether he's dead or alive and I honestly cannot say that I care."

She stared at him. What could be wrong with her father that his own brother cared so little about him? Then she caught herself. She knew nothing about her father; but she had spent five minutes alone with Duncan MacKenna and knew at least something about *him*. It wouldn't surprise her to learn that he cared nothing about anyone but himself. She looked slowly around the room. His eyes followed hers but he did not speak. She walked across the room to where an elaborate French porcelain vase stood on a delicate three-legged table. She ran her hand over it, remembering her uncle and his concern with appearances and his almost manic accumulation of "objects." She looked across the room and met Duncan's eyes. They stood without moving, looking at each other. He cleared his throat and it was he who finally broke eye contact. She took her hand from the porcelain vase and returned and sat down. She suddenly felt very tired.

"How did you find me?" he asked.

She didn't want to tell him. She was sick to death of thinking about the events of the past few weeks, and she surely did not want to talk about them. It had been her uncle's attorney who told her who her father was. She had asked him what she was supposed to do without a place to live and without money.

"Go live with John Stewart," he had suggested impassively.

"I will not. I have already lived far too long with the Stewarts," she had answered.

It was then that he suggested she go to her father's brother. She listened with surprise when he spoke of her father, who had come from a wealthy family, and of his twin brother, who was the pastor of a large church. It had given her hope and she felt she had someone to turn to for help after all. Now *that* hope was gone, along with everything else.

"It really doesn't matter how I found you," she said wearily. "I want nothing from you except for you to tell me where I can find my father."

He began again to rub his neck. Then it struck him and he fell into his chair, unwelcome memories flooding him as he looked at her. He knew now what was making him so uneasy; the girl looked exactly like his mother had looked when she was young, and the brooch she was wearing had been his mother's.

"I have no idea," he said, his voice cracking, no longer able to deny the reality of who she was. She must indeed be his brother's child. Doyle! Good Lord, could this really be happening? Was he really being forced to revisit a chapter in his life that he had closed the door upon long ago? But he could not push down the remembering, no matter how hard he tried.

His twin brother, Doyle, had been their mother's favorite, and Duncan had been their father's. On the surface. Duncan had been the obedient, studious one; Doyle had been the wild one who reminded his father of himself in his own youth. They looked so much alike that few people could tell them apart. When they were very young they had played tricks on people, each pretending to be the other. As they grew older, Duncan began to get into some minor scrapes, and he would lie and tell his father it had been Doyle. Doyle never revealed the truth but a slow hatred grew inside of him for his twin. As the years passed, Doyle came to resent his father, as well. He wanted his father to be able to see the truth without his having to tell him; the way their mother saw the truth. It finally drove a wedge between Doyle and his father.

When he was twenty, Doyle went West. After their mother died, he stopped writing. When their father became ill, Duncan wrote to his brother. Doyle wrote back saying that as far as he was concerned his father was already dead.

On his deathbed the old man had a change of heart and he made Duncan swear that he would find his brother and give him half of the considerable wealth he had accumulated during his lifetime. He did not want to face his maker with bitterness in his heart and he wanted Duncan to find his brother and make peace with him. Duncan promised that he would; but upon his father's death had immediately forgotten all about sharing any of his father's wealth with his brother, or contacting him in any way.

Duncan MacKenna regarded the young woman carefully. She was obviously the fruit of his brother's sinful loins. But what was she doing here after all these years? Did she think she was entitled to something from him?

"I'm sorry I can't help you," he said, seeming to regain control of himself as he sat, his fingertips poised cathedral-like under his slightly raised chin.

"Surely you must have some idea where I can find him. Can't you at least tell me that?"

His hands dropped to the desk in front of him, palms down, and he pushed himself slowly to his feet. "The last letter I got from him was more than five years ago. It was from Minnesota. Duluth, I think. Seems he was working for a logging company. Smitheson. Yes. The Smitheson Lumber Company. That was it." He walked to the door, his right hand on the door handle and his left hand hooked into his lapel. "I'm afraid I must say good day. I have many duties to perform and I have dallied long enough. The Devil finds work for idle hands to do."

Sarah stared at him, unbelieving. He had given her a small tidbit of information and now he was brushing her off like a pesky fly. She wanted to spit in his face but instead she turned and brushed past him and out the door without speaking. She was several steps down the hall when she stopped and turned and looked back at him. Her words were steady, measured, and not at all like those of the stammering girl who had first come into his office.

"I hope that when I find my father he is unlike you in every way. Don't bother to see me to the door. I can find my own way out of this house of God."

His eyes followed her dumbly as she strode the length of the hallway, her shoulders straight and her head held high. She pulled open the outer door, and without looking back again stepped out and slammed it shut behind her. He looked at the closed door, trying to fight down his growing discomfort. There was something coldly determined about her despite her initial nervousness, which she had quickly overcome. Would she find his brother? Would she urge him to return to claim his rightful share of their father's wealth?

"Damn you!" he shouted, his voice suddenly shaking and his hands trembling. "Damn you to hell, Doyle MacKenna!" As if it had been yesterday, he saw again the cold hatred in his brother's eyes; the same hatred he had just seen mirrored in the eyes of the young woman who was so clearly his brother's child.

CHAPTER 4

"**W**HAT does it say?" Katie was excited about the letter she had just handed to Sarah. It was postmarked Duluth, Minnesota, and maybe it would bring a smile to Sarah's sad face.

They were sitting across from each other in the tiny parlor of Katie's sister's house in a poor Boston neighborhood. They were poor people, but Brigitte and her husband had happily taken both Katie and Sarah into their home. Sarah was grateful, but she knew she could not stay; the house was barely big enough for two. Besides, this was Katie's family, not hers.

Family. What an awful word it had become for her. She had clung to her fantasy about her parents for as long as she could remember. Now her comfortable dream was shattered and she was left with the ugly truth that her mother had been a whore and her father had been so uncaring that he ran away to avoid responsibility for his own child. The only relatives she knew were her aunt and her cousin whom she hated, and now the horrid man who was her uncle and was no better than the rest of them. Worse, perhaps, because he hid behind a cleric's collar.

She did not understand why she even wanted to find her father. She already had a handful of useless, disgusting relatives who wanted nothing to do with her. Why go off seeking another one? Why open herself up to more hurt?

Why? Because she couldn't help herself. Even in her anguish over losing everything—including the man she thought had loved her—she clung to a faint glimmer of hope. Maybe her father was a good man after all. Maybe he had not known about her. Maybe her mother had kept her pregnancy a secret. If he had gone West to get away from a family whose members were anything like his brother, she wouldn't blame him. Maybe if she found him and told him who she was, maybe....

She tore open the envelope and read the words, her heart pounding, trying hard not to hope for too much. After she finished reading it, her hand fell into her lap and the letter drifted to the floor.

"What? What is it? Tell me. What does it say?" Katie begged.

Sarah looked at her, hopeless, wordless.

Katie wished Sarah would cry. At least then she would seem alive. It frightened her to see Sarah this way. Ever since she had been a little girl, Katie had been the one to whom Sarah had turned for comfort. She had spent much of her childhood in Katie's kitchen; helping her and listening to Katie sing Irish songs and chatter endlessly in her Irish brogue. Katie was never too busy to take a moment for the little girl. They had grown to love each other, but they both knew Katie could not be responsible for Sarah much longer. She had her own future to think about. She was getting old, and she had neither husband nor child. She was forced to rely upon her sister. How could she take care of Sarah?

"They have not heard from him in several years. He quit working for them some time ago," Sarah said without feeling, so accustomed to bad news that one more bit of it only confirmed that bad news was the only kind she would ever get.

"Quit? Where did he go? Did they say where he went?"

Sarah shook her head. "He was a timber cruiser, whatever that is." She leaned over and picked up the letter and read the last few lines from it. "Mr. MacKenna's last assignment was to estimate a stand of timber in an area near the town of Pine Crescent. We have not heard from him since he finished his work there."

Katie sat slumped on the settee, looking out of place in her sister's parlor. She was much more at home standing in front of a stove in a long, white apron, the appetizing smells of roasts and stews and puddings filling the kitchen. "Oh dear. Oh dear," she said, shaking her head sadly and wringing her work-worn hands. "I may never work again, but at least I have my family."

Sarah saw Katie's distress. "You mustn't worry so about me. I'll manage somehow. You have to take care of yourself, now. I've already been too much of a burden."

"Don't you go saying things like that. You have never been a burden to me. You've given me nothing but pleasure since you were a wee tot." Her eyes were soft and filled with kindness as she spoke.

"I will go there." Sarah spoke firmly, as much to convince herself as Katie that she had somewhere else to turn.

"Are you sure you ought to? You have no way to know if you will ever find him. He could be...."

"Dead? Perhaps. But I need to know." She stood up. "I will leave right away." Then she fell back onto her chair. But how? How could she go *anywhere*? She was penniless. She didn't have enough money to buy a train ticket to the next town, much less all the way to Minnesota.

Katie spoke hurriedly. "I have a little money saved and...."

"No! Absolutely not! I will not take anything more from you," Sarah protested, knowing she really had no choice but to accept.

"I want to help you, Child. Please let me do this for you."

After a long moment of painful contemplation, Sarah nodded slowly and said, "Alright. But I'll pay you back every penny, I swear."

"I know, I know." She patted the settee next to her and Sarah rose from her chair and came and sat down beside her. Katie's arms went around her, and she pulled Sarah's head down onto her shoulder.

Sarah could not cry; the tears were frozen inside of her. All she could do was let Katie stroke her hair, accepting the nurturing she so badly needed. She could no longer draw upon the sweet imaginings about her parents, which had sustained her for so long. She could no longer think about Steven and feel safe and secure. His love, too, had been nothing but sweet imaginings, vanished and gone with the first mention of her parents and her poverty. All she had left was Katie, and now she must leave her, too.

"I'll miss you, Katie, but I'll write to you, I promise."

"You'd better, because if you don't let me know how you're doing I won't get a moment's rest. And when you find that father of yours, you tell him for me that he was a fool to go away and leave such a dear girl as you are." She hadn't meant to remind Sarah that her own parents had deserted her, but it was too late to take back her words.

Sarah, however, wasn't listening. A flicker of hope was stirring within her. She would find him. Her father was out there somewhere. Out West in the timber. He was not dead. He was still alive and she would find him. She would find him if it was the last thing she ever did.

And when she found him, he would have a good deal of explaining to do.

CHAPTER 5

THE long train ride from Boston to Pine Crescent gave Sarah far too much time to think. Try as she might, she could not quiet the jumble of thoughts that assaulted her as soon as she settled into her seat. She had never before indulged in self-pity. She had always made the best of whatever life gave her; and although she often felt the stinging hurt of living with people who did not love her, she had always had her comforting images to sustain her.

She had always believed that her parents had met an untimely death, but that they had loved her and had made provisions for her in case something happened to them. There had been nothing remaining from her parents—other than her mother's brooch, because everything else had been lost in the fire. She was told that her mother had pinned the brooch to her blanket when she left her with her Aunt Lettie for the weekend. Her mother had been feeling ill, Aunt Lettie said, and she planned to spend a few quiet days alone with her husband. That weekend there had been a terrible fire in the house and her parents were both killed. Her father had been wealthy, or so she had also been told, so she would never have to worry about money.

Given those supposed facts, she had been able to build an imaginary world around them. Now she knew it had all been a lie. She was left with only the truth; a truth so awful that she almost wished for a blow to the head that would dull her senses and quiet her tormenting thoughts. Despite the torment, however, sometimes a feeling of euphoria would suddenly sweep over her at the thought of possibly finding her father. But then, just as suddenly, the sadness would overwhelm her again and she would feel the unwelcome stirrings of self-pity. Automatically she would bring forth the old comforting images; but then she would be jolted back to reality. The old images were a cruel lie, but they refused to die—no matter how forcefully she tried to push them completely out of her mind.

And if all of that had been a lie, who was she now? She had been led to believe she had been orphaned by a fire. She had not been; she was the daughter of a whore who was now dead and a father who ran away before she was born—but might still be alive. She had always believed she would inherit a small fortune when she turned eighteen. She would not. She was a pauper with nothing but the clothes she wore, a trunkful of clothing and a few pieces of jewelry. She had been betrothed to a man she thought loved her as much as she loved him. Now it was over between them. He had wanted nothing more to do with her when he learned of her misfortune.

Everything was changed. *She* was changed. But she had no idea what she had become. All she knew was that there were far too many moments when she felt useless, lost, unloved and abandoned; and worst of all, there were also moments when she felt unworthy of anything better.

She sat staring out the window of the train at the white bluffs and beyond at the tall buildings of the city of St. Paul. The Mississippi River was still frozen along its banks.

She felt a tug on her skirt and looking down saw a small girl smiling up at her. "Hello," said the little girl. She had long auburn curls and big brown eyes, and Sarah felt a sharp pang of remembering herself looking in the mirror as a child, wondering if she really was as pretty as Katie told her she was.

The little girl wore a green dress with an intricately smocked bodice and she was holding a rag doll for which someone had lovingly sewn a miniature copy of the green dress. As soon as the child had Sarah's attention, she put the doll carefully into Sarah's lap, and then put her hands behind her back and waited for Sarah's reaction.

A tall young man appeared and smiled apologetically to Sarah. "I'm sorry if she's bothering you, Miss." He swept the little girl up in his arms, along with the doll, and kissed the top of her head. "Come along, you little scamp. You can play dolls with Mommy and Daddy. The lady doesn't want you bothering her."

Sarah's eyes followed the man and the little girl to their seats. He seemed not to have noticed Sarah's silence, so intent was he upon delivering the child back to her mother, who took her and hugged her as though she had been gone for a very long time instead of mere minutes. She turned her head quickly back toward the window, trying to still the unwelcome thoughts that filled her at the sight of the devoted little family.

"Steven," she whispered against the cool window glass. She felt the hurt and then the shame and she closed her eyes, trying to concentrate on the rhythmic clacking of the train's wheels and wishing for some kind of an escape. At last it came—in the form of sleep.

She roused slightly at each stop when the porter passed through the car announcing each town along the way. Then she would let herself be lulled back to sleep until the next stop. It went on like that for much of the journey. She roused herself only to wander to the ladies lounge to freshen up, or to the dining car. Food tasted like sawdust but she forced herself to eat, if only the barest amounts.

When the porter finally announced their imminent arrival in Pine Crescent, she sat upright and peered out the window. The train was travelling between tall pine trees that towered over them on both sides of the tracks. The wheels made a sharp, piercing metallic screech as the train slowed, and she pressed her forehead against the window to see better, hoping to see signs of habitation. She frowned as the train approached an unimpressive-looking wooden building with a crude sign on top that read "Pine Crescent." A row of wooden buildings stretched toward the east away from the depot.

"I'm here," she thought, feeling an intense surge of disappointment. She had not known what to expect, but this was not it. She couldn't at first generate enough enthusiasm to rouse herself from her seat. She just sat there, staring out at the sign, reluctant to take the next step. Finally, with a great effort, she stood up, gathered her belongings and got off the train.

It had begun to rain, offering some slight relief from the black smoke and cinders the train was spewing. The air was thick with the acrid stench of burning coal. Half a dozen people waited on the platform to board the train heading north, several more were waiting for the mail to arrive, and several shabbily-dressed old men waited for the train to come in and liven up their dreary day.

Sarah stood for a moment, watching as a young boy unloaded suitcases and trunks onto a cart, listening to the raindrops hammering on the roof over the depot platform, vaguely aware that she must do something besides just stand there. She hurried into the building and found herself in a large waiting room with several small rooms off to either side. At the entrance to one of the rooms, a Dutch door stood open at the top.

A man was standing with his forearms resting on the ledge on the bottom half of the door talking to a well-dressed man in a dark brown Chesterfield coat and a brown derby. When they finished talking, the well-dressed man tipped his hat to Sarah and left the building to board the train, his gold-handled walking cane compensating for a slight limp.

The stationmaster looked at her. "John Smitheson. Owns the lumber mill in town." Then, worried that he had given her information she hadn't asked for, and thinking that she didn't care two hoots about who owned the lumberyard, he said, "Sorry Miss. May I help you?"

She did, however, care very much about who owned the Smitheson lumber-yard. It was the Smitheson Lumber Company in Duluth that had answered her letter about her father. She felt a thrill of excitement to learn that there was apparently a branch of that very company right here in Pine Crescent. She wanted to run after John Smitheson, but knew instinctively that she needed to move slowly. She was not yet ready to tip her hand. The letter from Duluth said they hadn't heard from her father. Did that mean the people at Smitheson's in Pine Crescent had not heard from him either?

"Is there someplace I could leave my trunk until I find a place to stay?" she asked, trying hard not to display any interest in the man who had just left.

"Stay?" He looked her quickly up and down, trying not to stare rudely, but unable to ignore her expensive clothing and carefully coifed hair. He was not accustomed to ladies arriving alone in Pine Crescent and planning to stay—certainly not ladies as beautiful as this one.

Sarah could not appreciate his look of approval. She knew his admiring look would turn to scorn if he knew the truth about her.

"Yes. I'll be needing a room. Is there a hotel in town?"

"Hotel? Yes, there's a hotel." He paused a moment before answering. "But, but I...I don't think you...."

"Thank you. I'll send for my luggage." She ignored his look of concern as she showed him her baggage claim ticket and walked away from the window, not waiting for him to say whatever it was he seemed to want to say.

She could no longer sit and let the train rock her to sleep in its iron womb. She had been jolted by the knowledge that she might be close to learning of her father's whereabouts, and she needed to continue to take action. She would take the logical next step and find a place to stay.

CHAPTER 6

S HE stepped out the door at the front of the station and raised her umbrella.
A road ran north and south in front of the depot, and a road led through
town toward the east, perpendicular to the front of the depot, then curved out
of sight. The buildings on either side of the rutted road were all made of wood,
and they appeared crude and temporary. She stood staring down the road. She
wasn't sure what it was she had expected Pine Crescent to look like, but she was
not prepared for the contrast between this place and the world she had known
back East.

Although the sky was leaden, the rain had stopped. She lowered her umbrella,
picked up her skirts and stepped gingerly down the wooden steps. When she
reached the bottom, she saw that the ruts were oozing with brown mud, and she
was about to step into several inches of it. She looked around and saw a wooden
plank laid across the road not far from where she was standing. She stepped
carefully onto it to cross the road, and then walked along the crude boardwalk
in front of the buildings on the south side. When she rounded the curve in the
road, she saw the hotel about twenty yards down the street on the opposite side.
It was indistinguishable from the other buildings—except that it was larger, and
it had a sign hanging from the wooden overhang with the word "Hotel" painted
on it in red letters.

She walked carefully along the boardwalk, greasy and slick with mud. Several
times she nearly lost her footing but managed to catch herself by using her
umbrella as a makeshift cane. When she was directly across from the hotel, she
looked across the road and noticed several women who had stepped out onto
the boardwalk under the hotel sign. They were looking down the street in the
same direction from which Sarah had come. There seemed to be something
unusual about the way the women were dressed, but she dismissed them from
her mind, looking instead at the mud she was going to have to step into in order
to get across to the hotel. With a sigh of resignation, she lifted her skirts and
stepped down.

41

She was so intent on her footing that she didn't notice the gang of rowdy men headed in her direction until they were almost upon her. The women in front of the hotel were calling to them, and the men were ignoring the mud and sloshing through it without a thought to what it was doing to their boots and clothing. They were laughing and shouting boisterously to the women. Sarah stood, her feet mired in the mud, skirts lifted, umbrella abandoned, directly in their path.

"Lookee here what I found!" shouted a big burly man with scruffy red hair and an unkempt red beard, who was suddenly looming over her.

She took a small step backwards, the mud sucking at her soft leather shoes, her skirts dropping into the mire and rapidly wicking up moisture. She struggled to keep from falling while the rest of the crowd of men swarmed around her, circling her like wolves around a dying fawn. Before her panic could fully register in her brain, a big man with white-blonde hair stepped out of the crowd, encircled her around the waist with his big hands, and lifted her free of the crowd and the mud.

He carried her at arms' length across the street and plunked her unceremoniously onto the boardwalk on the side of the street from which she had just come. Then he returned to pick up the umbrella, brought it to where she was standing, bowed, and then dropped the muddy thing next to her feet.

She was too stunned to do anything except stare helplessly into his icy blue eyes; eyes that seemed to look straight through her. As soon as he had deposited the umbrella, he turned and walked away from her as if nothing had happened. He was apparently far more interested in the women who were calling to him than he was in Sarah.

"Hurry on over, you jacks! First drink's on the house!" one of the women called.

Breathless with indignation, but finally able to rouse herself, she stamped her foot on the boardwalk and shouted at him in a voice that sounded to her like it belonged to someone else.

"What do you think you're doing, you brute? I want to go to the hotel!"

Hearing her voice above the din, he stopped walking and stood perfectly still for a moment, his back rigid. Then he turned and looked at her, his eyes travelling over her from the tips of her muddy shoes and mud-splattered skirt to her hat and then back down again. She felt the color rise to her cheeks and she opened her mouth to say something—but no words came. Then, in a voice clearly accustomed to being obeyed, he said, "You would do well to stay away from *this* hotel, Miss." His voice was scornful, and there was something so penetrating and cold in the look he gave her that she fell back a step.

Then he turned and walked back into the crowd of men, whose ranks parted like the waters of the Red Sea to let him go into the hotel first, the women crowding in behind him and seeming to ignore the rest of the men who followed them.

She watched, stunned and unable to move. She felt breathless, and she leaned back against the front of the building behind her, her hand groping and finding the cool smoothness of her brooch. She stood like that for a long time, unable to do anything but stare straight ahead. Then she bent down and picked up the muddy umbrella, and teetering slightly, walked clumsily back to the depot.

She stood outside trying to regain her composure before re-entering the depot. "What kind of place is this?" she asked herself. "Are all the men in the West this crude?" Would her father turn out to be nothing but a barbarian? Should she turn around and return to Boston? She stood outside the depot for a long time, trying to decide upon the most rational course.

She finally decided that leaving was not an option. She was here and she had better find a way to stay until she had accomplished her goal.

From now on, however, she would be more careful. She would be prepared for the worst; and if she had any fancy ideas about her search for her father being easy or pleasant—she would put them aside.

CHAPTER 7

HER resolve thus strengthened, and feeling somewhat better, she went inside the depot and found the station agent sitting at his desk in the room with the Dutch door. He looked up when he saw her, then got to his feet and walked over to her, his brow raised in question as he looked down at her mud-spattered hem and the muddy umbrella.

"Perhaps you could suggest lodging to me?" she began, trying to appear casual. "You were right about the hotel. There were some very strange men...."

He started to laugh, but when he saw that she seemed embarrassed, he said, "Lumberjacks. You probably saw some lumberjacks."

"Lumberjacks?"

"Yes. They're harmless really. Cutting season is over and they're coming in from the camps. They don't mean any harm, and they don't bother anyone. Anyone except them that wants to be bothered."

She remembered the women in front of the hotel, aware that they seemed quite happy to see the lumberjacks. She considered telling him about what had happened but immediately thought better of it. "Lumberjacks. Yes, that must have been who they were. I...I guess I was a little put off by them."

"Never you mind, Miss. Why don't you warm yourself by the stove?" He motioned to a pot-bellied stove standing in the middle of the waiting room. He took the muddy umbrella from her hand, grimaced, and then set it by the door. "We can deal with it later," he said. "I'll be with you in a moment." With that, he went through a door, closing it behind him.

She listened to his footsteps going upstairs, then heard him come back down and emerge smiling. "I told my wife there was a young lady downstairs looking for a place to stay and she right away put on a pot of tea and told me to send you on up."

He came over to her and held out his hand. "Richard Vogel's my name, and my wife's name is Clementine."

Sarah took his hand and said, "Sarah S...Williams. Sarah Williams," she lied, puzzled at herself for not telling him her real name."

"You go right on upstairs. It's real lonesome around here for poor Clemmie, and she can hardly wait to meet you. She gets tired of having no one to talk to except me." He laughed lightly and added, "I'm not very interesting I'm afraid, what with my head filled with train schedules and freight deliveries."

"I'm sure you're very interesting, Mr. Vogel," Sarah assured him as she walked to the door leading upstairs. "The train must be the thing that brings the world to your door." She felt hypocritical, talking about the world coming to his door when, in her true opinion, the outside world obviously had not bothered to pay the least bit of attention to this bizarre place.

Richard Vogel laughed ruefully. "If you say that to Clemmie, she'll agree with you that the train isn't doing a very good job of it. She thinks not enough of the outside world has arrived yet."

Sarah already liked Mrs. Vogel, and she gratefully climbed the narrow stairway to the Vogels' apartment.

Clemmie Vogel met her at the top of the stairs, a broad smile on her pretty face. "Land sakes alive! You're drenched with mud!"

"Richard!" She called down the stairs to her husband and his head appeared around the door. "Bring up the young lady's luggage so we can get her out of these clothes before she catches her death!"

She reached out her hand and Sarah shook it. "Sarah Williams is my name."

"Come right on in and make yourself at home."

Sarah looked down at her mud-caked shoes and at the hem of her mud-soaked dress. "I can't walk on your carpets with this disgusting mess."

Clementine blushed, embarrassed. "I don't have any carpets." But her face brightened again and she said, "Never mind that. We're used to mud around here."

Nonetheless, Sarah insisted upon taking off her muddy shoes, and she leaned against the door frame and took them off. Then she put them on the floor near the door, carefully avoiding the small, neatly-braided rag rug which lay inside the apartment door.

She followed Clemmie as she showed her to the spare bedroom. After her trunk was brought upstairs, she freshened up and put on dry clothing. Then she stood in the middle of the room and looked around, noticing for the first time the simple furnishings. They looked homemade, as had the rag rug by the door.

Not at all like the luxurious furnishings she was accustomed to seeing in her uncle's home. The room, however plain, was immaculately clean.

She walked over to the window and looked out. Her window looked out over the railroad tracks and beyond into the timber. There was nothing as far as the eye could see except the pines, tall and straight and endless. She closed her eyes and leaned her head back against the wall. "What are you doing here?" she whispered to herself, "and why did you lie, Sarah Elizabeth Stewart? Are you ashamed of even your own name?"

Before she could sort through that thought, she heard a gentle tapping on the door. "Come in," she called.

Clemmie peered anxiously around the side of the door. "I've made some sandwiches. I thought you might be hungry."

"That was very thoughtful of you, Mrs. Vogel."

"Clemmie. Please call me Clemmie." She led her into the dining room and motioned for her to sit down. Sarah was embarrassed because Clemmie had apparently gone through considerable trouble; but she tried hard not to show her discomfort. The table was covered with an embroidered cloth, and a shiny silver tea service sat on the table next to a silver tray of tiny sandwiches and a gold-rimmed porcelain plate filled with sugar cookies.

Sarah picked up one of the tiny sandwiches, thinking how strangely incongruous Clemmie's elegant tea display looked in such surroundings. She sensed Clemmie's need to appear gracious and civilized, so she said, "I must say you have managed to bring some good taste to this...this...." Sarah was unable to find the words to finish her sentence, and Clemmie laughed merrily at her difficulty. "I'm sorry," Sarah stammered, "I didn't mean...."

"Don't bother to apologize," Clemmie said, serious now. "I understand exactly what you mean. "It has taken me a while to get over my own disappointment. I had the romantic notion that the wilderness would be exciting; and that I was some kind of an adventurer who was helping to tame it." She laughed wryly. "It didn't take long for me to get over that silly idea."

"How long have you lived here?" Sarah asked.

"We came here about a year ago, just after Richard and I were married. My mother and father wanted me to wait and get married when I was older. They thought sixteen was too young." She blushed. "But Richard and I didn't want to wait. He was offered this job as stationmaster, and it seemed to be an exciting opportunity. Richard receives a good salary, I get to ride free on the train whenever I want to, and we get this nice apartment." She waved a hand, indicating the room. "It's comfortable, and I can't say I'm unhappy, but...." This time it was Clemmie who couldn't find the words to complete her thought.

Sarah nodded, but said nothing.

Clemmie was quiet for a moment, then said, "It's awfully lonely. Oh, don't get me wrong. Richard is always just a few steps away if I want to talk to someone." She sighed. "It's just...just that I miss Mother and Daddy and my friends. There are so few women here."

"Really?" Sarah looked puzzled. "I saw quite a few women outside of the hotel today."

Clemmie blushed crimson. "Those are...well, those are...soiled doves, Richard calls them. He would simply die if I spoke to any of them."

A wave of embarrassment swept over Sarah and she, too, reddened. She hadn't realized the women were whores. Whores. Like her mother. She didn't know what to say, so she changed the subject quickly.

"I surely do appreciate your letting me stay here."

"Think nothing of it! I'm so happy to have some company. How long will you be staying?" She looked thoughtful then, little lines forming a crease between her eyebrows. "What brings you to Pine Crescent? No one ever comes here except the lumbermen and the railroad men."

"I...I'm looking for someone," Sarah said. "My brother. I'm looking for my brother."

Clemmie was eyeing the black crepe of her dress. "Are you a widow?"

"Goodness no. Our...someone died, and...." She stopped, not having given any thought to what she would give for her reason if anyone asked her why she had come to Pine Crescent.

"One of your parents? Oh, I'm so sorry," she said, blushing again. "I didn't mean to pry."

"You aren't prying. It's a perfectly good question." She was stalling, trying to think of what to say. She didn't want anyone to know her real reason for coming West. She wasn't ready to tell her embarrassing tale to a stranger. Better to make up another lie.

"My mother died. Father died several years ago, and now that mother is gone...my brother...." She thought quickly, remembering an article about the outlaw Jesse James that she had read in a paper while on the train from Boston. "My brother, Jesse, is the only family I have."

She looked down at her lap and brushed imaginary crumbs away and said, "But it is for the best. Mother was very sick for a long time."

She was surprised at how quickly she seemed able to think up lies. She couldn't remember ever having told such a bold-faced lie before, and it occurred to her that she was going to have to remember what she lied about so she didn't trip herself up later.

"I see," Clemmie said, not seeing at all how someone could be glad her mother was dead—no matter how sick she had been.

She pushed the thought from her head. She didn't want to think badly of her new friend. "Where are you from?"

"Boston," she answered without hesitation. After she said it, she wondered whether she should have lied about that, too; but it was too late.

"What is your brother doing in Pine Crescent?" Clemmie asked, pretty certain no one named "Williams" lived in town.

"I don't know if he's in Pine Crescent. That's...that's just the last place he wrote to us from. I was hoping to find him here."

"Jesse Williams," Clemmie said thoughtfully to herself. Then she looked hopefully at Sarah and said, "The name isn't familiar to me, but I sure don't know everyone. Maybe Richard has heard of him. We'll ask him later. There are lots of men working in the lumber camps nearby. That's probably where he is."

She got up to go to the kitchen to refill the teapot, then hesitated in the doorway and looked back over her shoulder. "Is tea alright? I could make coffee if you'd prefer."

"No, no, tea is lovely," Sarah assured her.

When Clemmie returned to the table, she poured hot tea into their cups and passed the plate of cookies. "I hope you find your brother, but I hope you don't find him too soon."

Sarah smiled. "That's awfully nice of you."

She wondered how welcome she would be in their home if Clemmie knew what a liar she was—or rather, had suddenly become. And about her having given herself to a man who up and left her the minute he learned she wasn't rich.

But in that instant she decided she had to stop being so hard on herself. She was a stranger here, and in this rough place she doubted that anyone was going to bother to judge her.

"We women must stick together out here," Clemmie said. "We need each other. And we need many more of us if this town is ever going to be anything but a hellhole. Richard hates when I call it that. But it is. It's a hellhole. If our apartment were not so comfortable, I'd never be able to stand this town. You're lucky you don't have to stay here." She looked at Sarah and said with disappointed certainty, "You won't stay after you find him. You'll go someplace else, I just know it."

"I...I might. I...I don't know. I really can't say. It depends upon...." She stopped, not sure what it did depend upon. She stood up and went to the window.

"Are you alright?" Clemmie asked.

Sarah turned toward her. "I'm fine. I'm just feeling a little sad." She forced a smile to her face. "Why don't we look around your little town?" She frowned. "My last walk was cut short."

The truth was that she was feeling confused and disoriented. As if the change in her real identity hadn't been bad enough, here she was making up lies to change it even more. She was going to have to make up a story and stick to it.

Clemmie tilted her head to one side and looked puzzled. "Your walk was cut short? How?"

Sarah flapped a wrist, seemingly dismissing the incident as trivial. "It was nothing. I decided to come back and ask your husband about lodging instead of going to the hotel."

"That was certainly a good thing," Clemmie said, relieved. "The hotel is no place for a lady!"

Then she added brightly, "I know! We'll go to the general store. Mr. Peterson is expecting a new shipment of calico. Richard ordered me a new sewing machine from the Montgomery Ward catalogue. It came last week, and I can hardly wait to try it out. I need a new dress, and you can help me pick out the fabric and a pattern. You must know all the new fashions. You could help me." She blushed, realizing she was imposing upon her guest.

"I'd like that," Sarah said reassuringly. "It will be fun to look at some brightly-colored fabric." She glanced down at her dark dress. "I'm awfully tired of wearing black."

She didn't have to continue to wear black. She certainly wasn't mourning her uncle's death. The problem, however, was that even if she *did* have money for new clothes, she didn't dare come out of mourning. After all, hadn't she told Clemmie that her mother had just died? But then, did the people out here in the wilderness bother with mourning clothes? She doubted it.

"Good. Tomorrow, first thing," Clemmie said, unaware of Sarah's preoccupation. "I had better start Richard's supper. I don't think he'll want these little sandwiches. He's used to meat and potatoes." She giggled as she began clearing away the tea things.

Sarah stood, too, and began to help. Clemmie made a protest, but Sarah said, "Please. Let me help. It will feel good to be doing something after sitting so long on the train. I feel rather like a useless lump."

She thought about the man from the mud and felt the color rising to her cheeks as she remembered his hands on her waist. He, too, must have thought of her as nothing but a lump.

For the first time since that awful night when her uncle shot himself and ended the life she had known, she felt anger. Anger toward her dead uncle and the mud man, and yes, anger toward the father she was searching for. Who did these men think they were? Her father deserted her in her infancy. Her uncle stole her money just when she was nearly old enough to have it for her own. Her fiancée had made love to her and then abandoned her just because her money was gone; and gone through no fault of hers! And now some brute of a man had put his hands on her and picked her up and set her aside like a sack of grain! She glanced over at Clemmie, wondering if her thoughts were showing on her face.

Clemmie looked at her, at first smiling but then noticing something was wrong. "Why don't you go to your room and rest for a while. You look awfully tired, and you've had a long journey."

"Y...Yes," Sarah stammered. "I guess I'm not feeling very well. I really could use a little rest—that is if you don't mind."

"Heavens no! You go on and rest. When Richard has finished his supper we'll talk to him about whether he has heard of your brother."

"My brother?" Sarah caught herself quickly. "Yes. Yes of course. Jesse. We'll ask him if he knows Jesse."

She hurried to her room and closed the door behind her, not really tired having slept so much on the train. But she wanted to be alone again for a while to sort through her thoughts. She went to the window and stood looking outside. She had to think. Not only about what her story was going to be, but also about how she intended to go about finding her father. And if...no, *when*...she found him, what she was going to do about it.

She opened the window, pulled a chair over in front of it, and sat looking out at the pines. The smoke from the trains had settled, and now that they had stopped running for the day she could smell the pine forest. It was pungent and clean smelling, and soon she felt better, calmer. She sat quietly for a long time, breathing deeply and trying not to let herself feel anything except how peaceful it was here in the Vogels' guestroom looking out at the wilderness.

Nonetheless, she began to feel very alone, and she was all too aware of her need to learn to take care of herself. She wondered vaguely if she would ever find a man she could trust. She had been badly used by men who were supposed to be gentlemen, including her own uncle; who was the pastor of a church! Now here she was in a place where one of them felt he could pick her up bodily and move her around to suit himself! She was going to have to keep her guard up and her wits about her.

Now the lies she had told Clemmie seemed like wisps of meaningless air that no longer bothered her. After all, what choice did she have? She had been forced into her current situation against her will. Now she had to fight for survival while she looked for her father. If she had to make up a *million* lies in order to do it, then so be it. She would do whatever she had to do from now on; and she would answer to no one but herself.

CHAPTER 8

THAT night after they had visited for a while and the Vogels had gone to bed, Sarah stood alone in her room, again looking out the window at the timber. She tried not to think about the discomfort she had felt when, earlier that evening, Richard Vogel tried so hard to remember whether he had ever heard of Sarah's imaginary brother. Lying to people was one thing—making them extend themselves based upon one's lies was another. She felt restless and uneasy, unable to quiet her thoughts. She did not want to go to bed and toss and turn while she obsessed about one thing after the other, so she put on her shawl and went quietly down the stairs.

She had no idea where she was going; she only knew she wanted to escape from the dark, lonely silence of her room. She stepped outside and looked down the road through town. Most of the town was nearly as dark as her room. She looked up at the sky. The clouds had passed and there were stars beginning to twinkle overhead. She stood for a moment letting her eyes adjust, breathing the fresh, cool air. Then she made her way across the plank to the boardwalk on the same side of the street as the hotel, hoping this time to avoid the mud. Without understanding why, she headed toward the hotel.

As she drew nearer, she heard the tinkling of a piano, and the loud cacophony of voices singing, laughing and talking. As she approached the door to the hotel, her heart began to race and she stopped for a moment, eyes closed, breathing deeply, trying to calm herself.

Finally, somewhat recovered from her nervousness, she opened the door and stepped inside and stood for a moment, aware of the pungent smells of smoke and beer, and of the raucous, but not-altogether-unpleasant, din. Rather than being in a hotel lobby, she found herself in a brightly-lit saloon. A long bar ran the length of the room on the left, and over the bar hung a large portrait of a woman with hair the color of ginger. She was nude, except for a wisp of filmy fabric draped over her thighs. Sarah quickly averted her eyes.

There were tables scattered all along the right side of the room, and as she looked around at the people sitting at them, glasses were lowered to the table and curious faces turned to stare at her. There were at least a half dozen women in the room—some of them at the tables, and several of them standing at the bar. The piano stood against the back wall on the far end of the room, and a man sat on a small, round stool, his head and his back swaying as he played and sang "My Darling Clementine." Sarah wondered what Clemmie would think if she were here.

A plump woman with hair the color of the nude in the painting was standing next to the piano, one arm extended over the top of the piano and the other hand holding a fan with which she fanned herself slowly and deliberately. She saw Sarah come in, and she studied her carefully, the fan going faster. She did not, however, move from her observation post.

As the other occupants of the room became aware of Sarah, all heads began to turn in her direction. Sarah's hands nervously brushed the front of her dress, and she wished she had shed her mourning clothes in favor of something brighter. She felt like a black crow in a cage full of tropical birds.

She looked around the room, trying not to worry about how she looked. Her eyes were suddenly drawn to the tall blonde man standing at the far end of the room, one foot on the brass foot rail and an elbow on the bar. She immediately recognized him as the man from the mud. He had been listening to the piano player, and had turned toward the door only because so many of the heads in the room had turned in that direction. Their eyes met; his icy and disapproving and hers startled.

Sarah quickly pulled her eyes away from him to look at the pretty golden-haired woman standing next to him. She was wearing a low-cut dress, her bosom swelling halfway out of the bodice. The dress hung barely past her knees, revealing red stockings and high-buttoned shoes. Her hair was piled high on her head, a red plume sticking out of it in a jaunty angle.

Just then, the man with the red beard who had verbally accosted her earlier in the day got up from one of the tables and staggered over to her. "Sure as shootin' I figured you'd come lookin' fer me!" He took her by the arm and pulled her over to the bar before she could gather her wits to protest.

"Bartender! Give the little lady here a drink," he ordered. Then he turned and smiled widely at Sarah, exposing a gap in his mouth where his two upper front teeth should have been.

The tall blonde man set his glass onto the bar and spoke to his companion.

She put her hand on his arm as if in protest. Ignoring her, he strode the length of the bar, slapped the bearded man on the back and winked broadly at him. "Lila wants to buy you a drink, Red."

"Me? Hey, Lila!" the red-bearded man said, turning from Sarah to focus on the blonde woman. "I knew you was gonna figure out who was the best man around here!"

When he got to where Lila stood, he grinned broadly at her, but she ignored him. She was looking at Sarah, her eyes blazing. The bearded man took Lila's face in both of his burly hands and kissed her brusquely on the mouth. Lila grimaced and struggled to get away from him.

The woman with hair the color of ginger called across the room, "George! Give Lila and Red a drink!" Her voice was resonant, and she had stopped fanning herself.

Lila looked at her and started to make an angry retort, but seemed to think better of it. She accepted the drink from the bartender, lifted her glass and drank, and then looked up at Red with a forced smile. She pretended to listen to what he was saying, but her head was turned slightly so she could watch out of the corner of her eye. She watched the tall blonde man herd the newcomer outside, his hand cupping her elbow, and she lifted her glass and took another long drink.

"You seem to have a way of stepping into the mud, Miss, and one of these times I won't be around to get you out of it," the tall man said to Sarah as they stood facing each other outside the hotel.

She tried to retake possession of her arm, but he was far too strong for her. Finally, in response to the violent jerk of her shoulder, he released her.

"I can't help it if you happen to always be *in the mud.*" Her eyes were narrowed, and she spoke through clenched teeth, her anger rising.

He seemed completely unaware of her agitation. He casually leaned back against the building, his arms crossed over his chest, one knee raised, and the sole of one heavy boot against the wall. It made her furious the way he calmly looked her up and down.

"It is true what you say—about the mud. But then, there is no opera house in Pine Crescent, so what is a man to do?"

He's making fun of me, she thought. *I cannot believe such arrogance! Who does this idiot think he is?* "I don't care what you do or where you go. All I care is that you stop telling *me* what to do and where to go." With that, she stepped to the door of the saloon, opened it, and immediately felt her arm once again in his firm grasp.

"No," he said, the humor gone from him. "You are not going in there again."

"Leave me alone!" she demanded. She wanted to sound authoritative, but her voice cracked maddeningly.

"You don't want to go back in there." His voice had softened, but only slightly.

"What makes you think you know what I want? I have as much right to go into this hotel..." she pointed up at the sign that hung over the door, "... as you do."

"Hotel?" His eyes were wary as they explored her face. Was she even more innocent than she appeared?

"Why? Why do you want to go in there?"

"Because I'm...I'm looking for someone."

She was sorry the moment she said it. She hadn't even known why she went to the hotel. Her chin was lifted haughtily, but it was getting harder to hold it up because the truth was beginning to dawn on her. She wondered what Steven would think if he knew that a strange man had been obliged to keep her out of a brothel. Twice. It would no doubt reinforce his opinion of her.

Her opinion of herself was beginning to suffer as well. She had vowed that she would keep her guard up and her wits about her. A few short hours later and here she was again, letting this brute of a man tell her what to do.

"Who? Who are you looking for?" His voice had grown cold, intense. He didn't like the idea of this young woman looking for someone at Ginger's. If she was looking for a man and she found him in a whorehouse, chances were it wasn't going to be good news for anybody.

She didn't answer him. The anger in his voice made her suddenly nervous, and she decided she preferred it when he seemed to look through her, as he had done earlier that day. This new intensity of his was disquieting.

"Tell me who you're looking for. I know everyone in that room, and if whoever you're looking for is in there, I'll send him out. There's no need for you to go back in."

"I...I don't...." she stammered. A feeling of panic gripped her. What if her father was in there? Was she ready to face him? She had to make a quick decision, so she did. She would do this on her own terms and not be forced into action by this brute of a man. She would go back into the saloon and proceed at her own pace and in her own manner, even if she were temporarily without a real plan.

But before she could act upon her resolve, the door opened and Lila stepped out onto the boardwalk. "You comin' back in? If you ain't, Ginger says I gotta...."

"I will be there in a minute. Tell her to leave you alone." He waved a hand as if to dismiss her.

"It ain't Ginger I want to leave me alone!" Her voice became angry and insistent. "You said you was gonna stay with me tonight, and if I have to go with Red instead...."

"Dammit, Woman!" he growled, grabbing Lila by the arm and pulling her back into the saloon.

Sarah watched them go. The man seemed to think it was appropriate for him to be moving women from place to place to suit himself. Who did he think he was? Well *whoever* he thought he was, it was clear that she had better take this opportunity to go back inside while he was distracted.

She took a step toward the door. *I'll tell them I'm looking for my brother, the same as I told the Vogels. That way no one will know who I really am or who I'm really looking for. As to the rest of it, I'll decide later.* She reached out her hand to open the door at the same time as the mud man pulled the door open from inside. She stumbled backwards and lost her balance. He reached out a hand and caught her by one arm before she fell.

It infuriated her, and as soon as her footing was steady again, she swung one arm around and landed a blow to the side of his face.

He didn't even flinch. He took hold of her upper arms with both hands and pulled her up onto her toes so her face was inches away from his. "I told you Ginger's is no place for you. Where are you staying?" His calm voice contradicted the force with which he held her.

"Let me go, you idiot!" she commanded, trying to sound forceful but failing miserably.

"First tell me where you're staying!" he insisted angrily.

"I...I'm staying at the depot with the Vogels." She wriggled furiously in his grasp. "What business is it of yours? Let go of me!" Her voice rose and grew shrill. "I am not some cheap whore whom you have paid to do your bidding!"

She felt him go rigid, and the next thing she knew, he hoisted her up and over his shoulder and strode in the direction of the depot as though she was nothing more than a jacket tossed over his shoulder.

She was too astonished to scream, but she began pounding on his back with both of her fists as she hung there with her rear end in the air and her legs trapped against his chest. The hard ropy muscles in his back made her realize he could probably barely feel her blows. Steven flashed into her mind again, and in the middle of this strange trip she was taking she found herself wondering how two men could have such different physiques.

When he reached the plank leading to the depot, he crossed the narrow board as light-footed as a deer. He dropped her on her feet onto the platform in front of the depot, and she was so totally enraged that she started kicking him and beating on him with both of her fists.

He easily got hold of both of her wrists, and in one motion pinned her hands behind her. He circled one leg around the back of her legs, pulled her tight against him and held her there. She struggled for several moments, wanting to scream but afraid of waking the Vogels and having to explain these ridiculous events. Recognizing her own foolishness, as well as the futility of fighting against him, she went limp.

For a long moment he held her tightly against him, letting the smell of her fill his nostrils. She smelled of roses, all soft and delicate; not like Lila, whose scent was so cloying it sometimes made him want to go outdoors. He had never held a woman so beautiful and so elegant and with such high spirits. Who was she? Where did she come from? Who was she looking for? Who did she mourn in those black clothes? Black clothes that did little to hide her loveliness.

He had to fight to keep from nuzzling his face into her thick, rich hair, and felt in some strange way awed by her. She was clearly a proper young lady who needed protection from her own foolishness, which is what he thought he had done both times he had picked her up. Nuzzling her would not be in the way of protection, and he was enough of a gentleman to recognize it. He was ready for a woman, and he felt a twinge of annoyance that it couldn't be this one. Whoever she was, she was surely no whore, even though she had seemed mighty deter-mined to go into a whorehouse.

"I'm going to let go of you, Miss," he said with great effort, "and when I do, I want you to turn and walk into the depot and stay there. And if you come back to Ginger's, I'm going to think you're looking for a helluva lot more trouble than I have given you so far. I will then be more than willing to let you find it. Now get inside!" His voice was still hard and cold, but it held a new note that she could not identify.

When he released her, she stood a moment glaring up at him in the darkness, wanting to claw his eyes out. Then she turned abruptly and went into the depot without another word, ran up the stairs to her room and stood inside the door, her anger a palpable thing in the dark room. She undressed and went to bed, but it was a long time before she slept.

She awoke not long after in a cold sweat and sat bolt upright in bed. She had had a bad dream, and it took her a moment to remember what it was.

In her dream she had been standing in front of the bar at Ginger's dressed exactly like the whore, Lila. She was standing next to the man from the mud, just as Lila had been. He had his arm around her, and he leaned down to kiss her and he suddenly became Steven, who started laughing and pointing at her because of the way she was dressed. She ran from Ginger's and out onto the muddy road; but it wasn't the road through town. It was a muddy road through a thick forest of tall pines. Suddenly she was unable to move her legs because the mud had begun to pull at her feet and suck her under. She awoke just as the mud reached her chin.

She fell back down onto the bed, her heart pounding, praying she hadn't screamed in her sleep. She waited, but heard nothing from the bedroom next to hers. She was sure if she had screamed they would have heard her and come running. When she heard nothing, her breathing became easier and she lay very still. Strangely, the not-unwelcome image of the mud man's blue eyes kept invading her thoughts.

She rolled over and buried her face in the pillow, trying to conjure up the old happy images of her parents. So what if the image was false? Perhaps it would work anyway, and the images would bring her rest and comfort as they always had. But the old images refused to appear. In their place new images had formed; images of a mother in a rowdy saloon filled with painted women and crude men. And of a father not only without honor, but also without manners. She shuddered. Even, perhaps, without front teeth.

CHAPTER 9

SHE slept fitfully until morning, when she awoke with a start, feeling bewildered until she remembered where she was. A sense of gloom immediately settled over her. She groaned and turned her face toward the window. The sun was shining brightly and she remembered that today she was going with Clemmie to pick out dress materials. Perhaps the day wouldn't be so bad. Maybe she could find some pleasure from her first full day in this strange new place.

She got out of bed, poured cold water from the pitcher into the basin and bathed quickly, shivering from the cold water but not wanting to bother Clemmie to warm some for her. She dressed and went to the kitchen where Clemmie was preparing breakfast.

Clemmie stopped what she was doing and smiled brightly at her. "Good morning! Did you sleep well? Come and sit down. Breakfast will be ready in a minute."

Sarah did as she was bid and then gratefully accepted the cup of tea Clemmie offered her. "I slept well, thank you," she lied.

Richard walked into the room smelling of bay rum, his hair parted in the middle and slicked down on both sides, displaying prominent ears. Clemmie gave him a quizzical look and he looked at her as if to say there was nothing wrong with spending a little extra time on his toilet, gave her a peck on the cheek and then smiled at Sarah.

"Clemmie tells me you're going to help her pick out a pattern and some fabric for a new dress. That sure is nice of you."

"It's the least I can do after all you've done for me. I intend to pay you for my lodging, of course, but I really do appreciate your letting me stay here." Her brow furrowed and she looked perplexed. "I can't imagine what I'd have done if you hadn't."

"Oh bother," Clemmie said, flapping a wrist. "Don't you go worrying about paying us. We're just happy to have the company. Isn't that right, Richard?"

Richard hoped his wife would accept money from their guest, but he wouldn't be upset if she didn't. He was enjoying having such a lovely and refined young lady staying with them. It made him feel important. Besides, his wife looked especially happy this morning. "Clemmie is mighty pleased to have someone around besides me," he said. "I think she gets bored with my company."

"Oh hush, Richard. How can you say such a thing?" Clemmie scolded playfully.

They chatted amiably as they ate, and as soon as they finished Richard pushed his chair back from the table and stood up. "You ladies have a pleasant visit to the general store. I had best be getting downstairs. Trains won't wait while I dally up here in the kitchen with a couple of pretty gals."

Sarah and Clemmie started clearing away the breakfast dishes, but before they had finished they heard Richard's voice calling up the stairs. "Clemmie! There's a telegram from your mother. You'd best get down here."

"Oh my!" Clemmie said as she hurried to the stairs. "I hope nothing is wrong with Mother or Daddy. Excuse me. I'll be right back, soon as I know...." Her voice trailed off as she ran down the stairs.

"I hope everything is alright," Sarah called after her.

When Clemmie came back upstairs, she looked puzzled. "Mother wants me to come for a visit, but she says nothing is wrong."

"Don't you believe her?" Sarah asked.

"Well...yes...and no. I mean, she never asked me to come visit like this before. All of a sudden like this. I wonder if she's sick and doesn't want to tell me. Or maybe Daddy...."

"I guess I would just go. You'll know as soon as you get there if something is wrong. No sense worrying for nothing."

"Right. You're right, Sarah. That's exactly what I'll do. I'll take the train this afternoon." She looked apologetic and said, "Oh! I'm so sorry! I wanted to show you the town." She paused, then giggled and said, "Such as it is."

"Don't you worry about that. I'll get on just fine until you get back."

"Yes, yes of course you will," Clemmie replied. She hated to leave her new friend, but she was concerned about her parents. "I just hope nothing has happened to either of them while I've been stuck up here in this godforsaken wilderness." She caught herself and then looked fearful that she might be discouraging Sarah by being so negative about Pine Crescent. "I...I didn't mean...."

"Oh pooh!" Sarah said, seeing her discomfort and trying to reassure her.

"Don't worry about it for a minute. I'm here and I'm going to stay here. Even if it is a godforsaken wilderness."

***

That afternoon after the train left and Clemmie was on her way to Kansas City, Sarah stood on the depot platform uncertain about what to do next. Perhaps she should go to the general store by herself. She thought of the Mud Man. What if she ran into him again? "That's ridiculous, Sarah," she said out loud. Even if she did see him in town, surely he wouldn't try to remove her from the general store.

She left the depot and walked across the plank onto the boardwalk. The weather was very different from the gray, dripping gloom of the day before. She felt worlds away from Boston, and for a moment her thoughts went back there and she began to feel the painful ache that had lived inside of her for the past weeks. She shuddered visibly.

"I won't think back," she promised herself. She had come here by her own choice, and she wasn't going to let herself be dragged down with remorse about things that she could do nothing about. She thought about her quest to find her father, and her brow creased with worry and she felt a stab of apprehension. Looking ahead was no better than looking back.

"I'll stay in the present," she said aloud. "I won't look back and I won't agonize about what might be ahead of me. I'll just concentrate on doing what I must do today. Tomorrow will take care of itself."

She looked up at the sky. It was azure blue, and the air smelled fresh and clean. A slight breeze played at the edges of her skirt and at the tendrils of hair that fell around her face and neck. She stood looking skyward at the clouds floating lazily overhead. Everything looked different when the sun was shining, and she felt her spirits lift. "Today. Today is a lovely day," she breathed, half believing it.

There were people walking up and down both sides of the road. A wagon with its wheels creaking as it made its way through the muddy ruts tried to get around a wagon stuck in the middle of the road. She watched as two men slogged through the mud to help push the wagon, then crossed to the other side of the road and went into the barbershop. She wondered how long the mud would last, and if she could afford a more suitable pair of shoes so she wouldn't have to watch every step she took. She walked along the boardwalk until she was well past the hotel. The men she saw were dressed differently from the lumberjacks she had seen the day before, and they looked much less jovial than the lumberjacks. From the serious look of them, and from the clothes they wore, she assumed they must be farmers.

A sign on top of a building a short distance past the hotel read *Peterson's General Store, Proprietor Lars Peterson.* When she opened the door, a bell over the door jingled. There were two women looking at a table filled with kitchen gadgets, and four men leaned against the long counter smoking pipes and talking. They stopped talking and turned when Sarah came in, then nodded a greeting. She smiled and nodded back, then wandered around looking at the various displays, stopping at a table piled high with bolts of brightly colored calico.

"Aw gee, Pa! Why can't I?"

Sarah turned from the table and looked across the store to where a boy of about fifteen was pleading with his father, who was obviously the proprietor of the store.

"You're not old enough to go off into the timber, and even if you were, your Ma would turn over in her grave if I let you go."

The boy continued, stubbornly. "I don't want to be a storekeeper, Pa! I want to be a lumberjack!"

One of the men leaning on the counter laughed at the boy. "Why don't you go on over to the lumber yard? They're hiring some new jacks for the summer crew, and they're looking for someone to help Big Mary. You could maybe hire on as a cookee. I bet you could get that job." That brought laughter from everyone in the store.

The boy gave the man a scathing look and said, "I ain't gonna be no cookee. I'm gonna be a sawyer."

One of the men said, "You're going to have to get a whole lot bigger than you are now. But if you really want to get into camp as a sawyer, you're gonna have to convince somebody you know how to saw logs. Else you'd better settle for asking them to let you sling hash." That brought another round of laughter at the boy's expense.

Sarah's ears perked up and she pretended to be interested in picking out a length of calico from one of the heavy bolts on the table.

"I ain't bein' no cookee! That's sissy stuff! I'm gonna be a sawyer whether you like it or not, Pa."

"It may be sissy stuff, but I hear tell even Nilsson was a cookee when he first got to camp," one of the men said.

"That ain't true!" the boy protested. "That's just gossip."

"Now you watch your tongue, boy," his father ordered. "Don't you go talking to Mr. Lundgren that way."

"I ain't talkin' no bad way. It's just that...it's just that the people in town are always sayin' bad things about the jacks. Things that ain't true."

"And how do you know if they're true or not?" the man named Lundgren asked with a chuckle in his voice. "You ever had any dealings with any of them, other than selling them snuff or tobacco?"

All the men were laughing now, and the women had stopped looking at the merchandise and were laughing, too. That is except Sarah, who was listening intently.

The boy's face reddened and he clamped his mouth tight shut, afraid to say anything and be teased again. Then he thought better of it and said, "*He* ain't never been a cookee and *I* ain't never gonna be one neither. And that's that."

"I'll tell you, boy," One of the other men interjected, "The way I heard it, the first year Thor Nilsson hit the timber up in Michigan wouldn't nobody hire a sixteen-year-old who couldn't even speak English. He was so stubborn he managed to convince them he'd do any kind of work they wanted him to do, just so long as he could get a chance to prove himself." The man took a few puffs on his pipe, all eyes in the store now on him. "Worked two days as the cook's helper, and the third day the camp foreman saw him chop wood for the stove. He took him into the woods that day and found out the boy could chop down a tree almost as fast as two sawyers could saw one down. And that was the beginning of Nilsson's lumberjacking. So there ain't nothing wrong with going to camp as a cookee." Then he added, a chuckle in his voice, "That is if you don't have to keep on being a cookee."

Sarah watched the man as he spoke, aware of a kind of reverence in his voice when he spoke of some lumberjack named Thor Nilsson. In fact everyone in the room seemed somewhat awe-stricken by just the subject of lumberjacks. Her experiences with them had certainly not left her with any such reverence.

"Yeah, well this kid can barely lift a case of canned tomatoes," Lars Peterson said, looking at his son, "and if he picked up an axe he'd probably chop off his foot. He's been listening too much to the other boys around here who think they can go off into the timber and not have to stay and help their fathers."

"I hear tell the folks over at Smitheson ain't too happy about having to hire a boy." Another man, who had been listening to the conversation without speaking, said, "That lady cook of theirs has been in town three days already, trying to hire a helper. Too bad they're so set on keeping her. Men don't want to work for no female. Boys are the best she can get."

One of the women spoke then, looking at the men with disgust. "They keep her because she's the best cook in the pineries. Being a woman has nothing to do with it."

"That may be," one of the men allowed. "But I still don't get it. It's not just cooking. It has to do with giving orders. The cook is second in command to the foreman, and it's got to be a big problem when she's a woman. What man wants to take orders from a woman? And a *wee tiny woman*, at that."

All the women in the store looked at each other and raised their eyes heavenward, wondering how anything much would ever get done if they didn't give their husbands orders.

Henry Lundgren said, "Don't matter to them if it's a problem, I guess. They must figure having good food is so important they'll put up with most anything. I never heard of any jack from Camp Seven walking because of the food. And that sure ain't the case in most camps. Anyway, she'll probably have to hire a boy again whether she likes it or not. And soon's the kid gets some whiskers he'll be following the men off into the timber like they all do, and she'll be back again looking for another cookee."

"I don't care about their gosh durned cookee," the boy said sullenly.

"You watch your language and get back to work! You're not even fifteen years old, and you're not ever going to be as big as Nilsson. I heard enough about this lumberjack business. If you don't get these cases unpacked before lunch, I'll tan your hide and you can go to the timber as a horse harness!"

That brought another roar of laughter from everyone in the store except Lars Peterson's pouting son, and Sarah, who watched as he reluctantly began taking the cans from the case, banging them as loudly as he could as he put them onto the shelf.

Sarah walked casually to another counter, trying to hear better. She ran her hands over a stack of woolen shirts, her eyes on the boy, an idea taking shape in her mind. Then she wandered out onto the boardwalk and sat down on one of the chairs in front of Peterson's store. She sat for nearly an hour watching people as they came and went, paying particular attention to the lumberjacks that came along every now and then. As soon as they walked into town, most of them went either to the hotel or to the barbershop and *then* to the hotel.

She carefully observed their clothing and the bundle they carried over their shoulder. One of them carried only a stick, and she followed him casually into the general store and watched as he purchased a flannel shirt much like the one he was already wearing, a pair of socks, a pair of long underwear and a jar of snuff. Then he tied them all into a new bright red handkerchief, fastened it to the stick he carried, and left the store.

For the next several days, she wandered around town watching people. Sometimes she again took her place on the chair in front of the general store, and sometimes she sat in front of the only restaurant in town—which was across the road and a few doors down from the depot. People were curious about why such an elegant lady was hanging around town, but they were too polite to ask questions. Richard Vogel had spoken to some of them about her, and by the time she had been there several days most of them knew she was staying with the Vogels. She was relieved that the man from the mud seemed to have left town.

Clementine Vogel was still visiting her mother. She sent Richard a telegram telling him everything was all right and that her mother was simply lonely for her only daughter, and that she planned to stay another week. Richard Vogel was too busy to pay much attention to Sarah. He ate his meals at the restaurant, and Sarah kept herself alive by eating whatever she could find at the general store that didn't require cooking. She never really felt hungry, so she ate only when she grew weak and it reminded her that she had to eat to keep up her strength.

On the third day of her stay in Pine Crescent, she made up her mind what she was going to do. To implement her plan, she went first to the general store. She used some of her precious money to buy a pair of sturdy boots like the ones she saw most of the men wearing, a pair of heavy socks, a pair of long underwear, a pair of men's denim coveralls, a flannel shirt, and a length of white muslin.

Mr. Peterson raised his eyebrows when he saw what she was buying, so she smiled sweetly and said, "It's my brother's birthday and I want to surprise him with a set of new clothes. He's so unselfish he never spends any money on himself."

The lie seemed to satisfy him, but she again felt a twinge of guilt about the way lies slipped so easily off her tongue. Again, she consoled herself with the knowledge that lies were necessary. As soon as she had purchased her new clothing, she hurried back to her room over the depot, her heels clattering on the boardwalk and her bundle clutched against her.

She asked no one about Doyle MacKenna. She made up her mind that she must find a way to hide her real identity and her true reason for being in Pine Crescent. At the same time, she had to find a place to stay, a way to get fed, and a way to pay for them both. In other words, she needed a job. What better place to get a job than in one of Smitheson's lumber camps?

Once in the privacy of her room, she took the muslin and fashioned a binding to flatten her breasts, dressed in her new clothes and stood looking at herself in the mirror over the dresser. Satisfied that she looked like a young boy except for her hair, she took Clemmie's scissors from the sewing basket in the hallway and carefully began to cut her hair, trying to ignore the panic she felt as her thick auburn hair fell in clumps onto the floor around her. She took several deep breaths, trying to quiet her uneasiness.

She felt calmer as she stood staring at her reflection in the mirror. Her hair was now cropped short and her widow's peak was hidden by thick bangs that hung almost to her eyebrows. Not yet satisfied, she went to the lamp next to her bed, ran her finger through the blackening on the chimney and smudged a bit of it under her eyes, giving her a wan, sallow look. Still not satisfied, she raised the scissors and carefully snipped off half the length of her long, thick lashes.

She looked in the mirror and she saw a young boy looking back at her. He had neither past nor future nor identity, and she would have to invent them all for him. She could forget about being Sarah Stewart. Or Sarah Williams. Or Sarah anybody. Sarah was gone—and good riddance. She would find refuge behind this new face until she saw fit to come out of hiding.

She packed her belongings back into her trunk, taking only her brooch. She wrote a note thanking Clemmie for all her help, left a small amount of money and promised to pay her more after she had worked for a while. She did not explain where she intended to go.

She also wrote a letter to Katie, telling her she had arrived in Pine Crescent and hoped to find a job that very day. She told her not to be surprised if she didn't hear from her for a while, because she might not be able to write very often. She promised Katie she would take good care of herself, and told her not to worry.

Then she went downstairs, opened the door carefully to be sure Richard

Vogel was not anywhere in sight, and hurried outside and headed straight to the Smitheson Lumber Company. Her feet felt strangely buoyant in her heavy socks and boots. She was accustomed to light women's shoes, and the solid feeling of her new men's footwear gave her confidence—at least temporarily.

When she arrived at the lumberyard, she easily found the building she wanted from among the buildings and sheds that were scattered on the property because there was a large wooden sign saying "Office" above one of the doors. When she got inside, several men were milling around a table where a tiny woman half leaned and half sat against it. She was no more than four-foot-ten and she had her arms crossed over her chest and a look of disgust on her wizened face. Her hair had once been jet black, but was now streaked with gray, and it was pulled back into a tight bun at the nape of her neck. She was wearing a simple black dress, and she reminded Sarah of a sparrow perched on a limb.

"What do you mean you ain't seen no applicants? I need to get back to camp today, and I can't go without a helper. You don't have no trouble hiring jacks or yard workers. But helpers for me? You men all think you're too good to take orders from a woman. When you're hungry, seems I'm plenty good enough. I've a good mind to go up to Duluth and take life easy. If I never see another hungry lumberjack again, it'll be too soon!"

"Aw, simmer down, Big Mary! No use gettin' all fired up at us just because you can't find nobody who wants to work for you. It ain't our fault."

Just then, the woman spotted Sarah standing by the door. She looked Sarah up and down. Then she turned to the men and said, "See? Another kid. And he don't look dry behind the ears."

"You don't need to worry none that I'm not old enough, Ma'am. I'll be a cook's helper like you've never seen before," Sarah said as she strode over to the table and held her hand out to the tiny woman. Mary Bishop let Sarah pump her hand up and down, taken by surprise by this unusual display of self-assurance from a young boy. The boys she was usually forced to hire were always all arms and legs and stammering half sentences, and when they finally toughened up and gained some self-confidence, they were off into the timber.

The men were grinning as they went into small separate offices off the main room and returned to their work. Big Mary ignored them. It was nothing new to her to be teased by the men, both in the lumberyard and in camp. It didn't really matter to her, because she was the cook, and woman or no woman, she ruled her cook shack with an iron hand. The problem was hiring help; it was always one big pain in the ass, as far as she was concerned.

Big Mary motioned for Sarah to sit down, and she sat down across from her, her hands folded tightly on the tabletop, convinced that this boy would prove no more capable than any of the others she had interviewed during the last few days. "You know how to cook?"

"Yup. My Ma was a cook back East, and we cooked for some rich folks." Again Sarah marveled at how the lies kept coming, but coming they were, and she was grateful for that new and mysterious part of herself that was able to dredge up facts from out of nowhere. She hoped she could soon put aside her guilt about lying as easily as she could do the lying. Feeling guilty was getting to be a nuisance.

"We don't cook fancy in a lumber camp."

"Bread's bread, as far as I know."

"How old are you?"

"Fifteen."

"You don't look fifteen. You look about twelve."

"Can't help that. I'm a hard worker and I learn things real fast. Since my Ma and Pa are both gone now, I gotta find some kind of work." She lowered her eyes for a moment, trying to appear sorrowful.

"Gone? Where'd they go?"

"Pa died last summer. It was his heart. Then Ma got consumption and died last month."

Big Mary's eyes filled with sympathy, and Sarah felt emboldened. "I figure if I start out cooking, I can work in the camps until...until I get bigger. My Pa was real big, and he used to tell me he didn't start taking on any size until he was sixteen."

Big Mary looked her up and down, touched both by the boy's gritty self-assurance and by the hopeful look on his face. "Where back east you from, boy?"

"I came from Chicago just the other day. Right after things got settled. There wasn't any money left. Pa hadn't been able to work for a long time, and Ma earned just enough to feed us, and...." Sarah lowered her eyes to the table again before looking back at Big Mary with what she hoped looked like an effort to control her anguish. It was difficult to feign anguish when she was struggling to push down her own amazement at the tall tales she continued to invent.

She quickly said, "I had an uncle who came to the timber, and that's how I got the idea to come here looking for a job."

"What's your uncle's name? Maybe I know him."

"Uh, his name's William...Stewart Williams."

"Hmm," Big Mary said, raising her eyes to the ceiling and thinking for a moment before looking back at Sarah. "Never heard of him. But then, there's lots of timber and lots of men in it. What's your name?"

"Williams. My name's Williams, too."

"Ain't you got no first name?"

Sarah looked flustered, but only for a moment. She remembered the brother she had invented for the Vogels. "Jesse. Name's Jesse."

Big Mary was somewhat perplexed by Sarah's hesitation over names, but she attributed it to grief—and probably some nervousness.

As she continued asking questions, Sarah answered them carefully and thoughtfully. She would have to remember what she was telling this woman.

After about ten minutes, the front door opened and a boy walked in and stood looking around. Big Mary looked at him and then at Sarah. "Hmm. Looks like another prospect," she said, rubbing her chin thoughtfully.

Sarah stood up. "Is it okay if I wait around?" She hoped Big Mary wouldn't tell her to leave. She needed this job and she needed it right away.

"Sure. You wait. I'll let you know what I decide."

Sarah wandered over to a map that hung on one wall. It was a map of the state of Minnesota, with the timber regions identified by small green pine trees. The map was framed and covered with glass, and as she started to walk away she caught sight of her own reflection. It startled her, and for one brief moment she didn't recognize the boy in the glass.

A bulletin board hung on the wall next to the map. It was plastered with slips of paper containing job openings. Some of them were for jobs at the sawmills in Pine Crescent and in Hinckley, a large town northeast of Pine Crescent. Some of them were for sawyers in the various Smitheson camps, beginning in November. One of them was for a cook's helper at Camp Seven for the summer—the job Sarah hoped to get. One of them was for two cook's helpers and a bull cook to start in November. One of them was for a clerk at Camp Seven, beginning in October, and she began to read the list of qualifications required for that job. They wanted someone who could read and write, had neat penmanship, and was good with numbers. She knew she easily filled those qualifications, and those tasks appealed to her far more than working in a kitchen. And best of all, clerks were paid more than cook's helpers, according to the job slips. An idea began to take form. October was not all that far away, and if she hadn't found her father by then she'd maybe stay on and take the clerk's job.

She glanced over at Big Mary and her competing job applicant. The boy was fidgeting and Big Mary looked frustrated. Not wanting to eavesdrop or act too anxious, Sarah walked to the far side of the room and looked out a window facing into the lumberyard. There were piles of boards stacked around the yard, some of them ten feet high. Several sets of train tracks ran through the yard, and an empty flatbed railroad car stood waiting to be loaded.

Three men were standing next to one of the piles of boards. One of them had his back to her, but it wasn't difficult to recognize him. Her heart began to hammer. The Mud Man stood with his feet planted wide apart, his arms crossed over his chest in front of him. He was wearing black pants tucked into his tall-laced leather boots, and his brightly colored red suspenders matched the socks that formed cuffs over the tops of his boots. He wore a black and red checked wool shirt, and his hair glinted like gold in the clear light.

She watched in fascination as he nodded his head at what one of the men was saying. Then he dropped his arms, shifted uneasily, and put his hands into his pockets. He glanced to the left and to the right and then back over his shoulder. It was as though he could feel that he was being watched, and she stepped back away from the window just as he turned and looked in her direction.

Her heart was now pounding so hard she was afraid it would jump out of her chest. She leaned back against the wall next to the window, and for a brief moment wanted to turn and run from the room and never come back. She considered simply asking one of the men who worked in the office where she could find Doyle MacKenna. At that moment, it would have been easy to give up the whole crazy idea of taking a job as a cook's helper. She was seriously considering just such a retreat when she heard Big Mary call to her.

"Jesse Williams! You deaf?"

Big Mary had been calling to her, but she was still unaccustomed to being called by her fictitious name. "N...no, I'm not deaf. I...I was just thinking about something."

"Well stop thinking and get on over here."

"Yes Ma'am." She walked quickly to where Big Mary was now standing, her hands expectantly on her hips.

"Can you start today?"

Sarah swallowed hard. *Today*. She hadn't even considered what she'd do if she didn't get the job, or if she got the job and didn't have to start right away. How could she go back to the depot and face Richard Vogel looking like this? It *had* to be today!

"You bet I can. I'm ready," she gulped.

"Where's your things? Ain't you got no tussock?" Big Mary looked around the room, expecting to see Sarah's bundle of belongings.

Sarah reddened. "No Ma'am." She looked down at herself. "I spent most of my money buying these clothes. In Chicago we...we dressed a little different."

"Never mind," Big Mary said waving her hand. She wondered if maybe Jesse was the kind of boy who never thought ahead. He seemed awfully eager. But the truth was she was tired of people who lacked enthusiasm. Like the boy who had just left. It was hard to find fault with someone who had too much of it.

"I have to get over to Peterson's to pick up supplies before we leave for camp. You can get an extra change of clothes. Camp Seven ain't no pig sty where you can wear the same thing week in and week out."

"But...."

"I'll buy them for you. You can pay me back when you get paid the end of the summer." She wondered at herself. She usually didn't go out on a limb for a stranger. Something about this boy made her want to help him.

"I can't let you do that," Sarah protested.

Maybe that was part of the reason she felt the way she did about helping Jesse Williams. It wasn't merely that she felt sorry for him, although she did. She would treat him the same as she did every other cookee she ever hired. No better. No worse. No, sympathy wasn't why she was making exceptions for him. The truth was that he just didn't seem like the kind who'd take things for granted, but would, instead, appreciate anything that was given to him.

Big Mary reached up and put her hands on her new cookee's shoulders and looked sternly into his eyes, forcing him to look back at her. "Oh yes you can. You're working for me now, and you'll do as I say. You got that?"

Sarah nodded, unable to think of an appropriate response—not even a lie.

"Meet me over at the general store in an hour. You can help us load supplies."

Sarah walked out of the office wondering who "us" was going to be, but she was beginning to feel she could deal with each situation as it happened. As she left the lumberyard, a feeling of relief mixed with fear churned in her stomach.

She had thus far avoided coming face to face with the Mud Man again, she had a job, and she was on her way out of Pine Crescent to work in a Smitheson camp. She was going to be in a place where it would be logical for Doyle MacKenna to turn up. That is, if he was still alive.

She walked straight back to town to the general store, trying hard to carry herself like a man. She tried to mimic the walk of the men she had been watching for the past few days. It felt so foreign to her that she looked quickly around to see if anyone was staring at her. The people moving about in the road and on the boardwalk were not paying the slightest bit of attention to her. She squared her shoulders and breathed deeply, feeling strangely liberated, and almost confident.

"Inhale the smell of these pines, Jesse Williams," she murmured. "Fill your lungs and clear away the useless vapors that once belonged to that poor, helpless creature you used to be. Good-bye, Sarah Stewart, and good riddance! Hello, Jesse Williams. Welcome to...to this godforsaken wilderness!"

CHAPTER 10

BY the time she arrived at the general store, her feelings of liberation and confidence were gone and had been replaced by uncertainty and self-doubt. She leaned against the front of the building with her hands pushed deep into her pockets and her shoulders slumped forward. Remembering how the Mud Man had stood that night outside of Ginger's, she put the sole of one booted foot behind her on the wall, mimicking his stance. She wished now that she had taken some time to get used to her disguise before she rushed headlong into the unknown wearing it.

But it was too late. A wagon was just pulling up in front of the store, and seated next to Big Mary was the man with the red beard. Sarah felt the sharp intake of her own breath and had to make an effort to let it out again. This was the acid test; if he recognized her, it would be over before it had even begun.

Big Mary climbed from the seat directly onto the boardwalk. "I'll go inside and see if Lars has our stuff ready," she said, going into the store.

The red-bearded man got down from the wagon, tied the horses, then jumped up onto the boardwalk and shook Sarah's hand, his face beaming with a toothless grin. "Name's Red Scanlon. I'm the head teamster at Camp Seven. You must be the new cookee."

From the way he swelled with pride when he told her what his job was, she figured the head teamster, whatever that was, must be a pretty important person in a lumber camp.

Greatly relieved that he didn't recognize her, she said, "Yup. My name's Jesse. Jesse Williams. Pleased to meetcha." She felt a twinge of pride at the way she was talking. She seemed to have automatically adopted some of the vernacular of a rough and tumble boy. The words "yup" and "meetcha" had just popped out of nowhere. *Maybe I should have been an actress,* she thought wryly.

Just then three other men appeared in the road and stood next to the wagon. They looked at the empty wagon bed and then up at Red. "Ain't we ready to go? I'm sick of this goddamned town." The man who spoke was a burly man not much more than five-foot-six, nearly as wide as he was tall. He had a torso like the trunk of an oak tree, and there appeared to be not an ounce of fat on him.

Charlie DuBois was a Frenchman from the woods of northern Maine. When he was younger, he had been one of the most daring river drivers the timber had ever seen. He was agile and quick, despite his bulky frame. His low center of gravity gave him an edge, and he had managed to clear many a river that had become jammed with logs; jams that would crush a less able man. Now that the logs were hauled by rail because the timber had already been cleared next to the rivers, he worked with the cant hook to load the logs onto wagons or sleds, depending upon the time of year. He had a reputation for being moody and ornery, and the bright colors he always wore contrasted sharply with the darkness of his moods.

"Hold your horses, Charlie," Red said, frowning down at him. "Big Mary's checking on the supplies."

Charlie DuBois grunted and then looked at Sarah. "Who's this runt?" he asked Red, his eyes traveling up and down the length of her.

Sarah felt sudden panic. Had he been in the hotel that night? Did he recognize her?

"This here's Jesse Williams. He's Big Mary's new cookee."

This caused a burst of raucous laughter. These were men who were proud of their strength and their manhood, and being a cookee meant you were something less than a man; an object of derision. Sarah was prepared for this after seeing how they ridiculed the Peterson boy, and all she cared about was that this particular man seemed satisfied with Red's explanation of who she was.

After that, Charlie completely ignored her as he hoisted himself up onto the side of the boardwalk and sat with his feet dangling over the edge, pulled a pipe and a pouch of tobacco from his pocket and proceeded to fill his pipe and then light up.

One of the other men jumped up onto the boardwalk and looked at her for an instant before smiling a crooked smile. "Howdy. My name's Spike. Spike Anderson." He held out his hand and she shook it. He was a tall, bony man with a nose that was too large for his narrow face, and eyes that were too close together. Despite his homely face, she liked him immediately.

The third man had been standing in the road watching them. Or at least she thought he was watching them. He had one eye that wandered in all directions despite what the other eye was focused on. He walked closer to the boardwalk and turned his face up to her. "Name's Leverty. Sawtooth Leverty." He spoke in a low, raspy voice that put her teeth on edge as if someone was scratching their fingernails on a blackboard. "I'm new here, just like you. Us new men got to stick together." His smile sent a shiver of revulsion all the way through her. She found him so repulsive that she was unable to speak.

To her relief, Red Scanlon broke in. "Get your lazy asses in here and help with the supplies. If they ain't ready yet, we'll find out why not. Time's a wastin'."

In a flash, Charlie DuBois dropped his pipe and jumped up, grabbed Red around his middle and, half dragging and half lifting him, hoisted him over the edge of the boardwalk down onto the rutted road, which was dry and hard now that it hadn't rained for several days. "Who you calling lazy, you red-whiskered, toothless son-of-a-bitch?"

Red struggled to regain his balance and then scrambled back up onto the boardwalk, eyes blazing. He had one big hand on the top of Charlie's head, and Charlie lifted a leg to knee him in the groin.

Before his knee had time to hit its target, Big Mary stepped out of the store and saw the two men scuffling. She walked up behind Red and grabbed him by his suspenders, stretched them full out and then let them snap sharply against his back. "Dammit you jacks! Can't you act like grownups? Get moving and load these supplies. At the rate we're going, we won't get out of town until it's too dark to see where we're going."

The men sheepishly hung their heads as Big Mary herded them into the store. Sarah was amazed at the control the tiny woman seemed to wield over men who were so massive in size compared to her. Mouth agape, she followed the little troupe into the store. Without another word, they began carrying crates, sacks, crocks and miscellaneous supplies from inside the store, piling them onto the boardwalk and then packing them into the wagon.

"Who are you?" a voice asked as Sarah stood in the back room of the store lifting a sack of flour clumsily onto her shoulders and staggering under its weight. The Peterson boy was glaring at her. "Who are you?" he repeated, and without waiting for an answer, sneered, "Did they just hire you to be the new cookee at Camp Seven?"

"That's right. And who are you?" She acted like she had never seen him before.

"Shit!" he said, ignoring her question. "You ain't no bigger'n me. You can't even lift a sack of flour!" He stomped angrily out of the back room and toward the front door of the store. Paul Peterson was too angry to remember that he had not wanted anything to do with being a cookee for Big Mary. Now all he wanted was to be the one she hired, no matter what job he was hired to do. He didn't like the idea of losing his opportunity to another boy.

"Where do you think you're going, Paul?" his father called to him. "You're supposed to be helping load these supplies for Camp Seven."

"I ain't doin' no more nothin' for nobody!"

Lars Peterson moved quickly to intercept the boy before he could escape out the front door. He grabbed him by the ear and Paul let out a yelp. "I don't know what I did to deserve such a lazy, good-for-nothing son. What in thunder is the matter with you?"

"Leggo my ear!" the boy squawked, trying to pull away and nearly tipping over the large pickle barrel which stood in front of the counter.

"I'll let go of your ear, but if you decide to stop working again I'm going to pull it off and throw it to Old Man Henderson's pigs. And be careful of those pickles, you lunkhead!"

Paul Peterson glared at Sarah as she staggered past carrying her heavy burden out onto the boardwalk, trying not to crumble under the weight. The boy soon followed, carrying a sack of potatoes. He glared at Sarah as he tossed it onto the pile of supplies and said, under his breath so no one but Sarah could hear him, "You took my job, you little weasel, and you ain't nothin' but a weakling."

Sarah stared at him, tongue-tied. Judging the meekness of his adversary, Paul Peterson rid himself of his burden and held up his fists in a boxer's stance, pushing his face close to hers. They stood nose-to-nose for a moment, and Sarah stumbled backwards.

Big Mary came out of the store and saw what they were doing. "Quit fighting and get busy! You boys are just as bad as the men. They're all alike," she mumbled, walking over to the wagon, shaking her head back and forth and clucking her tongue. She examined the wagonload and then went back inside the store, still shaking her head.

The boy mouthed the word "coward" at Sarah and then swaggered into the store for another load, grinning with smug satisfaction.

I acted like a coward, Sarah thought, hating herself. Not really comprehending why, she felt sick with shame, and she swore she would fight back the next time something like this happened; with words, at least, if nothing else. Surely she could have won a verbal battle with a mere boy. She continued loading supplies, working as hard as she could. She was going to have to work hard—both at her job and at defending herself. She was pretending to be a man in a man's world, and it looked like self-defense was going to have to be part of her repertoire.

A short time later, Big Mary came out of the store and saw her standing deep in thought, staring off into space. "Dammit, Jesse! We ain't getting off to such a good start. If I have to talk to you one more time about something, you ain't coming to Camp Seven. You can stay here and try to find yourself someone *else* fool enough to hire you."

"Sorry, Ma'am," Sarah said, lowering her eyes to avoid the angry look on Big Mary's face. "It won't happen again."

"See that it doesn't," Big Mary said, scowling.

When the wagon was nearly loaded, Big Mary pulled her by the arm into the store and ordered her to pick out an extra set of clothes. Then she reached into the pocket of her black dress, pulled out a small black coin purse and paid for them.

Sarah nervously tied everything into her new red handkerchief and said, "Thanks. I'll pay you back as soon as I get paid."

"That's if you last long enough to get paid," Big Mary grumbled, then added, "Don't worry. You'll pay me back if you know what's good for you."

As Sarah followed her out of the store, she said under her breath, "I'm a liar and a coward, not a thief."

Big Mary turned to look back at her. "What did you say?"

"Nothing."

Big Mary turned away, seemingly satisfied, but eager to get moving.

The men had just finished loading the wagon, and Red Scanlon jumped up onto the seat and took up the reins. "You riding, Big Mary?"

"Nope," she answered. "I'll walk behind until after we eat. Ain't walked much lately. My bones need a stretch."

The men tossed their tussocks into the wagon, and Sarah did the same. Red flicked the reins and yelled, "Giddyap!" By the time the wagon was moving, the three other jacks were already far down the road ahead of them.

The road followed the railroad tracks north out of town for half a mile past the Smitheson lumber yard and sawmill, then crossed the tracks and turned sharply west. Sarah noticed for the first time that in addition to the two main sets of tracks, there were several additional sets of tracks running out of the lumber-yard into the forest. They appeared narrower than the main tracks.

"What are all those tracks for?" Sarah asked Big Mary.

Big Mary followed Sarah's gaze. "Those are the tracks they use to bring the timber into the mill. If it wasn't for those tracks there wouldn't be any Pine Crescent."

Sarah raised her eyebrows in question, as she looked sideways at Big Mary. They weren't walking very fast, but the pace was steady and Big Mary didn't slow down as they talked.

"In the old days the mills were all built along the rivers. The logs came down river to the mill. Soon's the timber was mostly gone along the rivers, they had to come up with some other way to get it to the mills. Seein' as how there's so much timber around here, Smitheson put a mill right smack in the middle of it and built railroad spurs leading into it.

The logs from all around here come by rail into what is now the booming town of Pine Crescent."

"Booming?" Sarah asked, trying not to sound sarcastic.

"You bet. For a town that's only been here a few years, it's growing by leaps and bounds."

Sarah glanced sideways at Big Mary, wondering if she really meant what she had just said about Pine Crescent being a booming town. Apparently she did, because her eyes were straight ahead and she sure seemed serious.

She glanced back over her shoulder at the "booming town" and felt a twinge of fear as she saw the wooden buildings recede in the distance. It hadn't been much of a town, but she had found a small measure of safety and comfort in the Vogels' apartment. She had no idea what kind of place Camp Seven would turn out to be. She was certain of only one thing; it was going to be even less civilized than Pine Crescent.

They traveled through the pines until they reached a cutover area near a river that snaked its way north and south. Sarah stared around her. Piles of pine branches, along with small trees that had been hacked to the ground to make way so the bigger trees could be cut, lay scattered among hundreds of ugly stumps. New growth had not yet taken over. She looked over at Big Mary to see her reaction to the ruin around them; there was no reaction. Big Mary seemed oblivious to the devastation.

After passing through the cutover area, they reached another river along which the lumber had been cut decades before and where aspen, poplar and wild plum now grew. As they entered the new-growth area, the atmosphere changed dramatically. Birds twittered in the branches of the young trees, their brightly colored feathers clearly visible among the buds that had just begun to open. Scattered profusely along the woodland edges, the delicate white blossoms of thousands of trillium brightened the forest floor. Now and then a rabbit scurried into the heavy undergrowth as the wagon clattered into earshot. Sarah could almost feel the vitality pouring into her from her surroundings as she lifted her face toward the sky and felt the warm spring sunshine. She ran her fingers through her hair and shook it, noticing for the first time how free it felt not to be neatly and fashionably coifed. The wafting breeze felt marvelous against her skin.

Big Mary looked at her new helper, but continued to walk without speaking. He was holding up well for a city boy. He had lost both of his parents, had come alone into the timber, and had so far held his own. *Oh to be so young and flexible— both in mind and in body*, she thought, reaching up and gently rubbing the back of her neck. It seemed not very long ago when springtime made her feel young again; it no longer held that power. She felt a twinge of envy as she watched Jessie, and she suddenly felt every minute of her forty-eight years.

She quickly turned her thoughts toward the cook shack at Camp Seven. She felt happiest when she was cooking for the men. It was there that she came into her own, and where she outshone the best of them. She knew she had become a better camp cook than even her father had been; and he had been one of the best. And she knew that being "best" at *anything* took some years.

The tote road passed over a rickety wooden bridge that spanned a narrow rushing river. There were logs scattered along the shore like giant matchsticks. "Why are those logs lying there like that?" Sarah asked.

"They were probably left after the last river drive."

"But why?"

"When the water got low in the spring they weren't able to get the logs downriver anymore. So they just left them."

"Why bother to cut them down if they're going to just leave them there? Isn't that a terrible waste of time? And of trees?"

"Waste? Look at all these trees." Big Mary made a sweeping gesture with one arm. "They ain't never going to get them all cut down. Besides, now that they use the rails they don't have that problem anymore. So you can stop worrying about the logs that didn't make it."

Sarah decided to stop questioning the local lumbering methods, because it was getting Big Mary all riled up, and that was the last thing Sarah needed right now.

They were now entering the deep pine forest, and the smell of pine became heavy and pungent. The towering trunks of thousands of giant white pines spread out in all directions, some of them more than three feet across, their upper branches intertwining and blocking out the sunlight. It was very dark and still, the darkness relieved only now and then by streaks of sunlight filtering down through the trees wherever a tree had fallen and made a space to let the light reach the ground.

Sarah looked down at her boot-clad feet and then ahead at the wagon and the men walking with long, easy strides far ahead of them. It all felt somehow unreal, and in her mind's eye she pictured cobblestone streets and shops and Steven and suddenly fear gripped her. "Oh God!" she groaned under her breath.

Big Mary heard her and stopped walking and looked at her, startled. "What? What's wrong?" She looked frantically around, wondering if the boy had seen something.

"N...nothing. I...I...." She had to think fast because Big Mary looked too worried to be put off easily. "I was just thinking about...about my mother. I'm sorry. I didn't mean to...."

Big Mary's face relaxed and she reached out and touched Sarah's arm. "That's okay, boy. It can't be easy for you, losing your folks and going off to a strange place. But don't you worry. You're young and you'll get over it." Her sympathy thus dispensed with, Big Mary started walking, her eyes once again straight-ahead.

Phew! Sarah thought to herself. *I'd better be more careful.* But she soon relaxed. She had gotten away with it by telling another one of those lies that seemed to roll so easily off her tongue. She walked silently beside Big Mary, and instead of ruminating over deception and possible detection, she forced herself to pay attention to her surroundings.

They walked without talking for another half-hour when finally Big Mary broke the silence. "Camp Seven's about twenty-five miles back in the woods. We'll rest and have something to eat around two o'clock. We'll make one quick stop at the Lawsons' and we'll reach camp somewhere around dusk."

"Who are the Lawsons?" Sarah asked, wondering if her legs would hold out for twenty-five miles. She had no idea how far they had walked thus far, but she was sure she had already walked farther this day than at any other time in her life.

"Tom and Sally Lawson. Their farm is about eight miles this side of Camp Seven. They're homesteading a piece of cutover timber land." She shook her head in dismay. "Now that's hard work if I ever saw it."

"Harder than working in a lumber camp?"

"I can't say it's harder than that. Not much is. But for a farmer trying to raise a family and feed them...." She broke off. "You'll understand after you've been out here a while. This ain't Chicago."

That's for sure, Sarah thought. She was getting tired and she had not even really begun to work, other than loading the wagon. Big Mary, who she calculated must be at least in her late forties—or maybe even her fifties—was acting like this walk was nothing but a Sunday stroll through the park.

Big Mary seemed to read her thoughts and said, "You can climb up on the wagon if you're tired."

Sarah looked ahead of her down the road at the three men keeping pace a quarter of a mile ahead of the wagon. "I can do it if they can," she said with more conviction than she felt.

Big Mary chuckled. "Don't be so sure. Those boys have been in the woods a long time. Can't hardly tire 'em out. I'm gonna ride in the wagon after we eat and you can, too, if you want to. That is unless you got something you got to prove to somebody."

Sarah glanced at Big Mary. Did that mean Big Mary wanted her to walk so she could prove herself? She wanted nothing more than to climb into the wagon and lie down, but she feared Big Mary might intend to judge her by her ability to walk.

Big Mary chuckled. "I was just messing with you, Boy. I don't expect you ever had to walk this far in Chicago. You're doing fine, but after lunch you can ride on the back of the wagon with the potato sacks. You'll think you're in your own bed."

Sarah looked away, trying to hide the eagerness she felt about the prospect of riding in the wagon. She dared not own up to the fatigue spreading over her.

Not long after, they rounded a bend in the road and she saw one of the railroad spurs crossing the tote road. "Couldn't we have taken a train?"

"The wagon's more convenient. They use these tracks to move logs—not people. Besides, the tracks don't run close enough to Camp Seven to make it worthwhile."

"I see," Sarah said, not seeing at all. She didn't understand it, but she guessed there was going to be much she didn't understand. "How many men will we be cooking for?" she asked, deciding to concentrate on her new job instead of trying to figure out the workings of this strange new world she had entered.

"There'll be seventeen men already in camp when we get there, and three of them, counting the Push, should be coming behind us before too long. They took some of the horses to town to be shod. Counting us, that's twenty-six."

Sarah grew quiet. Twenty-six people to feed. There were four jacks in their little group, so there were twenty more men to meet. Then she remembered something Big Mary just said.

"The Push? What's that?"

"He ain't a 'what.' He's a 'he.' The boss. In the timber we call the foreman the Push."

"The boss? I thought you were my boss."

"I am. But he's my boss, so that makes him your boss. The foreman runs the camp and everybody in it, including me. But if you're lucky, and if you do your job, he'll leave you pretty much alone. He's got plenty to worry about with the jacks, and he'd like nothing better than to leave the cook shack, and everybody in it, to me."

Sarah looked sideways at Big Mary. "Why does he have to worry about the jacks?"

"If it wasn't for a good foreman, nothing would get done right." She motioned with her head in the direction of the men. "Those louts don't know the first thing about what to do next. They won't do nothing but eat and fight unless somebody rides herd over them."

"Aw, come on. You said they've been in the woods a long time. They surely must know what they're supposed to do."

"Knowing ain't doing," Big Mary said. "But he keeps them under control like nobody you ever saw. That's where he got his reputation. He's as tough as the best of them; and if he wasn't, he wouldn't get the respect of the men."

Sarah pondered those words without saying anything. For a long time they walked without speaking. Finally Sarah asked, "How long have you been a cook in a lumber camp?"

"Long as I can remember. My pa was a cook in a camp back in the early days. After Ma died, me and my sister lived with him in whatever camp he was cooking in. My sister was six years older than me, and she got married and moved to Duluth when I was twelve. I got married when I was seventeen years old. I married Dan, one of my pa's helper, and when Pa died me and Dan took over. Spent our first winter together in a camp on the Rum River."

"Where's Dan now? Where's your husband?"

Big Mary walked for a while without answering, and then she said, so quietly that Sarah could barely hear, "He's been gone eleven years." Big Mary looked up into the canopy of pines. "Smallpox came through the camp in '81 and killed men left and right. Killed my Dan and my Danny, too." She was silent then, her eyes on the men walking far ahead of them.

"I'm sorry," Sarah said.

"You've got enough of your own sadness, Boy. Don't go worrying about mine. It's long past and I don't dwell on it. I was just answering your question." Big Mary hurried her steps, brushing away a tear so quickly that Sarah wondered if she had seen it at all.

Sarah looked ahead of them and saw the wagon moving faster. The tote road now followed along a high ridge, the high ground dry and hard, allowing the wheels to turn more easily. She glanced sideways at Big Mary, but now the little woman's expression registered nothing but the determination to reach her destination before dark.

After some time had passed, Big Mary said, "I been in a lumber camp as long as I can remember, and I can tell you they can be pretty God-awful. I'll never forget the first time Pa finally worked in a decent camp. I didn't know camps could be anything but filthy and disgusting, and when we found a good one, I thought we'd died and gone to heaven. It had gotten better by the time Pa...by the time me and Dan were working together without my father."

Big Mary walked along, remembering. She looked up at the sky again for a moment, seeking the sunlight of an opening in the canopy of the dense pine branches. Then she looked back at Sarah. "Those early camps were bad. "I remember one of them where the push was so bad that Pa and me only stayed a few days. Men were going down the road left and right, and the axe men...."

"Axe men?"

"The men who cut the trees down with axes. Didn't have sawyers until later. At first they used axes to cut down the trees, and let me tell you it was slow. Least I thought it was until I first watched a good man cut a tree down with an axe. Now the sawyers cut the tree down and the axe men just lop off the limbs and branches."

"They just leave them lying among the stumps? Shouldn't they *do something* with them?" Sarah interrupted, forgetting her resolve not to question the lumber-men's methods.

"Do what?"

"I don't know. Burn them maybe? It seems wherever the timber has been cut down there are dead logs lying everywhere, and branches and.... I don't know. Something." She caught herself again. After all, she really didn't know what she was talking about.

"That ain't the axe men's fault. That's the lumbermen's orders. They're in a hurry to get the timber out. They don't care what's left behind."

"So what does it mean, what you said before about going down the road?"

"Leaving camp. Quitting because you can't stand the conditions. It's tough enough in the woods in the middle of the winter without having to live with filth and vermin in camp like we had in some of those early ones." Big Mary noticed the fear her words caused Sarah, so she quickly added, "Don't worry, Boy. Ain't no filth and vermin in Camp Seven. And Dan and me were lucky enough to get into some decent places. We moved around a lot trying to find the good ones. We could afford to be choosy, because the camp cook's a pretty important person." Her tiny frame seemed to grow larger with pride. "If the food ain't good, the jacks will walk the cook, so a good cook can pretty much pick his own camp."

"Walk the cook?"

"Walking the cook means refusing to work until he leaves and they get someone who cooks better food. When Pa was cooking, and later Dan and me, we always had a happy crew. These jacks don't have much pleasure in their days, and food's the most important thing in the world to them. Leastwise, until spring. It's easier to find good camps nowadays. They've gotten lots better. Specially if you got a foreman worth his salt."

Sarah considered the remark about the vermin. "Vermin? What do you mean by vermin?"

"Lice. Bedbugs. Mice. Sometimes even rats. These men work from before sunup to after sundown all winter long, and they do it happily if they're fed good. They're even happier if they can sleep at night. You ain't never laid awake until you've laid awake scratching from lice and bedbugs!"

Sarah had stopped walking and her mouth hung open. Big Mary laughed so loud Red Scanlon turned around and looked back at them.

"Relax, Boy," she said. "I already told you there ain't no vermin in Camp

Seven. A mouse here and there maybe, but they don't hurt nothing unless they get into the food. It's part of your job to see they don't."

Sarah's mouth fell open even further. "How?" she gasped, finally. "How do I do that?"

Big Mary ignored her question and continued. "The bunks are made of cedar, and there's fresh cedar boughs under the straw. Critters hate cedar. And if a man comes to camp lousy, the Push makes him douse himself in kerosene oil and boil his clothes before he sets foot in the bunkhouse. Downright persnickety, he is. Him and the Finn get in that sauna..."

"Sauna?"

It was Big Mary's turn to grimace. "It's a real hell hole, as far as I'm concerned. But those two like it. It'd be great for plucking chickens, but ain't fit for humans. The Finn tells me they got those things everywhere back where he comes from. I guess those crazy Scandinavians like to torture themselves."

"But what is it?"

"It's a little shack the Finn built out behind the bunkhouse. First one I ever saw in my life, and I hope it's the last. It's got a small stove in it and a pile o' rocks they dump water on to make steam. Every Saturday night the two of them sit inside the damn thing, buck naked and cooking like pieces of meat. Then the crazy idiots get all soaped up and prance around outside throwing buckets of cold water at each other. That's what I mean by persnickety. The boss says it ain't healthy to be dirty like most of these jacks like to be."

She thought about her last remark, then said, "I ain't sure they're dirty because they like to be or because it's just too damn much work to stay clean out here in the timber. They get used to the dirt and their own stink. Every once in a while one of the other jacks tries the damn thing, but none of them ever go back for more."

Sarah screwed up her face in disgust, as much from the picture that was forming in her mind of dirty, stinking lumberjacks as from the thought of getting soaped up and having someone throw buckets of cold water at her. She made up her mind to stay away from this sauna place. She could hide behind her disguise as long as she kept her clothes on. It struck her that she might end up as dirty as some of them apparently were, for fear of getting undressed.

Big Mary continued to talk, almost to herself. "I'll never forget the Sunday two years ago when one of the new jacks called the two of them a couple of 'damned rosebuds.' Him and Jock had a sauna before supper, and when they came into the cook shack to eat, this guy got a whiff of 'em. I don't think he ever smelled soap on a lumberjack before."

Big Mary laughed out loud. "They dragged him outside, undressed him and threw him in the sauna and locked him in for over an hour. They went in once in a while just to stoke up the fire and throw more water on the rocks. He was pretty soon begging for mercy; but they just let him beg. When they finally let him out, he passed out in the snow and they had to carry him to his bunk. He went down the road the next day, and we ain't heard from him since."

"That's barbaric!" Sarah groaned.

Big Mary slowed her steps and looked sternly at Sarah. "Let me tell you something, Boy. A lumber camp ain't no picnic. Not even Camp Seven. You got all kinds of ruffians from all kinds of different places, and there ain't no law except the Push. One way or another he has to get their respect or he can't keep 'em in line. The tougher and meaner he is, the more they respect him, and the more logs get cut.

"I've even heard the men brag about a foreman who killed a man. One of the jacks had a bottle hidden on him, and one day in the woods he started sneaking drinks. Before anybody noticed that he was drunk, he got careless and caused a load of logs to shift and they fell on one of the other men. The logs crushed the man's legs and they both had to be cut off. When that happened, the foreman flew into a rage and went after the guy who caused the accident."

"What happened?" Sarah gasped.

"He beat him to death." She looked satisfied, as if the man deserved to be murdered and the foreman had every right to do it.

"Was he *our* foreman?" Sarah asked, as soon as she could get words to come out of her mouth. Her eyes were wide and filled with terror.

"No. Some foreman over in Wisconsin. But you're going to be hearing lots of stories about ours," she said, hurrying her steps. "Some's true and some ain't. The jacks compare horror stories to see which camp's got the toughest foreman in the timber. But you don't need to worry boy; you'll be damn glad to have the foreman we've got. And after you been in Camp Seven, you won't be liking it in no other camp. And that's for sure!"

Sarah shuddered, the next question dying on her lips. She had heard more than enough to shut her up.

CHAPTER 11

THEY stopped in early afternoon at the edge of a swollen creek to eat lunch. It took Big Mary, with some help from Sarah, less than ten minutes to spread their lunch out onto the lowered tailgate.

Big Mary grumbled the whole time about the quality of the food she had purchased at the restaurant in Pine Crescent. "Look at this bread. It's full of holes. And these beans are dry enough to pave a road." She began cutting two apple pies into quarters. "And just look at this crust! You men are lucky you don't have to eat this kind of vittles every day."

Red Scanlon, eyeing the food hungrily, came over and took a slab of pie and bit into it. Big Mary slapped at him with her knife. "You wait like the rest of 'em."

"I can't. I'm near starved. Flaky. Crust is nice and flaky," he said appreciatively, swallowing the rest of the piece of pie with one gulp. Then he swiped at the crumbs on his mouth with the back of his hand and walked over and sat down on the ground to wait for the rest of his food.

"Them ain't flakes. Them's chips," Big Mary groused, as she beckoned to the men to come and eat.

Sarah sat on a large rock close to the creek bank, sometimes looking into the rushing water, and sometimes watching the others. She barely tasted the food she was eating. She was too curious about her new surroundings. To her surprise, Red Scanlon took a five-gallon can from the wagon for Big Mary to sit on. She wondered at this show of chivalry, but Big Mary seemed not to notice.

"You too good to sit with the rest of us, City Boy?" At first Sarah didn't realize Sawtooth Leverty was talking to her until he repeated it louder. "Hey, City Boy. You think you're too good to sit with us?"

Sarah, embarrassed and unaccustomed to being called "Boy," looked at him and swallowed hard. His wandering eye made her want to turn away from him. It was too confusing to try to figure out whether or not he was looking at her. "N... no. I just...this is the first time I ever sat by a creek and...."

"You don't need to sit all by yourself," he said as he stood up and came over and sat on the ground next to the rock she was sitting on.

She got up as casually as she could. "I'm okay." She spoke without looking at him, and then wandered over to the wagon and pretended to look for something in her tussock. She could feel his eyes following her—at least one of them—and she looked around at the others to see if they noticed anything funny about his behavior. Everyone else seemed to be paying attention only to his food. She glanced at Sawtooth and he was grinning at her, one eye leering at her and the other wandering crazily in various directions. She shivered and walked over and sat on the ground next to Big Mary.

"You got much trouble with pelters where you come from?" Spike Anderson asked, directing his question to Sawtooth Leverty, who was now sitting alone by the creek.

All eyes darted in Sarah's direction and then quickly away, but it happened so fast that she wondered if it had happened at all. Everyone but Spike and Sawtooth sat silently, eyes riveted on their plates.

Sawtooth shook his head and said, "Nope. You have 'em around here?"

Spike answered, his face grim. "Had one over in Camp Twelve last year kill a man. Big, even for a pelter. He looked to be more'n six feet tall. The foreman made a bad mistake...."

"Mistake?" Sarah asked, wondering what a "pelter" might be.

"Yup. Mistake. Most foremen know better than to cut down a hollow tree without having a good rifle nearby. Should know damn well one of them pelters might be living there." Spike, his dark eyes intent, said, "Had that big old pine almost down when the pelter came crashing through the woods looking to take his afternoon nap. I can tell you, you ain't never seen jacks run so fast. Except one. Got his foot caught in a tree root. The crew went back the next day and found him, his guts spilled out all around him. Damned agropelter musta just up and grabbed him around the middle and crushed him to death."

Everyone kept eating as Spike told his story. Except Sarah. She stared at Spike, her face ashen. She had heard about Indians and about wolves and bears. But agropelters? What kind of horror was going to be visited upon her? Her eyes darted to Big Mary's face, and for one brief instant, she saw the corner of her mouth quiver upwards. So *that* was it. They were telling this tall tale to frighten her. Fine. It would serve her purposes to be the dumb new boy in camp. "Do they ever come into camp?" she asked, making her voice quaver.

"Sometimes. 'Specially if there's food left laying around," Spike said as though he knew all there was to know about the creatures.

"Gosh!" Sarah exclaimed, eyes wide and innocent.

"Eat," Big Mary ordered. "I been letting you men talk while you're eating, but don't go thinking you can keep it up. My rules ain't no different from rules in other camps. No jawin' at mealtime."

The men stopped talking and concentrated on their food. Puzzled, Sarah was also silent. She remembered the men in the general store saying the cook was second in command to the foreman, and from what she had seen thus far, it apparently was true.

"Besides," Big Mary said, her voice now slightly less authoritarian, "We need to stop by the Lawson place on our way past, and at the rate we're going we won't make camp by dark."

When they had finished eating and everything was stowed back in the wagon, Big Mary climbed onto the seat next to Red. "Come on, Jesse," she said. "Climb up on back."

Sarah did as she was told, and settled down onto the lumpy sacks of potatoes, her aching legs stretched out in front of her. She craned her neck around and looked at the men walking far ahead of them. Their strides were as brisk as they had been when they first left Pine Crescent. She was no physical match for any of these men, but maybe she could get by on her wits. And as long as she could keep them convinced she was stupid, she could probably pull off her disguise.

Big Mary and Red Scanlon rode silently, their bodies swaying gently with the motion of the wagon. Sarah looked to the east off into the woods, breathing in the strange, new smells. They were moving through an area of deciduous trees, and the buds were just beginning to open on the yellow birch and the sugar maples. She was startled by the loud, goose-like "kak-kak-kak-kak-kak" of a northern goshawk, resting in the limb of a large maple tree and disturbed by the sound of the wagon. Moments later, a fisher weasel skittered across a fallen log and disappeared into the brush at the edge of the road.

She glanced around at Big Mary, whose head bobbed every few minutes as though she had fallen asleep. Red stared straight ahead, the reins held loosely in his hands, the horses plodding along with little guidance. The three men had disappeared in a bend in the road ahead of them. Sarah let her eyes drift shut.

She awoke to hear Red calling "whoa" to the horses. She jerked herself

upright and rubbed her eyes and looked around. They had pulled into a farm-
yard. The three jacks who had been walking were nowhere in sight, and Sarah
figured they must have kept walking on ahead. Red got down to water the horses
at a cattle tank that stood in front of one of the small buildings.

A woman came out of the cabin, smiling as she wiped her hands on her
apron. Three small boys, all looking to be less than five years old, tagged along
behind her. Their clothes were patched, but the boys looked clean and well fed.

"Brought you that calico, Sally," Big Mary said as she got down from the
wagon and pulled a package from under the seat and handed it to the smiling
woman.

"I sure do appreciate that, Big Mary. You got time to come in and have
something to eat and set a spell while I dig out some money for you?" Sally
Lawson was lonesome for the sound of another woman's voice. She had not
visited with another of her sex for nearly a month.

"Can't. But I thank you. We ate back a ways, and we need to get to camp
'fore dark. And you don't need to pay me. Those vegetables you sent over from
your garden last summer was pay enough."

Sarah jumped down from the wagon and looked around the tiny farm. Sam
Lawson, who had been out behind the cabin plowing, came and shook Red's
hand and helped him with the horses.

"Howdy. How's things going over Camp Seven way?" he called to Big Mary.

"Can't say," she answered. "Ain't been in camp for a few days. I see you're
gettin' the plow in. Frost out pretty much?"

"Yup. Finally. Altogether I got nearly three acres cleared. Winter's here are
a lot longer than back in Iowa, so it's a lot slower than I thought it was going to
be."

"Longer and slower and harder," Sally Lawson added, trying to sound matter
of fact instead of like she was complaining.

Sarah strolled around the cabin and surveyed the field. It looked small and
insignificant, surrounded as it was by stumps and slashings, and beyond—the
timber. She wandered back to the cabin where a cat lay on the front stoop
sunning itself. She picked it up and it began to purr as she stroked its thick fur.

"Is this your kitty?" she asked the smallest boy, beckoning to him to come
to her.

He shook his head shyly and put his thumb in his mouth and slid around
behind his mother's leg. One of the bigger boys walked over to her. "Her name's

Missy," he offered. "She ain't really nobody's cat 'specially. She likes anybody who'll pet her."

"She's in the family way," Sally Lawson said. "You want one of them kittens when they come? Good mouser, the mother."

Big Mary was climbing back onto the wagon. "I don't want no cats in my cook shack. Hate 'em."

"I don't like them much, either, but they're better than mice," Sally Lawson said, hoping the boy holding her cat would take one of the kittens off her hands when they came. She hated it when Sam had to drown the new litters in the cattle tank. They had four cats on the farm, but one could keep only so many cats. They, like children, just kept on being born. She put her hand to her stomach, feeling the slight rustlings of her fourth child.

"We're hoping for a girl this time," she said, smiling." Then she added, "Me and Sam's hatching some chicks. We hope to have some eggs to sell by next fall. And some fryers come July, depending on how many roosters hatch."

She had a running argument with Sam about the future of the hatchlings that turned out to be roosters instead of laying hens. He wanted to let the roosters get big before they ate them, but she longed for the taste of young, tender fried chicken and potato salad, which reminded her of her mother and her older sisters, and of home.

"Good, good," Big Mary said smiling and motioning to Red to get the wagon back in motion. "Being able to get fresh eggs once in a while will be a real treat."

Sarah climbed back onto the wagon, her legs aching from the effort. As she settled down among the potato sacks, she looked at Sam Lawson. It was easy to see how proud he was of his little farm. As he turned to go back to his work, she wondered how long it would take him to clean up the mess the lumbermen had left behind. His wife stood with one arm clutching the package of calico Big Mary had brought, waving with the other, until the wagon was out of sight.

It had begun to grow dark when Big Mary sniffed the air and said, "We're almost there. Woody has got the fire going." She closed her eyes and smiled, breathing in the welcoming fragrance of the wood fire that signaled home-coming. "They're probably good and hungry by now. If I ain't there to feed 'em, they don't eat nothing but beans."

Red chuckled and held the reins tighter because the horses knew they were almost home and were impatient to get there. "You just think we can't get on without you, Big Mary. You know damn well Woody knows how to cook plenty good enough to keep the men from starving."

Big Mary bristled. "Woody cooks beans. Beans, beans and more beans, you boardbrain. They'll all be farting from here to next Sunday 'cause they ain't had nothing but beans!"

Sarah stifled a giggle as they turned the corner and headed downhill.

CHAPTER 12

BELOW them in a clearing next to a rushing stream lay the small woodland village that was Camp Seven. A cluster of log buildings was scattered around the clearing, and Sarah couldn't imagine what they all were.

She didn't have much time to worry about buildings, however, because her eyes were carefully surveying the group of lumberjacks greeting the newcomers. The three men who had been walking ahead of them were in the middle of the clearing, already surrounded by jacks. Her heart raced as she scanned the crowd of men. Then she breathed a deep sigh of relief. He wasn't there.

The wagon came to a halt next to a big hollowed-out log in front of the stable, the longest of the buildings. The log was raised up off the ground and filled with water for the horses to drink. She climbed down from the wagon, feeling stiff and achy. She began to rub the backs of her thighs, then glanced quickly around, relieved to see that no one was paying any attention to her. The men were all busy slapping each other on the back and laughing. Her eyes roamed with interest around the camp, and she felt a sudden urge to take off her shoes and go wading in the rushing water of the stream.

"Hey you! Boy!" A voice broke into her childish reverie. At first she didn't realize Big Mary was calling to her. She was going to have to keep her ears perked up or she'd forever ignore people when they called to her as "Boy."

"Jesse! Confound you, Boy! Get on over here before I have one of the jacks drag you by the scruff of the neck!"

She pulled her thoughts away from running barefoot through cool water and instead ran over to where Big Mary stood in the doorway of the cook shack. Big Mary called to Red Scanlon, trying to be heard above the voices of the men. "Hurry and get that wagon over here. We ain't got all night to unload."

Sarah followed Big Mary into the cook shack. "I'm sorry, Ma'am. I was just looking around."

"You'll have time to look around later. Right now I want you to get busy. I didn't hire you to stand around looking stupid."

"No Ma'am. You sure didn't."

The interior of the cook shack was dark except for one lantern flickering above them near the door. Sarah watched as Big Mary lit the rest of the kerosene lanterns, which were strung from the ceiling over the tables and the work area. Big Mary lovingly referred to the work area as her "kitchen."

Now that she could see, she stared around her new "home." The western end of the large rectangular room where they had just entered was the eating area. Four long tables ran lengthwise from west to east, and they were covered with bright blue and white checked oilcloth. Long, low backless benches stood on either side of the tables. Between the two center tables stood a large, pot-bellied stove in a low box filled with sand to protect the planked floor from the heat. At the far end of the room a huge black stove dominated the work area, or Big Mary's "kitchen." It was separated from the eating area by two-tiered counters with storage shelves beneath the work surfaces. A sink made from a hollowed-out log dominated the north wall, with a drain running outside.

In addition to the door they had just entered—which the men used when they came for meals—was a door leading into a storage room on the east and a door leading outside on the south. There were two openings between the counters that divided the eating area and the kitchen. Other than the doors and the two openings to access the tables, the entire work area was ringed with either work surfaces or storage.

Along the western edge of the cook shack, on either side of the entrance door, there was a row of cast iron coat hooks mounted under a long, high shelf. Several odd leather mittens lay on the shelf, and two seemingly abandoned woolen caps hung from the hooks. There were only two small windows in the entire building; one over the sink looking north into the camp clearing and one next to the south-facing door.

"There aren't very many windows," Sarah said as her eyes scanned the dark walls.

"Stays warmer in winter when there ain't so many openings," Big Mary explained.

"But isn't it gloomy working in here?"

"Gloomy? Hah! You won't have time to notice if it's gloomy. Did you think you were coming to work at a seaside resort or some such?"

"Well, no, but...."

Just then the door opened and Sarah looked quickly to see who it was. Was she going to feel panic every time the door opened? A small wiry man with a wooden peg instead of a right leg clumped across the wooden floor, surprisingly quick and agile for a man with such a handicap.

"This here's Woody Olson," Big Mary said waving a hand toward him. "Meet Jesse Williams, my new cookee. Or at least he's supposed to be my new cookee. He ain't been a bit of help so far. He spends a whole lot of time standing around with his jaws flapping."

Woody came over and shook Sarah's hand, winking at her. Then he said to Big Mary, "You want me to show him where to put all these supplies?"

Big Mary was bustling around the stove and she didn't bother to turn to look at them. "Yeah. Unless you want to leave the damn things on the wagon and let the vultures have at 'em."

Woody winked at Sarah again and beckoned to her to follow him out to the wagon, where they began unloading the supplies and foodstuffs.

He was a small man, fifty-two years old, his gray hair tied into a stub of a ponytail. He had lost his leg fifteen years earlier when a runaway wagon on an icy skid road careened into him, smashing his leg between the wagon and a tree. The doctors gave him an artificial leg after the stump healed, but he fashioned a peg for himself and threw the artificial leg into the fire.

"This here peg works better'n that damned contraption the doctors gave me," he said whenever anyone had the temerity to question him about his peg. As well as being the cook when Big Mary was gone from camp, he was the saw filer, the blacksmith and the general handyman around the camp. He had been one of Smitheson's fastest scalers until his leg was crushed. After they amputated his leg below the knee he could no longer work in the woods. But he would have a job in a Smitheson camp as long as he wanted it. In this case it wasn't an act of charity on Smitheson's part; he more than earned his keep.

Woody showed Sarah the springhouse, where the food for the camp was kept cold during the summer; the root cellar, where they kept canned food and root vegetables; the storeroom behind the cook shack work area; and the various storage areas for supplies used on a daily basis. She tried to pay close attention, but she felt bewildered and was convinced she'd never be able to figure out what went where.

By the time they had everything put away and Woody left to drive the wagon to the stable, Big Mary's bun had started to come loose and her brow was moist and she looked completely frazzled. "You finally done?" She asked Sarah impatiently as she jabbed loose strands of hair back into her unruly bun.

Sarah nodded, but said nothing. She had had to run to keep up with Woody Olson, and she had worked so hard and so fast that she didn't know if she could keep going without resting for a while. But from the look on Big Mary's face, she would not be resting any time soon.

Big Mary reached under one of the tables and tossed a folded white apron at her. "Put this on. I'll show you how to set the tables, but I'm only going to show you once, so pay attention." She pointed out the salt and peppershakers and the bottles of catsup and canned milk for the tea and the coffee. These items were to be placed along the center of the tables, one such group for every four places at the table. Next she showed her the individual settings. There was a tin plate for each man, placed face down with a tin cup upside down on top of it, with a knife, fork and spoon next to it. Sarah watched carefully, and then proceeded to finish setting one of the long tables. During the summer, when the crew was small, they needed to use only one of the long tables. It was a simple chore, but she was already fatigued and overwhelmed.

She was beginning to worry that this job might be too much for her. She was already stretched to the limit, and Big Mary seemed to think she was not doing anything either well enough or fast enough. She glanced up at the clock on the wall. It was past ten o'clock, and it seemed a long way until bedtime.

Then another thought struck her. Where was she going to sleep? Where did the men sleep? Would she be expected to sleep where they did? It seemed likely, and the thought sent new stabs of fear through her weary body.

"Phew," Big Mary said finally, brushing her forehead with the back of one hand. "Every time I go to town I end up working twice as hard to make up for it." She was clearly bothered by the late supper. "You can call the men now."

Sarah stared at her for a moment then said in a little voice, "How? What do I say?"

"Hell fire and damnation!" Big Mary yelped, her displeasure escalating. She scurried impatiently across the length of the cook shack, her tongue clucking the whole time, and stepped outside and rang the iron triangle that hung outside under the eaves of the building.

"I...I didn't know," Sarah said defensively, watching her helplessly.

"You don't know much, do you?"

"Guess not," Sarah said with a shrug. Then, with an effort, she gathered herself together and pulled her shoulders back. "But I'm a quick learner."

"Yeah, yeah. Get your quick-learning ass moving and let's get these men fed."

Sarah followed Big Mary back to the kitchen and then stood watching as the men began to file into the cook shack. She was waiting for the next orders, uncomfortably aware of her ignorance about what was expected of her, but at the same time nervously watching the faces of the men as they entered the room. They all seemed to have their own place, except Sawtooth Leverty, who stood waiting for the rest of the men to take their seats. There were other new men in camp, but they had already eaten in the cook shack and had been assigned their places. Woody Olson came in and sat down in the second spot nearest the work area, leaving four places empty; the two end places and the one directly across from him at his end of the table and one at the far end. Big Mary motioned for Sawtooth Leverty to sit at the empty place at the end farthest from the "kitchen."

"The Push just got back. Him and the Finn are helping Red put the horses away. He said to go on ahead and start eating," Woody announced as he sat down.

Big Mary grunted an acknowledgement to Woody, then she and Sarah began carrying food to the table. Sarah could hardly believe the massive quantities of food Big Mary had prepared for supper. There were fried pork and venison steak, both boiled and fried potatoes, baked beans, stewed tomatoes, cooked prunes and baking-powder biscuits. Big Mary kept complaining that she hadn't had time to bake any pies, but there were leftover cookies.

The men were silent as they ate, and Big Mary and Sarah had all they could do to keep enough food on the table. Sarah was so busy she didn't have time to maintain her watch over the entrance. She was at the stove loading up a plate of fried pork, her back to the room, when three men came in. Red and the Finn went to the table and sat down without speaking and began to eat, but the foreman walked over to the sink and stood scrubbing his hands. She turned from the stove and hurried out to the tables and looked at Red and the man who was just sitting down. Satisfied, she again concentrated on what she was doing, trying not to act as inept as she felt.

She failed to notice the man at the sink, who had turned and stood looking around at the men, drying his hands slowly on a towel. His eyes stopped at the new cook's helper, and as he stared at her, she felt his eyes on her. She straightened and turned to look at him and to her horror found herself looking into the eyes of the very man she had feared seeing; he stood drying his hands, looking as intently at her as she was at him.

The plate slid out of her hands and dropped onto the table, splashing its contents onto the oilcloth. Big Mary heard the noise and looked across the room to where her new helper had just made a fool of himself in front of the foreman. She saw Jesse staring stupidly at the mess on the table and wanted to scream at him, but feared that if she did her boss would criticize her for hiring such an incompetent fool.

"He ain't never worked in a lumber camp before," Big Mary said quickly in the foreman's direction, loud enough for everyone in the room to hear.

The man said nothing for a moment, but after some thought said, "I see you hired him anyway." Then he walked to the table, swung one leg over the bench and sat down. He watched as Sarah picked up the meat and put it back onto the plate and stood staring at the greasy puddle the meat had left on the oilcloth. Hesitating for only a moment, she lifted the hem of her apron and started to swipe at it. The men started laughing, but the foreman looked around the table at them and the laughter stopped.

"Use a dishcloth, you idiot!" Big Mary yelled across the room. "That apron's not for wiping up grease!"

Sarah, mortified, ran to Big Mary who was waving a wet cloth at her like a flag. She hurried back to the table, feeling her neck and her face grow warm.

"I thought you swore you weren't going to hire any more useless boys," the foreman said coolly to Big Mary.

"Who am I supposed to hire? Ain't had nobody else offer to come to work for me." Big Mary stood with her hands on her hips and her chin jutting forward, glaring at him. She was not accustomed to being criticized, and her small face was pinched and angry.

Sensing her authority being threatened, she looked around the table at the men, her eyes at first carefully avoiding the foreman, but her words clearly aimed at him. "I'm sick and tired of telling you men there ain't no talking at the table." Then she seemed to think better of excluding her boss from her scolding, and she pointed a finger at him and said, "And that goes for you, too, dammit!" With that, she spun around and marched over to the stove and started banging kettles around on top of it.

Sarah stood stupidly with the greasy cloth in her hand staring from Big Mary to the Mud Man and then back again, wondering what he was going to do about Big Mary's impertinence. She was sure his next words would be for the cook to fire her new helper and to follow said helper down the road unless she was willing to remember who it was who gave the orders at Camp Seven.

He was silent for several painfully long minutes, then slowly and deliberately he asked Red Scanlon to pass him the pork. He took a piece of it from the platter, put it on his plate, cut off a piece, put it slowly into his mouth and chewed for a while. No one moved and no one else tried to eat. Then, as if the thought had just struck him, he stopped eating and pointed at Sawtooth Leverty and then at Sarah with his fork. "It appears we have some new folks in camp. Tell us your name," he said, pointing his fork at Sawtooth Leverty again.

Leverty looked sideways at Big Mary, then cleared his throat and said, "Leverty. They call me Sawtooth."

The foreman nodded and then pointed his fork at Sarah again. She felt her stomach knot up as he spoke. "And you, Boy. You have a name?"

Sarah swallowed hard and said, "J...Jesse. My name's Jesse, Sir."

"Jesse? Is that all?" he asked calmly.

"Williams. Jesse Williams."

His eyes traveled slowly over her from head to toe, his face expressionless. Then he cut another piece of meat, put it slowly into his mouth, chewed it, looked over at Big Mary for a long minute, as if allowing her enough time to hear every word spoken against her wishes at the supper table. Then he said, making a sweeping gesture with his fork, "I want you men to say your names so Jesse and Sawtooth here know who you all are."

"I already met everybody," Sawtooth protested. He didn't like all the attention he was getting.

"That's fine. Let's do it anyway." He pointed with his fork again, this time across the table at Jock Lehtinnen. "We'll start with the Finn."

Several of the men glanced nervously at Big Mary, but they did as they were told, each man in his turn. Sarah nodded at each of them, knowing full well she wasn't going to remember any of their names, but also knowing full well that this was for Big Mary's benefit—not for hers. She could almost feel the heat from the anger visible in Big Mary's stiffened back as she fussed at the stove, trying to ignore what was happening behind her.

When they had gone around the table and it was his turn, the foreman looked calmly around the room and his eyes stopped at Big Mary's back. He stared at her for as long as it took for her to realize what was going on and turn around to face him. Then he looked away from her and back at the men seated around the table.

Finally, as if for emphasis, he looked at Sarah and said, "Nilsson. Thor. Like the Norse God of thunder. My father said I didn't cry when I was a baby. Seems I roared instead. Like thunder."

None of them had ever heard the story of how he got his name, but he was now looking around the table without a trace of humor, so no one dared to laugh.

After several tense moments he looked again at Big Mary, who was standing very straight and very stiff. "Did you make pie for supper?"

Big Mary looked back at him, and her stiffened shoulders relaxed slightly and she said, "There wasn't time. There's some cookies I made last week."

Without smiling, he looked around the table at the men. "Now that we all know each other, you can have some of those old cookies and you can keep your mouths shut."

The room was very still. Big Mary beckoned to Sarah to come and take the plates that were heaped with cookies. The men stared intently at the cookies as they ate, as if suspicious of them.

Except Thor. He would take a thoughtful bite, and as he chewed he looked casually around at the men. When he finished the first cookie, he took another and chewed it carefully as he sat watching Sarah and Big Mary clear away the dishes. His expression never changed and no one dared to meet his gaze.

As he and the men finished the molasses and oatmeal-raisin cookies, Sarah slipped unnoticed into the storeroom behind the kitchen and stood staring straight ahead at the shelf full of supplies in front of her, seeing nothing. She wasn't sure she was going to be able to stand being in Camp Seven. It had seemed such a good idea to come to a lumber camp and work until she could find out something about her father's whereabouts. But this was far worse than she had expected. She was working for an ungrateful wretch of a woman who answered to an even more ungrateful wretch of a man.

"Good God!" she cried with her hand to her mouth to muffle her words. "What kind of a place have I gotten myself into?"

She stood for a moment, uncertain about what to think or what to do. Then she spun around and faced the door leading back into Big Mary's kitchen.

"You've gotten yourself into this," she whispered, "and you are not going to turn back like some weak, cowardly, sniveling...girl! Whether you like it or not, you are exactly where you intended to be and you're staying. Even if the God of Thunder *does* make the rules!"

She smiled a weak, half-hearted smile and murmured, "Mud and thunder!" Then she left the safety of the storeroom, hoping for the best—but fully expecting that even though she wanted to stay and tough it out, she was probably going to be fired for causing so much trouble.

CHAPTER 13

S HE walked back into the main room just in time to hear Big Mary calling to her. "Dammit to hell, Jesse Williams! If you don't get out here right this minute, I swear I'm going to send you to bed with no supper." All the men were gone and Big Mary was filling two plates with food.

"Pour us some coffee," she said as she carried the plates to the table and set them down across from each other where the foreman and the Finn had sat. With a sweep of one arm, Big Mary pushed dirty plates aside as Sarah set the cups of coffee on the table and sat down across from her. Sarah didn't dare speak. She was waiting to hear that she was going to be let go. She was so nervous she could barely eat.

"You're skinny as a rail. Eat," Big Mary commanded, her voice less harsh than it had been.

Sarah half-heartedly lifted a forkful of beans to her mouth. They tasted far better than she expected, and she began to eat what was on her plate. She glanced across at Big Mary, who looked so pleased that she was eating that Sarah wondered if maybe she wasn't going to be fired after all. Why would Big Mary care if she ate unless she planned to keep her working?

"Are you going to make me leave?" Sarah blurted, unable to stand the suspense any longer.

Big Mary put down her fork, leaned slightly back on the bench with her hands cupping the edge of the table. She stared at Sarah without speaking and studied Sarah's face for a long time. Then she relaxed and picked up her coffee cup with both hands, put it to her lips and sipped, slowly. "What makes you think such a thing?"

"I...well, before when I...when I made a mess and...and all those times you yelled at me...."

"You'll make a whole lot more messes before you're done around here, and you can damn well bet I'll yell at you plenty more. Don't take it so serious."

"Then I can stay?"

"Stay? Of course you can stay. You worked hard tonight. You'll do just fine. Only thing is you need to relax and not take everything so hard. We won't bite. Not me and not Thor."

Sarah sat listening, wondering at how the little woman had softened, and if maybe she really had taken everything too much to heart. She was, after all, pretty worn out. Her head probably wasn't working too well because her body was so exhausted.

"You'll feel better in the morning and so will I. Let's get this mess cleaned up and go to bed. Tomorrow things will settle back to normal and we'll get you going on your duties. Oh, by the way, you'll be sleeping on the cot in the store-room. Come November, it'll be the bull cook's bunk and we'll need to send you up to the bunkhouse; but for now the cot in the back room is yours."

Sarah had been too busy to even notice that there was a cot in the storeroom. When she found it in the far corner, she fell onto it like a stone. If someone had told her she would fall asleep on a bed with a straw mattress in a tiny room filled with foodstuffs, with nothing but one blanket wrapped around her and her lumpy tussock for a pillow, she'd have told them they were insane.

Besides which, she was filled with gratitude that she was being allowed to stay. Despite the nap she had taken in the wagon, and despite the concerns that could easily have kept her tossing the whole night, she was so tired she fell asleep before her head hit the tussock. She was too tired to either think or to feel. She didn't even take her clothes off.

She awoke in the night unable to breathe. It took her a while to become oriented, and then she recognized that her muslin binding was rubbing under her arms and squeezing her chest. She sat up and winced with pain. Every bone in her body ached. It was pitch dark and she couldn't see what time it was. She missed her gold watch. It was at Clemmie Vogel's with the rest of the things that gave evidence of her true identity; except for the brooch, which was tucked into the folds of her breast binding. She was not ready to part with the one link to the woman who had given her birth—even if that woman was nothing but a whore.

She dragged herself from the cot and fumbled her way into the kitchen. She went to the match holder that hung next to the stove, struck a match and looked at the big clock on the east wall over the stove. It was after three. Big Mary had said she'd come and wake her at four, and she wondered if she should crawl back onto her cot and sleep for another hour. Grudgingly, she decided it wasn't worth the agony of waking up twice in one morning. Once was bad enough. She would forego the additional hour of sleep in favor of spending some extra time getting cleaned up.

Grimacing with pain and fatigue, she took a pan of water into her dark room, undressed, and gave herself as much of a bath as she could manage without the benefit of a decent bowl, a towel, or even bath soap. She was using the bar of lye soap from the kitchen sink, and she winced with pain when she touched the skin where she was chafed from her bindings. By the time she finished, her teeth were chattering, but she felt more alert. She bound herself up again, not so tightly this time, and dressed in her extra set of clothing. She hung yesterday's wrinkled ones on the end of her bunk, hoping some of the wrinkles would hang out.

She went back into the kitchen and found some baking soda on one of the shelves and used it to brush her teeth, and then brushed quickly through her short, tousled hair. Then she returned to the storeroom and cleared a small corner of a shelf next to her cot. She put her tooth brush in a small empty jar she found behind some boxes and placed it, along with her hairbrush, on what she decided was to be her personal shelf. A wave of sadness swept over her as she looked at the shelf. It was a pathetic reminder of how little she possessed.

"Stop it," she chided herself. She straightened and pushed her shoulders back. "Get to work and quit moping around."

She lifted her shoulders and hurried into Big Mary's "kitchen." As she lit the kerosene lamps and built the fire in the big cook stove, she thanked Katie silently for having taught her so many things about working in a kitchen. Her confidence began to return as she worked. The coffeepot was boiling when at exactly four o'clock Big Mary walked in.

"You're looking chipper this morning," Sarah said, noticing that Big Mary didn't look the least bit tired.

Big Mary looked around and saw how much Sarah had already done. "I feel fine. Slept real good. I was surprised when I woke up and saw the lights on over here. I thought maybe you'd still be asleep when I got up. How do *you* feel this morning?"

"Real good!" She squared her shoulders and said bravely, "Tell me what to do."

Big Mary began bustling around and giving instructions at the same time. She sent her to the springhouse for bacon, and then set her to work cutting strips from the huge slab so Big Mary could put them on the grill, where they immediately began to sizzle and fill the cook shack with an appetizing aroma.

"We'll set bread as soon as we get the men fed and off into the woods for the morning."

"Morning? Do they only work half a day?"

"They work until nearly dark. But we'll see them again this noon when we take flaggins out to them."

Sarah stopped what she was doing and looked at Big Mary. "I'm afraid to ask. What's *flaggins*? It sounds like we're going to go out and whip them."

Big Mary laughed so hard she almost dropped the bowl of flapjack batter she was carrying to the stove.

Sarah stared at Big Mary, perplexed. What was so funny?

Just then the door opened and Woody came in. He saw Big Mary convulsed with laughter and asked, "You been at the keg?"

"You can be damn sure I ain't been at no keg. You got a keg hiding someplace I don't know about?" She didn't wait for an answer. "Jesse here thinks flaggins is flogging. Can you just see it? Us coming out at noon with our whips to beat up on the jacks?"

"How am I supposed to know what *flaggins* are?" Sarah set the stack of tin plates she was holding onto the table so they clanged and clattered and one of them rolled onto the wooden floor. "How am I supposed to know all these things?" She looked at Big Mary and then at Woody and she felt tears sting her eyelids.

The thought startled her. She had not cried for as long as she could remember, despite all that had happened that gave her good reason to cry. Now she was about to cry over a *word*. She reached down to pick up the plate, hoping they wouldn't notice her discomfort. She wondered if maybe it was time for her monthlies, because that was the only time she ever felt weepy. The thought brought her up with a start. She had better put on some protection or she'd *really* blow her disguise.

"Don't let it bother you, Boy," Woody said reassuringly, interrupting her thoughts. "The Push told me the cook he worked for his first day threw a pan of dirty dishwater on his head when he asked what to do with it. He had trouble understanding directions because he couldn't speak English. Big Mary won't likely do something like that. If the worst thing she does is laugh at you, you'll live through it."

Without any of them noticing, Thor Nilsson had come into the cook shack and stood listening. When Woody saw him, he said, somewhat sheepishly, "You caught me tellin' tales."

Sarah turned to look at him, wondering what awful thing was going to happen now.

"At least you're telling the truth. It's the damnable lies everybody seems bent on telling about me that get under my skin." He slapped Woody playfully on the back, then walked over and tweaked Big Mary under the chin and said, "I see you're in a better mood this morning."

"Never you mind the mood I'm in," Big Mary said, slapping at him with the towel she had slung over her shoulder.

He poured himself a cup of coffee and looked at Sarah. "*Flaggins* is what we call lunch in the woods. It's a lumberjack picnic, if you have plenty of...I think you Americans call it imagination." He took a drink from his cup, frowned at Big Mary, and said, "If you can call it a *picnic* when nobody's allowed to talk." Then, grinning slyly, he left the cook shack carrying his coffee.

Sarah went to the log sink, pretending to busy herself so she could watch out the window as he headed toward the stable in the darkness. He did not look back, even though she suspected he knew she was watching him. She turned from the window and found Big Mary watching her.

"See? I told you he wouldn't bite. There ain't no need to be afraid of him."

"I...I'm not afraid. I just don't think it was very nice what he did to you last night," she said, trying to divert attention from herself.

Big Mary's eyes widened. "Nice? Nice? If the Push was *nice* we'd all be in trouble. Besides. I asked for it."

"You sure as hell did," Woody interjected from his spot near the stove where he was drinking his coffee. "Spouting off to him about breaking rules ain't real smart."

"Why can't the men talk while they eat?" Sarah addressed her question to Big Mary, but Woody answered.

"They got the same rule in every camp I ever been in. If the men talk, they dawdle and don't get done eating so they can get out to work."

"But at night they're done working. Why can't they talk then?" Sarah persisted.

"Because by then it's time for the cook and her helpers to get done cleaning up so they can get ready for the next day. Men sitting around half the night talking and eating would cause a big delay in the workings of the cook shack."

As Woody said this last, he put his cup at his place on the table and clumped out the door. "Speaking of work, I'd better get to mine."

"So if it's a rule and you just reminded him of it, why did he get so angry? And why was he so rude to you?" She knew at once that she had said too much and clamped her mouth shut—too late.

"Damn you, Boy. I'm beginning to think you ain't got no brains at all. If the Push decides to break one of the rules *right smack in front of the men*, it don't matter two hoots in hell about the damn rule. I ain't got no call ordering him around like he's nothing but one of the jacks. I got what I deserved, and I probably won't step on my tongue again for awhile." She tipped her head to one side, thinking. Then she chuckled and said, "But then on the other hand, I might."

"You really aren't one bit afraid of him, are you?"

"Afraid? Hell no. I already told you I ain't afraid, and I been telling you not to be. As long as you do your job, he won't bother you."

Sarah decided to let it go. She had to stop worrying about him. They had not fired her, and he had not recognized her. Those were the important things. If Big Mary was right, and she certainly seemed to know what she was talking about, she would be able to do her job and not be bothered by the foreman.

"What should I do now?" she asked, feeling better and eager to get on with her duties.

Big Mary shook her head in disgust. "I sure will be glad when you know what you're doing." She waved a wooden spoon at the clock. "The men will be coming in soon and you ain't even half done with the set ups. After breakfast when I'm done setting the bread dough we'll hitch up and get ready for flag...." Then she started to chuckle to herself.

Sarah ignored her and finished setting the table. When the men were seated she helped Big Mary relay the food to the tables. There were pots of baked beans, plates stacked high with buckwheat flapjacks, fried potatoes, fried bacon and doughnuts—which Big Mary called cold shuts.

She looked up at the clock, curious to learn how long it took for the men to eat. She wanted to get a feeling for her schedule. From start to finish it took them less than twenty minutes. She had never seen men eat so much or so fast. She barely had time to be nervous about Thor Nilsson's presence in the room before he and the rest of the crew were gone.

After they left, Sarah sat down at the table across from Big Mary. She was hungry and she ate more than she had eaten in days. The mixture of aromas from wood burning and food cooking had fired up her appetite. Big Mary watched with approval.

When she was satisfied that her new helper had finally eaten enough, she said, "If you're done eating, you better get a move on. The wood box is empty, and you don't have a lot of time to get the wood cut before it's time to get ready to load the flaggins cart."

Sarah choked on her coffee, and it took her several moments before she was able to speak. "Cut the wood? Don't the men do that?"

"The cook's helper does that. Woody keeps a woodpile out back behind the cook shack. All you need to do is split it."

Sarah sat for a moment, waiting for Big Mary to say she was joking, but no more words were forthcoming. How could it be true that with a camp full of lumberjacks she was the one who had to split wood for the stove? She got up and quickly cleared away all the dishes, her brow furrowed in concentration.

She had never split wood in her entire life. Toby had always brought the armloads of wood into the kitchen. She had never so much as touched an axe. The closest she had ever gotten to the woodpile behind the Stewart's house was when she was a little girl playing in the back yard. She would climb up into a tree and watch Toby swing the axe, either to cut wood or to chop the head off a chicken. Now she feared she would be having an intimate association with the resident woodpile.

She did the breakfast dishes, thoroughly rinsing off the soap so the men didn't get sick, as Big Mary instructed her. She propped them on the counter next to the log sink to dry. The knives, forks and spoons were put into a white grain sack and shook until they were nearly dry, then were dumped into a pan on the stove to dry the rest of the way.

When she was finished, she went out back behind the cook shack looking for the woodpile. It was behind the cook shack on the east, near the stream. Next to it was a tree stump with an ax stuck into it. Luckily, there were enough pieces of wood already cut and lying on the ground, and there were enough splinters of wood and bark scattered around the stump to make several hefty armloads. But from the way the cook stove sucked up wood, she knew it wasn't enough to last through supper that night.

She took off her cook's apron and hung it onto a tree branch, then walked over to take the axe out of the tree stump. To her dismay, she could hardly pull it out. She had to tug at it with both hands with all of her strength, and when it finally came loose with a jerk she fell over backwards and landed on the ground flat on her rear end. She quickly looked around, mortified and fearful that someone might be watching.

Much to her relief, no one was. She got up off the ground and brushed off the seat of her pants. Then, trying hard to remember how Toby split wood, she attempted to mimic his movements. Whenever she got a log positioned onto the stump, however, it fell over onto its side. When she finally got one to remain standing she swung at it and the axe flew out of her hand and bounced to the ground. She jumped backwards to keep it from landing on her foot. It had been sharpened recently and she knew it was dangerous. Not so much to the logs, she thought to herself, as to her feet. She picked up the axe again, and again she was unsuccessful and the axe ended up on the ground and the log ended up on its side, inert and in one piece.

Tears of frustration stung the insides of her eyelids. This was the second time she felt like crying since she arrived at Camp Seven, and she felt a wave of self-pity. She sat down on the stump and looked at the axe lying like a challenge at her feet. She jumped up, reached down and picked up the axe, fear gripping her. If the Push were to see what was happening, he would surely get rid of her. If he knew she couldn't even split wood she wouldn't last the day in camp. She looked around again, but the only movement was the smoke coming out of the cook shack chimney and the ripples in the stream at the edge of the camp.

Determined, she stubbornly repositioned the log. It took her almost an hour to get enough wood split to make an armload. She was clumsy, but she managed to begin to get a feel for swinging the axe. She would have to spend every spare minute—and she wondered how many of *those* there'd be—at the woodpile. She'd have to get up the next morning long before Big Mary or anyone else if she intended to keep enough wood in the wood box for the cook stove.

When she carried in the wood, Big Mary didn't say anything about the time Sarah had spent outside cutting it. All she did was look at Sarah and say, "Get on over and harness Old Bill to the flaggins cart." When she saw the look on Sarah's face, her own face softened. Wiping her hands on her apron, she walked out into the clearing and motioned for Sarah to follow. "I'll show you."

Relief flooded her, and Sarah hurried meekly along behind Big Mary. How many things would she have to do about which she knew absolutely nothing? And how much ignorance would Big Mary put up with before she sent her packing?

"During the season Paddy Roark works in camp in the morning and he'll hitch up for us," Big Mary explained. "But during the summer he goes out as part of the crew so we do it ourselves. Nothing to it, really."

"Which one is Paddy Roark?" Sarah asked.

"Don't you remember? All the men told you their names. He sits halfway down the table on the same side as the Finn. His hair's the color of a rusty kettle. Not flaming red like Scanlon's."

"I'm not very good at remembering names. Is he the one who blushes all the time?"

"Yeah, that's Paddy," Big Mary said as she deftly hitched the big bay gelding to the cart, then led him over next to the cook shack and tied the reins to a post outside the cook shack door.

After they had the flaggins cart loaded and had climbed onto the seat and pulled out of the camp clearing toward where the men were cutting the new road, Sarah inadvertently let out a sigh of relief.

"You can relax and enjoy the ride today, Boy," Big Mary said glancing at Sarah, "but you'll need to learn to handle a horse. We'll take turns going and coming. That way, we both get to relax part of the time. Sound fair to you?"

Sarah nodded and grimaced as she looked the other way. She didn't want Big Mary to see how discouraged she felt about all the things she was going to have to do. Helping Katie in the kitchen had been child's play compared to this. Thinking about it, though, she decided she had done pretty well so far—for a beginner.

Big Mary cleared her throat to speak, and Sarah expected to perhaps hear some words of praise. She didn't. "Tomorrow morning I'll show you the rest of your duties."

"H...how many more things could I possibly have time to do?" she asked. The words were barely out of her mouth when she knew she had made a big mistake.

"How many? How many? I can't believe you're so rattle-brained. So far you ain't done nothing but ask stupid questions and fumble around doing everything wrong!"

"B...but you said last night that I had worked hard and that...." Sarah stopped trying to defend herself. She knew she was only making matters worse.

"My advice to you, Boy, is that you'd better shape up and shut up. You'll have as many duties as I decide to give you. You'll do them, and you'll do them fast. And if you can't cut it—and I'm beginning to think you can't—you can get your lazy ass out of here and go back to Chicago!"

Sarah felt so intensely inadequate that it made her sick to her stomach. "I...," she began, her voice quivering, "I'm really sorry I've been so...so useless." She was having trouble getting the words out around the big lump forming in her throat.

Big Mary reached over and put her hand on her arm. Her anger seemed to have completely dissipated. "I'm sorry, Jesse. I didn't mean to sound so hard. You'll do just fine. It's just going to take some time. We need to be patient with each other." She needed to try harder to remember that the poor boy had just lost his mother, and he was trying hard to make his own way in the world. She had to stop being so unreasonable with the poor kid. She patted Sarah gently on the arm and then slowly pulled her hand away. "It'll be okay. You'll see."

Sarah nodded without speaking, and then sat silently, her head down, for the rest of their ride. They soon arrived at what Sarah could see was a pre-selected clearing in the woods. There were logs arranged to sit on, and a small pile of firewood. Big Mary showed Sarah how to build a campfire and they boiled water for tea and put the huge pot of beans onto the fire. Sarah was again surprised by the quality and the quantity of food Big Mary had managed to prepare for the outdoor meal. There was no bread, because Big Mary had been gone and hadn't had time to finish baking it; but she had made biscuits, and there were jars of oleomargarine and jam. Along with the baked beans there were boiled potatoes, slices of cold ham, canned tomatoes, oatmeal and raisin cookies and larrigan pie—Thor's favorite.

Again, the men ate without talking. Thor and Jock the Finn sat next to each other on a fallen log. Sarah tried hard not to look over at him. She had the feeling Thor was watching her, even though whenever she managed a discreet glance in his direction he seemed not to be paying any attention to her.

Sawtooth Leverty, however, *was* watching her. As she walked around serving food and pouring hot tea for the men, Sawtooth kept winking at her with his one good eye. She pretended to ignore him and she wondered why no one else seemed to notice his strange behavior. Perhaps she was just being paranoid and misjudging him because of the way he looked. She didn't want to be unfair, but he made her extremely uncomfortable and she wasn't sure why.

Two of the new men in camp finished eating and walked over to the edge of the clearing. Their voices grew loud and they began to push each other. At first it wasn't clear whether they were fooling around or were having a real dispute. Thinking the former, a small group of jacks finished eating and went over and started cheering them on. The two men, a big French Canadian named Pierre Letourneau, and a short, stocky German named Hans Freisenthal, were having an argument over who had cut the most board feet of timber during their careers as lumberjacks. It seems they had worked together other times in other camps. Their scuffle escalated and they started to exchange blows.

"You frog bastard," the little German growled fiercely, after he was almost knocked off his feet by a blow to the ear. He was nearly a head shorter than the Frenchman, but he was quicker, and he somehow got his arms around Pierre, pinning his arms to his side, and was about to give him a blow to the groin with his knee.

Without warning Thor jumped up, took several long strides over to them and jerked them apart. He put a hand on the back of each of their necks and smacked their heads together with a crack that made Sarah wince. Then he tossed them apart like several sacks of loose straw and said, his voice dangerously calm, "You get one warning. This is it." Then he turned toward the rest of the men. "Finish eating and get back to work. If you came here to be entertained, you chose the wrong camp."

Sheepishly, the two perpetrators picked their caps up off the ground and followed the rest of the men back into the pines. Thor stayed long enough to say something to Big Mary, but he said it quietly so Sarah couldn't hear him. Then he, too, walked into the pines and the trunks of the tall trees closed in around him.

Sarah busied herself cleaning up the site, wishing Big Mary would talk about the fight. When she didn't, Sarah finally said, "He could have cracked their skulls."

"Yup," came the answer, followed by silence. Then Big Mary motioned for her to sit down on one of the logs and eat. She did, the sun warm on her back. The food tasted better than any food she had ever eaten, and she wondered if it was the quality of Big Mary's cooking or the hard work she was doing that was making her so hungry. As soon as she had had enough, she stretched her legs out in front of her and rubbed the back of them. She was glad she didn't have to walk back to camp because she didn't think her legs would carry her.

"Don't be lollygaggin'," Big Mary scolded, getting up abruptly. We got work to do."

They finished loading up the flaggins cart, returned to camp, and immediately

began supper preparations. After supper, and after the supper chores, Sarah
managed to get out to spend one hour at the woodpile, trying to catch up with
the wood supply. By the time she went to bed that night, she was so tired she
almost didn't take the time to undress, but she remembered what it felt like to
wake up with her bindings still on. When she finally fell, exhausted, onto her cot,
she felt enormously grateful for her crude bed.

But then she suddenly remembered that in the morning Big Mary was going
to give her the rest of her duties and her eyes flew open. She lay staring up into
the black ceiling, fear and fatigue mingling in a crazy whirl in her head. "Oh
God," she groaned, turning over and burrowing her face into her lumpy tussock.
But even her troubling thoughts could not keep her awake. She was too drained
of life not to sleep.

CHAPTER 14

SHE awoke with a start, feeling the wetness between her legs that told her that her monthlies had indeed arrived. She staggered into the kitchen and looked at the clock on the wall. It was two forty-five. She groaned, feeling cheated of fifteen minutes of sleep. She had planned to sleep until three and then get up and go to the woodpile. She knew better than to go back to bed for so short a time. She would surely oversleep if she did. She bathed, fashioned a pad from her extra muslin, dressed and went to the kitchen.

"Oh Lord," she groaned, feeling a wave of weakness as she lit the lanterns. She felt exhausted, and having her monthlies added to her discomfort. The day was off to a bad start. She got the fire built and the coffee water boiling before she went to the woodpile. She managed to get enough wood chopped to last through breakfast.

She was putting it into the wood box next to the cook stove when the door opened and Thor strolled across the room to the stove, lifted the lid on the huge coffee pot and peered into the boiling water, then turned to look at her. It made her nervous to have him watching her. She brushed wood from the front of her, trying to aim for the wood box, and scattered wood chips onto the floor.

He frowned darkly at the mess she was making, then asked, "Why is there no coffee?"

She wanted to defend herself and tell him it was too early for her to be working yet, and that she wasn't supposed to have the coffee made until shortly after four. But she was too rattled to speak except to make some ineffectual noises about not having yet had the time.

Without speaking, he lifted the coffee container from the shelf. She watched him, dumbly, as he made the coffee, counting out just the right number of scoops of coffee into the pot.

The door opened at the far end of the room and Big Mary hurried in, followed by Woody. "Morning," Big Mary said. She seemed cheerful at first, but when she saw Thor making coffee, she frowned and glared at Sarah and said, "Ain't you made coffee? Does the boss have to come in here and do it for himself?"

"B...but...." Sarah stammered.

It was Woody who saved her. He pulled his pocket watch out of his pocket, looked at it, then looked sharply at Big Mary and said, "Give the kid a break. It's three-thirty. By rights, he should still be in bed." Then he looked at Thor and changed the subject by asking, "A couple of the new men were asking about the wannigan. Seems they need some liniment and tobacco."

Sarah looked over at Woody and her heart swelled with gratitude. At least she had *one* ally.

Thor nodded curtly to Woody, then walked over to the counter, opened one of the big jars and took out an oatmeal cookie. "Bring me a cup of coffee when it's done. I'll be in the clerk's shack. Then send anyone with questions over to talk to me." He shook his head in disgust. "Why don't the damn fools just ask me if they want something." He slammed the door behind him as he went out.

"They don't ask because he scares the living shit out of everybody," Woody said as he stomped over to where the cups were stacked and took two of them down. Then he looked at Sarah, who had begun nervously setting the table. "Don't let it get to you, Boy."

"I won't," she said, not at all sure it hadn't *already* gotten to her.

He began talking softly to Big Mary and Sarah tried to ignore them, hoping that no one would pay any more attention to her. A short time later, as she was busily setting up for breakfast, Woody headed toward the door with the coffee for Thor. He maintained his fast, choppy gait across the room without spilling a drop from the cup. He saw her watching him and stopped, looked down at the cups and then at her. "Not too bad for an old man with a wooden leg, eh?

"And a wooden head," Big Mary called.

He winked at Sarah as she opened the door for him. "She's ornery like that sometimes. You'll get used to it."

"What did you say?" Big Mary barked at him across the room.

"I said you're looking especially beautiful this morning," he called back to her, winking again at Sarah.

Sarah closed the door behind him and smiled to herself.

When the men finished breakfast and left the cook shack, Sarah cleaned up the long table and did the dishes. Then she started to go outside to cut some more wood.

"Where do you think you're going?" Big Mary asked.

"To get some wood."

"You ain't got time to get wood right now. You need to scrub the table and the benches and the floor. Be sure the water's hot and soapy. The men have drug in a ton of mud on the bottom of them damned lugged boots. Come summer you won't have to scrub the floor but twice a week or so. Except here in the kitchen. The kitchen floor gets done every night, but I've been letting you get by without doing it, seeing as how you ain't quite up to speed. From now on you need to do it every night before you go to bed."

Big Mary showed her where to find the bucket and she watched Sarah fill it with hot water and showed her how to shave slivers of soap into it and then swish the water around to made suds. "Scrub that table and the benches real good first, while the water's still clean. Then get the broom and sweep the floor and then use it to scrub with. I'll show you how if you can't figure it out." She seemed to have calmed down since her anger over the coffee.

Sarah began to scrub the long table. She was thankful she only had one table to clean, and one set of benches. The floor was more difficult for her. At first she had trouble handling the big heavy broom. She felt clumsy, but she finally got the hang of dipping the broom into the water, scrubbing, and then letting the excess water run down between the cracks in the floor.

After she had finished, Big Mary said, "Set the broom upside down out front to dry."

"I'll set it out back when I get the wood," Sarah said, again on her way outside to cut wood.

"You ain't going out back. Go find Woody and ask him to show you your duties up at the bunkhouse. There's another broom up there, so you don't need to take this one with you."

"Bunkhouse?" Sarah gasped. "I thought I was hired to help feed the men."

"You were hired to do what I tell you to do," Big Mary said, her anger rising again. "Let's not go getting all uppity and complaining every time I tell you to do something!"

Sarah wanted to scream, or to lie down on her cot and rest for awhile, or to hit the tiny woman over the head with the broom. Instead, she took the broom out front as she was told, and propped it against the side of the cook shack. Then she looked around to see if she could spot Woody. She saw him coming out of one of the small shacks at the far end of the clearing and she called to him. He beckoned to her and she hurried over to him, hoping for a few kind words to ease her misery.

"I'm supposed to ask you to show me my duties in the bunkhouse," she said, hardly believing she could be asking for more work.

"Come on, Kid," he said. "I don't have a whole lot of time."

She felt disheartened, all of her hopes dashed. Even he was going to be hard on her. "I'm sorry to bother you," she said, her voice choking up with self-pity.

"No need to be sorry. I just said I don't have much time. I didn't say I didn't want to do it." He seemed to notice how miserable she was, and his next words were gentle. "I'll help you whenever I can, but you need to buck up."

She nodded, trying to swallow the lump in her throat, but was unable to speak.

He put one hand on her shoulder and smiled at her. "It'll be okay, Boy. We ain't as hard as we try to make out." Then he straightened and said, "Follow me. You ain't seen nothing until you've seen a bunkhouse in a lumber camp."

She followed him as he led her to the bunkhouse. It was the biggest building in camp—except for the stable—and it stood on the eastern edge of the clearing. The cook shack and the long, low bunkhouse stood opposite each other on the northern and southern edges of the camp. She was beginning to learn what all the buildings were. When they got inside the bunkhouse, the unpleasant odor of stale tobacco smoke and dirty socks assaulted her and she gagged.

"My, my, ain't we persnickety?" Woody said, looking at her, but not without sympathy. "You'll get used to it. It smells like a daisy now compared to winter. During the season there's seventy or more jacks sleeping in here, farting and hanging their wet socks up to dry." He pointed overhead, where a wire was strung from one end of the ceiling to the other.

She longed to go back out into the fresh air to catch her breath, but she didn't dare. She knew she was taking Woody's time, and she couldn't continue to take advantage of his good nature. If she did, she feared he, too, might turn against her. Instead, she left the door standing wide open as she looked around the room. There were bunks along either side of the room, stacked two high. She could tell that only a small number of the bunks were occupied, because there was one blanket and one tussock on those.

"These are called deacon's benches," Woody explained, pointing at two long benches stretching along the ends of both rows of bunks.

In the center of the room was a pot-bellied stove with a large kettle on top of it, which he told Sarah she was to fill each day so the men had warm wash water the next morning. She wondered how one kettle of water could supply the summer crew, much less the winter one. From the number of empty bunks, she could tell the winter crew was huge compared to the summer crew. There was a big wood box filled with kindling and firewood. There were two low wooden boxes, one on either side of the stove, filled with sand, which served as spittoons. Sarah looked at Woody, hoping he would tell her that emptying those loathsome boxes would not be part of her duties.

He looked at her, read her thoughts, and then laughed. "Yup," he said. "You clean them whenever they need it."

She shivered and turned away from him, trying to hide her disgust.

At one end of the bunkhouse, next to the door, stood a washstand with a small square mirror hanging over it. There were several roller towels hanging on the wall next to it. He informed her that she had to hang a clean roller towel every day, and that it was her duty to wash them. She had no idea how she was supposed to do that, but again she didn't ask. Next to the washstand was a barrel filled with water, which Woody told her needed to be kept full. Apparently, some of the men washed in cold water. *If they bother to wash at all,* she thought grimly.

"You need to be sure there's soap in them soap dishes. And be sure to scrub those basins every day. You've got to sweep the floor every day, but it only needs to be scrubbed once a week unless we get a lot of rain. Can't help dragging mud in when it rains."

Just as in the cook shack, there were kerosene lanterns strung from the ceiling. "Keep them filled and clean. The Push don't like it when the chimneys get black."

"I'll bet he doesn't," Sarah mumbled under her breath.

"And oh yes," he said, almost as an afterthought. "Don't forget to sweep out the privies and scrub 'em down good twice a week." He looked around thoughtfully to be sure he had covered everything, and then he said, "You're on your own now, Jesse. I got my own work to do."

As he left, his wooden peg counting a brisk cadence on the bunkhouse floor, she stood staring after him until long after the peg and its owner had disappeared through the door. Once again, she felt tears working their way up through her misery.

"You baby," she said out loud, chastising herself. "You ignorant, stupid, inept, worthless...." She thought for a moment, then added, "Boy!"

She spent more than an hour finishing the bunkhouse, and that didn't include washing the roller towels. She'd have to find out where to do the laundry. It also didn't include emptying the spittoon boxes, which looked pretty grubby to her, but which would have to wait another day. She didn't know where to get fresh sand. She had a long mental list of things she needed to learn and she wondered if any of it would ever get to be routine.

She knew she had better get a routine going—and fast—because she couldn't possibly do all there was to do unless she had her schedule finely tuned, and unless her energy level magically increased about a hundredfold. *All this work for seven dollars a week,* she thought with dismay. She was only beginning to appreciate what her uncle had taken from her. She forced it out of her mind, because thinking about it was making her angry, and she didn't have energy to spare on anger.

She remembered how numb she had been on her way from Boston to Pine Crescent. It felt to her like eons had passed since then, and she wished she could recapture some of that numbness.

When she finished in the bunkhouse, she went back to the cook shack and found Big Mary standing in the doorway, her hands on her hips, looking impatient. "It's about time! Get on over to the stable and harness Old Bill to the flaggins cart."

When she saw Sarah's mouth drop open, she said, "I showed you yesterday. I don't plan to show you things more than once."

Seeing the tears suddenly well up in Jesse's eyes, Big Mary relented and said, as she headed to the stable, Sarah stumbling along behind her, "One more time. I'll show you one more time." She clucked her tongue impatiently and said, "Boys! I get so sick of 'em!"

The next several days were sheer torture for Sarah. And to make matters worse—if that could be possible, something happened that caused her to have trouble sleeping. It happened the second night after Woody showed her all of her duties in the bunkhouse. She did not have a lantern in the storeroom and she was growing accustomed to dressing and undressing in the dark. If she had a lantern she might have noticed the thing moving under her blanket. Instead, she undressed and crawled under her blanket and didn't notice she had company until something cold and moist curled itself around her leg. She screamed and jumped out of bed, stumbling and falling against the shelves, knocking things down as she groped along them to catch her balance.

She ran into the kitchen and stood in the dark, a fist to her mouth to muffle her cries. She tried to think what to do, but she was so terrified she couldn't think. Finally, after what seemed an eternity, she decided she had to light a lantern and get the thing—whatever it was—out of her bed.

She went and got the broom, and holding it and the lantern, went back into the storeroom. She set the lantern on a shelf, then went over to the bed and slowly and carefully lifted the blanket with the broom handle. A small snake lay in a coil against her tussock. She screamed again, but stopped herself in mid scream, afraid of waking someone in camp. She began to shake violently, and she dropped the blanket back over the snake and ran back into the kitchen, leaving the lantern on the shelf and the supplies she had knocked down scattered all over the floor. She went and leaned against the log sink, trembling and unable to think or to act.

After a while, she grew calmer and she looked out into the clearing. There was a full moon, and it lit the clearing enough so she could see that someone was out there. She shrunk back from the sink, hoping whoever it was couldn't see her. Then, realizing the lamp was in the storeroom and there was no light in the kitchen, she looked out the window again. Whoever it was would not be able to see her in the window without a light behind her.

It was Thor. He was standing next to the horse trough, his hands in his pockets. He was looking up toward the east, where the moon was hanging like a giant golden ball high above the trees on the other side of the stream. She stood watching him, fascinated by how motionless he was. She thought for a moment that she could call to him and he would come and take care of her snake. She immediately discarded that idea, knowing full well how much wrath would come down on her for being afraid of a little snake. But somehow his presence gave her comfort. She didn't know why or how, but the knowledge that he was out there, and that if worse came to worse he would take care of the situation, made her breathe easier.

She stood by the window and watched him for a long time. She thought it must have been nearly ten minutes before he moved, his long strides taking him in the direction of the clerk's shack. She wondered why he wasn't going to the bunkhouse to sleep, but she was too bone weary to think of anything but her own need for sleep.

She went back into the storeroom, calmer now. She looked around for something with which to pick up the snake, and decided instead to use the broom to sweep it off the cot into some kind of container. She found an empty wooden box with a sliding lid, which had contained rifle shells, and set it next to the cot. Using the broom, she lifted the blanket from the snake, which still lay curled next to her tussock. With one swift motion she swept the snake off the bed and it bounced into the box and she quickly slid the cover shut. Breathing hard from the excitement, she picked up the box and carried it at arm's length to the far side of the storeroom and set it on the floor behind several barrels. She didn't want to be able to see the box. Then she began to pick things up off the floor, not caring whether they were in the right places on the shelves.

Finally, she lifted her blanket and her tussock and shook them carefully to be sure there was nothing else in her bed. Then she blew out the lantern and crawled under her blanket. But she couldn't get to sleep for a long time. Every time she dozed off, she'd awake with a start, imagining she felt something. Twice during the night she got up and lit the lantern so she could check her cot because she was sure something was crawling around on her. When morning came she had slept little and she felt worse than she would have had she stayed up the entire night.

The following day was uneventful, and much to her surprise she managed to get through it without collapsing. She was too busy to think about how awful she felt, and after supper she hurried with her chores so she could get to bed early. She wanted nothing more than to be able to sleep. The next day was Sunday, and Big Mary said she could sleep until five.

The men seemed to be in an unusually jolly mood as they left the cook shack after supper that night. When the rest of the men had gone, Woody stayed and began helping Sarah clean up the supper mess. Sarah was puzzled, but Big Mary seemed to take his strange behavior for granted. Big Mary also seemed to be in a jovial mood. She was moving even faster than usual to finish her evening chores.

When everything was done except Sarah's nightly chores, Big Mary and Woody walked together to the door, laughing and talking.

At the door Woody stopped and turned to look at Sarah and said, "Come on up to the bunkhouse when you're done." Then he asked, almost as an after-thought, "Can you sing, Jesse?"

"Sing?" she asked, bewildered. She wanted to sleep, not sing.

"Sing. You know." He sang a few bars of a song she had never heard before, something about a lumberjack from Michigan.

"I guess so," she said, afraid to commit to having to sing for him, but filled with curiosity about why he cared if she could sing.

"Good," he grinned. "You can join me in song."

Big Mary slapped him playfully on the arm and said, "He's got this silly notion that he's some kind of canary. Truth is, he can't hardly carry a tune."

The insult didn't faze him, and he said, "We'll let the boy decide whether I can carry a tune." Then he looked at Sarah and said in a jolly voice, "Get on up to the bunkhouse soon's you can."

She hurriedly finished her chores, wondering all the while what could possibly be going on at the bunkhouse tonight, forgetting all about how tired she had felt only moments before.

CHAPTER 15

A S she crossed the clearing toward the bunkhouse, she heard music. But it wasn't just singing, as she had expected from what Woody had said to her. She stopped still and listened, wondering if it could just be her imagination or if she heard a fiddle, an accordion and maybe a harmonica. She began to run, and when she reached the door to the bunkhouse she opened it and stepped inside, her eyes lit with pleasure and surprise.

The men were sitting on the deacon's benches on both sides of the room facing each other. Several men lay on their bunks facing the benches, propped up on their elbows. Paddy Roark, the boy with hair the color of rust, was playing an accordion, his head bobbing and his foot tapping as one hand flew up and down the keys and one hand sped over the chord buttons as he pumped the bellows. Spike Anderson was sitting across from him playing a fiddle, his knee bouncing in time to the music, his eyes closed in pleasurable concentration. Lem Taylor, one of the scalers, was playing the harmonica. The Frenchman, Charlie DuBois, pulled a harmonica out of his pocket and began to play along with them. It was the first time she had ever seen anything but a scowl on his face. He wasn't actually smiling, but he was close to it.

Sawtooth Leverty was sitting with the other sawyers. She tried to look quickly away before he noticed her, but he saw her and he winked and slid over, patting the seat next to him. Sarah looked away from him, pretending she hadn't noticed. She felt ill at ease, but only for an instant. It was hard not to get into the spirit that filled the bunkhouse. She stood near the door, leaning back against the wall, watching and listening, fascinated.

They were playing a song about a lumberjack named Jim. Some of the men were singing, and others were just tapping their feet or clapping their hands to the music.

"Big Jim Taylor was a mighty man,
With hands the size of a Christmas ham.

127

Could chop down a tree and soon was done,
While a lesser man woulda just begun."

The words made her want to laugh, but the music charmed her, and she
soon stopped thinking about the lyrics. As she listened, her eyes traveled slowly
around the room, studying each of the men, surprised at how carefree and happy
they appeared. Before long, unable to resist the beat of the music and the lift it
gave her spirits, she began to tap her foot.

She had not noticed that Thor and Jock were not in the room, and was
surprised when the door opened and they walked in, their hair damp and their
faces pink and flushed. *The sauna,* she thought. *They must have been in that sauna
thing Big Mary told me about.* They had indeed, and when they came and stood next
to her against the wall, a clean soapy smell wafted from them. They nodded a
greeting to her, and she nodded dumbly back at them.

The four men were now playing an Irish tune she recognized from Katie's
repertoire, and she mouthed the words silently. When that song was finished, as
though it had been planned, Paddy rested his accordion on his lap and crossed
his arms over it, as if waiting for something to happen. Spike, too, put his fiddle
in his lap and waited. The Frenchman looked around, unsure of what to do,
and Lem shook his head at him when he put his harmonica to his mouth. The
Frenchman took the hint and tucked his harmonica back into his pocket and sat
waiting with the rest of them.

All eyes turned expectantly toward Woody, and he began to sing. As the
sweet, tremulous notes filled the room everyone grew silent. His clear tenor
voice was so sweet and pure that Sarah's eyes filled with tears. She blinked and
looked around at the others. Some of the men, too, were teary eyed.

She felt Thor stiffen beside her, and she looked sideways at him, waiting for
him to ridicule her. He wasn't paying any attention to her. He was watching two
of the new men, Cant Hook Jensen and Noah Watkins, who were apparently
getting a real kick out of seeing their comrades in tears. They were laughing and
pointing at Paddy Roark, who had taken a big red handkerchief out of his pocket
to blow his nose and wipe his eyes.

As if on cue, as soon as Woody finished singing, Thor, Jock, Red and Spike
simultaneously lunged for the two laughing men and dragged them out of the
bunkhouse. Everyone else crowded through the door and followed them into
the clearing. Cant Hook and Noah were no longer laughing, but were instead

struggling violently and swearing at their captors, but it wasn't having much effect. When they had them in front of the horse trough, Thor took Cant Hook by the wrists and Jock took him by the ankles and they swung him back and forth a few times and then threw him into the water. Red and Spike did the same thing to Noah. Then they held them under the water so long Sarah was afraid they had drowned them; but when they let go, the two men sprang up out of the water, sputtering, but greatly subdued.

Then the rest of the men, laughing and shouting and patting Thor and his cohorts on the back, all went back into the bunkhouse. She followed them, glancing back at the two men who had climbed out of the horse trough and were shaking themselves like two wet dogs. She heard the music begin again, and when she got inside one of the men had Big Mary at the far end of the room and was trying to get her to dance. She was resisting, rather coyly, but soon stopped her pretense and let him spin her around the room to a raucous polka. Soon half the men were dancing with each other, not caring who led or who followed. She went back and stood next to Jock and Thor again, but before long Thor quietly left the bunkhouse.

After he had been gone for a while, she looked at Jock, who was standing silently, watching. "Aren't you going to dance?" she asked.

"Nope. The Push told me to keep an eye out."

"Where did he go?" she asked, wondering why he didn't stay and enjoy the dancing and the music with the rest of the men.

"To the clerk's shack," he said. "He spends damn near every night in that blasted clerk's shack."

"Why? What does he do there?"

"The clerk's job."

"The clerk?" She wasn't sure she had heard him correctly.

"The clerk. The pencil pusher. Johnny Inkslinger. Whatever you want to call him."

"Don't we have one...one of those already?" She had seen the job posted at Smitheson, but it was to begin in the fall. She assumed they already had one for the summer but would need a replacement come fall.

Jock laughed. "Have you seen one anywhere?"

"I don't know. Would I know him if I saw him?"

He laughed. "I guess you wouldn't rightly know unless you saw someone with a pencil stuffed behind his ear and you asked what in tarnation he was doing with a pencil out here in the timber." He laughed again. "We don't have one during the summer. Smitheson makes us get by without a clerk until the regular season starts. Guess he figures the Push can do it, seeing as how there's not many men in camp during the summer for him to ride herd on. But the clerk's job isn't easy for Nilsson and he spends more time on it than he should have to. I think he's a damn fool for working all day and half the night, too, but I got nothing to say about it."

"Oh," she said, thinking how Thor did indeed seem to keep longer hours than anyone else did. "Do you know how to sing?" she asked, changing the subject.

"I sing, but not when anybody can hear me. My wife tells me my singing is pretty terrible."

"Wife? Are you married?" She had never considered that any of these men might have lives outside of Camp Seven. She wondered if he had been among the men at Ginger's that night, but she couldn't remember.

"A wife and six boys," he said, proudly. "They aren't big enough yet to come to the timber, but they're big enough to take care of their mother and the farm while I'm gone."

"Why are you here? Aren't you lonesome for them?" Sarah couldn't conceal her amazement that he would leave his family to work in the timber.

"Sure am. I'm a farmer when I'm not in a lumber camp. But it's hard to feed eight people on a farm around these parts. It's going to take a while to get enough land cleared to plant decent crops. But there's good money in the camps, so I work every chance I get."

"When do you see your family?" she asked, unable to comprehend such behavior.

"Not very much. But I don't need to do this much longer. Me and Nilsson are both leaving pretty soon." He scratched his jaw and looked as though he didn't quiet believe his own words. "We've been saying that for five years, but we're still here. One of these days, though, we'll both be gone."

"Gone? Does...does Nilsson have a family, too?" She pictured him standing next to Lila at Ginger's. Did he go to whores while his wife slaved at home on their farm? Did he have babies? She found those thoughts strangely disturbing.

"Thor? Hell no! He's carrying a torch that's damn near burned a hole in him. It'd be good if he *did* have a wife and kids."

She wanted him to say more, but he didn't, and just then the men started playing a bawdy song and everyone gradually stopped dancing and sat down again, laughing. When that song was finished someone started to tell an off-color joke and Big Mary got up and walked toward the door.

"This is about all the fun I can stand," she announced, nodding toward Sarah. "Come on, Jesse. You and me don't get tomorrow off like the rest of this lazy bunch."

Sarah said goodnight to Jock and was almost out the door when she heard her name. She stopped and turned around and Red Scanlon called to her from where he sat, "You sleep good last night, Boy?" Then he slapped his knee with his hand and started to laugh, and most of the other men started laughing with him.

So *he* was the one who had put the snake in her bed. She could still hear the men laughing as she crossed the clearing and waved goodnight to Big Mary as she went into her cabin.

"Damn you, Red Scanlon," Sarah said aloud. "I *just hate* being laughed at."

As she walked toward the cook shack she looked across the clearing to the little building standing about twenty feet to the west of the cook shack. She could see the light coming from the tiny windows. She knew this must be the clerk's shack and that Thor was inside working. Why was he leaving the timber? And when? And what had Jock meant about him carrying a torch that was burning a hole in him? She found the questions unsettling, and wondered at herself for being curious about him. She told herself that she had far too many problems of her own to go bothering about somebody else; especially the hard-nosed Push.

She thought about Red and the snake as she walked into the cook shack and went to the storeroom cum bedchamber. She lit a lamp and carefully examined her cot before she went to bed. She feared she might find another creature of some kind waiting to share her bed; but there was none. She hoped the snake in the box was dead by now, but she didn't want to look.

She lay awake for a long time, pleased with herself for having gotten through another day. The music kept playing over and over in her head, and mingled with the melodies were thoughts of how to get even with Red Scanlon.

The following morning, before she went out to cut the wood for the breakfast fire, she pulled the box with the snake from its hiding place behind the barrels and discovered that the snake had indeed died. She felt a slight twinge of guilt at not simply letting the poor creature loose in the woods, but it was too late now. Besides, it was an integral part of the answer that had come to her as she slept. She was prepared to give Red a taste of his own medicine.

She had devised her plan knowing that Thor never came to breakfast on Sundays because Big Mary had told her so. His habit was to take a plate of food into the clerk's shack and work there all morning. On Sundays the rest of the men ate later than usual and this morning they filed into the cook shack at eight o'clock. Many of them were without their flannel shirts, their suspenders bright and colorful against their drab underwear. There was a relaxed atmosphere around the table, even though the no-talking rule was in place—as it always seemed to be.

Breakfast was even more abundant than usual because they would eat only two meals that day; breakfast and a mid-afternoon dinner. On Sundays the men could wander into the cook shack and snack on whatever they wished, as long as they cleaned up their own mess. Big Mary told Sarah she was willing to let the men graze one by one on their day off, but she was not willing to clean up after them one by one. The Sunday kitchen privileges endeared Big Mary to the men, and although she pretended to be annoyed, she loved to see the pleasure on their faces as they wandered into her kitchen to help themselves to pie and cookies throughout the day and evening.

Sarah watched Red Scanlon out of the corner of her eye as he helped himself to the plates of food as they were passed around. He carefully filled his plate with flapjacks, fried potatoes, bacon, biscuits, beans and the fried egg each of them got because it was Sunday. Then he took the syrup pitcher and poured syrup on top of everything. Satisfied, he reached for his cup of coffee, which Sarah had brought to him. He glanced up at her, wondering why he was getting so much special attention, then lifted his cup to his lips. He sputtered and spat as something slid from his cup, brushed against his lips, down his chin, and then fell with a splat onto his plate.

"What the...?" he croaked, almost falling backwards off the bench but catching himself just in time by grabbing hold of the men on either side of him. He looked down at his plate and let out a holler that made Big Mary come running. Everyone else stopped eating and stared over at him. In the middle of Red's food, floating in a puddle of syrup, was the dead snake tied in a coil with a piece of string. He sat for a while staring at it. Then, without a word, he got up from the table, picked up his plate and cup, walked over to the sink and dumped everything into the slop bucket. Then he went to the counter and got a clean plate and cup and returned to the table, sat down, and beckoned to the man across from him to pass the flapjacks. Sarah came over and casually poured more coffee into his cup.

Big Mary stood transfixed, her eyes traveling around the table trying to figure out where the snake might have come from. No one touched his food, but instead sat watching Red refill his plate, pour syrup all over it again, take a drink of his coffee, and then scoop a huge forkful of the syrup-laden mess into his mouth. As he chewed, he looked around the table as though nothing had happened, and the rest of them started eating again, struggling to suppress their laughter.

When the rest of the men were done eating and had left the cook shack, Woody went over to Sarah, who was elbow deep in the sink washing dishes. He slapped her on the back and said, "That was damn good, Boy! I ain't seen Red that flabbergasted since the time somebody put a dead mouse in his snuff box."

Big Mary spun around and looked at them. "Jesse Williams! Am I to understand that you're the one who put that dead snake in Red's cup?"

Sarah turned to face her and nodded sheepishly.

She half expected Big Mary to fly into a rage, but instead, she started to laugh. "I'll be damned! I didn't think you had it in you!"

"I didn't either," Sarah said, smiling weakly. "But Red asked for it. He...."

Woody interrupted her. "There won't be no stopping him, now."

"What do you mean?" Sarah asked, thinking she had ended the whole business by paying him back.

"When somebody new comes to camp they're always the butt of jokes until someone newer comes along."

"I haven't seen him tease anybody else," Sarah said. "What about the other new men? Why doesn't he pick on them?"

"He does. They all do. You just ain't around to see it." He chuckled. "Most of the new men know it's part of coming to a new camp and they ignore it and let the other jacks go ahead and get it over with. It's just fun and nobody gets hurt. But you! You did such a good job getting back at him that now he's going to be forced to do you one a whole lot better. This could go on all summer." As he started toward the door he let out a malicious cackle. "Shit fire! This could get real good!"

Sarah looked at Big Mary, her eyes pleading.

"Don't look at me, Boy," Big Mary said, returning to her labors. "I ain't got nothin' to do with this. You got yourself into it and you can get yourself out of it."

Sarah busied herself with her after-breakfast chores, wishing whatever Red was going to do he'd do it soon and get it over with. This time she wouldn't pay him back. Maybe then it would end. She was deep in thought when Big Mary called to her.

"Thor ain't had his breakfast. Stop what you're doin' and take this plate over to him before he starves to death."

Sarah did as she was told, and when she got to the clerk's shack she knocked gently on the door. He didn't answer, so she opened the door a crack and peered inside. He was sitting at a desk, hunched over a large ledger. One elbow was propped on the desk with his head resting on his hand, his fingers spread and tangled in his hair. The other hand held a pencil that he was tapping on the desk over and over in a tattoo of frustration. He looked up when he realized someone was watching him, looked back down at the ledger, threw the pencil angrily on the desk, pushed his chair back and stood up.

"What do you want?" He walked to the window and looked out, his back rigid.

"Your breakfast...." She walked over and set the plate of food on the desk, and as she did, she glanced at the ledger he had been working on. The page was filled with labored, irregular letters, strange and unfamiliar, and numbers that she could just barely make out. Small pieces of paper were scattered on top of it.

He turned his head and saw her staring at the page in the ledger. "What are you looking at?" He sounded strange, and when she took her eyes from the page and looked at him, she saw that he was embarrassed. She looked back down at the ledger to avoid his eyes. It was somehow more comfortable to see him angry and giving orders than it was to see him embarrassed.

"I...I'd better get to work," she stammered, backing across the room to the door, then turning and stepping outside, closing the door quietly behind her.

Back in the cook shack, Big Mary was scraping the grill and humming. When she heard the door open, she turned her head for only a moment. "Did he eat?"

"I don't know."

Big Mary continued scraping.

"He has trouble doing the ledgers, doesn't he?" It wasn't really a question. Sarah knew about ledgers. Her uncle had been a banker. She had heard him talk about such things many times over dinner in Boston. He had many tales to tell about men whose businesses failed because of problems keeping the ledgers.

Big Mary continued scraping, but after several minutes she stopped and turned around and looked at Sarah, her forehead creased with deep frown lines. Then she nodded, looking worried. "Clerking is the only thing he can't do better'n any man jack of 'em, and it puts him in a real tizzy." She tossed the towel she was using over her shoulder and sat down at the table. "He manages to get it done somehow. Then in the fall, when the clerk comes, they get it all straightened out between the two of them."

"That's stupid! By then it must be such a mess nobody can figure it out."

Big Mary nodded in agreement. "I reckon that's the truth, but the lumbermen don't like to spend money if they don't have to. Smitheson ain't no different. He ain't hiring no clerk when the camp's not full."

Sarah fell onto the bench across from her, looking perplexed and annoyed. "Seems to me that's a pretty sloppy way to run a camp. Why does Thor put up with it?"

Big Mary had a meat fork in her hand and she pointed it at Sarah for emphasis. "Listen here, Jesse. It's none of our business what happens in the clerk's shack. We got all we can do to keep up with our own work. I don't want you to pay any attention to what goes on over there. If I ask you to bring him a plate, do it. Nothing more and nothing less. You got that?"

Sarah nodded. It was okay with her if he went along with Smitheson doing something stupid. "It just goes to show he's not infallible," she said, getting up to begin cleaning away the breakfast dishes.

"He's not *what?*" Big Mary asked, getting up, too.

"Never mind," Sarah said as she carried a pile of plates to the sink.

Just then Woody poked his head in the front door and called to her. "Soon's you're done, Jesse, come on out and I'll show you where you can do the laundry."

"I'll be out in half an hour," she said, hurrying to finish cleaning up. Then she looked at Big Mary. "Is that okay? I can do the rest of my chores later."

"Sure. You go on. Towels are stacking up and it's time you washed 'em before they start to stink."

Sunday was laundry day for everyone in camp, and Woody took her to the area the men called the "boiling-up grounds." It was out behind the bunkhouse and the men's privies. Every Sunday Woody supplied wood and water and set out several empty fifty-gallon lard cans. The men took turns using the tubs to scrub and boil their clothing.

Sarah had never washed clothes in her life. In her uncle's house and at school there were always servants who did such things. She let Woody show her how to scrub the kitchen towels and the roller towels on a washboard propped in one of the big cans. She thanked him for his help and then started to walk back toward the cook shack. As she walked, she was planning to set up her own "boiling-up grounds" out behind the cook shack. It made no sense to go all the way to the other side of camp, especially when she had so much washing to do.

Besides the roller towels from the bunkhouse and the towels and aprons from the cook shack, she had her own clothes to keep clean. She slept in her underwear now, the way the lumberjacks did; but she certainly didn't intend to wear them all week before she washed them. She would string a line from a tree to the side of the cook shack and hang the towels on it and they'd be easy to get to when they were dry. The best thing about having her own private laundry area was that she could secretly wash her bindings and private linens and then dry them behind her bunk next to the wall in her room.

Now that she had her laundry figured out, she felt better. She had jumped one more hurdle. All at once, for no apparent reason, she remembered the feeling of a soft cotton nightgown against her skin and she suddenly felt displaced and disoriented. She quickly looked around to get her bearings.

It was a warm, sunny day and the clearing was filled with activity. Red Scanlon and Paddy Roark were brushing two of the horses. Woody was cutting a man's hair, and there were two other men sitting on the ground talking and waiting their turn for haircuts. One of them called to her as she passed, asking if she'd found any more snakes in her bunk. A circle of men were seated on the ground in front of the saw-filer's shack playing cards and laughing because one of them had bet his whole supply of tobacco on the last hand and had lost.

When she reached the cook shack, she didn't want to go inside. She wanted to escape from this strange place; but there was no place for her to go. She walked out behind the cook shack and sat down on the bank next to the stream. She pulled her knees to her chest and wrapped her arms around them, then dropped her chin onto her knees and stared out at the water. She felt lost and alone, and all the little successes she had had over the past few days seemed suddenly meaningless and empty. What idiot couldn't learn this job? All one needed was a strong back and a weak mind. She looked at her hands, which were getting red and raw. *And tough skin,* she thought ruefully.

She let her head fall back so the warm sun could bathe her face, and she closed her eyes and listened to the sounds of the rushing water. Somewhere in the back of her mind she heard a little voice telling her it was not really so bad. She had come West for a reason, and that reason would have to be the thing that sustained her. Much had been taken from her. But much, too, had been offered; she might actually have a father.

She opened her eyes and looked across the stream and into the woods beyond. The new leaves on the trees shimmered silvery in the sun. She smiled to herself and stood up and stretched. She was young and strong and she would do whatever she needed to do. Nothing could stop her except her own laziness and cowardice; and she vowed not to give in to either of them ever again.

CHAPTER 16

ON Sunday night a week later, a late April snowstorm swept out of the north carrying with it forty-mile-an-hour winds and eight inches of blowing snow. Sarah heard the wind howl in the night and got up out of bed to look out the window over the sink. The snow was blowing sideways across the clearing and she thought dismally that it must snow year-round in Minnesota.

She went back to her cot and tried to sleep, but couldn't. It was after midnight and she knew she needed to rest, but it was no use. She finally got up and got dressed. She didn't dare walk around in her underwear for fear the storm might wake someone else, and whoever it was might come to the cook shack looking for something to eat. She wandered back and forth looking out the two windows, then went to the door and looked out. Through the blowing snow she saw a light burning in the clerk's shack.

"He must still be in there working," she said to the darkness. He had not been in the cook shack all day and Big Mary had had Woody bring his food to him in the clerk's shack. She lit a lantern and went to the stove and built a fire, an idea forming in her mind. As she made a pot of coffee she thought about the big ledger and about the clerk's job posted on the wall at Smitheson's.

She gathered bread and cold meat, along with some cookies and coffee, and went to bring them to Thor. When she stepped out the door, she was almost carried off by the wind. It was bitter cold and she had no coat. She had never expected to need one, but she was going to have to get one. *A really warm one*, she thought as she struggled sideways against the wind to the clerk's shack and banged on the door.

He opened it almost immediately and looked surprised to see her standing there. "Is something wrong?" he asked, looking over her shoulder.

"No. I just brought you some food and some coffee," she said, pushing past him into the room and setting it on the desk. He had a fire in the stove and she walked over to it to warm her hands.

"Why are you...? What are you doing up at this hour?"

"The storm woke me."

"Storm?" He hadn't noticed the change in the weather. He looked outside, still holding the door open. His surprise was obvious, but he simply closed the door and looked at her, then at the food and the steaming coffee and asked, "Did Big Mary send you?"

"No. Big Mary went to bed hours ago." The way he was watching her made her uneasy, but she made up her mind not to let him intimidate her. "Eat," she said, "before the coffee gets cold."

He sat down somewhat reluctantly and started to eat. She walked over to where a counter ran halfway across the room on the far end. There were shelves behind the counter filled with various items of clothing, a stack of blankets, jars of snuff, tobacco, liniment and other items. A wire screen was rolled back against the wall. There was a set of bunks in one corner and she wondered if he slept in the clerk's shack instead of the bunkhouse. There was a blanket folded neatly at the foot of the bottom bunk.

He never looked at her until his plate was empty, but when he finished and picked up his coffee he looked across the room to where she stood next to the counter. He seemed to have gained his composure and he said, "Okay. Now tell me what's wrong."

"Wrong?"

"Yes. Wrong. I've been a foreman long enough to know when someone has something on his mind. Is it Big Mary? Is she being too hard on you?"

He actually seemed worried that she was having some kind of trouble. Up until now she had been convinced Big Mary could drown her in the river and he wouldn't interfere.

"There's nothing wrong, Sir. Nothing at all. Except that...you see.... Well, the thing is that when I applied for this job at Smitheson I noticed you were looking for a clerk starting in October, and I thought maybe...."

His eyes darkened and the concern left his face. "This is not October." He stood up and walked over and put his empty plate and cup on the counter and pushed them toward her. "You're a cookee and you have all you can do to do *that* job."

She looked down at the plate and cup that he apparently expected her to pick up and take back to the cook shack. Instead of picking them up, she looked at him, determined. "When I went to school in Chicago I was real good at numbers. I thought maybe you could show me what to do and I could help you this summer and then you'd know if I could do the job this fall." She kept her voice firm and spoke quickly, not letting him interrupt.

He didn't say a word but just stood looking at her with no expression. Then he picked up the plate and cup, handed them to her again with a movement of his head toward the door. "Go back to the cook shack where you belong. I don't need your help."

She held the plate and cup and looked up at him, then reluctantly went to the door and opened it. "You're welcome for supper," she said, stepping out and slamming the door behind her and ducking her head against the wind as she hurried back to the warmth of the cook shack.

She had barely gotten to the kitchen sink to rinse off his plate when the door flew open and he stormed across the room toward her. She turned around and looked at him, but for some odd reason did not feel any fear. What could he do? He certainly wasn't going to beat her. And what else could he do to her that would be worse than waking up with a snake crawling around on her? He might send her down the tote road. She didn't think so. She knew she was doing a good job, even though no one had told her so. A week ago she might have cowered. Tonight she stood her ground, defiant.

He was unprepared for this new attitude. He began to say something, then stopped. When he finally spoke she knew it was not what he had come to the cook shack to say to her. "Big Mary's right. You are not like most of the boys who come here to work in her kitchen."

"Did she say that?" Sarah asked, wondering whether she was going to be praised or ridiculed.

He nodded. "Yaw."

She had never heard him say "yaw" before, and she nearly giggled. He had an accent, but he always spoke very careful English. She knew instantly that he must be nervous. Something told her that slipping into his native tongue made him feel somehow inferior, because he looked flustered and immediately corrected himself.

"Yes she did. She said you have a lot of spunk."

Was this praise? She relaxed somewhat and watched him walk over to the stove and pour himself a cup of coffee from the pot. "Do you want some coffee?" he asked.

She nodded and he poured another cupful and carried them both over, handed her one, then carried his toward the door. Then he looked back at her and called to her across the room, "You're welcome for the coffee," and was gone.

She just stood there, flummoxed, looking across the empty room at where he had been. She went to the door and opened it and saw the light still burning in the clerk's shack. She stood staring out at the storm and at the light as she sipped the coffee he had given her. Before very long the light went out and she waited for the door to open and for him to come out and head for the bunkhouse. He never came out, so she figured he must sleep in the clerk's shack instead of the bunkhouse. She couldn't blame him for that!

Then she, too, went to bed, and this time she slept soundly until it was time to get up.

The next morning when she went to build the fire she was startled to see that the wood box was full to near overflowing. Puzzled, she walked outside to the woodpile. Next to the log was a neat row of cut wood, stacked and waiting to be carried inside. She stood looking around, half expecting to see a ghost holding an axe. She went back inside wondering if this was going to turn out to be some kind of a prank. She was going to have to be on her toes this morning. But it wasn't a prank.

To her absolute amazement, Thor came into the cook shack just before breakfast, nodded to her and then said to Big Mary, "Jesse won't be cutting wood this morning. He is coming to the clerk's shack for fifteen minutes. I want to see if he is as good as he says he is with numbers."

"But...." Big Mary said, miffed that he was commandeering her cookee. Thor, however, looked so cheerful this morning that she didn't have the heart to object. "Oh, alright. But only for fifteen minutes. Don't you go keeping him any longer than that."

She jabbed a finger toward Sarah. "Don't you dally all morning or I'll come and drag you back here."

Sarah was too taken aback to say anything to either of them. She followed him meekly out the door and across to the clerk's shack. The snow had stopped, as had the wind, and the air felt almost mild. "What a strange place this is," she said to herself. "And what weird weather." But she couldn't help feeling nervous and excited about what was going to happen this morning. Was she going to be able to prove herself to him?

When they got inside, he waved her over to the counter where he had placed a sheet of paper and a pencil. She looked down at the paper and saw a long row of strange-looking numbers. She could tell what they were, but the way the numbers were slanted and formed looked very foreign to her.

He saw her confusion and said, "Can you read them? I want you to add the numbers I have written," he said. Then he asked again, "Are you sure you can read them."

"I think I can," she nodded as she ran the pencil quickly down the columns and added the numbers in her head as she went. "One thousand sixty three," she said as she scribbled the total and then put the pencil down on the counter and looked up at him.

Mouth agape, he stared at her. Then at last he said, "I'll be damned! Where did you learn to do that?"

"I told you. In Chicago. I was good at numbers in school." She had been good at numbers, all right, but not in Chicago. She had been at the top of her class in arithmetic at boarding school. The teachers had not encouraged her because they thought arithmetic was for boys. But she had loved numbers and she had sometimes even studied algebra problems in the library at school when she was bored.

"I'll be damned!" he said again, this time coming around the counter and putting an arm around her shoulder and leading her out the door and back toward the cook shack.

When Big Mary saw them coming across the room, her boss with his arm around her cookee's shoulder, she didn't know what to think. "You two look mighty damn cozy!" she said. "What do you think you're up to?"

"This boy," Thor said, taking his arm from around Sarah's shoulder and picking Big Mary up off the floor and spinning her around, all in one fluid motion, "is worth his weight in gold. You did one helluva job hiring *this one,* my little pea hen."

"Don't call me that, dammit!" she shouted, her hands pushing against his chest. "And put me down before I...."

"Before you *what?*" he asked. "No use trying to rile me up." He motioned toward Sarah with one of his big hands. "This boy is smart. You can keep him for now, but don't think you can lock him in your kitchen with your kettles." Then, to Sarah's surprise, he winked at her and was gone.

"Men!" Big Mary said, "I ain't never gonna figure 'em out!" She glowered at Sarah, who stood dumbly staring at the door. "Don't just stand there like an idiot! Get to work! You ain't managed to escape the kettles yet. And you won't. Not if I have anything to say about it."

Big Mary continued to mumble under her breath but Sarah wasn't paying any attention. She hurriedly resumed her breakfast-preparation duties, but couldn't help smiling to herself as she remembered Thor's words. She was sure she was going to be a clerk instead of a cookee. She felt proud of having convinced him that she could help him with a difficult part of his duties. Then she understood about the wood. She paused and looked up at the ceiling.   "Hallelujah!"   she breathed.

"What did you say," Big Mary called from the stove, clearly annoyed by the events of the morning.

"I was just telling myself to hurry," she lied.

"Good," said Big Mary. "Now you've got the right idea. The men will be in soon for their breakfast and none of them will give a damn whether you think you're hot stuff and don't have to chop wood like the rest of my cookees."

Sarah glanced quickly over at Big Mary and had a sudden insight. *She's jealous!* She had become certain that Big Mary and Thor had some kind of power struggle going on between them. Now she could see that there was more to it than that. It was becoming clear to Sarah that Big Mary had a special feeling for their boss, and that she didn't like the way her new cookee was winning him over. She made up her mind to be careful about the way she handled the situation. As if she didn't already have enough challenges, she promised herself she would take on one more; she would work so hard for Big Mary in the cook shack and for Thor in the clerk's shack that they would *both* be pleased with Jesse Williams.

She felt an unfamiliar warm glow of pride. She had come from a place where *no one* wanted her. Now they were fighting over her. She smiled to herself as the men filed in.

"Got any little surprises for Red this morning, Jesse?" Lem Taylor asked, laughing out loud as he turned around and gave Red Scanlon an evil wink.

She glanced over at Red. His brow was wrinkled in deep concentration, as though he was planning what his next prank was going to be. Without answering, she went to the kitchen and began carrying in the food. She may have had Big Mary and Thor Nilsson under control, but Red Scanlon was still determined to give her trouble. She wasn't going to worry about it. She would deal with it when the time came; the same as she had dealt with everything else that had so far come her way.

CHAPTER 17

WHEN Thor left the cook shack that night after supper, he told Sarah to finish her chores and come to the clerk's shack. "Is it okay if I go now?" she asked Big Mary eagerly after she had finished filling the syrup jugs and putting them on the table for the next morning.

"Go," Big Mary said, waving at her with a hand covered with flour from the dough she was mixing.

She hurried to the clerk's shack and found Thor standing behind the counter with his back to her, arranging one of the shelves. When he heard the door open, he said without turning, "I'll be right with you." When he finished what he was doing, he turned and saw that it was Sarah.

"You're early. I thought you were one of the men coming to get something."

"Nope. I came as soon as I was finished with my work like you said."

He rubbed his hands together and said, "Good! Then let's get to it."

He walked over and sat down at the desk and pulled a chair next to him and motioned to her to sit down. He opened the ledger and turned the pages until he came to the one he was looking for. He pointed at the neat, but foreign, words written on it. "I can do it in Swedish, but I cannot do it in English. By the time I figure these out," he said, pointing at the small pile of scraps of paper tucked between the pages, "so I can copy them into the ledger, half the night is gone."

She picked up the scraps of paper and looked at them. "These are the men's names. What are these numbers?"

"They write down how much timber they cut each day and what they take from the wannigan." He pointed to the supply shelves. He explained that the "store" was called a wannigan. "Everything gets recorded, but I can't read their writing."

She smiled. "I can read, but I can't read half of these. Most of this writing is a real mess."

He looked pleased. "Maybe that's why it's so hard for me to try to translate into my own language." He looked relieved, as though what she said vindicated him in some way. He turned and looked at her and she felt suddenly nervous, wondering if he might recognize her now that they were alone. But he looked away from her and back down at the ledger.

It made her feel somehow better to know that he *could* read and write in his own language, and that the problem had been one of translating. She knew he must be too proud to admit that he couldn't read and write English. She ignored that issue completely and began to ask questions, which he answered with some surprise because she caught on so quickly.

Once he looked at her and said, "You're a smart boy, Jesse. You don't ever have to worry about finding work in the timber. Most camps have trouble finding a decent clerk. Once you learn the ropes, I'll bet you can work anywhere you want to."

She reddened and said, "Thank you," wondering why praise from him felt so good.

After they had worked for nearly an hour, he slid his chair back and stretched out his long legs, reaching up at the same time with his arms. Sitting made him feel cramped and uncomfortable. When he relaxed again, he studied her face and said, "There's something familiar about you. Is there any chance we could have met somewhere?"

Panic gripped her and she looked intently down at the ledger page. "Not unless you've been to Chicago. I've lived there my whole life until I came here."

"Oh," he said, seemingly satisfied. "You must just remind me of somebody."

He continued explaining the ledger and the rest of the clerk's duties. The clerk kept records of the crew's work, wages and purchases. He recorded the number of logs cut on an individual—as well as on a camp-wide basis—for each day. He kept track of the number of days each man worked, because the men who weren't paid on the basis of timber cut were paid for the number of days they worked. Monthly reports were taken to Smitheson's in Pine Crescent.

The clerk also sold supplies to the men and kept supply and equipment inventories for the entire camp. He made sure the shelves were supplied with underwear, shirts, mittens, socks, mackinaws, rubbers, tobacco, snuff, painkiller, liniment, carbolic salve, castor oil, Vaseline and whatever else the men requested.

He took care of the mail, which Red brought back whenever he went to town. The clerk was expected to read the letters to the men who couldn't read, and to write letters for them. During the summer the men had to struggle with their own mail, or hope that one of the jacks in camp could read. They knew their temporary clerk—the Push—couldn't read their mail for them, but they were afraid to complain about it.

He wanted her to begin by spending one hour every night on the ledgers. If it worked out, they would try to find a way for her to spend more time, but they'd worry about that later.

By the time he finished explaining everything to her, Sarah was astonished at all the duties Thor had been trying to add to his own, and she wondered how much she would be able to do in addition to her cookee duties. She was grateful that he had cut the wood, but she wondered if he expected her to do as he had done, which was to go without sleep to do the extra work. She didn't ask. Instead she pointed at the bunks against the wall and asked, "Who sleeps here?"

"During the season, the clerk. And I always do." His face softened and for the first time since she came to camp, he smiled at her. "It smells better than the bunkhouse."

The smile softened his face. *Like the summer sun melting the edges of a glacier*, she thought as she watched him. Her stomach gave a strange little somersault. *My God! He's the most handsome man I've ever seen!*

She knew she had to say something but could think of nothing except, "You really *are* a petunia."

His eyes darkened and he said, "You've been listening to stories. You should not believe everything you hear."

"When do you want me to start my new duties?" she asked, flustered.

"Tomorrow," he said, getting to his feet.

A feeling of elation swept over her. "I'll come the same time as I came tonight. I'll finish my chores fast," and as an afterthought, "and thank you for cutting the wood." She felt herself grow red. She hoped he didn't think it strange for a boy to blush.

He seemed not to notice. "What makes you think I cut your wood for you?"

"If you didn't, please thank whoever did." She got up and left the clerk's shack without looking back at him, but could feel him staring after her.

In the days that followed Sarah looked forward happily to her hour in the clerk's shack every night, even though she had to work harder than ever during the day to make up the time she spent there. It was still cool enough sometimes at night that a fire was needed in the bunkhouse or the cook shack to take the chill off. She hated the bunkhouse chores, but didn't actually mind most of the cook shack duties. She had to admit to herself, however, that the clerk's duties were far more interesting. The one chore she happily gave up was cutting the wood. All she had to do sometimes was carry it in, and that was merely child's play.

The kerosene for all the lanterns, as well as that used on the saws during cutting, was kept in the tool shed. One afternoon when she went out to get the supply for the cook shack lanterns, she sat down on the stool Woody used when he worked with the grinding wheel. She fell fast asleep, her head leaning sideways against the wall.

Woody found her there and shook her awake, but he never told anyone about the incident. He liked Jesse. He had seldom met such a willing worker. Woody knew all too well that being on the low end of the totem pole in a lumber camp was enough trouble without somebody snitching when he worked so hard and was so tired that he fell asleep during the day.

Along with all of her other chores, Sarah was kept on the move bringing Big Mary supplies of flour, beans, peas, oatmeal, prunes, sugar, baking powder, spices, tea, coffee, oleomargarine or whatever else she needed. The only rest she got during the day was when Big Mary drove the flaggins cart. She learned to drive, and true to her promise, Big Mary drove one way and Sarah drove the other. At first, the minute Big Mary picked up the reins Sarah fell asleep sitting next to her.

But Sarah was young and growing stronger, and she soon stopped feeling sleepy during the day. It got to be second nature for her to get up at four o'clock and begin her work immediately.

She was, however, still annoyed at having to keep an eye out for pranks. She found frogs in the sink and mice in jars on the shelves. One night her boots were taken from the floor in front of her bunk while she slept and hung by a rope from a tall tree branch above the woodpile. She let it all pass. Payback only inspired the men to greater things. She had learned her lesson.

By the middle of May her routine was becoming finely tuned, including the hour's worth of clerk's duties she had taken on. It had become a challenge to her and she was beginning to win the battle. Even though she was up every night until well after eleven o'clock, she was beginning to get things under control. The aches and pains that had troubled her at first had finally left her. Her appetite got better and better, and because of all the good food she ate and the hard work she performed, she was gaining a finely muscled strength of which she was not even aware. Also unawares, she was learning the difference between strength and skill.

One day when she was doing her chores in the bunkhouse she happened to glance up at her face in the dark mirror that hung over the men's washstand. She took a step closer and peered at herself as her hand explored the line of her cheek. She remembered the last time she studied herself in a mirror. It had been at the Vogels' after she changed her identity. She hadn't recognized herself. Now she didn't recognize herself again. Her face was fuller, healthier, her cheeks pink and her hair shining with a luster she could not remember it ever having. It stunned her, and she stepped back and stood gazing at the image in the mirror.

"Who am I?" she asked quietly. "Who am I now?" She no longer knew. She only knew she didn't have time to think about it, so she stepped away from the mirror, telling herself that no one—including herself—would notice or care what she looked like; they would only notice whether or not she did her work.

CHAPTER 18

ONE warm, pleasant Sunday in early June, Sarah sat in the clearing in front of the tool shed enjoying the warmth of the sun as she watched Woody give haircuts to some of the men. After she had been sitting and watching for nearly an hour, Woody looked over at her and said, "How about you? You're starting to look like a shaggy dog."

Embarrassed, she put her hands to her hair as she felt the color rising to her cheeks. "No thanks," she said finally, rising to her feet and walking away as Woody and several of the men laughed after her.

She went into the cook shack and found Big Mary sitting at one of the long tables reading a week-old newspaper Woody had brought from town. She didn't look up when Sarah sat down across from her.

"Big Mary?"

"Hmmm?"

"Can I ask you something?" Sarah asked meekly.

"Oh alright, what is it?" Big Mary said impatiently as she looked up, clearly annoyed at being disturbed.

"Woody's hair...some of the men I saw in Pine Crescent wore their hair pulled back and plaited with leather, or twine or something...." she hesitated.

"So?" Big Mary asked brusquely. "What's so important about how Woody and the men in Pine Crescent wear their hair that you've got to come in here and disturb the only quiet time I ever get?"

"Do...do you think the men would tease me if I wore mine like that?"

Big Mary's eyes wandered over Sarah's face and then her hair. "It ain't long enough," she said, hoping that would be the end of the discussion.

"Is that all? If it were long enough would it be okay if I did it? Would the men think I'm a sissy? Would I get teased really badly?"

"What difference would it make if you got teased about your hair? They tease you about everything else under the sun. What would be news about being teased about one more thing?"

Big Mary was again focusing intently on her newspaper. Sarah decided she could safely let her hair grow again, as long as she kept it pulled back in a braid. She'd have to keep her bangs in place in order to hide the telltale widow's peak, but at least she could let the rest of it grow. She frowned as she got up from the bench and went back outside, wondering about this sudden reawakening of her female vanity. She had been sure she would never again care how she looked.

Really, Sarah! she told herself as she hurried out behind the cook shack to do the laundry, *it isn't as if you're going to make yourself glamorous. All you're trying to do is grow your hair back without anyone noticing. After all, someday you're going to be a woman again.* The thought brought her up short, and she remembered vividly the last time she had sat next to Thor in the clerk's shack.

She dismissed those thoughts and busied herself with the camp towels, scrubbing and rinsing them, then hanging them on the line to dry. As she worked she hummed an Irish tune she had heard Katie sing. She couldn't remember the words, but the tune stuck in her head sometimes, and often lately she found herself humming—either Katie's tunes or the ones the men sang in the bunkhouse.

Suddenly out of the corner of her eye, an unusual movement in the stream caught her attention and she turned to look more closely. A slippery brown curve broke the surface and disappeared. Behind it another curve appeared, and then another. She blinked several times, thinking her eyes were playing tricks on her. She imagined she saw a sea serpent, and it looked to be twenty or thirty feet long. Her first impulse was to run, but her curiosity got the better of her, and she edged closer to the bank of the stream to watch. She was so intent watching the water that she didn't notice Thor walk up and stand next to her, watching too.

"Otters," he whispered.

It startled her, and she let out a little gasp.

"Shhh," he said, pointing at the stream, where four small, sleek heads formed vees of ripples in their wake. Her sea serpent had broken into four pieces, each of them with a head.

"I've seen them in the late fall up on the lake just before it freezes over. They climb out of the water onto the ice with fish in their mouths, bite off the heads, and then go back for more. Sometimes they do belly slides down the banks along the edge of the lake. They are like children playing in the snow." He explained that they were river otters, traveling upstream to the lake three miles northeast of

Camp Seven, out of which the stream fed. They were soon out of sight around a bend and still he stood and watched.

She looked sideways at him and he turned to look at her, his eyes soft and unguarded. She had spent many hours with him at night in the clerk's shack, asking questions. He had taken to leaving her alone sometimes when she worked, confident that she knew what she was doing better than he did. Sometimes he laughed and sometimes he smiled, but he had never before looked so approachable. She wanted to reach out and touch his face. Instead, she took a small step backwards and away from him, then turned and ran into the cook shack, slamming the door behind her and leaning back against it, breathless. She pressed her palms flat against the door behind her, wondering at the sweet fluttering in her stomach.

A few minutes later she felt pressure against the door and she spun around and stepped back as Thor pushed the door roughly open, an expression on his face that was a confused mix of worry and annoyance. "What got into you out there?"

"N...nothing. I...I was just startled by...by the otters."

His eyes traveled over her face, unsure about the truth of what she was telling him. Then he said, "Don't go running off like that without saying something. It makes me think...I mean...I don't know what to think, and I...." He didn't finish, but instead turned abruptly and walked out of the room.

She stood looking after him, and she felt again the fluttering in her stomach. She went to her cot in the storeroom and sat down on it, her head down, her eyes on the planked flooring, her arms wrapped tight around her middle, rocking gently back and forth, trying to stop the unwelcome sensations. The change in him was wreaking havoc on her. There were still times when he was so cold it seemed to penetrate deep into her very soul. But now she knew the other side of him, and the contrast when he softened warmed her with feelings so intense that it was nearly unbearable.

She sat that way for a very long time, until finally she got up and went back outside to finish the washing. She heard the sound of music coming from the bunkhouse, but she did not go there and she did not go to the clerk's shack. She stayed busy until bedtime and then she went to her cot, slipped out of her clothing and crawled under her blanket and slept. She dreamed she was standing on shore looking out at the ocean and Steven was riding through the waves on the back of a sea serpent. She was waving to him as he rode away from her, farther and farther until she could no longer see him.

***

The next morning Big Mary was late coming to the cook shack, and when she got there she was holding the side of her face. Sarah looked at her and Big Mary dropped her hand and groaned. The side of her face was swollen to double its usual size.

"What happened?" Sarah gasped.

"Toothache. Can't hardly stand it."

"Why don't you go back to your cabin and lie down," Sarah offered. "You look really awful."

"That's how I feel. Awful ain't the word for it. But it don't matter how I feel. I've got to get the men fed." She went to the counter and started banging things around, but Sarah knew that her movements were a futile attempt to take her mind off her pain.

Moments later Thor came in and poured himself a cup of coffee. He didn't look at Sarah or at Big Mary. He seemed deep in thought about something.

"Somebody needs to take Big Mary to town," Sarah told him, not caring about his withdrawn attitude.

"What?" he said, looking up at her for the first time and then looking over at his cook.

"Big Mary needs to get to a dentist," Sarah repeated firmly.

"Is that right, Big Mary?" he asked, pulling himself into the present with an effort.

She didn't answer him except to groan and give Sarah an accusing look. But the pain was so bad she couldn't keep up her pretense, and her face contorted with pain.

He looked at Sarah. "Can you and Woody feed the men? I'll get someone to drive Big Mary to the dentist in Hinckley right away."

"I can manage without Woody," she said. "He needs to be the one to take her."

"Why?" he wanted to know. "The camp's full of men who won't be anywhere near as missed as Woody will be."

She said firmly, "He's the only one who'll care about seeing Big Mary gets taken care of. The rest of these louts are apt to just dump her someplace and go to a whorehouse."

The corners of his mouth twitched and he cleared his throat and said, "You may be right, Boy. What makes you so sure you know what the men will do?"

"Never mind," she said, "that's not the point." She tossed her head toward Big Mary, who was leaning back against the front of one of the counters, her eyes squeezed shut and her hands over her ears.

"Stop!" Big Mary groaned. "I got enough pain without listening to the two of you idiots arguing about who knows most about the jacks!"

He cleared his throat once more and said, "You sure Jesse? You sure you can do the work alone?"

"I'm sure," she said, not at all sure. She turned her back to them and took over the breakfast preparations. She didn't really know whether she could do Big Mary's job and her own as well, but she'd figure out something. If the men complained that it wasn't good enough she'd simply tell them to be grateful Big Mary was going to a dentist or the tooth might kill her and they'd be stuck with Jesse Williams as their cook. That would shut them up.

Fifteen minutes later Thor came back into the cook shack and got one of the cook's white aprons from the storeroom and began putting it on. "I put the Finn in charge of the men today. Tell me what to do."

She put a hand over her mouth to stifle a laugh.

He looked down at the apron, which seemed to be causing her glee, then looked back up at her. He didn't crack a smile, but she could tell he was having trouble not doing so. "I was a cookee once. Don't laugh. Just tell me what to do."

"Go."

"Go?"

"Yes, go. I can do this by myself. I just won't get everything else done. And I won't get to the clerk's shack tonight. You will have to live with that. It's only for a day. Go."

He took the apron off and put it back into the storeroom, and she could tell by his expression that he was grateful not to be stuck all day in the cook shack.

After he had gone, she was left again with that fluttering business in the pit of her stomach. He had seemed so vulnerable standing there waiting to be told what to do. It touched her in a way she didn't expect. *This is not good. You're at Camp Seven for a reason, and that reason is not Thor Nilsson. Remember that, before you get yourself more misery than you reckoned on.* As she bustled around the cook shack, her dilemma seemed to grow larger. She needed to find her father and she needed to do it soon. She needed to get away from Camp Seven while the getting was good, and before her feelings for Thor Nilsson got any more confusing.

The problem, however, was that in some little corner of her consciousness she was hoping to find a legitimate excuse to stay. She felt at home with her duties in camp. Although there were times when she longed for the feeling of clean white sheets against her skin, it was getting so that the routine of her work gave her so much satisfaction that the need for creature comforts paled beside it. She thought again about Thor's face as he stood waiting for direction. The memory filled her with an unfamiliar kind of contentment.

She managed to get through the day and get the men fed. The food, of course, was nowhere near as good as it was when Big Mary prepared it. The loaves of bread were not as nicely rounded on top, and were a little too brown on the bottom. But no one complained. One of the men snickered when he saw Thor ladling beans for the men during flaggins, and was rewarded by being assigned to pour tea for them. If any of the other men found it funny to see their boss doing flaggins duty, they wisely kept it to themselves.

Not until she had supper behind her, did she allow herself time to sit down and eat. Thor and Spike Anderson had stayed in the cook shack and were cleaning up the cooking area and doing the dishes, despite her protestations that she could do it by herself. Thor could easily have assigned kitchen duty to one of the other men but he knew how proud they were. He did not have the same kind of pride. And when Spike volunteered, there was no need to ask for more help.

Sawtooth Leverty lingered in the cook shack after he finished eating. "I can stay and help the boy," he offered.

"No need for you to stay. But you can go out and give Red a hand. I won't have time to do that." Thor spoke to him in a cold voice and Sarah wondered at his displeasure with Leverty. Did he find him as disgusting as she did?

Leverty looked annoyed. "I didn't hire on to work with no stinking horses."

Thor stopped what he was doing and gave Leverty a look that would have instilled fear in a smarter man. "You just lost your chance to volunteer. Get your ass out to the stable and help Red, and I'll be checking in with him to see that he's the one deciding when you're done."

Leverty paused, his mouth open to argue; but he clamped it shut again as he thought better of it. He left without another word and Sarah didn't doubt that he'd prove himself useful in the stable. She was learning that when the Push gave an order in the tone of voice he had just used, no man had yet demonstrated the will to go against him.

She started to rise from the table, but Thor motioned to her to sit back down and he poured her a cup of hot tea. She sat down again, thankful for the chance to rest for a few minutes.

As the men worked, they paid little attention to her. Spike was expressing his concern over their progress with the road construction. "You think we'll finish in time, or should we try to get a few more men?"

"We'll finish. We've made good progress. It's June. By late September we should be finished, as long as we keep moving at the same speed. Don't worry. The roads will be done a month before it's time to start cutting for the season. That'll give us time to give the men some time off. And I can stay and get some work done in camp."

Up to his elbows in dishwater, Spike said, "Leverty's one helluva sawyer. If we had a few more like him, I wouldn't worry. He works faster than any man I ever saw...except maybe you."

"He works fast," Thor said, ignoring the comment about his own ability, "but I don't like him." He glanced quickly over at Sarah.

She looked away, pretending not to be listening. She had picked up an old newspaper from under Big Mary's worktable and was pretending to read it.

"He's a liar," Thor continued, satisfied that Jesse didn't care what they were talking about. "I can put up with a lot in a man, but lying is one thing I can't tolerate. If you can't trust a man's words, you can't trust anything about him."

"How do you know he's a liar?" Spike asked.

"One day in the woods I asked him where he worked last, and he told me he worked for Gus Hawkins in a camp outside of Hurley."

"How's that make him a liar?"

"I know Gus Hawkins almost as well as I know you. He told me once that there were three places you'd never find him—Hayward, Hurley and Hell. Gus Hawkins wouldn't work within fifty miles of Hurley. I know it as sure as I know my own name." He lowered his voice, but Sarah heard his next words. "He's a liar, alright. I don't trust the bastard any farther than I could throw him."

She stared busily at the paper, pretending she hadn't heard anything they said, but her head was swimming. What would he think of her if he found out the truth? It was clear he hated a man who lied. How would he feel about a woman pretending to be a boy, and whose very presence in his camp was one big fat lie?

She got up from the table and began to set bread for the next day, while the men finished cleaning up and doing the table setups. Thor was the last one to leave the cook shack, because he took the time to fill all the lanterns and clean the chimneys. By the time they were finished, it was midnight.

When she got up the next morning, she was as tired as she had been her first days in camp, and she knew it was not so much from the extra work as it was the unfamiliarity of what she had to do. She had a new appreciation for Big Mary's abilities. Besides that, she had a new nagging fear of being found out; found out as a liar. She had worried about being found out before, but had come to take kind of an "if it happens, it happens" attitude. But things were different now. Now she realized she cared what he thought of her. And he hated liars.

Big Mary and Woody didn't get back to camp until the next night just before the men finished supper. Her face was no longer swollen, but the skin on her cheek had taken on a nasty blue-black color, and she looked flushed and feverish.

"You okay?" Thor asked as he came toward her from the stove where he had been spooning stew into a bowl.

"I'm better. Doc pulled the damn thing out, but he made me stay in town overnight. Says I got an infection and told me I'd better take it easy for a few days." Thor motioned to her to sit in his place. She did so, apparently too weak to protest.

Sarah watched, knowing Big Mary was not altogether comfortable with her boss waiting on her like a cook's helper. She wished he'd go back to the way he used to be; all hard and cold and concerned only with how hard everybody worked. She noticed smirks on several of the men's faces as they watched the Push playing nursemaid to the cook. Added to his behavior the day before, she figured there'd be talk in the bunkhouse that night about him being soft. She wished she could find an excuse to go to the bunkhouse before lights out so she could hear them talk about him.

The men often bragged about the Push and about how tough he was, and she got a mysterious kind of pleasure listening to them talk about him. She was curious to hear what any of his detractors—and there were a few of those, Leverty among them—might say about him tonight. She wanted to hear what the men who knew him and were loyal to him would say to refute them. But when she looked at Big Mary, she knew it would be another late night in the cook shack.

CHAPTER 19

THINGS settled back to normal soon, and the summer days began to grow hot and humid. On a steamy Saturday night in July, perspiration dampened her forehead as she finished her cook shack chores. As soon as she was done, she went outside to walk along the stream hoping to catch a breeze. She was beginning to feel at home outdoors and she no longer worried about being eaten by wolves. She sat down Indian fashion next to the stream and looked up at the sky. A full moon was just beginning its climb upward through the trees. She sighed, feeling relaxed. She had been working hard, eating well, and sleeping well during the past months. It was happening almost outside of her awareness, but as time passed she felt something new. It was a feeling, not quite of contentment, but something close to it. She pulled her knees up and rested her chin on them, her arms wrapped around her legs. She let her mind wander and for the first time in many days thought about her father. How strange that she had become so absorbed in her life at Camp Seven that days passed without her thinking about the reason she was where she was.

"Father," she whispered, almost as though she expected him to answer from somewhere in the shadows. A picture of him had begun to form in her mind. He had become, in her mind's eye, a mix of minister and lumberjack. She didn't know if he was an identical twin to the uncle she had met, but in her vision of him they were alike in appearance; although hopefully in no other way. She wondered now if she would actually ever find the man who was her father. She had begun to feel a slight uneasiness about finding him. At first it was something she had been unable to identify. But now, as she sat in the peaceful darkness, it was becoming clear to her. She was happy where she was. If—or when—she found her father it would have to end. Her life would change completely all over again.

She sat for a long time, thinking, until her thoughts grew random and scattered, then again became focused. This time—to her extreme chagrin—they settled upon Thor. She heard a sound behind her and she turned expectantly,

161

hoping to see him standing in the moonlight. Instead, Sawtooth Leverty stood six feet behind her. She jumped up and faced him. "What do you want?" She didn't bother trying to be polite. She hated him and she wanted him to know it.

He came slowly toward her. "Thought maybe you wanted some company. You look lonesome sitting all alone out here."

She started walking backwards away from him, then turned and began to run.

"Hey! Where you going? Come back and talk to me."

She paid no attention. She needed to go where there were lots of people. She ran until she reached the bunkhouse and went inside and stood inside the door in the shadows, trying to catch her breath. No one noticed her hasty arrival because they were all watching the two men who were sitting across from each other arguing about something.

"A pansy? You mean to tell me you think he's a pansy?" It was Red Scanlon, and he was pointing an angry finger at Charlie DuBois.

Charlie looked him straight in the eye without blinking. "Yeah! A pansy. Just because his precious cook gets a toothache, he puts on a Goddamned apron. What would you call a man who wears an apron?"

The room was silent, all eyes on the two men, waiting for one of them to crack. They seemed to have reached an impasse and neither of them spoke. They just sat and glared at each other.

Shorty Walker, one of the loaders who was sitting at the far end of the bench spoke up. "Hey, Charlie."

"Yeah, Shorty? You talkin' to me?"

All eyes turned to Shorty, who was exhaling a large wavering round circle of smoke up into the dark ceiling. Knowing he was now the center of attention, he crossed one leg over the other, leaned one elbow lazily on his knee and pointed the hand holding his pipe generally in the direction of the clerk's shack, where they figured Thor was probably working. He looked around the room, meeting each man's eyes in turn.

"Guess you ain't heard, DuBois," he finally said. "This foreman we got is one mean son-of-a-bitch; apron or no apron. Ain't that right, Tom?" He looked now at Tom Hopkins, one of the regular swampers, who was sitting halfway down the bench from the two men who had been arguing.

Every man in the room looked at Shorty, then at Tom, then at Charlie and then back at Tom again, waiting for him to answer. Some of the men coughed lightly, some of them shifted uncomfortably on the bench, and some of them sat with expressions that Sarah didn't understand.

Tom spit a long stream of tobacco juice into an empty can next to his chair. He seemed to puff up slightly as he straightened himself, wiped his mouth with the back of his hand, looked around at the men staring at him and waiting for him to say something. He leaned forward so he could look directly at Charlie DuBois and said, "Best you don't call him a pansy to his face."

The room buzzed with voices in agreement until Shorty stood up and looked at Tom and said, "I hear tell he killed a man over in Hayward over nothin' more'n a whore." Then, looking satisfied, he sat down again.

Sarah held her breath and pressed her back harder against the wall. She was afraid to leave and she was afraid to stay.

"She wasn't no ordinary whore," Tom said. "Thor Nilsson don't go around killing men just for the hell of it."

Half the men in the room nodded and Tom cleared his throat, aware that every eye in the room was now on him. "Happened over in Hayward back in the spring of '89."

"That Hayward's nothin' but a hell hole!" one of the new men who had never heard the story piped up.

Shorty glared at him and said, "Shut up! We don't need you tellin' us about Hayward! We've all been there."

Charlie ignored the rest of the men and gave Tom a nasty look and said, "How do I know this is a true story? I don't think all this shit you're always telling me about Nilsson is true."

"It's true, alright. My old saw partner, Jake Mooney, was there, and that's how I know. He told me the story many times before he left the timber. It was the first year Jake was in the same camp as Thor Nilsson. They were done with the cutting for the season and were heading out for the summer. Jake was going to the river drive on the St. Croix and Thor was going to work cutting a road for a new camp somewhere outside of Hayward. On this particular night Thor and some of the Jacks went to Crazy Lucy's to get laid. Most of the men got pretty wild that night, but not Thor."

Some of the men were nodding as if to say it was all true. They had heard the story many times because it was part of the lore in the northern camps. Thor Nilsson was known to whore the same as any man, but had a reputation for not ever losing his head over whores or liquor.

Tom went on, "There was this pretty little thing at Lucy's that night. Jake said no one had ever seen her before. She took a liking to Thor the minute she saw him."

"Yeah, don't they all," half the men in the room said in unison.

Tom looked thoughtfully around the room. "Funny thing. She was just the kind of woman Thor likes. Hair all bright and yellow and skin like the cream on top of a cat's dish." He was nodding for emphasis as he took out his tobacco pouch and filled his pipe as he spoke. "They egged him on, but he got all pissed off. Said his taste didn't run to children."

The men who had heard the story were again nodding in agreement, and the others were looking around with puzzled expressions on their faces. Sarah watched them, wishing she had never come into the bunkhouse that night.

"Jake said she didn't look to be no more than twelve or thirteen years old. Rumor was her folks died from diphtheria and that she-snake, Lucy, recruited her for her saloon. She hadn't been there more than a few days, and the poor little thing had kind of a stunned look on her face all the time, like she didn't really know where she was.

"Jake told me that when Thor walked in that night she just went straight to him, like she was hoping maybe he'd rescue her or something. Thor's got that look about him, like he's some kind of storybook hero with that yellow hair and handsome like he is."

"Like a pretty yellow pansy," Charlie DuBois said, nowhere near willing to concede his point.

Everyone in the room glared at him for a moment before all eyes turned back to Tom.

"He was all nice and gentle with her, like he can be sometimes with women—but he wouldn't take her to bed. He went over and asked Lucy where she got the little girl, and when Lucy told him he got that crazy, blazing mad look he gets. Jake said he was afraid Thor was going to do murder right then and there."

"Is that who he killed?" half a dozen voices in the room asked. "A Woman? Did he kill Crazy Lucy?"

"No, you stupid sons-a-bitches. Not a woman! He left Lucy's and went somewhere else that night. Jake didn't say where and it don't matter. What matters is that next morning everyone in town was buzzing about what happened over at Lucy's. Seems one of the whores had got herself hurt real bad.

Somehow Thor found out it was the little girl. Jake says he stormed over there and made Lucy tell him what happened.

"Sukie Crawford, one of the whores Jake always visited when he got to Hayward, was sitting with her and she told Jake this part of the story. Says she was bleeding from every opening in her poor little body. Her nose was broken and half of one ear was bit off. She said Thor just fell down on his knees by the bed and took the girl's hands in his and told her if she'd hurry up and get well he'd take her away with him to someplace nice where nobody could ever hurt her again. He knew damn well she wasn't going to get well, because Sukie told him the doctor had come and did what he could, but he didn't hold out a speck of hope.

"The little girl's face got all happy when he said he'd take her away, and then he made her tell him what happened—and who did it. It was one of the big jacks from up 'round Hurley. She said his name was Pete Slake. She started to cry and blame herself. She said she should have known what he wanted, but she didn't understand, and it made Pete mad and he went nuts.

"Well, Sukie thought Thor was going to cry, but he didn't. He just sat there, smiling and talking real nice to her and holding her hand and stroking her hair. He stayed that whole day, and come about midnight the poor little thing just kind of slipped off and never woke up again."

The room was silent and several of the men in the room crossed themselves. They were all either looking down at the floor or up at the ceiling. Sarah didn't want to hear any more. She felt sick to her stomach and she wanted to run from the room, but she couldn't move.

Tom lit his pipe, took a long puff, then took his watch from his pocket and looked at it. "Damn near nine o'clock."

"Hurry up, Tom! You ain't gonna get finished before lights-out if you don't quit your damn jerking off and finish the story!" Shorty yelled at him.

Everyone complained in unison, and finally Tom went on. "Don't take long to tell the rest. They found Slake a week later washed up on shore about five miles down the Chippewa River. No one knows for sure who killed him, but everyone in town knew Thor had gone looking for him. He found him in one of the bars down the street from Lucy's. At least twenty jacks saw Thor walk up to him and ask to talk to him outside. They said Slake looked kind of nervous and didn't want to go, but he went.

"The last anybody ever saw of Pete Slake was him walking down the road out of town, Thor's arm around his shoulder real buddy-buddy like. No one ever saw Thor in Hayward again, and next anybody heard he was in Minnesota. The authorities asked questions around town, but pretty soon the questions died out. I think everyone figured Slake deserved what he got."

A silence had fallen over the room and Sarah sensed that she should cover her ears from the rest of Tom's words, because even the men seemed to dread what was coming.

"Floated up to shore like a bloated, beached whale. Figured whoever killed him beat him bloody, cut off his balls and threw him in the river."

One of the new men jumped up and ran for the door. Sarah wanted to follow but didn't dare. Instead she pinched her eyes tight shut and fought against the gore rising in the back of her throat. She thought for a moment she was going to faint so she opened her eyes, hoping that the sight of the room and the men's faces would bring her back to reality. A reality that was awful; but not nearly as awful as the one she had just heard about.

Tom Hopkins stood up and stretched, his arms high in the air, a look of triumph on his face as he looked around the room and then purposefully gave a nod to Charlie DuBois as if to say, "So there!" Charlie didn't move nor speak. He just sat staring straight ahead, his face expressionless.

Sarah quietly stepped out the door and ran as fast as she could to the cook shack. When she got inside she found Thor Nilsson sitting across the table from Sawtooth Leverty. They seemed to be having a serious conversation, but they stopped talking and looked at her when she came in.

Without a word to either of them, she went into the storeroom and sat down on her cot. Thor's face swam in front of her, and she covered her face with both hands. How could she possibly have begun to have feelings for such a man? Then she started shaking and she shook so hard that she knew she had to do something to get control of herself. Maybe a hot drink. Yes, that was it. Some tea. But she couldn't. There was no way she was going to go into that room and look at either of those two unspeakably loathsome brutes.

CHAPTER 20

SHE sat like that for a long time, until she finally stopped shaking. She wasn't sure whether the incident with Sawtooth or the story about Thor had upset her the most. All she knew was that she hated them both. How can there be such horrible men in the world? Why does she keep meeting up with them? Her loathing spilled over to her father, wherever he was, and she wondered if she had better forget about this insane quest to find him.

A door slammed and she heard Big Mary's voice. She sat for a while longer, then decided to go into the other room. She would simply ignore the men and get herself a soothing cup of tea. Big Mary's presence assured her that she would be safe from having to talk to either Thor or Leverty. She stood up and went to the door to the kitchen and put her hand on the knob to pull it open. She pulled her hand away, hesitating, and then reached for it again and pulled the door open and left the safety of her room.

Big Mary and Thor were sitting across the table from each other and Leverty was gone. It was clear that they were talking about something serious—and also private—because they stopped talking as soon as they saw her.

"I decided to get myself a cup of tea. You want some?" she asked as casually as she could. They both shook their heads, glancing nervously at her and then returning to their conversation, their voices so low she couldn't make out the words except that once Thor raised his voice and she heard the words "good sawyer." She knew then what they were talking about. Leverty must have told them some lie about what had happened earlier that night by the stream. The way it sounded, Thor was defending Leverty to Big Mary because he didn't want to risk losing a good sawyer.

Sarah felt sick to her stomach again, wondering if they were discussing sending her down the tote road. She quickly forgot about wanting to run from Camp Seven and Leverty and Thor Nilsson, and began to worry instead about being forced to go. She figured if Thor had to choose between keeping Big Mary's cookee and a good sawyer, whom he needed badly if he was going to get the road finished, she was bound to come out on the short end. Just because she had helped a little with the clerk's duties didn't mean it outweighed the importance of the roadwork. The man had his priorities. She made her tea then said good night and went to her cot. She could hear the drone of their voices far into the night. She wondered if her stay at Camp Seven was actually coming to an end.

She felt uneasy for days after that, as though she was again on trial to prove herself to Thor. It didn't take her mind off her fear of Leverty, though, and she stopped walking alone around camp at night. Whenever she went to the clerk's shack she looked both ways before she stepped out the door. She would run as fast as she could when she was going from one to the other. She even took to pushing a heavy barrel in front of the door to the storeroom when she went to bed at night. For the first time in her life she was afraid to be alone. But as the days passed and Leverty completely ignored her, she started to relax again.

She began to wonder if the story that she had heard in the bunkhouse that night was really true. She remembered both Big Mary and Thor telling her not to believe everything she heard about him. The time they spent working together in the clerk's shack made her doubt that he could be so violent. He might be able to bang heads together to keep order in his camp, and he might bodily carry a strange woman to a place he thought was safer for her, but violent murder? She tried to convince herself that what had happened to that man Slake over in Hayward simply was not something he could do. She spent a lot of energy telling herself that his coldness and his authoritarianism did not extend to murder—even if that murder could be justified. After all, it wasn't like the foreman who had avenged the man whose legs had been crushed. He had been responsible for those men; Thor had no responsibility for the little whore.

Two weeks later as they were riding back to camp from flaggins, Big Mary said quietly to Sarah, "I'm not feeling so good. Think you can handle supper? I think I'll spend the rest of the day in my cabin. If I rest a while maybe I'll start feeling like my old self again." The infection from her tooth had weakened her. She had lost her appetite and she was so small she couldn't afford to lose the weight that she had lost as a result. It was taking a long time for her to get her weight and her strength back to normal.

Sarah nodded, remembering that Woody had gone to St. Paul to visit his sick brother, and that she'd be alone in the cook shack. But what difference could it make? Nothing had happened lately to renew her fear of Leverty; and besides, the men were all working in the woods. She told herself to stop being such a baby.

At about four o'clock, she was taking the loaves of bread out of the oven when she heard the door open. She turned, a hot pan of bread in each hand, and saw Sawtooth Leverty walking toward her. "Wh...what do you want?" Her voice was barely audible as she backed up against the counter, the hot pans of bread still in her hand.

"I came to say good-bye," he said in his raspy voice.

"G...good-bye? Where are you going?" She tried to sound curious instead of terrified, but her voice cracked.

"Where?" He laughed a deep throaty laugh and said, "I'm not sure yet. Out of here is all I know." His face darkened and filled with hatred. "I'm sick of working for that son-of-a-bitch Nilsson. Man don't get a moment's peace without him sniffing around to be sure everybody's busting his ass. I'm a damn good sawyer and I ain't never had no trouble finding work."

The truth was that the reason he had become such a fast worker was that it was the only way he could make up for the times when he slacked off. At Camp Seven, however, there was never any slacking off, and Leverty didn't like it. The night Sarah had seen them in the cook shack talking, Thor had sat him down and told him he had to work more steadily. If he couldn't or wouldn't do that he'd best take a hike. Leverty had chosen to take a hike and this was the day. He happened to know Jesse would be alone in the cook shack all afternoon. He was leaving, but he wasn't done with Camp Seven. Not just yet.

Shaking, Sarah turned and set the pans on the counter behind her then turned back to Leverty. "I'm sure you're a...a good sawyer." She paused, unsure about what to do, terrified at the way he was watching her with his one good eye, the other one darting crazily around the cook shack. "Well, good-bye...." Her voice cracked again as she held out her hand, reluctant to touch him but thinking it was better to act normal and shake his hand in farewell.

"You gonna miss me, Boy?"

He was only a few feet from her now, and the look on his face told her she was in real danger, but she wasn't sure what the danger was. What could he do to hurt her? What did he want? She didn't know. She only knew that her instincts were screaming at her to get away from him and to do it fast. She pulled her hand back and put it behind her, suddenly understanding that she must not let him touch her. She started working her way sideways along the counter, her back tight against it, hoping she could somehow get past him and run for the door. But he was so close she could feel his breath on her face.

"Why don't you give old Leverty a little kiss? You'll like it. I can tell you're the kind of boy ain't never gonna like women. I'm gonna show you why you feel that way." He reached for her.

With one hand she groped along the counter behind her and felt something familiar. It was the potato-peeling knife. She wrapped her fingers firmly around the handle, slipped it off the counter and down behind her right leg. Then, after only a moment's hesitation she whipped it around and jabbed it, with every ounce of her newly-acquired strength, into his upper thigh.

He let out a yell and fell backwards against the opposite counter and it gave her time to run. She could hardly get the door open because she was so terrified, and by the time she got outside he was right behind her. Blood was streaming from his leg and the look on his face was so awful she started to scream. But she was too scared and he was too fast and he grabbed her and spun her around and slammed her face hard against the side of the cook shack and began tearing at his belt.

"I was gonna be nice to you but now I changed my mind! I'm gonna give you a farewell you won't soon forget!"

Terror overcame her and her arms and legs grew weak and the fight drained out of her. Her head was spinning from the blow to her face and she felt the sick sensation of saliva forming at the back of her throat, and she knew she was going to faint. She opened her mouth and tried again to scream, but no sound came out. She felt dizzy, as if she was floating somewhere above herself.

Suddenly a loud *thwack* sounded over her head. Leverty released his grip on her, and she looked up and saw a quivering hatchet sunk nearly an inch deep into the logs above her head. She turned weakly away from the rough logs of the cook shack that were holding her up and saw Thor coming toward them, his face so filled with rage that she was afraid he was going to kill them both.

Leverty started shuffling sideways toward the road, clutching his bleeding leg. "The little son-of-a-bitch tried to kill me! I was only trying to defend myself," he pleaded, moving sideways fast, trying to compensate for the speed of the forward movement of his crazed foreman.

Thor didn't speak. He grabbed Leverty by both suspenders, lifted a leg and kneed him full force in the groin. Then he drew back one arm and slapped him on the side of the head, his hand open, and Leverty stumbled sideways and fell onto the ground. Thor reached down and pulled him to his feet, this time aiming a fist at his face.

She was having a hard time keeping her eyes open, and the three men who had run up behind Thor were little more than a blur. Spike Anderson grabbed Thor by one arm and Jock was struggling to get hold of the other. Red Scanlon threw his arms around Thor's middle and was trying to pull him away from Leverty but wasn't having much luck.

"Enough," Spike said in a low growl, as the three men struggled to hold him back. "Enough! You'll kill him!"

They finally got him under control, but it took all three of them to do it. As soon as Leverty saw that Thor wasn't going to be able to hit him again, he started running toward the woods, limping badly, still clutching his bleeding leg. Sarah watched numbly as Spike and Jock held Thor and Red ran after Leverty. Red soon caught the limping man and dragged him back to where the other men still stood holding Thor. Thor was breathing rapidly, fighting to control his rage.

"Tie the bastard up and throw him in the wagon and take him to Smitheson. They'll know what to do with him. Get him the hell out of here before I take my hatchet and finish him off."

Take my hatchet and finish him off! So it was true, she thought. He really did kill a man once and would do it again. These men were barbarians. All of them! She groaned as everything began to spin and float in front of her eyes.

No one had been paying any attention to her, but suddenly Thor looked at her and saw her eyes roll upward. He pulled himself loose from the men and with several long strides reached her just as her knees buckled and she collapsed against him.

"What's all the commotion? A body can't even be sick without you louts makin' enough noise to wake the d...." Big Mary stopped still in the middle of the clearing and her hand flew to her mouth as she saw Thor gather Sarah up, her arms dangling like a rag doll.

"Get the door," he said, his voice shaking and barely audible.

Big Mary saw the men dragging Sawtooth Leverty toward the wagon, and she saw that he was bleeding badly. Without another thought about him, she turned and ran as fast as her legs would carry her and opened the door to the cook shack. She hurried along behind them and watched numbly as Thor carried Sarah into the back room and put her carefully down onto the cot.

She looked at him, her face an agony of concern. "What happened? My God, what happened?"

"I'll tell you later. I'll get his clothes off. You go get a cold cloth." He hesitated. "Do you think he needs a couple of stitches?"

Big Mary peered closely at the side of Sarah's face, then shook her head. "No. He's young enough so's he'll heal fast."

Thor started unbuttoning Sarah's shirt and somehow she roused herself and managed to protest. He stepped back nervously, unsure about what to do next.

"Let him be. Get the cold cloth," Big Mary said, finally under control of her emotions and of the situation.

Sarah tried to sit up but she fell back down and her hand went to the side of her face. It hurt terribly, and when she pulled her hand away it was covered with blood. She saw Big Mary coming toward her with something in her hand, and she knew she'd better stay awake or they would try to undress her.

"I...I'm fine. If you just leave me alone for a little while...."

"Bullshit! You are *not fine*! You are all beat to hell and I want you to stay on that cot!" Thor's face had gone white and his eyes were wild. "Will he be okay?" he asked Big Mary, his hands locked in tight fists.

"Yes. He'll be okay," Big Mary said reassuringly, touching his arm. "Why don't you go outside and get some air?"

His eyes went frantically from Big Mary to Sarah, and finally his chest heaved and he took in a massive breath of air and ran from the room. Outside, he stopped and fell back against the side of the cook shack, his face contorted with emotion.

"Holy Christ," he mumbled as he turned and raised both arms high, hands clenched into fists as he hammered them impotently against the rough logs of the cook shack. "What if I hadn't gotten here in time? What if the men hadn't known enough to come after me?" A wave of cold revulsion swept over him as he brushed against the hatchet, still stuck deep into the logs just above his head. He reached up and pulled it out and looked at it in his hand. He grimaced as he remembered another man who had been the object of his wrath, and he pushed the hatchet back into his belt and started walking toward the road back to the work crews. His long legs moved faster and faster until he was running. Running away from the agony swirling inside his head and toward the safety of the timber.

Meanwhile, Sarah had fallen back onto the cot and turned her face toward the wall. Big Mary took her hand and pressed a cold cloth into it. "Hold this against your face, Boy. It'll stop the bleeding." Her voice was gentler than Sarah had ever heard it.

She did as she was told, then closed her eyes. She knew Big Mary was still standing by the cot watching her. She slipped into a restless sleep, remembering hearing loud footsteps in the other room and knowing someone had come into the storeroom. She remembered not caring who it was or why they were there and had drifted off again, and then felt a slight draft of air and the soft, feathery movement of another blanket being placed carefully over her. Again she slept.

She awoke later, the side of her face throbbing, and eased herself upright. It took her a moment to remember what had happened, and when she did, she remembered Leverty's attack less vividly than she remembered Thor's rage. She had been the cause of trouble in his camp, and now she would for sure be told she had to leave. It hurt her more than the attack had. She could hear voices in the other room and she sat and listened, trying to make out who it was and what they were saying. It was Big Mary and Thor.

"Might as well face the music," she said to herself as she got slowly up from the cot and walked toward the other room. She stood in the doorway and saw Thor nervously straddling a bench. Big Mary was sitting across from him. When he saw Sarah he jumped up so fast that he bumped the long table and splashed coffee from the cups in front of them.

Automatically, Sarah started toward the sink for a cloth to wipe it up, but with several long strides he reached her and grabbed her wrist. Without looking at Sarah, he spoke to Big Mary. "I don't want him here at breakfast." With that, he dropped her hand and stormed out of the cook shack.

Sarah stood speechless looking at the door that had just banged shut. Then she stumbled over and fell weakly onto the bench, facing away from Big Mary. The strength was gone out of her, and tears began to form. "I...I don't know where to go," she whispered hopelessly.

She spoke so softly that Big Mary couldn't hear her, so she got up and came around to where Sarah was sitting. "What did you say, Boy?" She reached over and gently touched Sarah's cheek. "That's nasty. You're gonna look like a piece of raw meat for a while." Then she looked more carefully at Sarah. "What is it? Does it hurt so bad?"

The tears had begun to slide down Sarah's cheeks, stinging her raw skin. She turned around and bent over and put her head into her arms on the table and began to sob.

Big Mary sat down on the bench next to her and put her arms around her. "It was awful, I know." Her voice became angry. "Men like that ought to be castrated!" Those last words made her gasp, as if saying them had some further meaning.

It made Sarah cry even harder because she knew exactly what Big Mary was thinking. Big Mary got up from the bench and went to the stove. "You just go on and cry all you want to. It don't make you less of a man just because you got to cry. You already proved you're no sissy, what with sticking that knife in him like you did. Besides, you ain't had a real good cry since you got here. Anybody who's lost his folks and then had to go through what you been through deserves a good cry. I'm gonna fix you a nice supper and then you're going to bed and you're gonna stay there 'til you're damn good and ready to get up. Just like Thor said."

Sarah sat upright and swiped at her tears with the sleeve of her flannel shirt. "What did you say?"

"I said lots of things, but mostly, I said you go ahead and cry."

"No. No, I mean about what Thor said."

"Thor? I don't...oh, you mean about not helping at breakfast?" Big Mary chuckled. "The man's getting soft." She turned from the stove and looked at Sarah, her face serious. "He don't like it when someone in his camp gets hurt. He thinks he should be able to prevent it."

Sarah sat watching her, awareness dawning upon her. He wasn't sending her away after all. He wasn't angry with her. Relief flooded over her and she stood up.

"I'm fine. I don't need the day off." She looked up at the clock on the wall. "Good grief! It's eleven o'clock! What happened to supper?" She turned and looked out the window. "I didn't even notice that it was dark already. How long did I sleep?" She grimaced and reached up to touch her face. It hurt when she talked.

Big Mary carried a plate of food over and set it on the table, then motioned to Sarah to sit back down. "Hours. You didn't even hear the supper commotion. I know, because me and Thor peeked in on you a couple times. You needed to sleep after that shock. Now you sit right down like I'm tellin' you. Don't go gettin' all rambunctious. Eat."

She sat down again and tried to eat, but chewing hurt her face. She put her fork down and put her hand to her face, smiling apologetically at Big Mary.

Big Mary got up again and went and ladled some broth into a cup from the huge stockpot at the back of the stove. Setting it in front of Sarah, she said, "Try that. It'll go down easy and you won't have to chew."

Sarah took a little sip, then closed her eyes and drank the hot, rich broth. When she opened her eyes again, Big Mary was looking at her fondly, the way a mother might. Sarah's eyes filled with tears again and she felt them sliding down her face into her broth. Leverty had tried to hurt her, and Big Mary and Thor had both taken care of her as if she really mattered to them. She thought suddenly of Katie, and she remembered all the times Katie had comforted her when her aunt or her uncle or her cousin had been cruel to her. She hadn't been alone then, and she wasn't alone now. She set the cup down and turned away so Big Mary couldn't see her tears.

Big Mary got up and went to the stove and began bustling around, pretending not to notice that her helper was bawling like a baby. She didn't want to embarrass him by watching; and God only knew how badly he needed to cry and get it out of his system. "That slimy bastard," she whispered to herself as she thought of Leverty attacking Jesse. "Thor should damn well have killed him when he had the chance."

CHAPTER 21

ONE evening the following week at suppertime the sheriff came to Camp Seven to talk to them about Sawtooth Leverty. Sheriff Jensen wasn't a large man, but he ate like a lumberjack and had an appreciation for good food. He was not against taking advantage of his position to get a meal cooked by Big Mary. After supper he sat with Thor, Big Mary and the cookee at the table and listened while Sarah told Jesse's story.

"The judge will be hearing cases in Hinckley sometime next week and he'll hear the case against Leverty at that time. You willing to come in and tell your story to the judge, Williams?"

"No!" she blurted. How could she do that? Maybe under questioning she'd break down and they'd find out the truth about her. Then what? "He didn't hurt me. Can't you just find some way so he can't work in any more lumber camps?" she asked hopefully.

"Pretty hard to do that," the sheriff said, looking at her with curiosity. "Oh, sure, word will get out. But from what I've been able to find out, he's a damn good sawyer and they need good sawyers all over the timber."

Thor looked carefully at the sheriff and said, "If Jesse doesn't want to take this any farther, it's okay with me. Leverty's no fool. If you let him go, he'll get the hell out of Minnesota, unless I miss my guess."

The sheriff eyed Thor, remembering the story he had heard about Pete Slake and the little whore. He didn't want some jack in his territory doing murder, no matter how bad the victim deserved to be murdered. He knew the jacks had some strange code of law of their own. But if this boy didn't want to press charges, there wasn't much the sheriff could do and he knew it.

Big Mary spoke, her eyes blazing. "Oh yeah, sure! Let him leave Minnesota and go to some other state and have him attacking *their* boys." But then she, too, remembered Pete Slake and grew silent. News traveled like wildfire through the timber, and bad news twice as fast. Justice would prevail. She wasn't going to worry about how. "I guess I agree with Nilsson," Big Mary told the sheriff. "If Jesse won't testify, I guess you're gonna have to let him run."

The sheriff laughed at that and looked at Sarah. "He won't be running very fast for a while, I'll tell you! You got him good, and he's pretty crippled up."

"Hah! Not much chance of that!" Big Mary scoffed. "These jacks heal faster than anybody I ever saw. You can't hardly hurt the bastards, unless you chop something clear off."

Thor shot a look at her and she added quickly, "Like poor old Woody's leg, and such as that."

"Maybe so," the sheriff agreed reluctantly. "They may be tough as nails under normal circumstances, but the boy stuck him with a kitchen knife."

"What difference does that make?" Sarah asked, wondering why it mattered what kind of knife she used, as long as it was good and sharp—which it had been. She felt a good deal of satisfaction about that sharp knife. Was she getting to be as bad as these wild men?

"I don't know much about medicine, but I know a bad infection when I see one. Leverty's got one helluva nasty one. It may not have started out as such a bad wound, but it's a damn bad one now. I wouldn't be surprised if that leg has to come off."

"Good," Sarah said, surprising herself with the venom in her voice. Although she wished she had the courage to expose herself to the law so they could put him in jail where he couldn't harm some innocent boy, news of the infection eased her conscience. The infection would mete out justice that the law could not.

Following the Leverty incident the camp buzzed as the men speculated about what had happened. They tried to coax Jock, Spike or Red into talking about it. They had, after all, been close to the actual event; but they stubbornly refused to talk about it. There was no use asking Nilsson, because the mere mention of Leverty's name sent him into such a black rage that no one had the stomach to bring it up. Going straight to the boy and asking him about it was also out of the question. Mentioning Leverty's name in Jesse's presence caused the boy such distress that they all kept a nervous silence when they were anywhere near him.

So because the truth was hidden from them, they made up their own truth, and the story grew all out of proportion. Jesse's bravery grew, the size of the knife grew, and the damage he had done to Leverty grew. As the story according to the jacks went, Jesse Williams—delicate for a boy—had a soft and gentle nature that had led his companions in Camp Seven to tease him and call him a sissy behind his back. Because he was such a "pretty boy," he had drawn the attention of a jack with a taste for boys. When the jack attacked him, the boy was as cool as a cucumber, and he reached for a ten-inch carving knife and sunk it deep into the man's groin and crippled him for life. As to what really finally happened to Leverty, no one ever knew. As soon as the sheriff let him go he limped in agony onto a train and left town. He was never heard from again.

Sarah knew nothing of the story that was growing up around the events of that awful day. She knew only that the teasing had stopped and that she no longer had to be on the lookout for assorted critters and foreign objects appearing in strange places. And it was hard for her not to notice the marked difference in the men's attitude towards her.

One day she remarked about it to Big Mary. It was a warm, sunny summer day and they were out in the root cellar cleaning and airing it out.

Big Mary chuckled. "It's because you passed muster."

"Passed muster? What does that mean?"

"It means you ain't no greenhorn anymore. You proved you could take care of yourself.

"I did?" she asked. "You mean...L...Leverty?" She hated even saying his name.

"Yup. The men respect somebody who stands up and takes action like you did." She chuckled with satisfaction. "I knew you were a good boy. I just didn't quite know *how good.*"

Sarah colored. "Anybody would have done the same thing. Besides, I wasn't so brave. I passed out cold."

Big Mary looked at her and said, her voice firm, "You passed out cold just as soon as it was okay to pass out cold. Not before. Give yourself credit for what you did. You've got damn good instincts and you can't teach that to a person. It's born in 'em. You can thank your parents for that. Now get to work."

Sarah looked at her for a long moment, then continued wiping off the jars and the shelves. *You can thank your parents for that. Parents,* she thought. It had occurred often to Sarah that the only visitor to Camp Seven since her arrival had been the sheriff. She felt pretty stupid for thinking her father might just come strolling into camp one day and announce himself. She was no longer, however, in any great hurry. Her priorities had shifted. She had come to Camp Seven because it offered a chance for her to look for her father. Now, after all that had happened, and because of how well she was taking to her duties, she had found a life for herself. She still hoped to find him, but for now she was content.

One of the reasons for her growing contentment was that she was finding more and more time to work in the clerk's shack. She had gotten fast and efficient with her other chores in order to allow more time for the clerk's duties. Clerking was more than satisfaction at learning a job well; it was fun for her, and it seemed to tap strengths she hadn't been aware of. She even went back through all the other ledgers she found in a drawer in the desk and studied what had been done before. She found some errors and it made her feel competent to know she could critique the clerks who preceded her—if only to herself.

She even rearranged the wannigan so it was more efficient. The things they sold the most were placed where they were most accessible. Winter caps and woolen mittens were stacked on the highest shelves to await the cold weather.

She loved it when the men wandered in after supper or on Sundays to buy things. When the men bought tobacco, snuff, socks, a shirt, underwear or a bottle of liniment for a sore muscle she'd make a note of it on their page in the ledger and in the supply log. It got so the men would linger for a while at the wannigan, talking to her about their families or the other jobs they had had. The boy, Jesse, was getting to be the one the men went to when they felt a bite of loneliness for family. He was like everybody's little brother and the crude, rough men developed affection for him.

She had completely taken over the main camp ledger, and whenever someone made a run to Pine Crescent or to Hinckley for supplies or equipment they came to her with the receipts. If she was in the cook shack, she'd stuff them into her apron pocket and record them later. All in all, she knew she was a good cookee and she was becoming a good clerk. There were fewer and fewer times when she considered the consequences of pretending she was a boy. It was becoming second nature to her to be Jesse Williams.

But amidst all the contentment, dark clouds began to form on the horizon. She had disguised herself as a boy in order to hide while she looked for her father. She had not intended to meet someone who made her feel very much like a woman. Now, along with hiding her identity, she must now hide her growing feelings for Thor.

One Sunday night she was rearranging the shelves in the wannigan when he came in. He looked flushed and his hair was damp, so she knew he had been in the sauna.

"Aren't you going to go listen to the music, Jesse? Woody's in rare form tonight."

"I...I have a lot of work to do."

"A boy needs to have some fun. You work too hard." He didn't press it though, and instead came behind the counter and began helping with the shelves.

He accidentally brushed against her and she smelled the clean soapy smell that always emanated from him when he had been in the sauna. Quickly, she finished what she was doing and said, with fake finality, "I'm glad that's done," and started toward the door.

"I thought you said you had a lot of work to do."

"I do. I did. I...I got done faster than I thought I would." She tried hard to sound convincing, but she knew she was doing a bad job of it.

"You going up to the bunkhouse to hear the music after all?"

"Nope," she said. "I've got some work in the storeroom that I've been putting off."

She was out the door before he could ask another question, and she ran, heart racing, into the cook shack and back into the storeroom. She stood with her back against the door, hoping against hope that he was satisfied with her excuse, and that he wouldn't come looking for her. She had never felt so completely vulnerable.

Thor, puzzled by her behavior, went to the desk and sat down. He casually opened the ledger and began paging through it, looking at the neatly written names and numbers Jesse had done. He no longer interfered much with what Jesse was doing. He was happy to be done with the clerk's responsibilities. It made his job a whole lot easier. But despite that, things were not going well for him. It was true he was satisfied with everything Jesse did, but little else in camp pleased him. He knew he was driving the men too hard. He was dissatisfied with the progress they were making on the road, and he did a poor job of hiding his dissatisfaction.

He didn't know it, but some of the newer men in camp had begun to talk about going down the road rather than working for such an unreasonable, surly boss. The men who had been with him for years tried to calm them down by saying it would pass, and that he was fighting his own private demons. Those who knew him well had seen it before. Such moods usually led to threats of returning to his homeland, but he had not yet followed through on those threats.

Most of them finally figured he never would. His foul moods always blew over
and he'd return to being his old self.

But for him, this was not like any other thing that had ever happened to
him. He felt out of control. He had used rotten judgment with Leverty. He had
known full well that Leverty was going to be trouble. He had even talked to Big
Mary about it; about the strange way he behaved around Jesse. But he had talked
himself out of it because he was so anxious to meet Smitheson's timetable with
the road. As a result, he had come close to causing a real catastrophe, and the
possibility of Jesse being raped by that pig, Leverty, made his heart pound and
his hands ball up into fists.

Too, the whole ugly matter brought back memories of the little whore. He
had tried to forget the pitiful little body in the bed at Lucy's, but the incident
with Jesse brought it all back as if it happened yesterday. He felt weak because
he couldn't control his thoughts. He was getting soft. He had developed a fondness for Jesse that was all out of proportion to feelings a foreman should have.
Tonight he had been disappointed when Jesse left the clerk's shack. He had
wanted to ask him to stay, but managed to control the urge. He had begun to
watch over him and worry about him more than he had any business doing;
especially since Leverty was long gone.

To add to the problem, Big Mary was sulking about Jesse. She kept telling
him how pleased she was that Jesse was doing so well with the clerk's job; but in
the next breath, she'd say she didn't like him taking her cookee away from her.
She complained that she'd have to hire three new cookees for the season, and
she was sure three of them put together wouldn't get as much done as Jesse did,
and certainly not as well.

He had been in the sauna for over an hour, trying to sweat the misery out
of himself. Even that hadn't worked. He closed the ledger and pushed his chair
back and stretched his legs out, crossing one foot over the other on top of the
desk. He linked his fingers behind his head and leaned back into them. But it was
no use. He couldn't sit still. He got up and started pacing around the room. He
went behind the counter and started counting the jars of snuff.

Finally, he gave a disgusted groan and said, "Damn! I need to get the hell out
of here for a while!"

His first impulse was to go to town—to Lila. But that thought didn't seem to
satisfy him. Besides, if he went to Ginger's most of the men would be clamoring
to go with him. If he didn't let them, they'd sulk for days. They already seemed

in a giant sulk and he didn't wish to aggravate it. He was unaware that his own behavior was bringing down the morale in his camp. It struck him then that he needed advice. Badly. "Gray Wolf," he said to himself. "I'll talk to Gray Wolf." Having made up his mind to go talk to his old friend, he felt better.

The following Saturday morning, an hour after the men had gone to the woods, he came into the cook shack where Big Mary was rolling out piecrusts and Sarah was scrubbing the benches and tables.

Big Mary looked up at him and asked, "What are you doing back here? Forget something?"

"Nope. Jock's taking over for today. I'm going to the Indians this morning. I'll be back late tomorrow night."

Sarah looked at him in astonishment. "Indians?"

"Good. It'll do you good to get out of here for a while," Big Mary said. Then, almost as an afterthought, she added, "Take Jesse."

Sarah stiffened, then pushed herself up off her knees and turned slowly around to look at Big Mary to see if she could possibly be serious; not just about letting her have some time away from work, but about sending her off into Indian territory to be scalped.

"Take Jesse?" Thor wasn't sure he had heard her right.

"Yup." Big Mary stopped what she was doing and looked him straight in the eye. "He's nothing but a kid and we've had him working himself to death and being attacked by...."

She didn't have to finish her sentence. The guilt worked on him. He hesitated for only a moment and then looked at Sarah and asked, "You want to come with me, Boy?"

"I...I'm scared of Indians," she said, looking at him with wide, frightened eyes.

"Not *these* Indians. They're peaceable. Isn't that right, Big Mary?"

Big Mary nodded, but Sarah was skeptical. "But I heard that...that Indians s...scalp people," she stammered.

He walked over and tousled her hair. "Might be a real temptation, all that hair. Get ready. Fix some sandwiches to take along. It's a long walk." He started toward the door, turning once to say, "Bring a potato knife so you can defend yourself."

"That ain't nice!" Big Mary called after him. Then to Sarah, "Pay him no mind. He didn't mean nothin' by it."

Sarah was looking slightly ill, but it wasn't because of the remark about the knife. She reached up and touched her hair where his hand had been, electric shivers running down her neck.

"You'll like Thor's friend, Gray Wolf," Big Mary said.

"I will? What makes you think so?"

"Everybody likes him. He's a real charmer."

A charming Indian? she thought. *What a strange way to describe an Indian.*

They busied themselves fixing food to carry with them and Big Mary said to Sarah, "It's a good thing he's going. He ain't been himself lately. Makes me think he's got that Swede gal on his mind again. I've been expecting him to say any day that he's leaving to go back home. It's a relief he's only going to the Indians. And if you go with him, I know he'll come back."

"Swede gal? Home? What are you talking about?"

Big Mary shook her head back and forth, making clucking noises and looking dismayed. "That man ain't never gonna be able to live his life until he gets that good-for-nothing female out of his head. It's like gangrene of the heart." Big Mary wasn't paying any attention to Sarah, and seemed to have drifted off somewhere into her own troubling thoughts.

"What Swede gal?" Sarah asked again, this time grabbing Big Mary's elbow and shaking it to get her attention.

Big Mary roused herself and said, "Ask him. He likes you. You'll have plenty of time to ask questions. He can't get too mad at you because he needs you to do his ledgers. You've got him over a barrel."

"Yeah, sure I do," Sarah said, not believing a word Big Mary was telling her about being able to ask him questions, but wondering mightily about the Swede gal. She remembered suddenly what Jock had told her one night in the bunkhouse. He said they were both getting ready to leave to go home. Her fear of the Indians abated and she felt a stab of jealousy that frightened her far more.

Thor came back in and put his backpack on the counter and started stuffing their lunch into it.

"There's molasses cookies for Gray Wolf," Big Mary told him. "Don't go eating them all before you get there."

He nodded impatiently. "Okay, okay. Don't worry. Jesse, go out to the wannigan and get a pack of Peerless for Gray Wolf's pipe."

She did as she was told and they met outside in the clearing, waved to Big Mary and were on their way. All she could think of was that she was going to be with him for nearly two whole days, and the thought of it caused a wave of happiness to engulf her that she would have been hard pressed to explain.

CHAPTER 22

"**H**OW long will it take to get to the Indians?" she asked as they headed west out of camp.

"Most of the day. It'll be dusk by the time we get there."

"Why are we walking? Couldn't we take a horse and wagon?"

"Following the roads is too round-about. Besides, I like to walk through the woods during the summer."

"Don't you ever get tired of being in the woods?"

He didn't answer right away. He was looking straight ahead, thinking. Finally he said, "Walking in the woods makes me feel like I am home again."

She said nothing, but wondered again about the "Swede gal."

It was already growing hot as they walked. There was no breeze and the smell of fires burning somewhere in the woods lingered in the air, a smoky haze lying heavily just above the trees. Thor sniffed the air. "It's close by."

"Maybe we shouldn't go. Maybe there's a forest fire."

He glanced sideways at her, a smile teasing the corners of his mouth. But when he saw that she was serious he said, "Don't worry. You'll soon get used to the smell of smoke in the timber. Late summer is the worst. As soon as the fall rains come, the fires die off."

"Where's the smoke coming from?"

"This time I think it's mostly from the south, although it could be coming from more than one direction. Sparks from a train maybe flew into some slashings. Or else somebody was careless with a campfire. With all the rubble left lying around, it's no wonder the fires don't up and burn down the whole damn state from St. Paul to Duluth."

"It's a wonder, alright, what with the way the lumbermen leave the slashings lying around everywhere like giant scrap heaps just waiting for a spark to come along." As soon as she said it, she was sorry because his reaction was instant anger.

"I only follow orders given to me by Smitheson," he said, stopping abruptly

187

and glaring down at her. "We've got a timetable to follow, and don't have time for a lot of housekeeping bullshit." He thought for a moment and was even more fired up when he spoke again. "You might not know it, but I'm not in charge of the Goddamned woods!" Clearly insulted, he turned and walked on ahead of her.

She was sorry she had criticized him, but she took several running steps and caught up with him and asked, "Don't they have a lot of forest fires where... where you come from?"

"Not like they do here. In Sweden we are more careful about the timber." He was calmer now, as if speaking of his homeland soothed him. "It comes from scarcity. In this country there's so much land and so much timber that everyone thinks it will last forever. It won't. In Sweden, each year we cut only as much as is replaced by growth in a year. We don't waste the way they do in this country."

"*They?*" she asked.

He glanced sideways at her, but apparently didn't catch the implication she was making that he was part of the "they" of whom he spoke. "In Sweden they must take care of the trees. It is not so here in America. They don't care if they destroy many of the trees even before they have a chance to grow. They're willing to sacrifice them to get at the big ones." He seemed agitated again and he hurried on ahead of her, walking so fast she couldn't keep up with him without running.

After a while he calmed down, but he still walked too fast for her. His speed surprised her. She had never walked with him before and didn't know the power of his stride. After a while he grew more relaxed, but he didn't slow down. His arms moved rhythmically at his sides at times, and at times he hitched his thumbs into the straps of the pack he had on his back. From behind him she could see the muscles moving in his back and in his legs and when he turned to look back at her he barely slowed his pace.

"You doing okay, Boy?" he called back to her once.

"Yup," she said dishonestly. She was getting a cramp in her right leg and she was afraid to tell him. She was afraid he might think she couldn't keep up, and that because she had annoyed him about the waste the lumbermen were creating he would send her back to camp and go on alone. She tried to ignore the cramp, but it finally got to be too much for her and she stopped and leaned over, trying to loosen its grip.

At first he didn't know she had stopped, but when he noticed he turned and looked at her worriedly. He walked back to her, his eyes questioning. "You said you were alright. You need to tell me if I'm going too fast for you."

"You aren't going too fast," she said in a rush of words. "I just...I just needed to tie my boot."

He shook his head in mild disgust. "You're a stubborn boy. Which muscle is cramping?"

Sarah avoided his eyes, ashamed of her weakness. "It's the back of my leg. Here," she said rubbing her hand over the back of her right calf.

He dropped his backpack onto the ground and knelt down on one knee in front of her. "Put your hand on my shoulder," he commanded. Then with both of his hands he began to knead the calf muscle. It hurt at first, but soon she felt the spasm begin to release. His head was bowed, and as he worked she stared down at his thick blonde hair and his broad, powerful shoulders. She didn't tell him the cramp was almost gone, because a feeling of such intense pleasure had taken hold of her that she didn't want him to stop. She looked away from him and into the trees, a dizzying warmth spreading through her and making her lower extremities grow weak.

He could feel that the muscle had relaxed, and he looked up at her and asked, "Better?"

She nodded and forced herself to take her hand from his shoulder as he stood up. After that he slowed his pace so that they were walking side by side for a while. When he was convinced she would be able to continue, he hurried his pace slightly, but not enough so she had trouble staying close beside him. It took all of her will to control her thoughts, and she had to force herself to focus on her surroundings instead of on him.

As the morning passed, she walked more easily. She remembered the day she came to camp and how hard it had been to walk so many miles. She realized now that the summer of hard work had strengthened her, and except for that one leg cramp she was able to walk with surprising ease. His nearness made her feel weak and helpless, but she knew she had grown physically stronger during her time at Camp Seven.

It was late morning when they passed out of the timber into an area of new growth a few miles this side of where he said they would cross the Rum River. When they left the cover of the pines, the smoky haze lifted and the sun beat down on them.

"You had better take your shirt off, Jesse. It's going to get a lot hotter." He stopped walking, dropped the pack, slipped his suspenders down and removed his shirt.

She shook her head nervously. "I...I can't. I...I'll get sunburned. Ma never let me out in the sun without my shirt because I always got so burned."

He eyed her suspiciously. "Burned? You don't look to me like you have skin that burns." He grinned and patted his chest. "Now *this* is skin that *burns.*"

Her eyes were on his fair skin, small beads of sweat glistening in the hair on his chest, gleaming gold in the sun. She pulled her eyes up to his face and knew very well that he didn't believe her protestations about the sun. She couldn't think of anything else to say and she felt again the now-familiar weakness in the knees. "I don't want to get burned," she mumbled.

"Have it your own way. Seems dumb to give up the chance to feel this sun on your back." He rolled up his shirt and pushed it into his pack. "We'll stop by the river before we cross. It'll be lunch time by then."

She wondered if she'd be able to eat. She was learning that whenever her head was filled with disturbing thoughts, her stomach wanted to stay empty. And her thoughts so far today were very disturbing.

When they finally reached the river, they had to climb down a steep embankment to get to it. It sparkled below them like a ribbon of silver, and she stopped and stared down at it, her eyes wide. He was halfway down the hill when he turned back and looked up at her, smiling as though he was giving her a gift. He spotted a patch of Great St. John's Wort a few feet from where he stood. He walked over and picked several of the yellow flowers and brought them back up to her. "Here," he said, "The Indians use them for medicine. They're good for your lungs." His eyes twinkled as he looked at her teasingly, then laughed and continued down to the riverbank.

She stood holding the yellow flowers, looking around at the clumps of them scattered along the riverbank. She descended the hill to the spot where he had dropped his backpack next to a fallen log. To her horror he stripped off his clothes and headed into the river, his naked back gleaming in the sun, the muscles of his legs and backside rippling as he moved. She was having trouble catching her breath but forced herself to act busy trampling the grass to clear a spot for them to rest and to eat. She didn't want to look at him but she was unable to keep her eyes from straying in his direction.

He was standing in the river with his back to her now, the water up to his knees, his head turned back to look at her. "Aren't you coming?" he called.

"I...I can't swim," she called back to him without looking in his direction, pretending she was busy with their lunch preparations.

"Come into the water anyway. It's cool and it will make the rest of the walk easier. You're missing something good." She shook her head without speaking and he finally shrugged his shoulders and said, "You can't swim and you can't stand the sun. You're in bad shape, Jesse. Best you just sit there and inhale those flowers." With that he walked into the river until the water was up to his chest, then relaxed and let the current carry him down river.

She felt a stab of fear that something might happen to him, and was greatly relieved when he turned and swam upstream against the current until he was back where he had begun. "Are you sure you won't change your mind and come into the water?" he called to her. "It's cool and feels real good." He reached up and wiped the water from his hair, his wet skin glistening and rivulets of water running down his body and shining in the sun.

She had never in her life seen a naked man, and she never expected that one could be so beautiful. The one time Steven had made love to her he hadn't taken off his clothes. Thinking about it, she felt a rush of shame. She forced herself not to think about Steven and what they had done. It proved not to be too difficult when she looked at Thor. She was glad he was too far away to see the look on her face, because she knew the hunger she felt for him must show. She had never felt this way about Steven; not before he made love to her and not after. She worried that she was making herself too vulnerable to her feelings. Maybe she should go back to Camp Seven and let him continue on to the Indian camp without her. But how would she find her way back to camp? And how could she find the strength to give up this time with him, even if she *could* find her way back?

He called to her again, stubbornly refusing to accept her reluctance to get into the cool water. *How could a boy refuse to go into the water? What was wrong with Jesse that made him so reluctant to enjoy himself when he had the chance*, he wondered, remembering how he felt in his own youth. When she didn't answer he shrugged and dove into the water and swam for a while longer, letting the current carry him, then swimming upstream against it. Finally he emerged from the water, ran his fingers through his wet hair and stood with his face to the warm sun, letting its heat spread over him.

She looked away as he put on his pants, unable to control the hot sensations that assaulted her. She felt totally helpless against what she felt. And she didn't care.

He walked up the riverbank to where she was sitting and dropped onto the grass. He sighed deeply and lay back against the log, his arms folded behind his head. "When I am in the water I can close my eyes and pretend that I am home. In the summer me and my friends would sometimes sneak to the lake during the day when we were supposed to be cutting hay." He seemed to remember something and the peaceful look left his face, replaced by tightly drawn brows and a slight flush of emotion. He reached over and picked a blade of grass and began tearing it into small pieces.

"Are you hungry?" she asked, trying to find something for them to do besides sit next to each other while her feelings ran rampant over her.

He shook his head, gazing intently at the blade of grass he was scraping with his index finger and thumb. "You eat. I'll eat a little later." He looked around as he plucked at another blade of grass, then turned onto his side facing away from her and began to speak in a distant voice, almost to himself rather than to her.

"I didn't mean to stay so long in this country. Sometimes when I am in the river or in the woods I think about how good it feels and it makes me fear that I will never go home again. When I first came to this country I ached to see my mother again. Now it has come to be more of a memory than a hurt, and I fear that I will never see her again. And perhaps my grandfather won't know who I am when I return."

She waited for him to continue, yearning for—and at the same time dreading—the sweet pain his words kindled in her.

"It is hard to go from a place you love...and from someone you love." He turned back toward her, resting on his elbows, one knee bent. He was watching her face now, and he seemed to come back to the present. "What about you, Jesse? You never talk about your mother and father. It must be sad for you to come alone to the timber without anyone to go home to."

What would he think if he knew the real truth? Being alone and unloved was part of who she was. She had no place or no one to go back to. She couldn't talk about her past to him and her present was a huge lie. "I'm okay," she said as she got up and sat on the log and looked down at him. How could she tell him the truth? That she wanted him to stop thinking about the woman who lived in a place he called home.

She knew she had to change the subject—and quickly—before her face betrayed her. "I wish I knew what I was going to do...." She hesitated, then added, "when I'm grown up." She could no longer look at him and she stooped and pulled out a blade of grass and examined it carefully, just as he had done.

Thor cleared his throat nervously because Jesse looked like he was going to cry. It troubled him that the boy had such tender emotions. Yet, for some strange reason, it seemed to fit him. His brow creased and he thought for a moment before he spoke. "When I first came to America I was very young and very stupid. You're lucky, Jesse. You're very smart. I've lived by my muscles. You'll do just fine by using your head. Brains are of more use than muscles."

"How can you say you live only by your muscles?" she protested. "You are the Push! You know everything there is to know about a lumber camp. The men respect you." She felt her face grow warm, but she continued. "So do I."

The pleasure on his face from her words was only fleeting. "If I am good at what I do, it is because of Gray Wolf."

She was pleased to hear him speak of his friend who was an Indian who lived in the timber, not someone who would lure him back to Sweden.

"If you're good at what you do, and if your good friends are here in the timber, why do you want to go back to Sweden?"

Her question puzzled him. "To Sweden?" He shook his head in disbelief. "Sweden is my home. I *must* go home. Sometimes I think it will be very soon. Then when I am almost ready, I tell myself I do not yet have enough money. Money. Always I want more and more." His face registered self-disgust and he said, "I wish I did not need this damn money."

"Who is the 'Swede gal' Big Mary talks about?" She had spoken without thinking, and she quickly looked away from him, wishing she could swallow her tongue.

His gaze was penetrating. "Big Mary has no business talking about...." He didn't finish his sentence. He had made the mistake of telling Woody and Big Mary about Annika when they had shared a jug of whiskey one cold January night. He seldom drank too much whiskey, but when he did, he talked too much.

He stared at her for a moment longer, and then he sat up and looked down at the river. His knees were bent, his arms draped over them, one hand gripping the wrist of the other hand. A bee buzzed in a nearby wild flower, and he watched it, deep in thought. Then he looked up at the sky, cerulean blue, with a few fluffy white clouds floating lazily overhead, blocking the sun for an instant. He seemed to be traveling across a great distance and it was a long time before he said anything. When he spoke his voice was soft and dreamy, and she wished even more that she had not asked that awful question.

"Annika. Her name is Annika." He said the name with reverence, and Sarah felt a pain so intense that it seemed to engulf her and wipe away every good feeling she had ever had.

"When we were small children," he continued dreamily, "we went together to tend the cattle in the high pastures with our older brothers and sisters. At first, and for many years, she was my friend." He grew silent then, a smile threatening at the corners of his mouth. "Her laughter is like the little bells they ring in church to make music."

His smile was unlike any she had ever seen on his face. She could not bear to look at him. She knew in that moment that she had never really loved Steven. She knew because what she had felt for him, and what she had felt when she lost him, could not compare in even the slightest measure to the bittersweet, agonizing despair she felt now.

He turned toward her, stretched out, and leaned on one elbow as he plucked at another blade of grass. His eyes had become soft and unguarded and without thinking she let herself gaze into them and was lost forever.

"Have you ever loved a girl, Jesse?"

She barely heard the question, and all she could do was shake her head weakly, her eyes still glued to his. Fortunately for her, he looked away and sat up again, this time with his back to her.

"Her hair is golden—like the sun."

Sarah reached up and nervously touched her own hair. It was not beautiful, she thought, like Annika's or Lila's. It was not golden, but instead dull and boring and brown.

"It was on a day just like this one..." he continued, nodding up at the sky, not noticing her sudden preoccupation with her hair. "When we first made love, the wildflowers were blooming. We were very young." He was silent again for a long time.

Sarah didn't want him to say anymore. She wanted to jump up and run away from this place and never again lay eyes on him. She hated this pain. She wouldn't listen anymore. She put her hands over her ears then took them down and listened despite herself.

"We promised ourselves to each other. We were to be married." His voice suddenly changed and his back visibly stiffened. "She married someone else."

"Why?" she breathed, again against her will. How could a woman choose someone else when she could have had him?

"Land. Annika wanted land."

He looked back at her over his shoulder. The telling of this part was easier for him because it renewed the deep anger. He was comfortable with the anger. "Olaf Hanson's father has much land. It will all belong to Olaf and his sister when his father dies." His face grew sad, the anger gone now. "My father has no land. My grandfather is very stubborn and will not give up the farm. Most of my uncles and aunts have gone away and gotten their own small farms, but my father will not leave my grandfather. When grandfather dies the farm will be divided among all of them; it does not matter that my father and mother stayed to help him. The land will be divided, and then when my father and my aunts and uncles die it will be divided again among me and my brothers and sisters and my cousins. There will be very little land for me." He hesitated. "Or for Annika."

He hesitated again, then spoke as if renewing a sacred vow. "That is why I must go back."

It made no sense to her. She understood now why Big Mary called Annika "that good-for-nothing Swede gal," but the rest of it made no sense.

"Why must you go back? For what?"

"You can't understand, Boy. You're very young, and you have never been in love with someone the way I was in love with Annika."

At least he had said "was." But it was small comfort. It was plain that he intended to go back to Sweden. It was senseless, and his next words made even less sense to her.

"When she told me she was going to marry Olaf Hanson, it was like someone stuck a peavey hook into my chest. I will not ever forget it. On the ship coming to America I made a promise to myself that I would earn enough money to go back to Sweden and marry someone from my village. Someone younger and more beautiful even than Annika."

"Who? Who are you going to marry?" She felt like she was rolling down a hill, and there was no way to stop the painful, downward momentum.

"She has a little sister. Gretchen was only seven years old when I left, but she will be very beautiful. I will marry Gretchen and Annika will be sorry. She will hurt the way I have hurt. And it will be too late. I'll be a rich man in our village, with a young and beautiful wife. Annika will be old, probably with a herd of little ones hanging onto her skirts." His thoughts seemed to give him great pleasure. He let out a long breath and said, "Oh yes, she will be very very sorry."

"H...how do you know Gretchen is not already married to someone," she asked, anger rising in her chest, pulling against her effort to remain calm.

"If she is, then I will find someone else."

Sarah stared at him for a moment, her mouth agape, astonished. She couldn't stop herself. She jumped up and glared down at him. "That's the most stupid thing I ever heard!"

He, too, jumped up, his eyes ablaze. "Who do you think you are that you can call me stupid?"

"I'm the smart one. Remember? You said so yourself."

"Why you little...." He stopped his hand in midair, surprised that he was actually ready to lash out against the boy's words by striking him.

She flinched and took a step backwards, but couldn't stop her words. "You're working yourself to death in the timber so you can go home and marry someone you don't even know so you can have revenge on that...that Annika *baggage*." She hated the stupid woman! Not only because she had rejected him and broken his heart, but because she still had the power to draw him back to her.

"Who are you calling a baggage?" His face was tight with an animal-like fury.

She managed to stop herself from saying more, and she turned and stumbled down toward the river. When she reached the edge of the water, she was gasping with the effort it took to calm herself.

He, too, was trying to calm himself, but it wasn't easy. Who was this whelp of a boy to challenge his dream of revenge? "Maybe you are not as smart as I thought," he shouted angrily down at her.

Her breathing grew steadier but her anger and frustration didn't abate. She climbed hurriedly and clumsily up the bank, her cold words contradicting the blazing heat in her eyes. "When I get married, it will be to someone I love and respect. Not to someone I am using to get revenge; revenge upon someone who does not deserve another moment of my life."

"I have dreamed of revenge for ten years!" he shouted back at her, his nose inches away from hers. "You cannot take my dream away from me with your high-blown ideas and fancy words!"

Her eyes traveled over his face, as if by staring hard enough at him she could discern his logic. Finally she spoke. "Dream?" Her words were scathing. "You don't have a dream, you fool! You have a nightmare!"

With that, she ran down the riverbank again and stared, unseeing, out at the water, wanting to be somewhere else; anywhere but here with him.

As the minutes passed she grew calm, and what she had done began to dawn on her. She had behaved like a jealous woman—which was exactly what she was. How was she going to explain herself? And how was he ever going to forgive her and be her friend again?

And worse, underneath those thoughts lay the bigger question; how could she bear it if he went back to Sweden? Then reality struck her like a blow to the stomach. *What does it matter? What does any of it matter? Our paths may have crossed for a while, but how can there be a future for us? I have destroyed any chance I may have had with him.* She thought about Lila and her golden hair, and about Annika, and about Gretchen. *I am not beautiful, and I do not have golden hair. And I am not only a liar, I am a cruel critic of his dream, and now he hates me*

Thor stood on the crest of the riverbank looking down at her, his anger blurring his vision and making his heart hammer against his chest. His first impulse was to strike the boy, but that impulse dissipated quickly as he remembered why they were together today in the first place. He had put Jesse at risk by ignoring Leverty. This trip to visit Gray Wolf was to serve two purposes: he wanted to see Gray Wolf and clear his thinking; and Big Mary wanted Jesse to have some pleasure to make up for what had happened to him. What did it matter that the boy had wounded his pride?

He was not such a fool that he didn't know how people felt about his plan to return to Sweden for revenge. Jesse Williams was not the first person to scoff when he shared his story with them. Besides Big Mary and Woody, he had also confided in Gray Wolf nine years ago in Michigan when they first worked together in the same camp. It was after Gray Wolf had taken him under his wing and was teaching him to speak English. Thor had begun to talk about himself, and about the reason he had come to the timber. Gray Wolf had told him in no uncertain terms that he was a fool to continue to let Annika run his life. No; Jesse was not the first person to tell him he was a fool. But Jesse had said it better, and for a reason he did not fully understand, the boy's words struck a chord no one else's ever had.

For now, though, he knew he had to put his feelings aside. He began to unpack their lunch, and then he called, "Jesse! Come up here and eat. We must hurry."

"I'm not hungry," she shouted back.

"You must eat or you can't travel. Come on. Let's call a truce."

His calm willingness to call a truce surprised her as much as anything else that had happened that day. Perhaps he was right. Perhaps she could put her opinions aside and try to get along with him as best she could. Perhaps she could stop feeling the way she did, now that she considered him a fool.

But when she got up to where he was sitting, and she sat on the log to eat her sandwich, she knew her hope was in vain. When she looked at him she had no sense that he was a fool. She sensed only how deeply he must have felt about Annika, and how deeply he had committed himself to finding relief from his pain. If it worked for him, and if it made his life what he wanted it to be, who was she to judge him?

Especially when she had not the slightest clue about what she was going to do with her own life. He had come to the timber to earn enough money to get revenge. She had come to the timber to find a father who had not cared enough about her or her mother to stay with them. Which of them was the greater fool? She was not at all sure.

They ate in silence, and after they had packed everything up once more, they walked along the river for about a quarter of a mile to where some rocks formed small rapids, making it possible to cross. After he had crossed, Thor saw her hesitating and stood impatiently waiting for her to make up her mind to chance a crossing. Even from across the river she could sense his growing annoyance with her, so she took a deep breath and started across the rocks. She almost lost her footing once, but managed to get across safely. The minute her feet hit the far shore he was off into the woods again and she lost sight of him in the heavy brush. Every now and then she caught a glimpse of his red suspenders, but then he would be lost again from view.

As she walked, she wanted to try to recapture the feelings she had earlier in the day, before they had their argument by the river. But those feelings kept being disturbed by the picture in her mind of a woman in Sweden, and of a young couple making love in the wildflowers in a place far away.

After another hour, she saw Thor standing very still not far ahead of her. They were in a forest of mixed pines and hardwoods. He waited until she was close to him, then held up his hand in a sign for her to listen. She heard a tapping sound, which accelerated as they listened. His eyes were scanning the trees overhead, and suddenly he pointed high up the broad trunk of a large maple tree. "Logcock," he said.

It took her several moments before she spotted the large pileated wood-pecker hammering away above them. He seemed undisturbed by the intruders beneath him, and he glided soundlessly to another tree, his ebony wings showing a flash of pure white. She caught a glimpse of gleaming scarlet on its head and let out an exclamation of awe at the size of his wing span, which she calculated to be nearly three feet. She watched him for a few minutes, then, seeing that Thor was moving on again, reluctantly continued through the woods after him.

They reached the Indian camp on the southeastern edge of the big lake shortly before dusk. The sun was setting on the far side of the water, and Sarah's breath caught in surprise at seeing so large an expanse of water emerge from the forest. The entire sky was streaked with pink clouds, and the sight made her stand still for a moment, awed by the wild beauty.

A cluster of teepees lay scattered near the shore beneath birch, maple and ash trees. Several dogs came running, barking wildly and followed by half a dozen children. The children recognized Thor, and he hoisted one of the small boys onto his shoulders. He waved and greeted people as he passed between the teepees, heading to where one stood apart from the others near the shore.

Next to it, a newly-constructed birch bark canoe stood on the ground, inverted, and a man and a woman were on their knees on opposite sides of the canoe spreading it with gummed pitch. Aware of the commotion and the approaching visitors, they stood up from their labors and looked at them. They both smiled at Thor, and the man stopped what he was doing, then walked toward them. He clasped Thor's hand in one hand and clasped his shoulder with the other.

"You're a sight for sore eyes, Boy. What in thunder brings you here? You run Smitheson plumb out of timber?"

Thor laughed and playfully slapped the man on the back. "How are you, you wily old bastard? I came to see if you were still here." He looked over at the Indian woman and raised a hand in greeting. The woman was large with child. "I wondered if White Feather had snared you permanent or if you had headed West. But I can see it looks permanent."

The man smiled and shrugged. "I don't know why I let her do it, but she caught me." Then he laughed. "She's a good woman. Probably the best thing that ever happened to me." The woman was quietly watching them.

"And who's this?" he asked as he looked at Sarah and reached out his hand to shake hers.

She let him take her hand, which had grown ice cold. She looked at him but couldn't speak, merely nodding dumbly at him. He was not an Indian. He was a white man. He was a good head shorter than Thor; but he was stockier, with a broad chest and muscular arms. He wore fringed buckskins and moccasins and his thick gray hair was plaited with a buckskin thong and hung to the middle of his back. His skin was tanned and weathered. A jagged white scar made a diagonal slash across his left eyebrow and would have made him look fierce but for his dancing gray eyes. A small hatchet encased in a leather sheath, hung from a strap around his waist.

She looked down at the hatchet, then at the deep cleft in his chin, and then into his gray eyes. She remembered a similar face; a face illuminated by the sun streaming through a stained glass window. The awareness flickered and then solidified, and she knew as surely as she had ever known anything in her entire life that she was looking into the face of Doyle MacKenna, her father.

CHAPTER 23

"I...I expected an Indian," she said, struggling to find words. She looked at the hatchet again and then at Thor. "I suppose you learned your hatchet trick from Gray Wolf?" She wasn't sure how she was maintaining her composure.

Gray Wolf grinned at Thor and slapped him on the back. "Have you been showing off again?"

"Not exactly," Thor replied, as he walked toward White Feather and the canoe.

Sarah watched Thor walk away and then looked at Gray Wolf, cleared her throat and said, "I think I'll look around." Reality was beginning to press in upon her, and she wanted to run.

"Come and meet White Feather first," Gray Wolf said, putting his hand on her shoulder and guiding her toward the canoe where Thor now stood talking to the Indian woman.

"White Feather, this is Jesse," he said.

White Feather looked at her and smiled. "Welcome," she said and then quickly resumed her work.

Sarah watched her deftly applying the pitch, thinking how beautiful she was, even in her advanced state of pregnancy. Her skin was golden and her black hair shone. Her black eyes were almond shaped, slanted slightly upwards, and her nose was long and straight. Sarah nearly laughed about her earlier fear of being scalped.

"And how's Big Mary?" Gray Wolf asked, half to Thor and half to Sarah, who was still watching White Feather with a wry smile.

"She's feeling pretty good now. She just got over a bout with a bad tooth," Thor said.

"So how'd you talk her into letting the boy go traipsing off into the woods with you? You got a short crew?"

"Usual summer crew. No more, no less. It was Big Mary's idea that I take him along. I guess she figured she could get on without him for a day or so, now that she's got her strength back."

Gray Wolf was unconvinced. He knew there was some other reason why the boy was with him, but would find out later. "We've eaten, but we'll take the other canoe and catch some fish so you and the boy can eat."

Thor looked at Sarah, who had begun to back away from them. He frowned, aware for the first time that she was acting strangely. "You want to come fishing with us?"

"N...no. I...I think I'll just walk around a little."

"Suit yourself," he said, shrugging.

White Feather had stopped spreading pitch, and her eyes followed Sarah as she walked away from them. Then her hand moved to her stomach as the child stirred within her.

"I am going to talk to Many Crows," she said softly to Gray Wolf.

He looked at her worriedly. "Is something wrong?" First the boy had acted in a peculiar manner, and now White Feather all of a sudden felt the need to go talk to the medicine man.

Without answering, she made her way toward the center of camp, her head held high and her movements graceful despite the obvious shift in her center of gravity.

Gray Wolf shrugged again as he watched the visitor and his wife walk away from them in opposite directions. Then he turned and looked at Thor. "I don't know what's going on, but all three of you seem to have a lot on your minds. He put his hand on Thor's shoulder. "Let's see if we can catch you folks some supper."

As the men sat in the canoe, their lines in the water, Gray Wolf said, "Out with it. I can tell you've come for a reason. You didn't come here with the boy just because you needed a stroll in the woods."

As he had many times in the past, Thor wondered at the sixth sense Gray Wolf possessed. He told him about the Leverty incident, and Gray Wolf remained expressionless, concentrating on his line in the water.

When he got to the part about the knife, a faint smile crossed Gray Wolf's face and he said, "The boy's got guts."

Thor nodded and continued. When he finished his story Gray Wolf thought for a moment and then said, "I've had men like that in camp more often than I care to think about. One thing's for sure; I always got rid of them—quick."

Thor's eyes were avoiding Gray Wolf's. "I wasn't sure about him."

"You were sure. You just didn't want to face it."

Thor nodded, the guilt plain on his face. "You're right. I guess that's why I'm here."

Gray Wolf raised an eyebrow in question.

"My judgment wasn't good. Now I don't feel like I can trust myself."

"No sense falling apart because you made one mistake."

"*One mistake?* Do you have any idea what it would have been like if....?"

He didn't finish his sentence and Gray Wolf was silent for a while, watching his face carefully before he spoke. "You know, Boy, just because somebody hires you on as foreman doesn't mean you're God."

Thor's eyes grew dark. "I never said I thought I was God. I just feel like...."

"You just feel like you should be able to protect every poor helpless kid who gets fucked by some asshole in calked boots. You can't. You're one man, and there are too many assholes. Don't be so arrogant!"

It was the last that stopped him, and he sat quietly, his head down, chastened and silent.

After a long time Gray Wolf said, "I'm sorry, Boy. I don't mean to make you feel bad. But you've got to be realistic. Nothing happened to the boy. You were lucky. Learn from it."

Thor looked up and studied Gray Wolf's face, hoping for a sign of what it was he was supposed to learn.

Seeing his confusion, Gray Wolf said, "Trust yourself next time, Son. When something inside is talking to you loud and clear you've got to listen."

As he spoke Thor sensed that Gray Wolf's words held meaning for both of them. But he was busy with his own muddle and he wanted to stay with it, hoping Gray Wolf would lead him toward some kind of resolution. "Maybe I should never have let a boy who looks like Jesse come to camp."

"Sounds like maybe that's right."

"The problem is, now I don't know what I'd do without him. He works harder than anybody I ever saw. Not only that, I was planning to have him stay on this winter as clerk. The boy is as smart as a whip. He can add a row of numbers quicker and righter than any man I ever knew." He was talking fast now, his words refuting his own determination that he should not have let Jesse come to camp in the first place.

Gray Wolf pulled a large walleye into the boat, took it off the hook and let it flop around in the bottom of the canoe. He spoke as he carefully baited his hook and tossed the line back into the water. "It sounds to me like there's something about this boy you aren't telling me."

"Shit! I don't know! I like the boy, that's all. Too much maybe. Maybe I'm no better than Leverty. Maybe that's what's got me all fired up. Maybe...." Thor pulled in his line and dropped his pole into the canoe then crossed his arms over his chest and stared off across the water in disgust, his jaw set in a hard, stubborn line.

Gray Wolf didn't speak right away. When he did he said, "Let's think about this for a while. You know as well as I do that your taste doesn't run to boys. There's another answer here somewhere. We just don't know yet what it is. How long can you stay with us?"

"I must get back tomorrow," Thor answered sullenly, disappointed because he had expected his friend to give him answers—not questions.

"That's not very long, but maybe it's long enough." They sat in silence waiting for the other to speak. After a while Gray Wolf also pulled in his line and dropped his pole into the canoe. "We have enough fish. Now we will talk about *my* problem."

"*Your* problem? I thought your problems were solved. Looks to me like you're all settled down." He was surprised to see White Feather with child. He never pictured his friend as a family man, but a woman carrying his baby looked like the beginning of a family to him.

Gray Wolf's eyes were troubled. "Does look that way, doesn't it? Wish I felt that way.

They had seen each other in Pine Crescent during the spring, but Gray Wolf had said nothing about having settled down with White Feather. Thor was under the impression he was just passing time with the Indians until he decided where to go next.

"She's a good woman, White Feather. I've been happy here, away from the lumbermen. White Feather and her people have a way of life I would like to live."

"Isn't it a little late to decide you aren't happy?"

Gray Wolf looked even more deeply troubled as he spoke. "It's not so easy. I'm confused. I hate the way the lumbermen are knocking down the timber, leaving nothing behind but food for the fires."

He looked toward the teepees clustered along the shore. "The Indians don't destroy the land. They're a part of it. It feeds them and shelters them. They bend to it—to its seasons, and to its tempers. Not like the White Man, who's always fighting against it to make it fit his own idea of what it's supposed to be. It's like we're having a Goddamned war with the land itself."

He sat silent for a while, and when he continued his voice was quiet, his face puzzled. "But I'm not an Indian. I'm not an Indian and I can no longer be a lumberman. I'm in the middle."

"I don't understand...."

"The thought of being a father puts things in my head that were never there before."

"What things?"

"Things like having a farm, and...."

"A farm? You? On a farm?"

"What's so strange about that? My grandfather was a farmer. I'd probably have been born in Scotland on a farm if the English hadn't chased him off his land. When the English came into the Highlands and drove the Scots off, taking the land to raise their herds of sheep for wool, my grandfather had no choice but to leave. He could have gone to Australia with his brothers, but he came to America. If it weren't for the English I might still be wearing a skirt and playing a bagpipe."

Thor laughed at his mental vision of Gray Wolf wearing a skirt, but Gray Wolf ignored him. He was shaking his head sadly. "The English took land from the Scots for sheep, and the Americans took land from the Indians for timber. I get sick of all this taking. It makes me want to buy my own piece of land. Maybe a piece of cutover timberland. That way I wouldn't have to destroy trees to plant crops. The trees would already have been destroyed."

"You could always go to Australia and buy land, seeing as how you don't like it here."

"I'm an American," he snapped. Then more calmly, "This is where I'll buy land when I decide to do it."

All this talk of settling down made Thor uneasy. Gray Wolf had always been a man who followed a different path than most men, guided by whatever urge made him want to be somewhere other than where he was. Now here he was wanting to settle down and become a farmer like any ordinary man. "Do you intend to take White Feather to this land with you? And what will happen to her and to this land of yours when you get a cockeyed notion to go somewhere else again?"

Gray Wolf spat over the side of the canoe. "Don't you think I've thought about all this? I'm not sure White Feather will leave her people and I'm not sure I want her to."

"So we finally come to the heart of it. You want to settle down and you aren't sure you've chosen the right woman."

Gray Wolf looked at the younger man, then began to laugh. "Don't it just beat all hell? Here I am asking advice from a stubborn jackass who don't know crap about choosing the right woman."

Thor looked threateningly at Gray Wolf. "Don't call me a jackass."

Gray Wolf thought back to the younger Thor, whom everybody had called a dumb Swede. It hadn't taken long to figure out that this boy was far from dumb. "I'm sorry. I didn't mean to imply that you're stupid. I just meant you aren't too smart about women."

"Smart? Now I suppose you're going to tell me you've gotten smart about women all of a sudden."

"No," Gray Wolf replied, serious again. "Not smart. It's more like I'm learning to appreciate them. Especially the good ones. The thing that's troubling me is that I'm not sure it's fair to take White Feather away from her people. Her father has tried to help his people keep the old ways. How can I take her away to the White Man's world?"

"Why can't you stay here?"

"And there we are back again where we started."

"I still don't understand."

"I'm getting old, Boy. That's the truth of it. I want to sink my roots down somewhere before it's too late." He looked again toward the shore. "I'm going to have a son. I must think about him, and about what I want his life to be. I don't want him to live in a world in which he doesn't have a place. The way I have done." He had talked a circle around it, and had finally landed in the middle of it.

Thor felt helpless. He could not argue with Gray Wolf about a son. He knew even less about sons than he knew about women.

***

Later, after Thor and Sarah had finished eating fish with wild rice and berries sweetened with maple sugar, they sat by the fire. Gray Wolf was smoking a pipe, and he offered Thor a puff, which he took, grimaced, and handed back. Gray Wolf handed it to Sarah, and she shook her head. White Feather also refused the pipe and sat quietly listening to the men and now and then looking thoughtfully at Sarah.

It had grown dark, and a sliver of moon was rising in the starry, black night. The water lapped softly against the shore. Sarah sat with her knees pulled up, her chin resting on them, her arms hugging her legs as she stared into the glowing fire. The men talked quietly together, filling each other in on what had happened since they saw each other last.

She was very quiet, but no one seemed to notice. Every now and then she shifted her eyes from the fire to stare at Gray Wolf, listening as he spoke. She had found her father and now she had to figure out what she was going to do about it. She was sure of only one thing; she *did not* want to tell him who she was. She wasn't ready. Telling him would destroy all she had built for herself at Camp Seven. If she confessed her true identity, she'd probably be kicked out of the lumber camp. And she certainly did not want to come and live with her father in a teepee!

Besides, he probably wouldn't want to be bothered with her. He kept talking about having a son, and it seemed very important to him. She wanted to ask what he would do if this child turned out to be a daughter instead of a son. But she couldn't. It would bring him too close to a truth she could not yet reveal. She looked up at the sky and tried to calm her thoughts. There was plenty of time to make a decision. For now she needed to let her mind rest, so she asked where she was going to sleep.

White Feather led her into their teepee, where she laid out a soft bearskin and pointed to it. "You sleep here."

Sarah nodded and said, "Thank you." She sat down on the fur and unrolled her blanket. She had forgotten to give Gray Wolf his tobacco. She called to White Feather just as she bent to go through the opening of the teepee. "I brought tobacco for Gray Wolf."

White Feather returned and reached for the package without smiling. "Thank you. I will give it to him."

Sarah watched White Feather go, then wrapped her blanket around herself and lay listening to the soft drone of the men's voices. Sleep was very far away. She was still awake when the other three came into the teepee, but she pretended to be asleep. She opened her eyes just wide enough to see White Feather put down an animal skin for Thor next to her, then roll out her own and Gray Wolf's bedding across from them. She lay very still. She was with her father. She was no longer an orphan. She wondered how long it would be before the reality of it actually struck her, because surely it had not yet.

She slept fitfully and was relieved when the darkness softened into dawn so she could leave the tent. Thor was sound asleep on his stomach, one arm folded under his head. His other arm was stretched toward her and she had fought to resist the urge to touch him. She rose quietly and slipped out of the teepee without waking anyone. No one in camp was stirring, except a few dogs barking in the distance.

She walked out of camp and along the shore until she was satisfied she could not be seen through the trees. Then she removed her clothes and her bindings and stepped carefully into the water. She walked out to where it reached her middle, then sank down into the cool water. She needed to wash away all the emotions that had assaulted her as she lay in the teepee.

Thor breathing softly only inches away from her had been nearly as disturbing as the realization that her father lay several feet away next to an Indian woman who carried his child. One moment it all seemed unreal and the next moment it seemed altogether *too* real.

After a while, reluctantly, she got out of the water and dressed. She walked back to the camp and sat with her back against a tree and watched the sun come up over the big lake. The haunting cry of a loon calling to its mate echoed across the water. She looked up and saw White Feather coming toward her.

Something about the Indian woman was different this morning, and she spoke with a deference that made no sense to Sarah. "Come. You must eat with my family and with Many Crows. We are eager to sit with you and share our fire."

Sarah stood up, too taken aback to think of refusing. She followed White Feather between the scattered teepees to where the old chief sat smoking. He looked at her and nodded. There was another old Indian sitting next to him, whom White Feather introduced as Many Crows. White Feather's mother was by the fire and a young girl was helping her.

Several kettles hung suspended over the fire from a tripod. The old woman stirred the contents with a long reed. White Feather gave Sarah a wooden spoon and two wooden bowls. One was for tea and the other for the food, which was passed around in buckets and shallow trays made of birch bark. They ate venison, fish, broth, rice sweetened with maple sugar and fresh berries. Sarah suspected it was not their usual breakfast fare.

Breakfast lasted nearly an hour and Sarah wondered why she had been invited without the two men. She did not, however, feel comfortable asking questions. Many Crows sat watching her, his eyes almost never leaving her face. She wondered if these Indians were able to see through her disguise. If so, why were they treating her with such respect, almost as if she was some kind of visiting royalty?

The young girl never looked directly at her and all at once Sarah wondered if they were thinking of Jesse as a potential suitor. Could that be the reason they were treating her so well? It seemed bizarre, but then, everything was bizarre these days. Besides, what else could it possibly be that had them acting this way? She relaxed and tried not to think too much. Thinking only spun her in circles, and there was no way to resolve anything. She turned her attention to the food. She didn't feel hungry, and she had to force herself to eat to be polite.

Meanwhile, Thor and Gray Wolf made their own breakfast of fish, tea and rice, and Gray Wolf ate two of the molasses cookies Big Mary had sent for him. "Don't you want one?" Gray Wolf asked, holding one out to Thor.

"Big Mary told me they were for you. I don't want to get sideways with her over a cookie."

They both laughed, and then Thor asked, "Why has White Feather taken Jesse to her parents' teepee?" Gray Wolf had told him where he was, but not the reason for it.

Gray Wolf dunked a molasses cookie into his tea, grinning with pleasure. "The only thing I miss about the timber is Big Mary's cooking." He patted himself on the stomach. "I've lost most of the flesh she put on me, but I'd be willing to put it back on again if it didn't mean living with a camp full of jacks."

"You aren't answering my question."

"Tell me about the boy."

Thor felt the conversation was getting all disjointed, and he couldn't figure out why Gray Wolf kept answering a question with a question. "What about him?"

"Where did he come from?"

"Chicago. His parents were killed in a fire and he had to find work."

Gray Wolf had a faraway look in his eyes. "That's probably not true."

"Not true? What the hell...."

"White Feather sees things I don't see. I don't know if it's because she's an Indian or because she's a woman. She took Jesse to her parent's teepee so the medicine man could have a look at him. When we woke up this morning, she told me she had a dream in the night. She believes this boy is the spirit of my mother. She thinks my mother is trying to learn about White Feather and if it is good that White Feather is giving me a son."

"What the hell are you talking about? Have you gotten senile living out here in a teepee?"

"Shut up and listen to me."

Thor clamped his mouth shut and waited for an explanation for this apparent lunacy.

Gray Wolf reached into a leather pouch that was lying beside him and pulled out a small, oval picture frame. "She told me I must look again at this picture. I showed it to her once, a long time ago, and she remembered it. This boy looks so much like my mother that it's hard not to think something spiritual is going on."

Thor took the picture and looked at it. Dumbfounded, he jumped to his feet. "Jesus! It's the woman from the mud!"

"Mud? What mud? What are you talking about? This is a picture of my mother!"

"Your mother?" Thor looked more closely at the picture, then handed it back to Gray Wolf and fell back down, cross-legged onto the ground, Gray Wolf watching him, just as dumbfounded.

Thor reached for the picture again and looked at it for a long time, then handed it back to Gray Wolf. The expression on his face had changed from confusion to understanding. He started talking very fast, telling about his encounters with the mud lady.

"She was wearing the same brooch," he said, jabbing at the picture with one finger, "and she said she was looking for someone. She must have been looking for you!"

Gray Wolf stared at him. It was all coming together now. "Lorna. It had to be Lorna. I gave her my mother's brooch, and she must have given it to...to her daughter. How old is he...she?"

"Fifteen. She...he says he's fifteen."

"No," he said shaking his head. "She's older than that. She has to be...she has to be somewhere around eighteen years old. Do you remember my telling you about being in love once, a long time ago? With a girl in Boston?"

Thor nodded, remembering Gray Wolf talking about himself, trying to get a lonely, angry boy from Sweden to talk about *himself*. "But you didn't say anything about a daughter," Thor protested, frantic to understand.

"I know. That's because I knew nothing about a child. I asked Lorna to marry me but she wanted me to stay in Boston. I said I wouldn't stay anywhere near my father and my brother, and that if we were to be married she would have to come away with me. She refused to leave and I refused to stay. This girl must be.... I had no idea! I don't understand why Lorna never told me. I have no idea if she's alive or dead. I don't understand why this girl didn't simply come to me and tell me.... She's dead. Lorna must be dead." He sat silent, his face a mask.

Thor felt the rage building in his chest. Jesse, or whoever she was, had made a fool of him. He colored slightly as he thought about his nakedness by the river. He knew she was too delicate to be a boy. How hard he had agonized over his behavior towards her.

He had ignored his gut about Jesse the same way he had ignored it about Leverty. Had he known? It didn't matter much to him now. All that mattered was that he intended to confront her with her lies, drown her in the big lake, and then go back to Camp Seven without her.

He started to say just that when he saw the determined expression on Gray Wolf's face and knew he was making up his mind about something. When he did that, there was no changing it. Murdering the Mud Lady was not going to be an option.

"Did you tell her my real name?" Gray Wolf asked.

"No, of course not. You made me vow never to tell anyone who you were or where you were. You said you didn't want your family to find you."

"I didn't. But I didn't know I had a child. She can't possibly know who I really am unless someone told her my name."

He looked angrily at Thor. "You'll say nothing. I'll handle this in my own way."

"Say nothing? Why the hell not? She's made a Goddamned fool out of me! What do you expect me to do? Ignore it?"

Gray Wolf's eyes penetrated the depths of those of the younger man. When he finally spoke it was through tight lips. "This girl is my daughter. Remember that. It has nothing to do with you. It has to do with *me*. You owe me this."

Gray Wolf had never once in all the time Thor had known him spoken of any debt of gratitude. But it was there, and Thor knew it. The man who had taught him to speak English, and to get along in a strange new world, and to whom he owed whatever success he had in the timber, was calling in his chits.

Angry and reluctant, but finally resolved, his shoulders slumped forward and he said, "What do you want from me?"

"I'll find a way to tell her who I am. The decision will be hers what to do about it. It's pretty clear that she's come West to find me. I'll let her find me. Then we'll see what she wants to do about it."

As far as Thor was concerned, at least one of his problems had resolved itself; he no longer had to worry about his growing fondness for a *boy*. "You'd better hurry and get it over with," Thor said, rising to his feet. "We're leaving in an hour."

He went down to the lake and sat on the shore staring out at the water. The lake stretched farther than the eye could see, reflecting the pink light of dawn in its quiet waters. "Home," he said at last. "It's time to go home."

When Sarah returned, she was strangely subdued. She looked at Gray Wolf and then her eyes sought Thor and saw him sitting alone down at the lakeshore.

"Sit with me," Gray Wolf said. "I'm anxious to hear about you helping with the clerk's duties. Thor tells me you're pretty good with numbers."

She sat down, too confused about the goings on in the Indian camp to exert any will of her own. Gray Wolf, too, seemed to have changed toward her in some way she could not comprehend.

"There isn't much to tell. Numbers are easy for me, and I think I can...I think I can learn to do the clerk's job. If I stay at Camp Seven I'd rather do that than work in the cook shack." Then she added, "Not that I don't like working for Big Mary."

He laughed. "I sure do miss that little pea hen. My mouth waters just thinking about the meals she puts on the table. By the way, tell her Doyle MacKenna said hello, and that I'll come by soon to get some of that larrigan pie."

Her eyes darted to his face. Why had he suddenly decided to reveal his real name? "Gray Wolf" had seemed sufficient up to now. His face told her nothing, and he continued talking, reminiscing about his days in the timber.

Finally he said, "I'll go see if Thor's about ready to leave. I won't be long."

When he reached the place where Thor was sitting he looked down at him and said, "I told her who I am."

"What did he...she say? Did she admit who she is?" He was still staring out at the water as he spoke.

"No. She didn't bat an eye. She's a cool one." He felt a certain pride in that fact. "Don't let on you know who she is. I want her to be the one to make the next move."

"Why? Why don't you just ask her who she is and what she's doing here? Why make it so damned hard? How the hell am I supposed to keep pretending he...she...."

"You already knew Jesse wasn't a boy."

"What? That's a lie!" He jumped up from the ground and glared at Gray Wolf, his hands clenched into fists at his sides.

"Think about it. You as much as told me there was something about the boy you were attracted to. Remember?"

Thor didn't speak, but something passed across his eyes.

"Just be sure you keep your mouth shut," Gray Wolf said, putting his hand on Thor's shoulder and studying him carefully. "Look, I know this isn't going to be easy for you, but I'm begging you. Please. Do this for me."

Thor stiffened, but only for a moment. "Okay. But then we're square."

"No more cookies and tobacco?"

"You know what I mean, you old bastard!"

Gray Wolf frowned and looked over his shoulder to where Sarah still sat alone in front of the teepee. "Yes, I get your meaning," he said, "and I think you get mine. This girl is my daughter and it doesn't look to me like too far a stretch for you to think about bedding her."

Thor took a step backwards and stumbled against the tree, his mouth agape. Steadying himself he said, "What makes you think I'd even consider bedding that...that lying bitch!"

"Shut up and listen," Gray Wolf said, the smile gone. "You came to camp yesterday full of talk about how smart she is and how hard she works. Have you forgotten all that?"

"Yesterday I didn't know she was a woman."

"We've already been through this." Gray Wolf's face had gone ashen and his left eye twitched dangerously. "I'm telling you once and for all. Keep your mouth shut and keep your hands off my daughter."

"I'll keep my mouth shut. And as for touching your...your daughter...." Thor turned abruptly and began to walk away, then stopped and looked back over his shoulder and growled, "I'd rather bed a skunk!"

CHAPTER 24

As they made their journey back through the woods toward Camp Seven, Thor was too infuriated to speak and his silence festered into seething anger. She had made a complete fool of him. Worse yet, he was powerless to do anything about it because of his obligation to Gray Wolf. He must continue to be made a fool of until God only knew when.

Gray Wolf had not only dumped his problems and the responsibility for them back into his own lap, but he had burdened him with *her*. She was in his camp to stay until she was ready to go—whenever *that* might be. He could feel the angry raging of his own blood turning his face red and making his ears buzz. He looked back over his shoulder, wanting nothing more than to have lost her somewhere far back in the woods; yet knowing full well he would never let anything happen to Jesse whether she was the woman from the mud or the man in the moon.

At first Sarah didn't notice his strange behavior. She, too, was deep into her own thoughts. She felt whipped, as though everywhere she turned some other awful blow was struck at her. She had found her father among the Indians, about to become a father again. This time, however, he was apparently glad of it. She could not understand why she felt such acute pangs of jealousy.

As the hours passed, her thoughts became more and more confused. One minute she'd want nothing more to do with him—ever. She would leave him with his adored new family and never darken the door of his teepee again. The next minute she'd want to be with him, and to feel the touch of his arm around her shoulder again. She had known he might be married—or even dead, for that matter. Surely she couldn't turn and run the minute she found him just because he seemed happy with his new life. Surely after all she had been through to find him she could at least see it through to some kind of resolution. Running away would resolve nothing. She had come West to challenge him because he had run from her and her mother. Was she now going to do the same thing—run?

She began to feel the strain of walking so fast, and it finally dawned on her that Thor was crashing ahead like an angry bull, walking so fast she could not possibly keep up with him. Several times she called to him, far ahead of her on the trail, and he would slow down—without once looking back at her—until he sensed that she was close behind. Then he'd be off again and she would have to run, stumbling and cursing to herself, unable to see him through the trees. She had to force her legs to continue to move beneath her.

What had Gray Wolf said to him? Amid the jumble of her thoughts, she felt she finally had the answer; Gray Wolf had told Thor that it had been a stupid mistake to keep Jesse Williams in camp. He should have let him go at the first sign of trouble between him and Leverty. Then he would still have his good sawyer and the road would be on schedule. Now, once again, she feared she was going to be sent away. She had been around and around that same issue many times before. Would he send her away? Would he let her stay? Each time the matter had been resolved in her favor and she had been allowed to stay. But this time it seemed different. From the look of it he was enraged beyond anything she had ever seen; and his rage would do what it always did. It would harden into ice.

When they got to the river, to her surprise, Thor waited on the other side while she jumped over the rocks. He was angry; but not so stupid as to risk letting her fall into the river with no one there to rescue her. As soon as she was across, however, he turned and resumed his rapid pace. When they reached the place where they had rested the day before, Sarah stopped and looked longingly at the trampled grass next to the log. Had they really been there only yesterday? It felt like ages ago.

"Thor!" she called to him. "Can we rest for a while?"

He neither stopped nor slowed his pace nor in any way acted as though he heard her.

"Please? Just for a little while?" She called louder this time, but still got no response.

She no longer cared. If he intended to leave her there to be eaten by wolves, then so be it. She could not go on. She was physically and emotionally exhausted. She spread her blanket and sat down on it with a deep sigh of relief and leaned back against the log. "I'll just sit for a little while," she whispered to herself. But she kept nodding off, her head dropping forward, and she finally gave in and slipped down onto the blanket, curled up with her head cradled in her folded arms and fell asleep.

He kept walking for nearly half a mile. When he realized she was going to stop and rest without his permission, he turned back. He reached the log, breathing hard—not from the effort of his rapid pace throughout the day, but rather from anger and frustration. When he got to the log she was already asleep. He was furious, but short of using force to wake her and make her keep moving, there was nothing he could do but wait.

He opened his pack to get something to eat, took one bite of one of the sandwiches left from the lunch Big Mary had packed for them, then tossed it toward the river for some wild creature to feast upon. He wasn't hungry. He was too angry to be hungry. He considered taking a swim but was too angry even to do that. Usually he was comfortable with anger. His anger had fueled him for over a decade and it had always inspired him to some kind of action; but now there wasn't any action he could take. He was trapped. And it was *her* fault. He looked down at her, his heart beating so fast in his chest that he wondered if he was going to fall dead beside her. It would serve her right to wake up and find him dead. A corner of his mouth turned up at the foolishness of his thoughts and he began to feel more calm.

As he stood watching her sleep, he thought she didn't resemble Gray Wolf in the least—except for the cleft in her chin. He hadn't noticed it before, and he felt a sudden urge to reach down and touch it. Her resemblance to the picture of her grandmother, however, was startling. He remembered how beautiful her hair had been when he first saw her in Pine Crescent, and he knew it must have been difficult to cut it off. It was beginning to grow again, and although it was far shorter than it must have been when she was able to coil it up so elegantly, it was still thick and rich.

Much to his discomfort, he thought about how her hair had smelled of roses, and how he had thought of her that night while he was making love to Lila. He felt a sudden sweet ache as he looked at her eyelashes, once again long and feathery. She must have cut those, too, or he would have noticed Jesse William's long eyelashes the first time he laid eyes on him. They now lay against her cheeks, and her cheeks were flushed slightly pink, probably because he had made her walk so fast for so long. How could he not have known who the boy really was? How could he have been so blind? He looked away, down toward the river, trying to deny the feelings he found so strangely sweet and yet so unwelcome.

"Damn you, whoever you are," he growled under his breath.

She made a small sound in her throat and shifted her position, but she didn't waken. Even in sleep her movements were feminine and graceful, and he cursed himself for not having allowed himself to see the truth.

He suddenly felt a stirring in his groin, and he groaned and stumbled clumsily down the riverbank. He fell onto his knees and splashed cool water wildly onto his face. He kept filling his cupped palms and splashing furiously, waiting for the cool water to chill the heat of the passion he had no choice but to feel— and yet was being cruelly forced to deny.

She heard the noise he was making and sat up, her eyes wide and startled until she remembered where she was. Thor was down at the shore splashing like an angry grizzly bear. She rose calmly and walked slowly down to the river and knelt beside him, ignoring him completely as she drank from her cupped palms. She didn't have to look at him to feel the tension in the air between them. He bolted up from where he had been kneeling and with long strides climbed up the riverbank and started through the woods once more.

She scrambled up the riverbank and gathered her blanket into a tight roll, fearing she might not be able to catch up with him if she dallied. It took every ounce of strength she could muster to stay close behind him the rest of the way back to camp.

By the time they reached camp, her anger nearly matched his. She wanted to strike him, but she remembered her efforts to resist him on the boardwalk in Pine Crescent. She knew she was stronger now than she had been then, but she knew she was no match for him. She could rain blows upon him until she was blue in the face and he wouldn't even feel it.

It was long past suppertime, and she followed him into the dark cook shack and went directly to the storeroom and slammed the door, fearful that if she stayed in the room with him she would explode into a rage to match his. She was too uncertain about her future at Camp Seven to risk provoking him further. The events of the day since they left the Indian camp made it clear to her that his fierce mood was all because of her.

She could hear him banging things around in the kitchen, and she knew he was probably hungry. They had not eaten since breakfast; but she did not intend to help him find something to satisfy his hunger. He could starve to death for all she cared. As for her appetite, it had abandoned her, as usual, at the first sign of emotional turmoil.

She waited until the noises stopped and then went into the dark kitchen and crossed to the log sink and looked out the window. The clearing was silent and empty and she could see no sign of him. She stood staring out at the darkness and it was then that the full force of what had happened crashed down upon her.

"Oh my God!" she cried softly. Her hands went to her mouth to muffle her next words. "Gray Wolf is my father!" She backed slowly away from the window, her palms pressed one over the other covering her mouth. She bumped against a counter behind her, stopping her backward movement. Then she stood, frozen, as a confused mix of emotions swept over her.

She could see her father's face as they sat cross-legged on the ground around the fire. She could still hear the sound of his voice and smell the tobacco drifting up from his pipe. The picture was so clear that she could almost feel his presence in the room. She dropped her arms to her sides and let out a sigh that turned into a groan of frustration.

"Now what? What should I do now?"

Her eyes scanned the clearing again, but there were still no signs of life. She was the only one awake in the camp, except probably Thor, and she wished morning would come so she could get to work and she wouldn't have to keep on thinking. She went to her cot to lie down but she couldn't rest. Thoughts of her father and what she should do next kept forcing everything else out of her mind.

She awoke the next morning to Big Mary standing over her, her hands on her hips and her angry eyes blazing. "Are you dead? Get your lazy ass out of bed! You just had a vacation and don't go thinking you can stretch it out any farther!"

Sarah bolted out of bed, nearly knocking Big Mary over. "Wh...what time is it? I...did I oversleep?" Then she remembered that she didn't dare let Big Mary see her in her underwear without her breast bindings. Luckily, Big Mary hadn't bothered to bring a lantern into the storeroom and the windowless room was dark, except for the dim light coming in from the doorway to the kitchen.

"It's four o'clock," Big Mary said, turning to go back into the kitchen, remembering that her cookee had never before failed to be up before everyone else. Her initial anger dissipated and she said, looking back over her shoulder. "I'll start the coffee while you get dressed."

She ignored Thor when he came in to get his morning coffee. She thought for a moment that he didn't seem quite as angry as he had the night before; but luckily she didn't have time to think about him. She was grateful for her work. If she moved fast enough, her mind stayed calm and she could focus on whatever task she was performing. It was only when she slowed down that the thoughts came racing back. For the entire day, except for the ride to and from flaggins, she moved as fast as she ever had. And during the rides, she kept asking Big Mary questions that she knew would keep her talking. She wanted to avoid any unwelcome silences.

By nightfall she was too tired to think, and she slept that night like a baby. It went on like that for days, and finally thoughts of her father receded somewhat and her life at Camp Seven returned to normal. That is, except for her relationship with Thor. He had changed toward her, but she couldn't quite figure out in what way. Overtly he became again much the same as he had always been. But she felt a tension that had not been there before.

Her concern that he was going to make her leave Camp Seven because of something Gray Wolf had said proved to be unwarranted. She was greatly relieved, because she didn't want to have to find another job in order to stay in the timber. And she had made up her mind that she wanted to be near her father until she decided what to do. Staying on would buy her the time she needed, so she tried to ignore her concerns about Thor and his changed attitude toward her.

Ever since their journey to the Indian camp he had stopped coming into the cook shack when she was alone. He seemed to know when Big Mary arrived in the morning and it was only then that he came in for his coffee. He would merely nod to Sarah, get his coffee, and then leave again. During mealtime in the cook shack the room was full of men and it was easy for him to ignore her. During flaggins he would often keep working and not come to eat. Big Mary didn't like it, and the first time he skipped flaggins she sent Jock to get him. He caused such a ruckus over her telling him what to do that she never did it again.

The men, however, were happy with the change in him. He remained hard driving and demanding, but he seemed deep in his own world and that world seemed to be somewhere other than on their efforts. He seemed to have lost his former compulsion to finish even more miles of road than Smitheson was expecting, and the men decided he was finally satisfied with their progress.

Red, Spike, Woody and Jock often discussed Thor's strange withdrawal. They thought they knew exactly what was wrong with him; he was getting ready to go back to Sweden. What they could not possibly know was *why*.

In the middle of a hot, stifling night in early August he awakened from a sound sleep, let out a long, low moan and reached down and used his hand to relieve himself. He moaned again, half from pleasure and half from helpless frustration. He had just dreamed he was back in Pine Crescent and Doyle

MacKenna's daughter had entered the saloon and walked directly to him and taken his hand and led him upstairs. He had dreamed they were in Lila's bed, wildly embracing, and he awoke just as he was ready to enter her.

The dreams had started the night they returned from seeing Gray Wolf, and now they came to him several times a week. He hated the dreams. He had had many such dreams in his life, but they had never focused on one woman so completely. They had always been random; sometimes it was Annika, and sometimes it was Lila or some other whore. He detested the mixture of physical pleasure and self-loathing the dreams had begun to give him.

He had no room in his life for this woman. She was stealing his sense of purpose. For more than ten years the reason for his very existence had been clear as crystal. His direction was straight and true, like a compass needle pointing north. Now the compass needle of his life was spinning out of control. No matter how hard he tried to make it again aim directly toward Sweden and sweet revenge, it kept coming back again and again to Jesse. It was as if true north was lost to him, and the clear need for revenge had changed to the bewildering need to possess a woman he was determined to hate.

If it had been simple animal hunger he'd have gone to Lila and spent a night in her bed. However, the desire that had begun to wake him in the night and destroy his concentration during the day was not a simple thing. These feelings knocked him completely off balance. There was no way he could satisfy the need he felt for her—short of betraying his friend. Not only that; it also meant giving up the dream of revenge that had been his life's blood since he left his homeland.

Despite the heat of the night, he dragged himself from his bed and went to the sauna and built the fire. While the coals were getting hot he filled buckets with water, stripped, and then sat on the log bench and let the heat penetrate his tormented body. For him, sweating in the sauna was not like sweating from the heat and humidity of August. The sauna purged him.

But later, standing behind the sauna dousing himself with buckets of cool water, waiting for the relief he needed so badly, it did not come.

His hair was damp and his skin tingled as he walked across the clearing toward the cook shack. He needed a cup of strong coffee. He was too deep in thought to notice that there was a light in the window and he opened the door and went inside.

She was there, setting the table. Her mouth fell open when she saw him, and she stood, wide-eyed, a stack of tin plates pressed against her middle. She, too, had been unable to sleep because of the heat. They stood staring at each other for a long moment, his eyes filled with surprise—and something else. He clenched his fists until the knuckles were white, opening and closing them, fighting to restrain himself.

As she watched him she felt fear unlike any she had ever known. She had been afraid of Leverty—but this was different. What she feared now was that harm was going to come to her from someone she had begun to have strong feelings for. It felt like the worse kind of betrayal. It wouldn't be so bad if he just made her leave camp, as she had so often feared he might. This was far worse. He seemed to be fighting to keep from...from what? Striking her?

Panic-stricken, she turned and ran out the side door. She went directly to the woodpile, and without thinking pulled the axe from the stump and stood holding it poised in front of her. Her breath came in short gasps and she felt suddenly weak. She let the axe head fall to the ground, her hands still clutching the handle. What was she going to do? Hit him with the axe? She felt ridiculous. She leaned on the axe handle and looked up at the sky, letting her head fall back wearily.

"Sarah, Sarah, Sarah," she mumbled. "What are you thinking?" Did she actually intend to attack him with an axe? "Are you losing your mind?"

Then she heard the muffled sound of the cook shack door slamming shut and the sound of his footsteps running across the clearing. Whatever it was he had intended to do to her, he must have decided against it. She lifted the axe and raised her arms and sunk it back into the stump. When her heart stopped pounding in her chest and she felt her sanity returning, she blinked several times and then looked over at the stream, flowing peacefully next to the camp without regard for the goings on of its human neighbors.

She remembered the night they had stood together watching the otters. She remembered the pleasure that filled her so often in the clerk's shack when he had come in while she was working. She remembered thinking how beautiful and pure the lines of his face were when he let down his guard and smiled.

Even more clearly she remembered her feelings by the river when he had swum naked in front of her. She remembered all too well the fluttering in her stomach and the feelings she had begun to have for him back before their return journey from the Indian camp.

Must she now fear him? Was he so angry with her that he could no longer control it? But why? It simply made no sense. What on earth had she done to make him so angry? What had Gray Wolf said to him? Even more confusing, what had she done to cause White Feather to hold her in some strange kind of esteem?

Her head swam with confusion and so she did what she had so recently learned to do. She went back into the cook shack and began to work so hard that there was no time to think. By the time Big Mary came into the cook shack that morning, Sarah had finished her own chores and had done half of Big Mary's breakfast preparations.

Big Mary kept watching her out of the corner of her eyes wondering what was driving Jesse these days. And Thor, too. The two of them had begun to act like crazy people. Big Mary was worried. And scared. Was something sick going on between her boss and the boy? Was she blind to Thor the same way they had all been blind to Leverty? She shook off the thought.

No! It's not possible! She thought to herself. *Or is it?*

CHAPTER 25

H E went to the clerk's shack and packed his rucksack. Then he went into the bunkhouse and walked quietly over to Jock's bunk and shook him awake.

"Wh...what's wrong?" The Finn sat bolt upright and looked at his foreman, his eyes wide with alarm.

"Come outside," Thor whispered. "I don't want to wake the rest of the men. We have to talk."

Jock groped for his pants and stumbled into them, banging sideways into the bunk in the process and sputtering to stop from letting out a noisy stream of cuss words. Then he followed Thor outside without bothering to put on his shirt or his boots. Thor headed toward the horse trough and Jock protested saying, "If we're going to take a hike I can't do it without my boots." Thor glowered at him, so he followed without further complaint.

"So what's up?" Jock asked when they finally stood face to face.

"I'm leaving."

Jock raised one eyebrow, skeptical. "Yeah, sure. I've heard this before."

"No. I mean it this time. I'm leaving this damned timber and I'm going home. I need you to take over as Push."

"When? When are you leaving?" Jock asked, seeing as how it looked like this time Thor meant business.

"Now. This morning."

"This morning? Isn't that kind of sudden?"

"It's nowhere near sudden enough," he said, his eyes darting toward the cook shack, then back again to Jock's face. "I want you to have Woody pack up the rest of my things and send them to town. There's not much. An extra set of clothes, a heavy jacket and some other winter gear. You want my calked boots?"

Jock looked down at Thor's feet and then at his own. "Are you nuts? Your feet are damn near twice as big as mine."

"Try them on. If they don't fit, find someone else who can use them. I won't be needing calked boots."

He was going to Sweden with enough money to buy a nice piece of land and get back to farming. He wouldn't be working in the timber any longer. Something stirred in him as he remembered standing on his grandfather's land in early spring, reaching down to pick up a handful of earth to test its moisture. He missed working the land, and he had been working so hard for so long that he had almost forgotten what it meant to him.

"And tell Red to have the boys at Smitheson get ready to square up with me. I'll pick up my money and the rest of my gear before I get on the train."

"How's that going to work?" Jock asked, puzzled. You'll be in Pine Crescent long before the supply wagon. Red said he was going in to get supplies on Friday. Today's only Wednesday.

"I'm going to see Gray Wolf."

Jock, still looking puzzled said, "You just saw Gray Wolf."

"I know that," Thor answered, growing impatient with all the questions. "I'm going again. One last time."

"And the rest of the men? Aren't you going to say good-bye to them? And what about Big Mary? You just gonna walk away without so much as a by-your-leave?"

Thor grunted, as if Jock's opinions didn't deserve further reply.

"I don't like this," Jock said. "Most of us have been together for a long time. We're like family. What do you think it's going to do to the men to have you just up and run off without bothering to explain? It's not like you." Jock cocked his head to one side and squinted at Thor as if he could see inside his head. Then he seemed to come to a conclusion. "You're sick. That's it. You're sick and you don't want to admit it."

Thor laughed wryly at that and said, "Look. I know it's sudden, but something.... I've got to go, and I can't explain. You just have to trust me and do as I ask." His eyes were steady. "You're a good man, Jock. You've been my right hand for a long time, and I've always been able to count on you. Besides that, you've been my friend. If I ever come back to this place I'll look you up." He paused, wishing he could explain, but knew he didn't dare. "Will you do as I ask?"

Jock nodded and his shoulders sagged, as if he had lost the energy to argue. "Guess there's not much I can do but agree."

Thor held out one hand and shook Jock's, slapping him on the opposite shoulder with the other. Then he turned and walked away, his boots crunching on the gravel, his pack slung over his back.

He half ran the entire way without stopping to rest. Now that he had finally made up his mind to go, he was desperate to get out of the timber. The sooner he saw Gray Wolf and said good-bye to him, the better. First, though, there were issues blocking the road between them; like stumps still standing in a new roadbed where they didn't belong. He needed to clear them away.

He was going to tell Gray Wolf of his growing feelings for Jesse—or whatever her name was. He didn't want to blame Gray Wolf for his sudden departure, but he needed to be honest with him. He could no longer be so close to her, day in and day out, without risking the danger of exposing his feelings. He had already come too close.

He didn't want to think about her, so he moved fast, focused on his progress through the woods. He reached the Indian camp in mid-afternoon.

The camp was quiet and empty, and the temporary birch bark coverings had been removed from all the teepees. "Damn!" he said out loud. He had forgotten that the Indians moved from their main summer camp to the rice camp to gather wild rice sometime in September. It was plain to him that they had gone.

But when he looked down by the lake he saw smoke, and he saw that Gray Wolf's teepee still had its birch bark covering. He hurried through the deserted camp toward the smoke, and when he was almost there he saw Gray Wolf sitting in front of a small fire. Thor walked over to him and Gray Wolf turned and looked up at him. He nodded, but didn't speak, merely lowering his eyes to again stare into the fire.

Thor sank down on the other side of the fire, legs crossed Indian fashion, and waited for Gray Wolf to speak. He waited for what seemed like hours but was in fact little more than five minutes.

When Gray Wolf finally spoke his voice was flat and expressionless. "White Feather has gone with her people to the rice camp."

Thor nodded. "I forgot it was time for them to go. Why didn't you go with them?"

"White Feather doesn't want me."

His voice was strange and Thor felt a niggling fear. "How can that be? I thought the two of you...." He couldn't finish, because Gray Wolf looked over at him with such pain in his eyes that it stopped his words.

"Bad medicine. She says I'm bad medicine."

"Don't tell me you believe that!"

"I don't have to believe it," Gray Wolf said, still without expression. "It's enough that *she* believes it."

"Why?" Thor asked. "What makes her think you're bad medicine?"

"She had the baby. A boy."

"Did she take him away with her? Is that why you're sitting here moping like an old woman?" Maybe if he got Gray Wolf riled up he'd get some of his old fight back.

"Dead. He was born dead."

Thor didn't know what to say. They sat silent for a long time. Then finally Gray Wolf began to speak in a strange, low monotone, and as he spoke he stared out across the water, his eyes unseeing.

"White Feather was convinced that the spirits had sent Jesse to us to see if our union was a good one. When I tried to explain the truth of who Jesse was it only made it worse. She said I should go and make peace with this daughter of mine or the spirits would not allow me to have another child. I told her she was crazy, and that the world didn't work like that. She became very angry and told me not to anger the Gods by speaking with such disrespect. I told her that her Gods had nothing to do with me. I told her that I am a White man, and we have our own God."

He looked at Thor, his eyes leaden. "At least I used to think we did."

Silence again. Then after a while he continued, his eyes scanning the waters of the big lake. "She wouldn't listen to me. She went every day to talk to Many Crows, and when I wouldn't go and talk to the girl she went to live in her parents' teepee. I figured she'd come around after the baby was born."

After another long silence he said, "Last week Many Crows came to me and told me the baby had been born dead, and that they were going to bury him that night. He told me I had to come and see him right away or it would be too late for me ever to lay eyes upon him."

A visible shudder ran through Gray Wolf and Thor wondered how long it had been since he had eaten. His voice sounded weak, as though he could barely get out the rest of his words. "I tried to give White Feather something to put in the spirit bundle. She wouldn't take anything from me."

"Spirit bundle?"

"When an Indian is in mourning he keeps a spirit bundle. Something from the...from the deceased; a lock of hair...." He paused, his face showing some emotion for the first time since Thor arrived. "His hair was not black. It was the color of the girl's hair."

"The girl's hair?"

"Jesse. Jesse Williams' hair."

"Christ!" Thor muttered under his breath. Then he said, "You've got to get away from here for a while. Come back to camp with me. You can stay there until White Feather has had a chance to come to her senses."

"No!" Gray Wolf said sharply. "I need to stay here. The burial grounds are close by, and I...."

"For God's sake, Man! Don't be crazy! Your son is gone."

The words struck Gray Wolf hard. *Your son is gone.* It sounded so final. No one had said any words of sympathy to him. No one had come to comfort him. He had no one here except White Feather, and she had withdrawn from him completely.

"White Feather believes his spirit will stay in the spirit bundle until she has finished carrying it, and that sometimes it will come to the burial grounds. Then when she is finished with her year of mourning, his spirit will fly to the land of his forefathers." He said it as though he was trying to understand it, or perhaps even believe it.

Thor felt his anger rising. "If you believe he has a spirit that flies around looking for forefathers, what makes you think he won't fly to Scotland? You have no way to predict where or when this spirit might appear, so it makes no sense for you to sit around here turning into a madman!"

This last finally penetrated Gray Wolf's delirium and he began to laugh. Then he said, "You unholy son-of-a-bitch! Don't you Swedes have a God?"

"We have the same God as the rest of you. I just do the best I can and hope I don't end up burning in hell for letting him do *his* job and expecting him to let *me* do mine."

His harsh down-to-earth words seemed to be having an impact, so he continued. "Come with me to camp. You can make peace with your daughter. Just like White Feather wants you to. Then you can go back and tell her and the two of you can start all over again."

Thor had a sinking awareness that he was ruining his chances to get away, but Gray Wolf's problems had taken priority over his own. For several long moments the two men sat staring at each other; Thor trying not to think about the woman who would still be in his camp when he returned, and Gray Wolf letting Thor's words sink in.

As if trying to rid himself of some unpleasant vision, Gray Wolf suddenly shook his head and asked, "What in hell are you doing here?"

"I...never mind. I just had the urge to see you and it's a good thing I did. You're a real mess."

He was. He hadn't bathed or shaved for days, and his hair was wild and unkempt, the long plait partly undone and strands of hair hanging over his eyes.

"What do you say? Are you coming with me?"

Gray Wolf didn't answer at first, seeming deep in thought. Then he lifted his head and brushed the hair from his face with both hands. "Maybe you're right. I could use some of Big Mary's cooking." Then he added, almost as an after-thought, "Funny. I spent many years alone in the woods when I was cruising the timber for Smitheson. Now I can't seem to stand being alone. Age. I guess I'm getting old. Maybe it's time for me to settle down permanent."

"I thought you already had, and look what happened," Thor said, fearing Gray Wolf was going to become maudlin again.

"Don't be so hard on the meanderings of an old man's mind, you young whippersnapper." Gray Wolf rose somewhat unsteadily to his feet. "I'll be ready shortly. Let me get cleaned up some or I'll scare the bejeezus out of your men."

"Hah!" Thor scoffed. "It'll take more than even the mess you've turned into to scare the bejeezus out of those jacks."

He wondered how he was going to explain his aborted departure for Sweden. Well at least when he got back to camp Gray Wolf would be there to protect him from Jesse—or protect Jesse from him.

As he sat waiting for Gray Wolf to get cleaned up and gather his gear, the reality of what he was doing slowly came to him. "Shit!" he said, jumping up and kicking at the dirt to put out the fire. He had nearly made a clean break; and now here he was, ready to walk right back into the wolves' den. He looked down toward the lake where Gray Wolf had stripped off his buckskins and was submerged up to his head in the water. He watched for several minutes and then shrugged resignedly and let out a long, deep sigh. He owed Gray Wolf a lot. How could he desert him at a time like this? He sure couldn't do it just to save his own selfish neck.

"Shit!" he said again, finally accepting that there was no turning back.

CHAPTER 26

THE stir caused by the two men when they walked into camp early the next morning was nearly as wild as the stir Jock had caused when he told them Thor was on his way back to Sweden. It was just after breakfast and the men were gathering their equipment to go into the timber. Red and Paddy were harnessing the teams. When Thor told the men simply that he was back and that Gray Wolf would be staying for a while, the men cheered.

Sarah was working at the sink and heard the cheers. She looked out the window and saw that there was a crowd gathered up near the bunkhouse.

"Something's going on, Big Mary!"

Big Mary ran to the window and saw what was happening. "C'mon!" she shouted, and the two of them ran out into the clearing.

"Now what in hell do you suppose...." Big Mary said as she neared the crowd of men. She forced her way into the middle of the crowd, pushing men aside to confront Thor.

"What in thunderation is going on?" She glared up at him, hands on hips, heel planted and toe tapping, at first not seeing Gray Wolf among the crowd.

"I'm back," Thor told her matter-of-factly.

"I can see that. You go, you come. Nobody tells me anything. I have to figure it out by seeing it with my own two eyes. I thought I deserved better from you."

Gray Wolf stepped forward, paying no attention to her tirade. He picked her up, spun her around and then set her down and tweaked her chin. "Did you miss me, my little pea hen?"

She punched him hard in the stomach. He staggered backwards, feigning injury. "If I've told you once, MacKenna, I've told you a thousand times! Don't call me that!"

Sarah stood apart, watching them.

"You men better get to work," Thor said, his words aimed at Jock. "We'll be out to help as soon as we get some shuteye. We've been up all night."

"Does that mean you're going to take over again?" Jock asked, hopefully.

"That's what it means," Thor answered flatly, none too happy about the reality of the situation.

Sarah followed Thor and Gray Wolf into the cook shack and watched her father's bravado dissipate and his face turn as dark as the unlit corners of the cook shack.

Big Mary, now that she had settled down some, saw it too. She motioned for Gray Wolf to sit and brought him a cup of coffee and sat across the table from him.

Thor leaned against a counter, his arms crossed over his chest, refusing to meet Sarah's eyes.

"He died," Gray Wolf said, struggling to hide his emotion.

"Died? Your baby died?" Big Mary asked, not sure she had heard right.

Gray Wolf nodded.

She looked at Thor and he, too, nodded. "White Feather? Is she...is she...?"

Gray Wolf shook his head. "She's okay I guess. She left me, so I don't really know."

"Left you?" Big Mary asked, incredulous. Again she looked at Thor for some kind of confirmation, but he was staring up into the ceiling as if he saw something interesting there.

"You'd better tell me what happened," she said sympathetically. "Tell me all of it."

Gray Wolf let out a long sigh and began to relate the events of the past week and Big Mary sat listening without interrupting.

Sarah leaned sulkily against the log sink, listening too. She wanted to feel sorry for him, but instead felt anger burning in the pit of her stomach. This tough, hardened man—half lumberjack and half savage—was nearly inconsolable at the loss of his Indian family. What about the loss of his other family? What about that innocent and abandoned baby in that other family?

Angry tears stung her eyes, and she muttered something about having work to do in the clerk's shack. She wondered vaguely why she bothered to say anything, because clearly no one was paying the slightest attention to her. She ran out of the cook shack and stumbled across the clearing to the safety of her ledgers; and to the shelves of objects needing to be moved from place to place and then back again.

She wasn't sure how long she had been there, or how many times she had moved the snuff to where the tobacco had been and the tobacco to where the snuff had been, when she heard a sharp knock at the door. She ignored it. Maybe if she didn't answer, whoever it was would simply go away. But the knock grew more and more insistent, and with a great effort at controlling her quavering voice, she called, "Wh...who is it?"

"Are you okay in there?" It was Thor, and he sounded more impatient than concerned.

"What do you want?" she called, wondering why he didn't just open the door and walk in. Since when did he knock on the door of the clerk's shack?

"We want to use the bunks. We need to get some sleep."

She went to the door and threw it open. Thor and Gray Wolf stood waiting, neither of them looking directly at her.

She brushed past them saying, "It's your camp. Do whatever you want."

"Call us when you and Big Mary get the flaggins cart loaded," Thor called to her departing back, ignoring her insolent behavior.

Back in the cook shack, Big Mary looked at her, lines of worry creasing her brow. "You okay, Boy?" She came toward her, then hesitated and said, "We keep forgetting about you losing your family and how this must remind you all over again." She reached out to touch Sarah but pulled her hand back self-consciously. "I know what it's like to hurt, Jesse," she said gently. "Seems when men have some kind of trouble they always forget about everybody but themselves."

Sarah swiped at her eyes with her sleeve, unwelcome tears again stinging her eyelids. "I'm not crying. I'm...I'm okay," she said, unable to keep her voice from trembling. "I'd better get to work," she said, and began to scurry around the cook shack as if she had a deadline to meet.

Big Mary watched her for only a moment, then shook her head in dismay and busied herself with her own chores. "There's too damn much misery in the world," she mumbled under her breath.

Back in the clerk's shack, although they both needed to sleep, they lay in their bunks unable to rest. Finally Gray Wolf got up and went to the window and stood staring out.

"Can't sleep?" Thor asked from the top bunk.

Gray Wolf nodded without turning. "I was wondering why you came to see me so soon again. You never did tell me." They had barely spoken on the way back from the Indian camp, each of them saving their energy for the long walk, their thoughts deep into their own misery.

Thor jumped down from the bunk, ran his fingers through his hair, then raised both palms and shrugged. "It doesn't matter. The important thing is that I came."

Gray Wolf turned from the window and looked at him. "It matters. Tell me what you're up to."

"Nothing," Thor said without meeting his friend's eyes and instead going behind the wannigan counter and studying the shelves of supplies as if he cared how they were arranged.

"Out with it."

Thor spun around and this time looked squarely at him. "I was going home."

"Home?"

"Yaw. Home."

"You mean home to Sweden?"

"Don't act stupid. You know where my home is."

"So when are you leaving?" Gray Wolf asked, not without humor.

"I changed my mind, dammit! Can't a man change his mind?"

"Changed your mind? It's because of me, isn't it?" he challenged. "When you saw the sorry state I was in you decided you needed to hang around and take care of me."

It was the first spark Thor had seen in him since he arrived at the Indian camp and found him staring morosely into the fire. Gray Wolf slapped the top of the table with the palm of his hand and yelled, "I won't have it! You've been saying for a decade that you want to go home, and I'm not going to be the one who stops you if you've finally made up your mind.

Then, as if a sudden insight had come to him, he walked over to the counter and looked steadily at Thor and said, "Why? Why now all of a sudden did you get a gnat in your ear to go back to Sweden?"

Thor tried to shrug it off. "No reason. It's time, that's all."

"I see," Gray Wolf said, as if he knew what was going on even though Thor hadn't told him.

"Good," Thor said. "As long as you know already, you can mind your own business. I'm going to get some sleep." With that, he climbed noisily onto the top bunk and turned his face to the wall.

Gray Wolf sat down on one of the chairs and stared across the room at him, but Thor never moved and soon Gray Wolf's head nodded and he, too, crawled into bed and slept.

When the men came in for supper that night, instead of giving him the place at the table that Leverty had vacated, the entire crew shifted and made room for Gray Wolf across from Thor.

That unusual show of respect by the men gave Sarah mixed feelings. She grudgingly had to admit that he must have earned it; but at the same time she resented the fuss everybody was making over him. She began to get the uncomfortable feeling that she wanted everyone to punish him for deserting her and her mother. It made her ashamed, and yet she couldn't help herself.

After supper Thor, Jock, Red, Woody and Gray Wolf stayed in the cook shack and Thor pulled out a map he had drawn. As she and Big Mary finished the evening chores, Sarah kept half an ear focused on what they were saying.

Thor stood next to the table, one foot up on the bench, one hand curved over his raised knee. With the other hand, his index finger traced lines on the map. "These are the roads we cut this summer," he explained to Gray Wolf. He ran his finger along a line representing one of the auxiliary roads leading from the main feeder line. "This branch is the last. We'll need to get the stumps out at the north end but the men should be able to finish in less than a week."

He looked at Jock with satisfaction and said, "We did it." Then he folded the map and tucked it into his shirt pocket and sat down straddling the bench. The rest of the men sat down, too.

"We'll start cutting the beginning of November, as usual depending upon when we get the first hard freeze," Thor said, his words directed at Gray Wolf. "I'll let most of the men go next week and we'll run with a skeleton crew until the men start coming back into camp for the regular season."

He turned to Woody. "There's plenty of fix-up work for us to do. I noticed a lot of junk piling up in the dingle room."

"Yeah," Woody agreed, embarrassed. "There's some things I can't seem to get to."

"Do you want me to be part of that skeleton crew?" Gray Wolf asked.

"Might as well," Thor said, aware that Sarah was straining to hear—even though she was pretending not to. "For a while, anyway, until you decide where you're going next."

Gray Wolf looked at Thor and then across the room to where Sarah was wiping plates. She pretended she hadn't been paying attention, but their eyes met and he called to her. "How about you, Boy? You staying?"

She answered without looking at him while she rubbed an imaginary spot on the plate she was holding. "I haven't decided," she said.

Gray Wolf looked at Thor and made a movement with his head that made Thor say to Sarah, "It's up to you. Woody will take over the cooking for the summer and you can work with him."

"What about Big Mary," she asked, as if the idea of being in camp without her was unheard of.

"She always goes to Duluth to be with her sister during the break between summer work and the regular season." He looked at Big Mary. "Isn't that right?"

"Yup. And I can't wait to get out of here. You men don't appreciate me, but after a month of eating beans you're all so hungry for some real food that I get some respect—at least for a while." No one seemed to notice that she was complaining, and she wondered if the tension that lingered in the room just beneath the surface had anything to do with her helper.

Thor continued, his eyes on Sarah. "You can stay over the break or you can take the month off. It's up to you."

"I told you," she said, with unaccustomed sharpness, "that I haven't decided whether I want to stay. Or if I want to come back...."

Gray Wolf got up from the bench and walked over to where she was standing. She backed up until she was pressed against the log sink, but he paid no attention to her obvious withdrawal from him and put his hand on her shoulder. "What are you talking about, Boy? Thor tells me you're the best clerk he ever had. Of course you're coming back."

She pulled away, bumping clumsily against a counter and dropping the plate onto the floor. He reached down and picked it up and handed it to her, willing her to look at him; but she averted his eyes.

"Leave him alone," Big Mary said. "He's old enough to make his own decisions without you louts bossing him around." She looked first at Thor and then at Gray Wolf, who had gone back and stood next to the table, his face now void of all emotion. "Seems to me the two of you have plenty to do to keep your own lives on an even keel without messing with Jesse's."

She looked at Sarah and said, "Take some time off. If you decide not to come back, you need to let them know over at Smitheson so they can hire another clerk." As far as Big Mary was concerned, that was that.

Sarah nodded to her, hung the towel on the sink to dry and went to her room. She sat on the edge of her cot with her head in her hands staring down at the floor, wanting nothing but to be gone from Camp Seven and away from all this troubling and stinging resentment that baffled her with its intensity.

The following week was filled with even more activity than usual. She had to be sure the men's work records were current so they could be paid before they left camp. That made it necessary for Thor to come into the clerk's shack to work with her some of the time. Since their trip to the Indian camp he had avoided coming into the clerk's shack when she was alone. But now that Gray Wolf was in camp, his behavior had changed. He was all business, and the anger that had seemed to overcome him at the sight of her had evaporated. But the easy camaraderie they had begun to share before they took that fateful journey to visit Gray Wolf was also gone.

While the men remained to finish the roads, she only saw Gray Wolf during meals. He was usually jolly and cheerful; but there were times when an undercurrent of sadness surfaced and his pain was unmasked.

The day the men pulled the last stumps, they came into the clerk's shack after supper to get their pay and to say good-bye to Jesse. They all wanted to know if he was going to be Camp Seven's Johnny Inkslinger, but she said she wasn't sure.

The next morning, while Thor and Gray Wolf were out inspecting the finished roads, she announced to Big Mary that she was leaving that morning with the men and going to Pine Crescent for a while.

"Sounds like a good idea to me, Jesse," Big Mary said gently. "You ain't been looking so good. I think you need to get the hell out of here, and go have some fun." Big Mary had stopped worrying about Jesse and Thor, and sometimes felt ashamed for even having thought there could be anything going on between them.

"Fun?" Sarah scoffed. "Fun?" she repeated with disdain. "I don't think I even know what that is."

"Now don't you go feeling sorry for yourself," Big Mary scolded. "All you need is a little time to yourself. Use your money to buy yourself something nice. Maybe a new shirt. That's it. Buy a new shirt and go to town and meet some nice girl and get yourself a kiss."

Sarah couldn't help it. She started to laugh.

Big Mary grinned at her and said, "See? All you need is a little fun. You can still laugh, so you ain't a total loss."

She paid Big Mary the money she owed her for her extra set of clothes, said good-by to the little woman, and climbed onto the seat next to Red.

As they rode she tried to ignore the ribald conversation going on among the men in the back of the wagon. It got so bad that Red looked back over his shoulder and said, "Watch your mouths. The boy don't need to hear that kind of talk."

"Oh, poor baby!" Paddy Roark said. "We better not soil his tender little ears!"

Sarah turned around, feeling the heat rising to her neck and her face. "It's not the dirt that bothers me, you fool. What bothers me is listening to you talk about throwing away the money you've worked so hard for."

"Throwing it away!" the men said in unison, laughing at her. "What do you know about the value we get for our money by getting good and drunk and poking Ginger's girls?"

Red pulled on the reins and brought the team up short and handed Sarah the reins. "Hang on to these, Boy."

Then he jumped down and walked calmly to the back of the wagon and lowered the tailgate. "Get out," he commanded, motioning to the men.

"Aw come on, Red," Paddy wheedled. "Don't go getting your shit in an uproar. We're just having some fun."

Red reached into the wagon and grabbed Paddy by his shirt and pulled him out of the wagon. "I told you to get out and I meant it." He pushed Paddy so hard that the younger man stumbled and fell onto the ground. In the meantime the other men scrambled out of the wagon, seeing that their teamster wasn't fooling around.

"Okay, okay," several of them mumbled, holding up their hands in a defensive posture. "We're going."

Red climbed back onto the wagon seat and took the reins, flicked them, and then set the horses into a fast trot. "We'll let 'em cool down for a while and then we'll let 'em ride again," he told Sarah with a sly grin.

"You don't need to protect me," Sarah protested. "I'm getting used to the way you jacks talk. I can take it."

"Sure you can," Red said, glancing sideways at her, "but if Big Mary finds out I let the men talk garbage in front of you she'll have my ass in a sling."

"Who do you think is going to tell her?" Sarah teased, at last seeing the humor in the situation. After what she'd already been through, what could a few foul-mouthed lumberjacks say that could possibly hurt her?

What she didn't see, however, was the way those in charge of Camp Seven had begun to look after her. She was too deep into self-pity, and too focused on the adulation they gave Gray Wolf, to recognize the care the people at Camp Seven took of her.

Later when Gray Wolf and Thor got back to camp and found Jesse gone, Gray Wolf grew sullen and refused to eat supper. Thor found him out behind the cook shack sitting on the ground staring into the blackness. The evening air was chilly, the moon and the stars hidden under a thick layer of dark clouds.

Thor sat down on the ground next to him and neither of them spoke at first. It was Gray Wolf who finally broke the silence. "Go get her," he said, his voice flat.

Thor turned to him, thinking he hadn't heard right. "Get her? Get her? What are you talking about? I can't just go get her. Who the hell do you think I am that I can just up and go get her?"

Gray Wolf glared at him, clearly determined to have his way. "You're her boss. Go find her and bring her back."

Thor jumped to his feet and began pacing back and forth in front of the older man, his breathing fast and his fists clenching and unclenching in helpless fury. How had he gotten himself into this? Why had he suggested that Gray Wolf come to camp with him? Why hadn't he just gone home to Sweden the way he planned?

Gray Wolf got to his feet, too, and put his hand on Thor's arm to stop his lion-like pacing. Even in the darkness Thor could see the unyielding force he was up against. "Tomorrow you'll go to town and find her. You told me she stayed with the Vogels at the depot before you hired her. Maybe that's where she went."

"Goddammit!" Thor bellowed. "I'm not going to follow her and...."

"You forget," Gray Wolf interrupted, his voice filled with uncharacteristic venom, "that you owe me."

It was the one thing he couldn't fight. His shoulders fell and he stared at Gray Wolf, a sick feeling growing in the pit of his stomach. "I'll go," he said through clenched teeth, "but after I do this one thing we're even. You understand my meaning, old man?"

Gray Wolf reached out a hand so fast that it caught Thor completely by surprise. He clutched a handful of shirt and pulled the younger man toward him, spraying spittle as he spoke. "We're even only if you get her back! Do you understand *my* meaning?"

Just as suddenly as he had grabbed his shirt, he dropped his hand and stepped back several paces. "What's happening to us? I thought we were friends. Look at us!"

Thor relaxed, his own arms dropping helplessly to his side. "It's nuts, us getting all riled up like this. I'm sorry. I'll try to find her and convince her to come back. I know what it means to you to lose...to lose another...another...."

Gray Wolf didn't wait for him to find words, but instead nodded and turned away and headed toward the clerk's shack. He called back over his shoulder, "I appreciate it. I mean it. She might listen to you. She's already written *me* off."

Thor caught up to him and asked, "What do you mean 'written you off?'"

They went into the clerk's shack and Thor lit the lantern and they sat down across from each other at the table. Gray Wolf seemed to want to talk.

"Don't you see?" he said. "She's decided not to have anything to do with me. My only hope is to try to convince her I'm not a worthless piece of shit."

"Dammit, Man! You aren't making any sense!"

"We both know she knows who I am, but she doesn't give a damn. Ever since I got here she's been backing off farther and farther. What other reason could there be for her not wanting to admit I'm her father? She probably figures any man who'd sire an Indian baby isn't worth...."

"Now just a minute," Thor said. "You've got no reason to jump to that conclusion. She's never said a word about...."

"Haven't you been paying attention? Every time someone mentions White Feather or the boy she turns pale and looks the other way." He was nodding his head. "Yup. She hates me for having an Indian for a son."

"Then why don't you just let her go?" Thor asked, wondering why anyone who believed as he did would want to expose himself to more of the same.

"I need to prove something to her, and I can't do it if she isn't here," he said, as though it made all the sense in the world. "Go get her. Bring her back."

"But...."

"I understand why White Feather left me. She was right."

Thor didn't respond. He didn't like to think about all that, because if it hadn't happened he'd be gone from the timber and on his way home.

"I have a score to settle with Lorna."

"Lorna? I thought it was White Feather you...."

Gray Wolf ignored him. "I don't know whether she's dead or alive, but I owe it to her and to this daughter of hers...ours...." He stopped talking and stared up into the dark rafters.

Thor felt his frustration mounting. He got to his feet and went behind the counter and took down a jar of snuff and pretended to read the label. "You sure have gotten yourself in a mess over these women," he said finally, unable to hold in his bitterness any longer.

"Hah! You should talk!"

"Me? I'd never let a woman tell me what to do! How can you compare my situation with yours?" He slammed the jar down with such force that it cracked open and snuff spilled all over the counter.

Gray Wolf laughed scornfully. "Think about it, you idiot. Think about why it is you keep threatening to go back home. It sure isn't because you've got a hankering for your mother's lutefisk!"

Thor was using his hand to sweep the mess into a trash bucket, his face a sullen mask. He wished Gray Wolf didn't know him so well, but was thankful he didn't know him well enough to know that not only was he going back home for revenge upon a woman—he was going back home to escape his feelings for one more of the damned creatures.

But did he really intend to go home? Ever? He looked around the room and felt a sudden, strange emptiness. Could it be that he, too, hoped he could get Jesse back? He thought about his troubling dreams, although he had only dreamed about her once since Gray Wolf came with him to Camp Seven.

He and the Mud Lady were upstairs again at Ginger's, about to get into bed. Just as he began to undo the buttons of her bodice the door flew open and Gray Wolf appeared. He was blazing mad and was holding a rifle aimed directly at Thor's heart. The dream had ended there, and he had not had another one.

He had felt intensely relieved and was able to convince himself that the dreams had been only temporary insanity, caused by being too long in the timber. After all, he was a normal man with the usual appetites, and she was a woman.

Gray Wolf was studying his face from across the room. "What are you so deep in thought about?"

Thor shook his head and wiped his hands on the side of his pants. "Nothing."

"Don't give me that. You were thinking real hard about something."

He was. He had nearly convinced himself he had delayed his departure only because Gray Wolf needed him. Or so he had convinced himself. Now he stood staring up at the shadows on the ceiling over the desk where they had worked together on the ledgers for so many hours. He felt an intense and overpowering longing to wrap his arms around her and let what was left of his resolve to go home melt away into nothingness.

Aware that Gray Wolf was expecting some kind of an answer, he said, "You think you know everything, but this time you're wrong. I wasn't thinking about a damn thing. And even if I was, it's none of your business!"

"Fine. It's none of my business," Gray Wolf said as he stood up and went to the door. Then he turned briefly and jabbed a finger at Thor. "Go find my daughter and bring her back." Then he was gone, the door slamming violently behind him.

CHAPTER 27

BY the time Red dropped her off at the train depot in Pine Crescent, Sarah was sure of one thing; she needed to get away from Jesse Williams. She needed to take off her men's clothing and look into the mirror and see a woman.

It wasn't that she was sorry about the time she had spent as Jesse. Being Jesse, after all, had made it possible for her to find her father. It had served its purpose. What to do about having found him, however, seemed to her not to be Jesse's job. *Sarah* was the one who needed to sort out what to do now that she had found him.

She was beginning to think that maybe she should simply reconcile herself to her orphan status once and for all. She was a grown woman now. People grow up and eventually leave their parents, don't they? Don't they say good-bye and travel across continents and oceans and never see parents and family again? She'd never had them in the first place; but even if she had, she'd perhaps have left them by now.

And hadn't she found people who were almost like family to her? Look at the Vogels, and Big Mary, and Woody—and, yes, even Thor Nilsson. They had all looked out for her in one way or another. Maybe now she could accept being an orphan. Camp Seven had taught her she could make a place for herself in the world without parents to love and to guide her. But that realization didn't help all that much. She was still awfully confused about what to do next.

She was sure about one thing, though. She needed some distance between herself and Jesse Williams—and Camp Seven. She wasn't ready yet to make a move she could not undo. She would put the matter of her father on a back burner for a while. She would get back into her own skin, and then, well....

***

Inside the depot, she folded her arms on the closed bottom half of the Dutch door leading into Richard Vogel's office and smiled at him. "Hello, Mr. Vogel. How are you?"

Richard Vogel turned from his desk, and then stood up and walked over to her looking puzzled. "Do I know you, young man?"

She smiled at his consternation and said, "Don't you recognize me?"

"No. I most certainly do not." But then, squinting and looking more carefully at her, he gasped, "Sarah? Sarah Williams? Is it you?" He pushed the lower half of the door open and stepped out into the waiting room and looked her up and down.

She nodded uncomfortably. "Is Clemmie at home?"

He seemed not to have heard her. "Well, I'll be.... Where have you been? Clemmie's been worried sick about you."

"I'm sorry if I caused her to worry. I should have let both of you know where I went. It's just that...I was.... I was working in a lumber camp." She stopped there; not sure what more she should tell him.

"A lumber camp? Good Lord, Woman! What were you thinking?"

"I guess I was thinking they wouldn't know I wasn't really a boy. You didn't, did you?"

"No. You sure could have fooled me." He nodded toward the door leading upstairs. "Go on up. Clemmie will be glad to see you. That is, if she doesn't faint dead away at the sight of you."

Then he thought better of it and said, "I'll go on up and warn her. She...." He colored slightly and said, "She's in a somewhat delicate condition."

"Is she ill?" Sarah asked, regretting barging in on them like this if Clemmie was not well.

"No. Not exactly ill. She was at first, but now.... She's in the family way."

"How nice," Sarah said, breathing a sigh of relief, but then immediately feeling worried. If Clemmie was unwell and she couldn't stay here with the Vogels for the time being, where would she go?

"I guess. Sometimes I don't think it's all that wonderful. Oh, she's better now. It's been nearly six months. But the first few months were...kinda unpleasant."

"I'm sure she's very happy," Sarah said. She didn't know what else to say. Her experience with her father's baby was dismal, and she had little knowledge of anyone else's. She thought gloomily that she had learned more about lumberjacks in the past six months than she had learned about regular people in her entire life.

He motioned to her to follow as he hurried ahead of her up the stairs, calling to Clemmie. By the time he reached the kitchen door, with Sarah halfway up the stairs behind him, she was standing in the doorway with a puzzled expression on her face.

"Yes? What is it, Richard?" She looked over his shoulder and saw the apparition standing behind him. She stared down at Sarah, her eyes wide with disbelief. "Sarah? Sarah, is that you?"

Sarah nodded, wondering if Clemmie could really be as glad to see her as she appeared to be.

"Oh!" Clemmie breathed, then ran down the steps to meet her and threw her arms around her with a happy cry. Then she took her by the arm and led her upstairs, all the while asking one question after the other, not leaving any space for answers. "Where have you been? Why didn't you write to me? I've been worried sick! I thought something awful must have happened or I'd have heard from you, or you'd have sent for your trunk."

Richard interrupted and said, "I'm going back downstairs. It looks like you two have a lot to talk about."

Clemmie ignored him, her attention on Sarah. "Come and sit down and I'll fix you some tea and something to eat, and you can tell me all about where you've been and why you look so...so strange." Her hand went up to cover her mouth. "Oops! I didn't mean that. But you really do look...well...."

Sarah laughed and sat down at the kitchen table, her index finger tracing the embroidered flowers on the tablecloth. "I can't argue with you about that," she said looking down at the threadbare knees of her pants. "I must look pretty pathetic."

"Oh pooh! I'm thrilled that you're here. I don't care one bit how you look."

"I don't want to be any trouble."

"Trouble? Trouble? This is the best thing that's happened to me since...." Clemmie patted her stomach, which had grown to the size of a watermelon. "Since I learned about the baby coming."

They heard noises on the stairs and turned to see Richard and a young boy dragging Sarah's trunk through the door. "I thought maybe you'd like to have your things," Richard said as they carried the heavy trunk into the room where Sarah had spent her earlier visit. They came back into the kitchen and the boy went downstairs while Richard stood in the middle of the room and asked, "Would you like me to fix you a bath?"

"Yes, a bath!" Clemmie exclaimed. "Wait until you see how Richard fixed up the spare room for me. It has a tub and everything."

He took a large copper boiler from a hook high on the pantry wall, lifted it onto the stove, and then filled it with several buckets of water that were standing on the floor behind the stove.

He was about to lift the stove lid when Sarah hurried over and said, "Let me take care of the fire."

"Of course not!" he protested gallantly.

Without thinking she brushed him aside brusquely, as Big Mary might push someone aside who was infringing upon her territory around her stove. "You won't believe what I've been doing. Building a fire so I can have a bath is nothing."

He shrugged and let the lid fall back into place on the stove. "If you insist."

"If there's one thing you learn in a lumber camp, it's how to build a fire."

"A lumber camp? Is *that* where you've been?" Clemmie wondered if she had heard right.

Richard turned around just as he was going out the door and said, "If you call me when the water's hot, I'll come back up and see it gets into the tub."

Clemmie nodded to him and waved him away impatiently. "Have you Sarah? Have you really been in a lumber camp?"

Sarah finished stoking up the fire. "Yes. Believe it or not, that's where I've been."

Clemmie looked as though Sarah had said she had been sojourning in hell.

"I need to get out of these clothes so I can think straight." Sarah said, the prospect of a bath making her men's clothing feel even more oppressive.

"I know!" Clemmie exclaimed, as if she had just had a sudden revelation. "Your brother. You found your brother, Jesse. You must have been there with him. That's it, isn't it?"

"No," she said flatly. "I don't have a brother." In her mind's eye she saw White Feather standing next to a birch bark canoe.

All at once she felt the urge to spill the whole sordid mess, as if she were getting rid of rotten food by dumping it into the slop bucket at Camp Seven.

"I'll tell you the whole story, Clemmie, just as soon as I get a bath. Right now all I want to do is get out of these clothes and take a good long soak." Maybe after that she'd be able to think straight, and talk straight.

"You don't have to tell me anything at all if you don't want to," Clemmie said politely, her face plainly showing that she didn't really mean a word of it and wanted to hear absolutely everything.

"I think it's high time I tell *somebody*," Sarah said. "It sometimes feels like I can't think straight anymore. Maybe talking about it will help."

Sarah finished her tea, along with some fresh bread and some cheese. Then Clemmie took her into her old room and showed her the tub, which sat behind a screen. Sarah let out a groan of pleasure at the sight of the tub. There was a mirror on the wall behind it, with a shelf under it that held combs and brushes and several jars of bath salts.

"Help yourself to whatever you need," Clemmie said, after Richard and the young man had come back upstairs and filled the tub. She motioned to the bath salts and to the bath linens hanging on bars on the wall. "Enjoy your bath. Soak as long as you like. I'm going to sew for a while. Wait until you see the darling little nightgown I'm making. I've finally mastered my sewing machine."

"I'm sorry, Clemmie. I've been so rude! You haven't had a chance to...."

"Never mind all that," Clemmie assured her with a flap of the wrist. "Right now what you need is a bath. This baby isn't going anywhere. We'll have more than enough time to talk about it before it gets here."

The door closed and Sarah stood looking around her. It was almost too much to bear. She began to tear at the layers of men's clothing she had worn for what seemed an eternity. She tugged violently at the breast bindings and they became tangled and she had to slow down and carefully unwind them. Then she crumpled them up in disgust and tossed them into the wastebasket. She didn't want to look at them ever again.

She poured a handful of lavender bath salts into the tub and then stood naked, letting the fragrance of the warm steam float up and over her. She felt the tension beginning to ease from her body as she stepped into the tub and slid down into the water, letting it surround her in a fluid, sensual embrace. She breathed deeply, closed her eyes, and gave in to it.

When the water began to cool and she was ready to get out of the tub, she looked at her hands, turning them over slowly and noticing that they were red and raw. "My goodness! I've ruined my hands with lye soap!" She wondered dismally if she'd ever look like a lady again.

The first thing she did after her bath and a shampoo was fix her hair the way it had once been. Because she had let it grow and had worn it in a braid it was now long enough so she could create a semblance of her old coiffure. She pulled it back off her face so that the widow's peak was again visible. As she looked into the mirror she saw that her skin had taken on a new color. She looked healthier than she ever had. She touched her cheeks with her fingertips, then turned from one side to the other, examining her face. It was indeed a woman's face, and she barely recognized herself.

Even with Clemmie's willing help it took her most of the afternoon to get her clothes in order. She was thankful that the camphor she had put into the trunk had kept the insects away, but they needed a good airing. More troubling, however, was how poorly they fit.

"Oh Clemmie," she wailed. "Look at how fat I've gotten! Nothing fits me anymore!"

Clemmie dropped her head back and laughed. "You don't know what fat is," she said, patting her own stomach. Clemmie looked her up and down, her head cocked to one side, a finger resting on the side of her face. Then she reached out and tugged at the waistline of the dress Sarah had just put on. "Look at this," she said. "You certainly haven't gained any weight here. The waistline is way too loose."

Sarah pulled at the bodice of the dress, annoyed. "But look at this. It all seems to have settled in my bosom. I certainly didn't eat *that* much!"

"That isn't from food, my Dear," Clemmie said with a teasing smile. "That's maturity. It seems you've spent the summer disguised as a boy while you grew into a woman behind your back."

Sarah groaned. "I feel betrayed by my own body!"

Clemmie looked at Sarah, her pretty face suddenly serious. "There have been many times during the last months when I felt my body was taking a journey against my will. I'm sure before it's all over I'm going to wish many times that I could turn back. I sit in church on Sundays and try to accept that my life is following a pattern that God has willed for me. Sometimes I believe it and sometimes I don't. I think I've finally come to accept something my mother has always told me. It does no good to fight against the inevitable." She put her hands on her stomach, feeling the baby stir. "You're a woman Sarah, just as I am, and being a woman comes in a package that includes blood and babies and breasts."

Sarah stared at Clemmie, the words resonating inside her head. Then she put a hand on Clemmie's arm and said, "I'm ready to talk."

"Good," said Clemmie.

They went into the parlor and sat sideways on the loveseat facing each other. Clemmie had an expression of patient anticipation on her face, and Sarah's face was filled with nervous uncertainty.

"I don't know where to begin."

Clemmie squeezed Sarah's hand. "At the beginning, Dear. Begin at the beginning."

"The beginning. Yes, that's it. I'll begin at the beginning."

She talked for nearly two hours, explaining everything that had happened, beginning with that awful night when she crept down the stairs of her aunt and uncle's home in Boston and learned that her whole life had been a lie. She told Clemmie her real name. She told her about the father who had deserted her, and about what her mother had become. She told her about the uncle who had stolen her inheritance and the uncle who had refused to help her. She told her about her former fiancé—but not *everything*, of course. How could she?

She only told her that the man whom she had loved had betrayed that love the minute he learned her money was gone; even though she had nothing to do with the loss of that money. She told her about coming West to find her father, and about how she got the idea to go to work at Camp Seven, and all that had happened since.

She hadn't realized how badly she needed to talk, and once she began, she couldn't stop. She did manage, however, to gloss over the part about beginning to care too much for Thor.

Clemmie listened, thunderstruck, alternatively gasping and asking a question now and then, but usually simply nodding in stunned disbelief. The part about stabbing Sawtooth Leverty caused Clemmie to clasp her hands over her mouth and let out a scream of horror. Other than for several such outbursts, she listened with rapt attention.

When she started telling Clemmie about the last days in camp, and how her father's sadness over his "other" family had such a strange effect upon her, the tears began. Clemmie slid close to her on the loveseat and put her arm around her shoulder and gently pulled her head onto her shoulder, stroking her hair with one hand.

"Sh, sh, sh," Clemmie whispered. "It must be terrible finding out after all those years that you really do have a parent, and then having to watch him grieve over the loss of a child when he seems to have so casually abandoned *you*."

Sarah nodded, the tears now flowing uncontrollably. Clemmie had hit the nail on the head and now all the resolve she had felt yesterday about accepting that she was an orphan seemed to be gone and in its place was an awful, soul-wrenching hurt.

"But don't you see? You don't know anything about the circumstances of his leaving your mother. You're assuming some things about him that may not be true."

"How could he not have known about me?" Sarah sobbed. "My mother wouldn't have willingly gone off and done what she did if she had any other choice."

"You don't know that, Sarah," Clemmie insisted gently.

"Yes I do!" she said, her sobs subsiding. "I can feel it. In here." She pressed her crossed hands over her heart.

"Could it be that you feel that way because you *want* to feel that way?" Clemmie asked. "Maybe you're protecting yourself. Maybe it's easier to convince yourself that he never cared about you and doesn't care now, than to risk opening your heart to him and being hurt again."

Sarah stared at her, not wanting to believe the words, but knowing somewhere deep inside that Clemmie was right.

"Maybe you're right. I...I just don't know." On the wagon on the way to town she thought she had it all figured out. Now she had to face the very real possibility that she had only been fooling herself.

"I don't want to put thoughts into your head, Sarah," Clemmie said quickly, seeing the confusion on her face. "All I'm saying is that I think you should consider the possibility that you could be all wrong about your father." She patted Sarah's knee and stood up. "It seems to me you've had your mind on this long enough for one day. Let's take a walk, and I'll tell Richard his supper is going to be late."

"Isn't all of this too much for you?" Sarah asked, worried that she was leaning too heavily on Clemmie in her delicate condition.

"Not at all! I'm just fine."

"Honestly?" Sarah asked, thinking Clemmie might be pretending for her sake.

"Honestly." Then Clemmie paused, thought a moment, and said, "Except for my legs. I was sick for the first three months and as soon as I began to feel better the veins in my legs began to pop out. Mother says she had the same trouble when she carried me." She reached down and lifted her skirt to exhibit her wrapped legs. "You should see them without their bandages! No, maybe you shouldn't. You might never want to be a mother."

"I don't think there's much danger of that happening," Sarah said, smiling ruefully. "I'll be ready in a moment. I need to go wash my face. I hate it when I cry."

Clemmie looked sternly at her. "Be grateful for your tears. Sometimes a good cry is the best medicine."

Sarah nodded and smiled. "You're right. I really do feel much better."

"Good! Then go ahead and wash those tears away and let's be on our way."

Richard saw them when they came down the stairs and he gave Sarah an admiring whistle. "You certainly do look fine. Wherever you've been, it agreed with you."

Sarah blushed and Clemmie said, "My own husband..." she gave him a look of mock admonishment and continued, "can't take his eyes off of you."

Richard cleared his throat. "Now, Clemmie...."

"Never mind, Dear. It's just what the doctor ordered for Sarah right now, so I'm not going to be angry with you." She playfully patted him on the cheek and said, "We're going for a walk. I want to show Sarah the new part of town, and we're going to have an ice cream cone. Your supper is going to be a bit late. I'm sure you don't mind."

He frowned at her and asked, "Are you sure you should walk all the way to the ice cream parlor?"

"Yes, Clemmie, are you sure?" Sarah said, turning toward her. "Maybe we should stay here and...."

"Nothing doing," Clemmie said firmly, taking Sarah's arm and leading her toward the door. "I'll lean on you if I need to. I can't think of a single thing I'd rather do."

Sarah looked over Clemmie's shoulder at Richard and said, "I promise I'll take good care of her."

He looked skeptical, but he nodded and said, "Very well. But don't stay gone too long or I'll have to come looking for the two of you. I don't want you running off and taking Clemmie with you."

"Richard!" Clemmie said reproachfully. "Sarah had a very good reason for doing what she did, and it was none of our business where she went. All that matters is that she's back. Don't you dare make a fuss and spoil it for us."

"I'm not making a fuss," Richard protested. "It's just that I figure I deserve some kind of an explanation." He had been thinking about Sarah all afternoon, wondering if she might be a bad influence on his wife.

"I'll explain later," Clemmie said with a toss of a hand in his direction.

She saw the worried expression on Sarah's face as they walked out the door. "Don't worry. I won't tell him any of the juicy parts. What he doesn't know won't hurt him."

As they crossed the road onto the boardwalk, Clemmie said eagerly, "I never did get a chance to show you around Pine Crescent when you were here before. There's much more to show you now. Just wait until you see the new businesses that have come to town since you left. There's a millinery shop, a dress shop—and of course the ice cream parlor."

"All this in so short a time?"

"Yes. And that's not all. There's a boarding house run by a widow from back east. A respectable boarding house, too. No whores allowed. And we have a lawyer. And there's a doctor coming next month. In fact I hope he's here to deliver the baby so the doctor doesn't have to come all the way from Hinckley."

"That's wonderful. Why all this growth in only one summer?"

"Settlers. There's getting to be more and more of them. As the timber comes down, the farmers move in. And as soon as there are men who bring their families with them—not like the lumberjacks and the railroad men who come alone—they begin to need things besides saloons and brothels. Isn't it exciting? And they're building a Lutheran church. And the school is nearly finished. Why, before you know it, Pine Crescent will be as big as Hinckley!"

"Maybe I should try to find a job right here in Pine Crescent," Sarah said thoughtfully. She had shared her past with Clemmie, but hadn't touched on the future. Probably because she had no idea what she was going to do. She knew she didn't want to go back to Camp Seven, but beyond that, she didn't have a plan.

"I think that's a wonderful idea! Then we can see each other all the time. I want you to be the baby's Godmother."

"Clemmie!" Sarah stopped and looked at her. "Do you really mean it?" She looked thoughtful. "But what about Richard? Will he approve?"

"Approve? Of course he will. And even if he doesn't, he hasn't any choice. He gets to choose the Godfather."

"I think I'm going to like Pine Crescent," Sarah said, squeezing Clemmie's arm.

She felt accepted. She was beginning to have an appreciation for the people in the West. She had a growing sense that one was judged by what one was today, and that folks didn't bother much about what you were before you arrived. And they certainly didn't judge a person based upon the exalted status of some dead ancestor.

They were standing directly across from the hotel when Sarah looked across the street and let out a little cry of panic.

"What? What is it?" Clemmie asked, alarmed.

"It's Red Scanlon and Paddy Roark! From Camp Seven! My God! Where can I hide? They'll see me!"

Clemmie followed Sarah's gaze to where the two lumberjacks were coming out of the barbershop and heading toward the hotel. She immediately relaxed and took Sarah's arm and guided her back into motion. "Don't be silly! They'd never recognize you in a hundred years, especially from across the street. Just keep walking."

Sarah did as she was told, but she whispered nervously, "They're watching us."

"Of course they are," Clemmie said impatiently. "Look at you. They're men. They're *supposed* to notice women who look like you.

"But then, on the other hand, if they're gentlemen, they're supposed to look the other way when they see a fat pregnant lady." She giggled. "We probably have them all confused about whether to look or not."

"You're a rascal, Clemmie Vogel," Sarah said, unable to suppress a giggle of her own, despite her apprehension about being recognized.

The two men disappeared into the hotel and Clemmie and Sarah continued walking. "You know, Sarah, there's something about your stay in Camp Seven that you didn't 'fess up about."

"What? I told you everything that happened. If I left something out it's because it wasn't important." She stopped walking and looked at Clemmie, who was eyeing her suspiciously. "Honestly, Clemmie, what are you talking about?"

"I didn't want to bring it up before, but now that you're feeling better...."

"Out with it! What are you talking about? What could I possibly be keeping from you? I've bared my entire soul to you!" Sarah was hurt that Clemmie could even think she wasn't telling her everything. She had lied plenty, but not to Clemmie—at least not this time.

Clemmie's face broke into a mischievous grin and she turned and started walking again. "You spent the whole summer with Thor Nilsson, and you can't tell me you didn't find him irresistible—even just a little bit?"

"Clementine Vogel! What in the name of heaven are you talking about? And who ever heard of somebody being a 'little bit' irresistible?"

She had purposely not spoken of her feelings for Thor; partly because she didn't want to seem a fool—and partly because she was as yet too unsure about what she really felt to be able to talk about it with any kind of clarity. She had presented him as simply the boss and nothing more.

"Listen here, Sarah. Don't you go trying to pull the wool over my eyes. I've *seen* Thor Nilsson." She sighed and placed one hand over the other and pressed them dramatically against her breast. "He's...he's absolutely the most handsome man I've ever laid eyes on."

"Clemmie! And you a married woman!" Sarah said, trying to find a way to change the direction this conversation was taking.

"I'm married, not blind! And you spent the whole summer with him. Don't try to tell me you didn't notice what he looks like. I've seen him in a crowd of lumberjacks, and he's like...well, he's like...like a magnificent palomino stallion prancing around in a herd of mules!"

"Clemmie!"

"Don't *Clemmie* me. Out with it. Tell me what's been going on."

"Going on? Nothing! Nothing has been going on! How could you even think such a thing?"

They stood challenging each other stubbornly for a few moments, and finally Sarah's face softened. Clemmie was turning out to be a very wise lady.

"He thinks I'm a boy, remember? How could anything be going on? Besides, he...he's in love with someone back in Sweden." She paused and looked into the road where she had first seen the Mud Man. It all seemed so very long ago. She sighed a deep sigh and was quiet.

Finally, after several minutes when neither of them spoke she looked back at Clemmie and said, "He's going back to Sweden. He thinks he needs to get even with her for marrying someone else."

"Oh pshaw," Clemmie said, fluttering a hand at Sarah and taking her arm and starting to walk again. "He's been saying that ever since he came to the timber, but he's still here."

"And what makes you so certain you know what Thor Nilsson is planning to do?"

"Everyone knows the story of Thor Nilsson and his Swede woman. It's all part of the lore. Folks around here haven't had much else to talk about up to now. The lumbermen and the railroad men. That's been about it. And when one of them looks like Thor Nilsson, well…. He *looks* like the stuff of legends. Don't you think? A veritable golden Viking God!"

Clemmie feigned a swoon and Sarah looked at her with disgust and said, "Ugh! You're making me nauseous."

They had just reached the front of the new millinery shop and Clemmie stopped and pointed at the name on the window. *Agnes Witherspoon, Milliner.* "Never mind. Let's go inside. You can tell me all about Thor later."

"But there's nothing to tell, I swear to you…."

Clemmie opened the door to the millinery shop, patted Sarah on the cheek and said, "Don't ever get into a serious poker game, my dear; if you do, you'll lose all your money."

CHAPTER 28

THE next morning Sarah wrote a long letter to Katie and sent her the money she owed her, along with a little extra. Then she and Clemmie spent the day together. They looked at the baby clothes Clemmie had sewn and the ones her mother had sent from Kansas, they walked to the site where the new church was being built and they strolled through town.

However, amid the pleasure of having nothing to do except relax and enjoy herself, feelings of uneasiness kept intruding. While she had been at Camp Seven she had a place to stay and plenty to eat and she had gotten paid for it. Her money wouldn't last long though, so she had to find some kind of work—soon.

***

At supper that evening she talked to Richard about possible jobs in Pine Crescent. He said, "I don't know, Sarah. There don't seem to me to be very many jobs for women around here. A man and his wife own the restaurant and they handle everything by themselves. Same thing for the ice cream parlor. And Mrs. Witherspoon doesn't have anyone working for her in the millinery shop except the boy who helps me around here sometimes. She has him deliver things for her and he brings her supplies when they come in on the train. Maybe you'd have better luck in Hinckley. That's a much bigger town." He looked thoughtful for a moment, as if he had just remembered something. "Did you tell Clemmie you did some clerking while you were working for Nilsson?"

Sarah nodded. "Yes. And I liked it a whole lot better than working in the kitchen or the bunkhouse, I can tell you."

Clemmie wrinkled her nose in disgust at the picture she had formed in her mind of the bunkhouse from what Sarah had told her.

Richard continued, "George Hermann came in today and bought a ticket to Hinckley. Said he was leaving Smitheson because he got a better offer from the Brennan mill up there."

"Really?" Clemmie asked eagerly, looking from her husband to Sarah and then back again. "Wasn't he one of the bookkeepers?"

"Yup. Maybe there's a chance that job is open. He told me it all happened kind of sudden. Seeing as how you worked for Nilsson as his clerk, maybe they'd consider hiring you. I don't see any harm in asking."

"I will," Sarah said. "I appreciate your telling me about it."

"Think nothing of it. I like seeing Clemmie happy, and having you around seems to do that."

Sarah had grown silent and Clemmie asked, "Is something wrong? Don't you feel well?" Sarah folded her hands in her lap and looked down at her plate. "I guess I'm not very hungry." She pushed her chair back and looked apologetically at Richard. "I just remembered. I can't ask Smitheson for a job. Someone will recognize me and then...."

"Oh hogwash," he said. "If someone recognizes you as the boy who worked at Camp Seven, deny it."

"But...." she protested.

"If you worked hard enough to satisfy Big Mary and Thor Nilsson, there's no question you can satisfy Smitheson. They won't care where you came from as long as you do your job. Just tell them you have the kind of face that reminds people of someone."

She looked back and forth from Richard to Clemmie, and both of them seemed to think it was a perfectly logical approach to take. She slid her chair back to the table. "I'll do it," she said.

The next morning she dressed carefully, her hair somewhat more conservative than she liked it. Clemmie told her she looked very nice and very businesslike, so right after breakfast she headed for Smitheson's.

The road was busy with groups of jacks coming and going, all of them looking at Smitheson's for work in the camps. They looked at her as she passed, but merely smiled politely and walked on. She decided jacks looking for work were less unruly than jacks looking for a good time at Ginger's. She was relieved she didn't recognize any of them, but she feared it was only a matter of time before she would. But she couldn't worry about that now. Her main concern was to find a job.

When she got to the lumber mill, she went directly to the office where she had first met Big Mary. She went inside and was surprised to see the room crowded with lumberjacks. Luckily, none of them were from Camp Seven. They stared at her, but she ignored them and walked directly to the job board to see if they were advertising for a job that sounded like the one George Hermann had vacated.

There were dozens of openings for lumberjacks and cookees at the various camps, as she had expected. She examined the board carefully, and sure enough, in the upper right hand corner was a notice that they were looking for an assistant bookkeeper in the office. The pay was more than three times more than she had earned as a cookee, and she calculated that it would be enough for her to get by on.

"Can I help you, Miss?" a voice asked over her shoulder.

She turned and looked into the eyes of a short, stout young man with a round face and a receding hairline. His shirtsleeves were rolled up and he had a pencil stuck behind his ear. He was rudely looking her up and down.

She gave him a look that told him she didn't like being ogled and said, "Yes you may. I'm looking for the job of...."

He didn't let her finish her sentence. "A job? For whom? For your husband?" He was still staring at her, but he kept his eyes on her face.

"If I *had* a husband, he could find his *own* job. I'm looking for work for myself. As a bookkeeper."

Most of the men in the room were listening with one ear to their conversation. It was quite a novelty to see a woman in a lumber mill office looking for a job; and a beautiful woman, at that.

"We don't need a bookkeeper," he said brusquely, aware that all the men were waiting to see how he was going to handle the situation.

She reached up and took the thumbtack out of the advertisement for the assistant bookkeeper, jammed the thumbtack vigorously back into the board and handed him the slip of paper. "It says here that you're looking for an assistant bookkeeper to start next week, and fortunately for you, that just happens to fit my schedule."

"Smitheson doesn't hire women," the man said, forcefully tacking the paper back onto the board. Then he turned away from her. That was that, as far as he was concerned.

At that moment, the front door opened and Thor Nilsson walked in. He had driven in with the wagon to drop Big Mary at the train for her trip to Duluth to visit her sister. His next stop was Smitheson, where he was going to check if Jesse Williams had told them whether or not he was coming back to Camp

Seven. It was to be the first step he took in trying to find her and bring her back to Camp Seven. The last thing in the world he had expected was to find her so fast—and to find her out of her disguise!

He made his way through the crowd to where Sarah stood glaring at the back of Smitheson's chief accountant. It would be difficult to say which of them was more astonished to see the other, but it was Thor who managed to speak first. "We meet again," he said with forced politeness.

She couldn't think straight, because the sight of him affected her in the most unimaginable way. It was that damnable fluttering in her stomach again. She struggled to get a grip on herself, but when she opened her mouth nothing came out.

He stared at her for a moment, and then made a motion with his head toward the job board. "If you're looking for a hotel again, they don't put ads for hotels up on Smitheson's job board."

Damn you, she thought. He was so infuriating! "I was hoping to find a job. Mr. Vogel at the depot tells me George Hermann has left and I was hoping to get his job." *Why in the world am I telling him this?*

In the space of several seconds he had assessed the situation and decided she must no longer intend to pretend she's Jesse Williams. There sure wasn't much sense trying to bring her back to camp.

Besides, there was no way she could come to camp looking like this! The men would riot!

He motioned with his head, this time toward the accountant who had dismissed her so summarily. "What did he say?"

Was he going to help her? He looked downright concerned. "He said Smitheson doesn't hire women."

"Hey, Peter," he called to the stout man, who turned around and looked at him.

"The young lady wants to apply for George's job. What did you tell her?"

"I told her Smitheson doesn't hire women, if it's any of *your* business." He never did like Thor Nilsson. He was too arrogant and pushy for a thick-skulled lumberjack.

Thor was still trying to think, and trying not to let her know how shaken he felt. If he helped her get this job, at least then she'd stay in Pine Crescent. Maybe that would halfway satisfy Gray Wolf. He was trying hard not to consider his own satisfaction.

"You're wrong, Peter my friend. Smitheson *does* hire women. Big Mary's been with us for how long now?" Thor went over and put his arm around Peter's shoulder and patted him patronizingly.

Sarah could see that the little man was furious, but he couldn't seem to think of anything to do or to say. Neither could she.

"Is John in his office?" Thor demanded.

"Yeah," several of the lumberjacks said in unison, fascinated by the goings on between the Push from Camp Seven, the fat little accountant, and the woman who had the guts to be asking for a man's job.

"Come with me, Miss.... I'm sorry, I can't remember your name."

That's because I never told you my name, you brute, she thought. Did he know who she was, or did he simply remember her from the mud. Surely if he knew she had been pretending to be Jesse Williams he wouldn't be able to keep that knowledge from exploding into the room. She hadn't the faintest idea why he was trying to help her, but she didn't know what else to do but to go along with him.

"Sarah Stewart. My name is Sarah Stewart." She said it so softly he could barely hear.

"What did you say?"

"Sarah Stewart is my name," she said again, this time loud enough so everyone in the room heard it.

"Follow me," he said, walking over and knocking on one of the closed office doors.

Peter's face was growing redder by the minute. He brushed past several of the lumberjacks, pushing them aside and trying to ignore their smart-aleck sneers. Nilsson was actually trying to go over his head!

Thor didn't wait for an answer, but instead opened the door without waiting to be invited in. John Smitheson looked up from his desk and then stood up and walked around it, smiling broadly, his arm outstretched to shake Thor's hand. "What in tarnation are you doing in town, you malingering son-of-a-bitch? You got my roads done?"

Then he saw Sarah. "Sorry, Miss. I didn't mean to use such inappropriate language in front of a lady." He was limping slightly, and Sarah remembered him as the man with the cane who had been at the depot the day she arrived in Pine Crescent. He seemed not to remember her.

Peter Knox pushed his way around Thor and addressed his boss in an icy tone. "Mr. Nilsson seems to think I should hire this..." He jabbed a fat finger in the air in Sarah's direction, "this woman as my assistant."

"Calm down, Peter," John Smitheson said, giving him a stern look. "It's not good for you to get all riled up like this."

The accountant took a deep breath. It was growing more and more apparent that he was going to be overruled. He did some quick mental gymnastics and decided resistance wasn't very politic. "Of course, if Mr. Nilsson is prepared to vouch for the young lady's ability...." he said, quickly making a hundred and eighty degree turn in his sentiments regarding hiring women. "We can't pay her the same wage as we'd pay a man if we hired a new one."

"I don't see why not. We pay Big Mary the same wage as any other cook in the pineries. This doesn't seem any different," Thor insisted.

Sarah could only stand dumbly listening to what was going on around her. Why was he doing this for her? He couldn't possibly know she had pretended to be a boy. If he knew she had fooled him, he'd be flying into an uncontrollable rage over having been deceived.

He was talking, his tone smooth and convincing. "I think you should give the young lady a chance. This town can use a few more women," he said, winking so Sarah couldn't see it.

The accountant looked resolved and a trifle cowed. John Smitheson said, "Sure. Whatever you say. If you want us to hire this young lady, then we'll give it a try. Have her fill out an application, Peter." Thor was about to protest, but John held up a hand and said, "It's just a formality, Nilsson. She can fill out the necessary papers on Monday morning when she comes to work."

"Good," Thor said amiably, satisfied. He turned toward Sarah. "Anything else I can do for you, Miss Stewart?"

"N...no. Thank you. I...." She didn't know what to say to him, so she turned to John Smitheson and said, "Thank you, Sir. You won't be sorry."

"I'm sure I won't," he said, glancing at Thor as he shook Sarah's hand. "See you on Monday."

"Seven sharp," Peter cut in, trying to once again assert some authority.

Sarah nodded to him and left the room without looking at Thor again.

After she left, John Smitheson closed the office door and motioned for Thor to sit down. "Okay. What the hell's going on here? You looking to bed that pretty piece?"

Thor thought about it for a moment and then said, "I don't think so. This is going to be a tough one for me to explain to you."

"Try," John said, leaning back in his chair and folding his arms over his stomach, his fingers linked. Thor Nilsson may have been his best foreman, but he was going to have to explain why he was meddling in their hiring of a book-keeper—which wasn't any of his business.

Thor shifted nervously in his chair. "It has something to do with Gray Wolf...."

"How is the old buzzard? Still out in the woods with that Indian woman? What was her name? White something. He brought her in here once. Beautiful woman."

"Her name's White Feather. No. He's back in camp."

"What's he doing back in camp? He sure can't be looking for a job. He's got enough money stashed away to buy me out and have some left over."

"White Feather had a baby boy, but he died."

John paused for a long moment. "I'm real sorry to hear that," he said. "I lost a son myself, you know. Poor little guy died of pneumonia when he was barely two years old. Tell Gray Wolf I'm real sorry."

"I'll tell him. He's taking it real bad, so I talked him into coming to Camp Seven and helping out for a while. Figured it would do him good to be working. Get his mind off things."

John cleared his throat, "Now what's all this got to do with the woman?"

"I need to ask you to trust me on this one. I can vouch for her and her ability, but I'm not free to talk about how. It has to do with Gray Wolf, like I told you."

John Smitheson was studying his face and Thor shifted uneasily again. Finally, John stood up and said, "Okay. I trust you know what you're doing. But if this thing doesn't work out, I'll have to let her go."

Thor stood up, too. "That's more than fair."

"Did you need to talk to me about anything else?"

"Oh yes. I almost forgot. Do you know anything about Big Mary's summer cookee, Jesse Williams, coming back to camp this fall as the clerk?" He'd better follow through on the Jesse business or someone was going to get suspicious.

"I think he was here a few days ago. Someone told me he came in and said we needed to find another clerk for Camp Seven."

"Did he say where he was going?" Thor asked, knowing damn well where he had gone, but continuing to fill in the cracks of Jesse's departure.

"Not as far as I know. You might ask Peter...."

"No. It's okay. He must have gone back to Chicago."

John put his hand on Thor's shoulder and walked him to the door. "You planning to be in town for a while?" He smiled a knowing smile. "The jacks tell me Lila's carrying a pretty hot torch for you and isn't too happy that you haven't been in to see her since last spring."

Thor frowned. "I get the feeling I'm pretty much done with whores. Must be getting old."

John dropped his head back and laughed, then straightened again and said, "And I suppose hell's about to freeze over!" He saw Thor's expression change and said quickly, "Now don't go getting all excited. If you're staying in town for a few days we need to talk about the roads, and about how many men you need to start the season."

"Why don't we do it now. You got time? I'm not sure how long I'm staying. One of the horses looks to be losing a shoe and I have to take him over to the livery stable to have it fixed. I might have to stay over."

That was only partly true. He wasn't sure how much longer he'd be hanging around town, or whether he'd be much in a talking mood if he did. He could feel himself getting madder and madder about the web of lies he was being forced to spin. He might need to get the horse's shoe fixed and get out of town fast, before he wrapped his hands around the throat of a certain lying female and strangled her.

CHAPTER 29

"**I** got the job," Sarah told Richard and Clemmie as they ate lunch together that same day.

"That's wonderful!" said Clemmie, clapping her hands together gleefully.

Sarah smiled to herself as she thought about the events in the office at Smitheson's, and Clemmie asked, "What's so funny?"

"Nothing. I was just remembering the look on the accountant's face when Thor...when Mr. Nilsson told him to hire me."

"Then I guess you've told Mr. Nilsson the truth," Richard said without looking up from his plate.

"The truth?" Sarah asked innocently, perfectly aware of what he meant, but annoyed at what seemed to be his change in attitude.

"Yes." He raised his eyes and looked straight at her, not bothering to disguise his disapproval. "About how you were pretending to be someone you weren't."

Clemmie gave him a stern look and said, "Now, Richard. That's not fair."

"It's okay," Sarah said, not wanting them to fight about something she had done. She looked at Richard and said calmly, "He didn't seem to recognize me, so I didn't bring it up. I thought it best to follow your advice."

"*My* advice?"

"You said I should deny I had pretended to be Jesse Williams if someone recognized me. I figured not bringing it up was the same thing."

"I see," Richard said, getting up from the table.

Clemmie put her fork down and gave her husband a look that would have put a layer of ice on top of a pail of hot water. "You did tell her that, Richard."

"I guess I did," he admitted grudgingly as he left the apartment.

After the door closed behind him, Clemmie said, with undisguised disgust, "Men!"

Sarah felt uneasy. "Now that I have a job I'm going to see if I can get a room over at the new boarding house."

"Absolutely not! Don't pay any attention to Richard. He's just having a hard time finding a place in his thinking for a woman like you."

Sarah thought about that for a moment and then said, "Why don't I stay until I'm settled into my new job. Then I'll leave."

"This is my house, too. I don't see why I should let him rule our home as if I'm nothing but an indentured servant."

"But Clemmie...."

"Men!" she repeated. "He thinks nothing of Ginger's girls servicing men right here in the middle of town! But when a woman tells a few untruths in order to get a job where she doesn't have to lie on her back with her feet in the air just so she can eat, he gets all uppity and judgmental about it."

Sarah studied Clemmie, not quite able to believe what she had just heard. "Have you and Richard been arguing about me?"

Clemmie looked away. "Maybe just a little." Then with her jaw squared and her mouth set in a stubborn line she said, "As far as Richard is concerned, there are only two kinds of women; good little wives and big bad whores. There's no in-between."

Sarah sat helplessly, not knowing what to say. She felt terrible. The Vogels had been so kind to her, and now they were fighting because of her. Finally she managed to say, "I'm so sorry, Clemmie."

"It's not your fault," Clemmie said quickly. "We've had these fights lots of times. He's such a blind fool. Sometimes I just cannot endure that man and the way his mind works."

"You don't mean that, Clemmie."

Clemmie's chin lifted defiantly. "Oh, but I do mean it."

"It's awfully nice of you to defend me, Clemmie, but I can't let you keep doing that. I don't want to see you and your husband at odds over me. It's unfair to you both. I should be settled in at Smitheson's with my job within a week or so and then I'm leaving. Besides, when the baby comes you won't have room for me."

Clemmie wanted to argue, but she knew Sarah was right on both counts. She couldn't fight a running battle with Richard in her present condition, and the spare room had to be converted into a nursery. But she wouldn't always be pregnant, and when she was back to her old self again, well then.... She reached across the table and covered Sarah's hands with her own. "As long as you know that you're my friend and that you're important to me. This business between

Richard and me has been going on ever since we first came here. You just gave him another reason to show his true colors. If he doesn't stop being such a stubborn mule, I'll take the baby and go back to Kansas to live with my parents." She got up and went to the stove and busied herself filling the teakettle from the reservoir on the side of the stove.

Sarah rose and pushed her chair in and stood with her hands on the back of it. "Don't you dare leave Pine Crescent! Now that I've decided to stay, you must stay, too." Then she smiled mischievously and said, "Besides, if you really do decide to get rid of your mule, you might consider going after that Palomino stallion you find so...what did you call him? Magnificent?"

Sarah raised her arms to defend herself against Clemmie, who was coming toward her brandishing a long-handled kettle, but wasn't going to be able to use it as a very effective weapon because she had sunk into a fit of giggles.

After they had cleared away the lunch dishes, Sarah suggested that they spend the afternoon doing some sewing for the baby. Clemmie refused, saying Sarah needed to take some time for herself before starting her new job. "Besides, I think I'll lie down for a while." She pressed her hands against the small of her back and arched backwards. "I'm feeling a bit achy, and I'll feel better after I rest."

"That's a good idea. I think I'll go to the dress shop and see about having some of my clothes altered. I'm tired of having the buttons on my bodice pop open."

"You go on ahead and do that. I'll see you later this afternoon."

A short time later, as Sarah walked along the boardwalk toward the dress shop, it occurred to her that she hadn't thought much about her father during the last few days. Finding a job had been good for her, even if she had to grudgingly admit that she had Thor to thank for it. She still couldn't figure out why he had helped her so graciously. When they had met last spring, he had been anything but gracious.

How, she wondered, would he act the next time she saw him? She didn't doubt for a moment that she would see him again, given they both still worked for Smitheson. She decided not to worry about it as she made her way along the boardwalk, smiling at people she passed.

It took her completely by surprise when a woman stepped out of the millinery shop and stood squarely in front of her, blocking her way. She took a small stumbling step backwards, caught herself, and then looked at the woman, startled.

"Wh...what are you doing?" she asked. She didn't realize who it was at first, because she wore a simple dark dress and a dark hat that partly covered her yellow hair.

"I knew I'd see you around here again one of these days," Lila said, looking Sarah up and down disdainfully.

Sarah felt an inexplicable surge of anger, replacing the pleasant feelings of only moments before. "Well now that you've seen me, let me pass." She tried to step around her but Lila kept stepping the same direction as Sarah stepped, effectively blocking her way. Sarah gave up trying to get around her and looked directly at her and said, in a voice that was far more ladylike than she was beginning to feel, "May I ask why you won't let me pass?"

"Where is he?" Lila asked, ignoring Sarah's question.

"Where is *whom*?" Sarah asked.

"You know very well *whom*," Lila sneered. "Thor! Where is he?"

Sarah's lips parted but no words came. Finally she managed to pull herself together enough to say, "Thor Nilsson? How should I know where he is? Let me pass. I don't have time for this nonsense."

Lila was blocking the boardwalk so no one else could pass, and a small group of interested onlookers began to gather on either side of them on the boardwalk, as well as down in the road next to them.

When Sarah realized that they were drawing a crowd she snapped, "I have no idea where Thor Nilsson is. Furthermore, I don't care. Now let me pass."

"You're a dirty liar," Lila sneered, reaching out a hand and giving Sarah's shoulder a push.

Sarah was again knocked slightly off balance and her temper flared. She had been through too much and had held too much inside for too long. Added to that, she had spent the summer in the crude, colorful world of the lumberjack.

Through clenched teeth she said, "Get out of my way, you jack-jumping Jezebel!"

People behind Sarah had stepped aside to let a man through to where the two women stood nose to nose.

"You looking for me, Lila?" Thor asked, having arrived just in time to hear her question and Sarah's response.

Sarah spun around and saw Thor, an amused expression on his face. "You...

you certainly do get around," she said, surprised that she was able to say anything at all.

"It's a good thing for you that I do," he said, his amusement increasing moment by moment.

"Well now that you're here, you can tell this...."

"Jack-jumping Jezebel?" he offered.

"Oh! You! You...." This time she couldn't find words, and she turned and tried to push her way through the onlookers. But nobody moved.

"Where've you been all summer?" Lila asked Thor, her voice so petulant that Sarah stopped trying to get away and turned to look at her.

Then her voice grew rancorous and she said, "I figured you was prob'ly with that...that uppity bitch." She tossed her head toward Sarah, who was looking first at Lila and then at Thor and then back again at Lila, completely stupefied by the goings on.

"Turns out I was," Thor said mischievously, trying not to look at Sarah.

"You were not!" Sarah shouted, aware that she was behaving like a fool, but unable to control herself. He was acting as if he *did* know she had pretended to be Jesse. But how could he?

The people around them were grinning and nodding knowingly and Sarah wanted to sink beneath the boardwalk and disappear. What a way to begin her new life as a citizen of Pine Crescent; standing in the middle of town fighting with a lumberjack and a whore! And listening to the lumberjack telling everyone within earshot that he had spent the summer with her!

"Is she better'n me or something?" Lila challenged, her face growing red with indignation.

"She's pretty damn skilled," Thor said, barely able to keep from bursting into laughter.

"Oh for God's sake," Sarah groaned, throwing her hands in the air in helpless frustration and then trying again to push her way through the throng now gathered around them. To her horror, as if things weren't already bad enough, Lila lunged for her and Thor had all he could do to grab her and hold her back before she did some real damage to Sarah's face.

"Cat fight!" somebody yelled, and the crowd began to grow even larger.

Thor had his arms around Lila's middle from behind, and she was screaming and kicking and flailing her arms. "You and your fancy clothes!" she screamed.

"You ain't no better'n me. He was mine until you came along, and you ain't havin' him!"

It was all like a bad dream, and Sarah stood and stared at her for a moment, and then said, with icy calm, "Settle down, Lila. You win. I've decided to let you have him."

Lila's eyes grew wide and she stopped struggling against Thor, who let go of her, as surprised as she was by what Sarah had just said. He began to sputter and choke and then he burst forth with a roar of laughter that infuriated Sarah to the point of absolute madness. She strode over and pushed Lila roughly aside, then raised one foot and brought it down with all the force she could muster on top of one of Thor's boots.

He looked down at his foot and then at Sarah, and with a twinkle in his blue eyes said, "You'll have to do better than that."

She was hopping mad and she sputtered, "Don't you dare laugh at me, you... you...."

"Let me see.... If she's a jack-jumping Jezebel, that must make me...hmmm...a Jezebel-jumping jack." Then he doubled over, his arms clutching his middle, convulsed with laughter.

Lila just stood there looking helpless and confused, and Sarah, too furious to even attempt speech, turned and tried once again to push her way through the crowd, her face and neck hot with repressed fury.

Thor stopped laughing and grabbed her by the arm from behind and she was forced to turn and face him. "Come on, Jesse...I mean Miss Stewart. I didn't mean to laugh at you, but it's the first time I ever saw a lady behave worse than...." He couldn't finish because he was laughing uncontrollably again.

Sarah stared at him for only an instant, realizing finally that he knew all about her disguise. But she was too angry to think about what that meant. Instead, she hauled back and punched him squarely in the jaw.

"That does it, you hothead!" he said, picking her up and tossing her over his shoulder, just as easily as he had done the night they met in Pine Crescent for the second time. He paused for a tension-filled moment and glared at the crowd blocking his path.

Magically, they all stepped aside to let him pass, as they had refused to do for Sarah. He carried her off to the sound of men cheering and calling after them, "Attaboy, Nilsson. Show her who's boss!"

No one was paying any attention to Lila, and she burst into tears as she stumbled from the boardwalk into the street and across to the other side where she scrambled up onto the boardwalk in front of Ginger's and then inside to safety.

Sarah kicked and pounded with both hands and feet and screamed until she grew hoarse, but it did little except make him walk faster, and no one seemed to be bothered by her distress. One man even tipped his hat to her as they passed. By the time they had traveled the quarter mile to the livery stable there was no one in sight to help her...even if someone had chosen to do so.

Thor decided quickly to take her to the livery stable where he had left the horses. He could think of no other place where they would be reasonably alone. He realized they were in a somewhat delicate situation, and suddenly Gray Wolf's face popped into his mind.

When they got to the livery stable, he called out, "Ezekial? Are you here?" Then he remembered that the owner of the livery stable said he couldn't fix his horse's shoe until morning, because he had to go out to one of the camps. *Good,* he thought. *Now we can be alone while I try to straighten out this she-cat.*

He carried her inside, looked around and spotted the ladder leading into the loft, oblivious to her shrieks and the blows she was landing on his back with her fists. He carried her effortlessly up the ladder and dropped her unceremoniously into a pile of hay.

She tried to scramble up, but her feet got tangled in the hem of her skirt and she fell backwards. He was standing over her, laughing again, and she lunged for his legs and knocked him off balance and he was unable to keep himself from falling on top of her.

He rolled off of her, not intending to hurt her by flattening her with his weight, but in one swift movement she was on top of him, straddling him, hitting at him wildly with both hands. In a movement just as swift, he grabbed both of her arms and rolled her onto her back and pinned her arms over her head. Now *he* was straddling *her.* She tried to rise up, but it was no use. She lay still, breathing hard, her eyes wild and filled with animal rage.

He was breathing hard, too, but he was no longer laughing. Things were not going as he had planned. They seemed to have crossed over into dangerous territory, and he wasn't sure he was going to be able to get back to safety.

Sarah could hear the horses below them snorting and moving about, made skittish by the presence of humans tussling in the loft above them, and she grew acutely aware of the smell of dust and the scent of the warm summer earth still lingering in the hay.

Thor was still straddling her, but even in the dimness of the windowless loft she could tell that something had changed. His hands were still holding hers down over her head, but their fingers had somehow become entwined, and all of a sudden he leaned over and kissed her searchingly. Then, just as suddenly, he let go of her hands and sat up. His breathing was labored and the effort he was making to control himself was palpable in the dark loft.

"My God! I've got to get out of here!" she cried, struggling to sit up. But then she gave up and fell weakly back into the hay. Neither of them spoke for a long moment, their breathing the only sound in the darkness. Sarah tried to think. She tried to put her thoughts into some kind of order about how he knew and when he knew, but her thoughts kept drifting aimlessly like dust motes in a shaft of light.

As for Thor, his brain had become useless. He couldn't think. He could only feel—and try to fight what he felt.

Then, as if they both knew exactly what they were doing, they reached for each other. Arms and legs and mouths became tangled together in an embrace fueled by the fires that had smoldered for far too long, but had finally burst into flame. Clumsily, he fumbled at the buttons on her bodice. Then he stopped what he was doing, and gasping for breath from the effort it took to restrain himself said, "If you want me to stop, you've got to tell me now!"

She let out a small whimper and nuzzled her face into the hollow of his neck. He smelled of something spicy from the barbershop where he had been that morning, and of wool grown damp from the heat of his body. She touched his neck with the tip of her tongue. He tasted of salt, and of fresh cedar boughs and of the crisp fresh air of the northern forests. She grew slightly dizzy and felt herself slipping down, down, down into a place from which she knew it would be difficult to return. She groaned, the only answer of which she was capable.

He moved his mouth back onto hers, wanting her more than he had ever wanted a woman. He slid his hand into the soft warmth of her breasts and felt her body arch upward. They clung together like two drowning souls, mouths frantically searching, tongues entwined as if they could never get their fill.

He pulled up her skirts, hotly aware of his erection against her smooth bare thigh. Then he hesitated, forcing himself to consider her virginity. It was no use, and when she didn't resist, his fingers slid into her wetness, searching. He found what he sought and the sweet pain of his touch made her cry out. He could wait no longer and he thrust himself into her.

In some obscure part of his brain he recognized that she was not a virgin. He wondered vaguely if Gray Wolf would kill him deader if she were. Somehow it didn't matter. All that mattered was the way she was arching herself toward him with each thrust, matching his intensity, surpassing it. She bit his lip, and he tasted blood. He winced and paused, then he bit her back, gently, and began to thrust again—not gently.

Then something was happening to her that she didn't quite understand. Something far beyond her control. She arched her back and pushed harder and harder upward again and again in a crazy crescendo until she shuddered and said over and over again, "Oh my, oh my, oh my!"

His movements slowed and he groaned softly and withdrew, rolling off of her and onto his back into the hay. She lay very still, wishing he had not moved away but would hold her in his arms. She wanted to talk to him—to try to explain why she had let this happen. Her feelings were out in the open, raw and oozing, like a bad burn, and she wanted to share them with the man who had brought them upon her.

But instead of moving toward her, he sat up with his back to her, his head down, his elbows on his raised knees and the fingers of both hands tangled in his hair. "No! Dammit all to hell! No!"

She jumped up and began groping in the dim light with her buttons, fighting the lump in her throat and trying not to wonder why he had suddenly grown so cold. Then she remembered what he had said about hating liars. Was that it? Was he sorry because he had made love to a liar? Her thoughts were now rushing at her—assaulting her. "Why did you help me get a job if you hate me so much?" she blurted.

He stared at her as if he had just returned from someplace far away. "Hate you? Help you?" He looked bewildered. Then he seemed to come back to himself. "You'd never have gotten that job if I hadn't walked in at exactly the right time," he said.

"What do you care?" she cried. "What do you care about...about anything! Besides, I didn't need your help!" She flopped down onto the hay and tried to tie a shoelace that had come loose during their tussle, her mind awash in hurt and confusion.

"Bullshit!" he roared, jumping to his feet. "You might be a damn good liar, but you aren't *that* good. If I hadn't shown up you'd have been out on your fanny in the cold before Peter Knox had time to give his balls a good scratch!"

"You arrogant swine!" She scrambled to her feet. "I don't have to stay here and be insulted and abused by you!"

He stared at her, his face distorted with emotions ranging from bewilderment to anger to helpless frustration, and then around again in a circle. Had he actually abused her? His thoughts were again spinning out of control. He threw both arms into the air and pumped his fists, letting out a yell that was loud enough to be heard in the next county. Then, also struggling to tie one of his boots so he could get the hell out of there, he lost his balance and fell into the hay.

"Damn you, Woman! You're driving me out of my mind! First you tell me a pack of lies and come to my camp pretending you're a boy and throw the whole damn place into a turmoil, then...." He got up again, this time having the struggle with the fly of his pants.

"I did not throw your camp into turmoil!" she hissed, then raised her voice to a timbre that matched his and shouted, "I did everything anybody told me to do, and I did it well! Is it my fault that...that piece of scum Leverty came after me?"

"That's another thing," he said, jabbing a finger at her. "I nearly killed a man over you!"

"Well really," she said, her voice suddenly calm and as cold as ice, "What's one more murder to you?"

They stood glaring at each other, both of them breathing hard, but this time not from lust.

Finally he said, "I did not kill that man, but he deserved what I *did* do to him. It was his choice not to live without his...." Silence, then, "He drowned himself. I had nothing to do with that part of it. I'd do exactly the same thing again. That poor little girl didn't deserve what he did to her. I'm glad he drowned himself. It's one less piece of shit in the world."

It didn't matter to her if he was telling the truth. All she knew was that they had made love and he seemed to have forgotten all about it. Here they were, standing in the hay screaming at each other in the same spot where they had lain passionately together only moments before.

She suddenly remembered Lila asking him if Sarah was better than she was and she got a sick feeling in the pit of her stomach. He hadn't enjoyed their lovemaking. It had been just an animal release for him and it was less than nothing to him now that it was over. For all she knew he might have done it out of revenge for her having duped him. She couldn't stand thinking about it, so she let out a small cry of frustration and scrambled down the ladder.

He knew he should stop her and make her understand why he couldn't let himself acknowledge what he felt for her. There was Gray Wolf and his promise to him. There was his promise to himself to go back home. What could he do? He didn't know what to do or what to say and knew only that what he had said thus far was all wrong, and what he had done was far worse than wrong.

"Goddammit!" he swore, letting the anger carry him away into a black rage until he found himself safely again in more familiar emotional territory.

CHAPTER 30

SHE hurried to the depot where Clemmie was in the midst of preparing supper. She looked up when Sarah came in, suddenly alarmed. "What's wrong? What happened?"

"I can't talk about it right now," Sarah said, her eyes full of fire. "I...I'll explain later."

Clemmie moved toward her and held out a hand to touch her, but pulled back when she saw that the fire was mixed with pain. She looked her up and down and saw how disheveled she was. "What happened? Have you been hurt?" she asked, alarmed now.

"No. No, it's nothing like that. I don't want to talk about it yet. Please try to understand. We'll talk later." She started toward her room and then turned and said, "Don't say anything to Richard."

Clemmie shook her head and said worriedly, "No. Of course I won't. I...I'll wait until you're ready to tell me what happened. As long as you aren't hurt...."

Sarah turned and ran into her room and slammed the door behind her, threw herself onto the bed and stared up at the ceiling, her breath coming in short gasps. "I hate you, Thor Nilsson!" she said aloud, not even caring if Clemmie heard her. Then she rolled over onto her stomach and let out a soft moan.

"No, I don't hate you. I love you. Oh Lord," she groaned. "What have I done!"

The torment she felt was almost more than she could bear. She wasn't sure she'd be able to live in her own skin any longer. Should she board the train and simply go away? But go where? The only life she could hope for was here in Pine Crescent, where she would at least be able to support herself. Her mind raced wildly until she knew she had to get control of her emotions. She got up from the bed and went to the window and opened it. Breathing deeply she smelled the familiar scent of pine. It calmed her somewhat, so she pulled a chair over in front of the window and sat quietly. She slowly became aware that the worse was over. Nothing she could possibly do could be any more shameful than what she had already done.

It was nearly dark when Sarah heard a gentle tapping on her door. "It's me, Clemmie. I brought you some tea and a little something to eat. May I come in?"

"Sure. Yes," Sarah said. She stood up and lit the lamp on her dresser, suddenly aware that it had grown dark. She must have been sitting by the window for several hours. She accepted the tray and sat down on the bed, motioning to Clemmie to sit in the chair. She badly needed the tea, but didn't have the stomach to eat the sandwich. "I'm really sorry I acted the way I did," Sarah said as she sat on the edge of her bed sipping the hot, soothing liquid.

"Do you want to tell me what happened?" Clemmie asked hesitantly. "You don't have to. I just thought maybe...."

Sarah sighed with resignation. "There's no sense trying to keep it from you. I'm sure by now everyone in town is talking about it."

Clemmie reddened. "Well, actually, Richard did hear something."

Sarah groaned.

"He didn't say much," Clemmie offered hurriedly. "Just that someone in town saw you and one of Ginger's girls...well, saw you talking...."

"Hah!" Sarah said wryly. "Talking would be putting it mildly."

She stood up and put her tray on the bedside table. "What time is it?"

"It's after six. I was going to call you for supper, but I decided you probably needed some time to yourself."

"I guess I did need to pull myself together." She looked down at her wrinkled dress just as Clemmie reached over and plucked a piece of hay from the folds of her skirt. Sarah blushed crimson and sat back down on the bed. "I might as well tell you what happened. Better for you to hear the truth from me than to listen to the rumors that are going to be flying around." She paused. "I had a run-in with your stallion and made a complete fool of myself."

Clemmie looked more interested now than worried. Her friend had, after all, survived whatever had happened. How bad could it be? "What were you and this woman....?"

Sarah interrupted saying, "Her name's Lila. We had a fight."

"You had a fight? What in the world about?"

"Not what. Whom. We fought over Thor Nilsson." All at once, the whole thing struck Sarah as terribly funny and she began to laugh. "I think I won."

"Tell me everything," Clemmie urged, sitting now on the edge of her chair.

Sarah told her about the fight and Clemmie squealed, "You called her what?"

"A...a jack-jumping Jezebel."

Clemmie gasped. "You didn't!"

"I did. And as if that wasn't bad enough, Thor said that then he must be a Jezebel-jumping jack and...."

Clemmie was now laughing too hard to hear what Sarah was trying to say, so she waited. When Clemmie again had control of herself Sarah told her about the rest of their altercation, and about his carrying her to the loft at the livery stable. Then she stopped, uncertain about whether to go on. "I don't think I should tell you the rest."

"Oh, but you must!" Clemmie cried, still wiping tears away from her laughter of only moments before.

"He...he kissed me." She decided there had to be limits to what Clemmie could accept about her.

"Oh!" Clemmie moaned, sinking back into the chair with both hands clasped to her chest. "Oh!" she said again.

"Did you kiss him back? Are you going to marry him?" Clemmie asked.

"Marry him? Good God no! Actually, I hope I never lay eyes on him again," she lied vehemently.

"That doesn't seem very likely," Clemmie said. "You're destined to keep running into each other." Then she seemed to be considering something. "Did he tell you he knows who you really are...or were?"

Sarah stood up. "He knows, but I have no idea how or when he found out." She thought for a moment. "Maybe he just put two and two together."

"Two and two?" Clemmie asked.

"Jesse quits his job as a clerk and then I show up and apply for a job as a bookkeeper. Maybe he.... Oh, I don't know! Is Richard furious?"

"Who cares how Richard feels. Tell me more about what happened and how you figured out he knew the truth."

"He called me 'Jesse' by mistake. That was the first indication. After that, well, it just became clear that he knew." A hot flush of shame swept over her. "I think I'd better find another place to stay right away."

Clemmie stood up. "Don't be absurd. Did someone see him carry you into the stable?"

"I...I don't think so."

"Well then don't worry about it. They can only *suspect* he carried you to...to his cave." She started to giggle. "All anybody knows for sure is that he carried you away. He may have taken you for ice cream, for all they know. There's no way for anyone to know he spirited you away so he could...so he could kiss you."

"Oh sure," Sarah said, but realized what Clemmie was saying was true. People could guess, but they couldn't know. Surely Thor wouldn't say anything, would he? What was he thinking now? Wasn't he too wrapped up with his 'Swede gal' to even care what happened with another woman? Her thoughts were in a terrible state of confusion. His lovemaking had seemed so...so real. Could it have meant nothing to him? Or was he afraid that being tangled up with her would force him to give up his stupid notion about going home to get revenge? Was that it? Or was it the lying business? If he really hated her for lying, how could he...?

"Don't be so worried," Clemmie assured her, seeing her distress. "I think you're going to be surprised by what people say."

"What do you mean, surprised?"

"By tomorrow morning everyone in town will know you're Thor Nilsson's woman and you'll be famous in Pine Crescent."

Sarah groaned and put a hand to her forehead. "Oh Lord! This is awful!"

"There's not a female alive who wouldn't gladly roll around in the hay with that man. Quit complaining."

Sarah looked at her in disbelief. "You're disgusting, Clementine Vogel! And we didn't exactly roll around in the hay. I told you he just kissed me and that was all." She hated the lies she was once again forced to tell, but how could she do otherwise?

Clemmie smoothed the front of her dress over the bulge that was growing larger every day. "You sure have added a new kind of excitement to my life, Sarah Stewart. I guess now I'd better stop hankering over that Palomino stallion. It looks like you've gone and closed that door for me. "Oh well," she said as she tossed her hands hopelessly into the air. "He probably wouldn't be interested in me right now anyway." She sighed. "I guess I'd better be content being a good little wife. Which reminds me, I'd better get back to Richard or he'll be worried about me. He thinks I get too upset over you. It's so annoying. I'm not so fragile that I can't be a good friend."

"And you surely are that," Sarah said, hugging her. "I think I'll come out, too."

"Are you sure? You don't need to make an appearance on my account."

Sarah frowned. "Should I not want to show myself? Is it that bad?"

Clemmie laughed nervously and said, "It isn't that it's bad. It's just that...."

"That I'm disgraced and should hide myself? Is that it?"

"No! Of course not! I just thought maybe you didn't want to deal with my husband on top of everything else you've been through."

"I appreciate your concern," Sarah said, without sarcasm, as she walked over to the door and opened it. Then she winked and said, "Let's confront the fire-breathing dragon together."

Clemmie laughed and followed her into the kitchen where Richard was sitting drinking a cup of coffee and reading the paper.

He looked up when the two women came into the room and said with a sly grin, "Well hello there, Miss Stewart. I hear you had quite a day."

"I did indeed. This morning I found a job and this afternoon I found out that I'm vying with a whore for Mr. Nilsson's affections. Fascinating, isn't it? Especially given that I don't give a hoot about his or anybody else's affections."

It caught Richard so by surprise that he coughed and sputtered and spit coffee all over the front of himself.

Clemmie didn't know what to say, so she just clamped both hands over her mouth and tried not to giggle.

Sarah smiled innocently at Richard and said, "I'm going outside for some fresh air." She held a hand up to Clemmie. "Don't worry, Dear. I'm going to sit out on the train platform. I'm not quite ready to venture into town."

"May I join you?" Clemmie asked. "It's a nice warm evening and I could use some fresh air, too."

Richard looked as if he was going to try to stop his wife, but immediately thought better of it and got up to clean up his mess and pour himself some more coffee. "Women," he mumbled as the door closed behind his wife and their visitor. Then he smiled to himself. "She's quite a woman," he admitted. "I can see how Nilsson could be taken with her." Then he chuckled. "Yes sir, she's quite a woman."

They sat outside for over an hour, but Sarah began to feel too weary to sit any longer. It had been a long day.

Later as she lay in bed her thoughts went back to that afternoon, which already seemed eons ago. There had been something primitive in the way he made love to her. The one time she had made love with Steven she had vowed not to let it happen again until after they were married. She knew she had ruined herself for another man, but she trusted that Steven would marry her. That wasn't anywhere near what she felt after making love with Thor. This wild man of the timber had made her blood scream in her veins and a fire rage throughout her entire body. Steven Caldwell, an educated physician, had done little to arouse any response in her except shame and determination not to let it happen again. If she felt shame about having made love with Thor it was only because of the niggling fear that perhaps she was just like her mother. The thought disturbed her in no small measure. She knew it mustn't happen again, but the reason wasn't that she didn't *want* it to happen again. Heaven help her; she *longed* for it to happen again!

She sat bolt upright, then got up and went to the window, forcing herself to remember how far she had come. "I simply will not let it! I want to be respectable. I want to be able to hold my head up." She would stop thinking about Thor and what had happened between them. She would put all of her energies into her new life in Pine Crescent. How strange life can be, she thought. Two men had put her life into turmoil and had driven her here. She thought bitterly of her uncle and of Steven Caldwell. Now two *different men* had her going around in circles.

"Curses on the whole pack of you!" she said aloud, looking out into the darkness. She felt a steely new determination. There was nothing to be done about her uncle and about Steven because that part of her life was finished. As for her father and Thor, although she didn't know what to do about them, there was one thing she did know; they were not going to destroy her. She would not run away like a frightened doe.

This time, come hell or high water, she would stand her ground!

CHAPTER 31

WHEN Thor got back to camp, he tried to avoid talking to Gray Wolf. It wasn't hard, because the weather suddenly turned cold and the camp began to fill with men. Within a week there were seventy-five men working at Camp Seven. Two men, in addition to Jock, were elevated to straw boss, directly under Thor. Seventy five men were too many for one man to manage alone.

Not only was the camp filled with men, but Red Scanlon now had fifty horses to care for. In addition to the horses that Smitheson owned and had been in camp for the summer, they leased additional horses from farmers in the area. Ten men were kept busy helping Red with the teams.

Big Mary settled quickly into the busy winter routine. Her bull cook was a burly Irishman who helped ride herd on the six new cookees. She thought about Jesse more than once, but as the season got into full swing she came to accept his absence. Thor said Jesse had gone back to Chicago and she had no reason not to believe him. It saddened her, but she soon got over it. She had been seasoned to overcome sadness.

Thor knew he couldn't avoid Gray Wolf forever, and early in the evening on the second Sunday after the camp filled with men, he went looking for him and found him behind the cook shack staring out at the cold black stream that flowed next to the camp.

"You've been avoiding me," Gray Wolf said matter-of-factly without turning, sensing Thor's presence.

Thor stood quietly behind him. He knew the time had come for them to talk. Gray Wolf had been so hot under the collar about him bringing his daughter back to Camp Seven that he had half expected to be met on the road by Gray Wolf before he even got back to camp. He had attributed Gray Wolf's surprising calm to his other miseries. Now, however, it seemed they were going to have to finally confront the matter of Jesse Williams.

Gray Wolf spoke again, softly. "Big Mary tells me you told her Jesse went back to Chicago, but I know that's a lie."

"She took a job in the office in town," Thor said as he sat down next to Gray Wolf and let his eyes scan the waters of the stream.

"Smitheson's. I already know that."

Thor glanced sideways at him. "How's that?"

"Bad news spreads fast."

"Bad news?"

"You were supposed to bring her back here, not help her stay away."

"I didn't know what else to do. It was pretty clear to me she was done pretending to be someone she's not." He knew full well who she really was and was having a heap of trouble keeping his mind clear of her.

"I've decided to buy a farm," Gray Wolf said out of the blue.

"What?" Thor asked, astonished. Was he going to bring up that settling-down business again?

"There's a nice piece of land up north a little ways. I've had my eye on it. It's high. Not marshy like a lot of the land around here. One side of the property slopes down to a lake. Real pretty."

"What's that got to do with the girl?"

"My father hated farming," he continued, as if they had not been talking about Sarah at all. "When my grandfather died, he sold the old place and built a shoe factory." Gray Wolf shrugged and said, "I guess it was the right thing for him. Made him rich. But I hated the place. I spent a lot of time with my grandfather on the farm, and I guess it stuck with me." Staring at the stream he appeared deep in thought.

Then he seemed to make up his mind about something and said, "The older I get the more I get the urge to settle down. Farm's a good place to stay put." He was silent then, and Thor continued to watch him, wondering what was coming next.

Finally Gray Wolf smiled wanly and said, "You're looking at me like I've lost my mind. I haven't. You know I've been thinking about this for a long time. We talked about it when you came to camp with the boy...girl. Anyway, I'm going to try to get White Feather to come with me."

"You told me White Feather wouldn't have anything more to do with you."

"She's had some time to think."

"She wanted you to make peace with your...your daughter. How will you explain that you didn't?"

"I'm going to tell her the white man's God works in strange ways, and that so far making peace with my daughter doesn't seem to be in his plan."

"Sounds pretty far-fetched to me. White Feather's no fool."

"It may be far-fetched, but it's as close to the truth as I can come right now."

Then, again changing the subject entirely, he asked, "How do you like the new clerk?"

Thor grunted. The new clerk was a twenty-one-year-old with a long skinny nose and a face full of pimples. "He's not real smart."

"Not like Thor Nilsson's woman," Gray Wolf said without emotion.

It was as if Gray Wolf had struck him and Thor sucked in his breath, waiting for the real blow to come. When it didn't, he could think of nothing to say.

Gray Wolf continued, "It's all the men talk about in the bunkhouse at night. How Smitheson's new bookkeeper got tangled up with a jealous whore out in front of one of the shops in Pine Crescent, and how it ended with the man they were fighting over tossing the bookkeeper over his shoulder like a sack of grain and carrying her off to God only knows where."

"I...." Thor's gut was tight with the knowledge of how badly he had betrayed his friend, but at the same time he couldn't fathom why Gray Wolf was remaining so calm. Was he simply too wrapped up in his own problems to think straight?

"I don't want a woman to come between us, Boy. Not even my own daughter. I understand there's things a man can't help doing."

"Doing? What makes you think I did anything except get her away from a bunch of nosy folks?" His voice was too loud, too filled with protestation to be convincing.

He could no more control his outward behavior than he could control what he was thinking. It was impossible to suppress the feelings he got whenever he thought about her and about that afternoon. Those feelings had almost driven him to town more than once during the past days. He wanted to explain everything to her, and it was tearing him up that he couldn't. He had to get hold of himself. As long as no one had actually seen him take her into the stable it was still between him and the woman. He could take his time dealing with it. He could wait for all of this business with Gray Wolf and his daughter to somehow shake itself out.

Gray Wolf was again looking off into the distance, his eyes searching for something that wasn't there. When he spoke again his voice was low. "Sometimes it's hard to do the right thing. I didn't, you know. Do the right thing. I left a woman I loved alone to bear a child, and to raise her as best she could. In my own defense, I didn't know about the child, but that's a hollow defense—if any. I've known for years that leaving Lorna was wrong. I just didn't know why. Not until the girl came here." His eyes returned to Thor. "Do you get my meaning?"

"I'm not sure. I...Sarah...." Thor began.

Gray Wolf interrupted. "Sarah? Is that her name?"

"Didn't I tell you?"

"No. Information from you has been mighty scarce. Sarah what?"

"Stewart. Sarah Stewart."

Gray Wolf winced and said, "Lorna's sister was married to a man named William Stewart. I hope she wasn't forced to live with that son-of-a-bitch! He'd have made her life miserable. I hate to think what it would have been like living with that cold-hearted prig of a man and that lame-brained sister of Lorna's."

"You started to say something about...about Sarah."

"Nothing. It doesn't matter."

"I know you well enough to know there's something you're not telling me, but if you aren't going to talk about it...." His eyes were dark and angry but somehow he seemed unsure whether to actually confront Thor.

"Listen, Boy. Sarah Stewart is my daughter. She came here to find me and she found me. I can't figure out why she's keeping shut about it, but I guess that's her business. But one thing I damn sure *do* know; she didn't come here to get tangled up with one more shiftless bastard."

Then he seemed to deflate, his shoulders drooping; the contours of his face settling into wan resignation. As if disgusted with his friend's behavior, half wanting to know more about that behavior and yet not really wanting to know, he got up and walked away leaving Thor staring blankly after him.

The next morning Gray Wolf was gone, but Thor had little time to worry about his absence or the strange conversation they had had about Sarah. The cutting was now in full swing and he had so much work to do that he barely had time to think. When he did have time his thoughts went to Sarah, and he had to force himself to stop thinking. The only way to do that was to pick up an ax. The new cook's helpers found the woodpile always stacked to overflowing, and had no need to chop wood themselves.

In the middle of many endless, dark and lonely nights, bone weary but unable to sleep, he would go to the woodpile and chop wood like a man whose sole purpose was to commit suicide by chopping wood until his heart stopped.

CHAPTER 32

SARAH arrived at the Smitheson Lumber Company office at six forty-five on Monday morning, determined to get off on the right foot. If being on time was good, then being early was even better. She paused for a moment before she opened the front door. She could feel her heart pounding in anticipation, and she steeled herself. After all, she had managed to pull off her job as cookee under far worse conditions than these. She told herself sternly that she must calm down and everything would be alright. She inhaled deeply of the crisp morning air and opened the door.

Inside, the place was empty except for an elderly man who was sweeping the floor. She thought at first that he was hunched over because of his task, but when he realized someone had come in, he looked up but remained hunched over.

"Mornin' Miss," he said, raising his eyes with an effort to look at her. "Ain't no one about yet except me."

He shuffled over to a closet and put his broom away, then shuffled over to the door and reached up and took his coat down from a hook. "Fire's goin' and it's nice and warm. Now that someone's here, I'll be gettin' on home."

She took off her coat and hung it on the hook from which he had taken his, then went over and sat down on a chair with her hands folded in her lap and waited. According to the clock on the wall, it was exactly seven when the door opened and Peter Knox walked in.

"Ah. You're on time. That's good." He looked around the big room. "Where's Henry?"

"Henry?"

"Yes. He's always the first one here in the morning. He gets the fire going so it's warm when the rest of us arrive. Then he comes back in the evening and cleans up the place."

"He left as soon as I got here."

Peter Knox frowned. "And what time did you get here?" He looked suspicious, and she wondered why.

"Six forty-five. I wanted to be sure to be on time."

"Hmpf!" he said, taking off his coat, not bothering to hide his obvious displeasure. "He's supposed to stay until we get here."

"I guess he figured someone was here so it was alright to leave," she said, trying not to sound defensive.

"He's too trusting," he said. "He doesn't know you and he shouldn't have left you alone in here."

She couldn't decide whether Peter Knox didn't trust her or didn't trust the old man's judgment; but whichever it was, her new supervisor annoyed her. It was a bad beginning to her first day.

"Should we get started?" she asked, changing the subject. She was not going to let him know she was bothered by his attitude.

He showed her the small office that was to be hers and told her to look around while he talked to John Smitheson, who had just arrived. She felt a sudden twinge of pride. Her own office! She went into the main room to retrieve her coat so she could hang it on her own coat hook. She sat down at the desk and rubbed her hands over the wooden desktop. Then she started opening drawers and taking a mental inventory of the supplies she had to work with. By the time Peter Knox returned ten minutes later, she knew where everything was.

She followed Peter into the main room. There were two other men working in the office besides Peter. He introduced her to them, and they smiled politely and went about their own business. From the looks they gave her, she knew they weren't expecting her to last long in her new position.

Then Peter spent the morning acquainting her with Smitheson's accounting system, and it wasn't long before Peter's mood began to soften. He was clearly pleased with how quickly she picked up on things, and his earlier resentment of her began to dissipate as he realized how much help she was going to be to him. The man she replaced had been diligent and plodding, but he was often confused and seldom, if ever, showed any initiative.

At exactly twelve o'clock, John Smitheson poked his head into her office where she and Peter were still working and said, "Would you two like to go to town for lunch?"

"No thank you," she said quickly. "I brought something with me." She could see that Peter was disappointed. From the size of his rotund middle, she knew food was important to him. "You go on ahead. I'll eat lunch here at my desk."

When he seemed reluctant, she added, "You've shown me so much that I'd like to take some time to let it all soak in." That seemed to satisfy him.

"There's a small kitchen next to my office," John told her, "and a small stove that we use to make tea or coffee. Help yourself."

After they had gone, she got up and found the kitchen. The other two men were already sitting at the small table in the center of the room, and they had a pot of water heating on the stove.

"Mind if I join you?" she asked.

"Pull up a chair," Hank Olson said without smiling.

The other man, Charlie Hokenson, said, "You want coffee? We only got water cooking for tea, but we can...."

He started to get up from his chair, but she held up a hand and said, "Don't get up. Tea is just fine." She sat down and unwrapped the sandwich she had brought. They also had sandwiches, but they each had three of them.

When the kettle started to whistle, Charlie got up to make the tea and then set three cups on the table and poured it. "You take milk or sugar?" he asked politely.

"No thanks," she said, smiling. She was aware of some tension in the room, so she decided to confront it head on. "I don't suppose you men like it much. Having to work with a woman, I mean."

It caught them off guard, and they both stopped chewing and looked at her, neither of them knowing quite what to say.

"I understand," she said pleasantly. "But you'll find that I'll do my share and won't bother anybody."

They looked embarrassed, and Hank cleared his throat and said, somewhat defensively, "We didn't say anything about you not being welcome."

"I know you didn't," she said, giving them her most engaging smile. "And I really appreciate it. I just wanted you to know that I can see how you'd feel uncomfortable having a woman think she could do this job as well as a man."

They looked at each other quickly, then back at her. "We didn't say...."

"All I ask is that you give me a chance." She looked from one to the other, her brown eyes imploring. "I don't expect any special treatment." She nodded toward the stove. "And I'll take my turn making the tea."

She had approached the matter so straightforwardly that neither of them could think of any reason not to give her a chance. They had never had a woman speak to them with such directness. They sat thinking for a long minute, and it was Hank who finally spoke. "You're welcome here, same as any man." Then he grinned, and his eyes lit up like those of a little boy who had just been told he could have a cookie. "Except you're a whole lot prettier." He hadn't meant to say that, but it cleared the air and made all three of them laugh.

They ate their lunch and got acquainted, Sarah prodding them with questions and avoiding talking much about herself. By the time half an hour had passed, the tension was gone and the two men had almost changed their minds about working with a woman.

After lunch Hank stepped into Charlie's office for a moment and said, "I think I'm going to like having a woman around here. Kinda brightens things up."

"Me too," Charlie said. Then he grew thoughtful and said, "I'm not so sure my wife is going to like it, though."

"I'm going to break it gently," Hank agreed, "but I probably won't tell Ida Mae what she looks like."

"Smart man!" Charlie said, both of them laughing as Hank left to go to his own office.

Things went well in the afternoon, but by the end of the day Sarah was exhausted from the effort of learning a new job and meeting so many new people. Besides the men who worked in the office there were the mill hands that came in and out of the office all day, along with other men who came and went and about whom she knew nothing. It was a busy place, and she wondered if she could possibly ever get to know who all the men were. She didn't dare close her door because she felt she had no right yet to ask for privacy. She had no way to know it, but the novelty of having a beautiful woman in the office was attracting men into the building who normally didn't show up except on payday.

Throughout that day and the rest of the week the curiosity seekers kept stopping at the office and innocently passing the door to her office, looking for an excuse to talk to her. At first it annoyed her, but by Wednesday afternoon she had grown more comfortable with her surroundings. As she began to relax, she found the situation somewhat amusing.

On Saturday afternoon John Smitheson stepped into her office. "How's it going?" he asked with a friendly smile.

"Fine. Good." Then she frowned slightly. "It's been awfully busy around here. Is it always like this?" She had wanted to finish something in one of the ledgers, but there had been so many men coming and going and stopping to talk to her that she had fallen behind in her work. Admittedly she couldn't work as fast as she knew she would eventually be able to, but she knew she could do far more than she had gotten done that week.

He laughed and said, "I'll tell you what, Miss Stewart. Why don't you shut the door to your office during the day."

"Would that be okay?" she asked, not wanting to be presumptuous about her territory so early in her employment.

"I think it's the only way you're going to get anything done," he said. "The men seem to be rather curious about you."

She felt the color rising to her face. "They're only trying to make me feel welcome."

"Do you? Do you feel welcome?" he asked, sounding sincerely concerned.

"Yes. Yes I do. Everyone has been very nice to me."

"Good. Then shut your door." He said it kindly, as if wanting to protect her in some way.

"I will," she said, nodding. "Thank you."

"By the way," he said, almost as an afterthought. "I seem to remember seeing you at the train depot way last spring. At least, I think it was you."

"It was," she admitted.

She said nothing about what she had been doing since then, and he was too polite to ask. He did, however, suspect there was a story here somewhere. He suspected, also, that it had something to do with Thor Nilsson and Gray Wolf MacKenna.

Just then Hank poked his head around the door. "Oh! Excuse me, Sir. I didn't know you were in here."

"I was just leaving. I'll see you both on Monday," he said as he walked out.

"You ready to go?" Hank asked.

"I guess so. There are some things I hoped to finish, but...."

"You've worked long enough. I'll walk you home. Ida Mae made me promise to be home on time. It's my oldest son's birthday and we're having a little celebration."

Hank and his family lived in Pine Crescent, but he was the only one in the office whose wife was willing to live there. The other wives insisted it was too isolated and that there was absolutely nothing to do and nobody to do it with. The rest of the men were forced to commute back and forth from Hinckley.

He and Sarah always walked home together at night. He enjoyed talking to her and she was happy for the company. As they walked together on this particular evening, she asked, "Do you happen to know anyone who lives at the new boarding house?"

"The pastor of our church, Axel Wolff, is living there temporarily. We hope to be able to build him a parish house one day, but for now we had all we could do to raise enough money to build the church and pay him a small amount. As far as I know he's quite happy with the accommodations. Most of the other men who stay there are railroad men who are only in town part of the time. I haven't gotten to know any of them. Are you thinking of moving out of the Vogels' place?"

"Yes. Their baby is almost due, and I think it's time I got a place of my own." The wind was raw and cold against her face, and she took the muffler she wore around her neck and put it on her head, winding it an extra time around the lower part of her face. "It's getting awfully cold," she said, hurrying her steps.

He looked up at the dark sky. "Yes, and it looks like it could snow. We could use some."

"We could?" she asked, still baffled by Minnesota's weather.

"It's dry," he said. "If it doesn't snow and get colder the jacks will have a tough time in the woods."

"I should think it would be easier to work if there wasn't so much snow. And it seems to me it's plenty cold enough."

"You'd think so, but for them this is warm. If it's too warm they sweat and their clothes get wet. When their clothes get wet it's miserable working. If a winter is too warm we lose a lot of the jacks. They just up and leave. They can deal with the cold much better than they can deal with wet clothing."

She thought about Camp Seven, and about Thor, and she felt the familiar quickening of her pulse. They had reached the road in front of the depot, and Hank stood and waited while she went to the door. She turned and waved to him before going inside. "See you on Monday," she called.

He waved back and said, "Yup. Enjoy your day off."

She did enjoy it, much more than she would have if she hadn't worked so hard all week. She set off to find a room the first thing the next morning. She went directly to the boarding house. It was a square, flat-faced wooden building, built during the past summer while Sarah was at Camp Seven. It stood just past where the road curved out of sight if one stood in front of the depot and looked east. Across from it and beyond were the new businesses Clemmie had been so excited about. At the far end of the road stood the Lutheran Church.

As soon as Nell Clarke, the owner, opened the front door, wiping her hands on her dazzling white apron, Sarah knew she was going to like the boarding house. The inviting aroma of food cooking on the stove wafted into the entrance hall and mingled with the smell of furniture polish. There were eight rooms for boarders on the second floor, and the downstairs level consisted of a large dining room, a parlor, a kitchen and Nell's quarters in the back. Within half an hour, Sarah had arranged to take one of the rooms. She went back to the Vogels and gathered her belongings and had Richard's assistant bring them to the boarding house for her. By mid-afternoon she was busy getting settled into her new lodgings when there was a tap on the door and Nell invited her to come down to the kitchen for a cup of tea.

Nell Clarke had been a widow for only two years. She told Sarah that her husband was killed by a widow-maker in the Wisconsin timber.

"What's a widow maker?" Sarah asked in astonishment, wondering if someone in Wisconsin went around killing husbands for some reason.

Nell explained, "When they cut down a big tree sometimes the upper branches get tangled with a tree standing next to it. When that happens, the tree doesn't fall in the right direction." She looked away from Sarah. "It happened one day when Karl and his partner, Sven, were sawing down a big white pine. The severed trunk twisted off the stump and fell and crushed my Karl. Sven said it happened so fast Karl didn't have a chance to get out of the way." She looked sad for a moment, but brightened quickly and said, "I guess it could have been worse. He didn't see it coming and he died instantly. He didn't feel a thing."

"I'm really sorry, Nell. It must be awful for you."

"I suppose it's pretty awful, but the men who work in the timber know the risks they're taking. There really aren't many accidents, considering the danger involved. I remember Karl telling me about watching a tree crash to the ground, knocking loose a branch high on the neighboring tree. The severed limb plummeted down and landed about fifty feet away and exploded like a mortar shell. Luckily no one was hit. Someone could easily have been impaled by flying splinters."

Sarah looked stunned, and all she could think about was Thor out there in the timber. She had no idea it was so dangerous; and she had spent a whole summer in a lumber camp!

"If you stick around these parts long enough you're going to hear of somebody getting hurt or killed. And seeing as how you work in a lumber mill, well...."

"Why ever did you come here? To the timber. I should think you'd want nothing to do with it ever again."

Nell shrugged. "My brother Lars, I guess. He's all the family I've got. Him and Pauly. Karl and I never had children. I lost three babies when I wasn't very far along. I couldn't seem to carry a baby through to the end."

Lars Peterson, the owner of the General Store, was her brother. He was the one who had convinced her to come to Pine Crescent. He told her there was nowhere else in town for people to stay and that the town was growing and she would no doubt prosper if she offered nice lodging, good food and reasonable prices. She had some money of her own from when their parents died. They had left Lars enough money to open his store, and because she and her husband had simple needs, she had saved her share. Now she wanted something to do with her time besides taking care of an empty house so she came to Pine Crescent and started the boarding house.

"What about you?" Nell asked. "Are you from around here?"

"My no! But it's a long story and I'd better not get into it right now. One of these days I'll tell you all about it."

"No need," Nell said, feeling that perhaps she was being too forward with her new resident. She stood up and got the pot of tea and was about to pour some more into Sarah's cup.

Sarah held her hand over her cup and said, "No thank you." Then she stood up and said, "I'd best be getting upstairs to put my things away."

Sarah wondered if she had hurt Nell's feelings by refusing to talk about herself, especially after she had told Sarah so much about her own life, so she said, "The next time you and I have tea together you must let me tell you about why I came out here. I've been feeling pretty sorry for myself, but after hearing your story I can see that nobody out here has had an easy life. Otherwise they'd probably have stayed where they were."

Nell smiled, relieved that Sarah had warmed to her after all. "I'd like to hear all about it." She couldn't help adding, "I'm dying to know how you ended up as a bookkeeper in a lumber mill. Especially since you're...."

"Only a woman," Sarah said, finishing her sentence for her.

"Well, yes—and such a pretty one, at that. I don't imagine the men get much work done with you around."

Sarah laughed. "Believe me, they barely notice me."

Nell grinned and said, "I certainly hope you don't think I'm dumb enough to believe *that.*"

As Sarah left the kitchen, a tall thin man wearing a dark suit and a cleric's collar was coming down the stairs. As he approached her, he held out his hand. "You must be Miss Stewart. How do you do? I'm Axel Wolff, the pastor of the Lutheran church."

She took his hand and shook it briefly and said, "I'm pleased to meet you," and then hurried upstairs. She couldn't have explained it, but there was something about him that she didn't like, and it wasn't until she was back in her room that she realized what it was. She was thinking about her uncle and putting Axel Wolff in the same category. She decided she had better give him a chance. He couldn't possibly be anything like her uncle or he wouldn't have come to this wilderness. A self-centered, hedonistic man would find little in Pine Crescent to attract him.

That evening when she went down to dinner there were only four other people in the dining room. Nell had told her that she had room for eight residents, and that now that Sarah had taken a room she was full up. Nell motioned for her to sit to the left of Axel Wolff, who was seated at the head of the table. The men all stood up as she took her seat.

"Pastor Wolff tells me you've already met," Nell said, nodding toward him. Then she motioned to a man with slicked-down black hair and a thin mustache who looked to her like a gambler. "This is Martin Mischke. He works for the railroad." He nodded to her and she nodded back. "Gordon Oberland works in the barber shop, Horace Smith owns the tobacco shop, and Walter Cunningham is staying with us for a while to see if he wants to make Pine Crescent his permanent residence. Isn't that right, Mr. Cunningham?"

"Walt. Please call me Walt."

Just then a girl of about twelve came in carrying a large bowl of steaming soup. "And this is Effie. Her daddy owns the barber shop, and her mother lets her come and help me."

Effie blushed as she set the soup down in front of Axel Wolff.

"You folks enjoy your dinner," Nell said, and then she left the room and went into the kitchen to finish the rest of the dinner preparations.

Sarah ate with relish because it was the first really good meal she had had since she left Camp Seven. Clemmie was a dear friend and a generous host, but she was an unimaginative cook. After dinner they all went into the parlor for coffee.

"I understood you had eight residents," Sarah said to Nell, who had just brought in a tray with the coffee.

"Yes, but they're seldom all here at the same time. It can be pretty quiet sometimes," she answered as she hurried out of the room and back to her duties.

Martin Mischke tapped the ashes from his pipe into an ashtray and began filling it with tobacco from a leather pouch. "It's not always quiet. It gets pretty noisy sometimes," he said, as if he liked it that way. "We get some good card games going some nights. Do you play cards, Miss Stewart?"

"No, I'm sorry. I've never learned any card games."

"Then we must teach you," he said as he lit his pipe.

"Perhaps the young lady doesn't wish to learn your games," Axel Wolff said in a condescending tone. He clearly did not approve of card playing.

Martin Mischke ignored him and looked around at the other men, purposely avoiding the pastor's eyes. "Would you like to play this evening, Gentlemen?"

Sarah felt a strong urge to carry the coffee tray to the kitchen and help Nell and Effie, but she immediately thought better of it. If she wanted to be a working woman in a man's world she was going to have to resist behaving like a cook's helper.

"Euchre?" asked Walter Cunningham enthusiastically. "How about euchre?"

"We'll need Miss Stewart to play. We need four players," Gordon said, looking at Sarah.

"No matter," Martin Mischke said. "We can play with only three of us. We'll play call-ace."

Sarah declined, saying she'd rather watch them play. She turned to the minister, wondering why they were excluding him. "Why don't you play?" she asked innocently.

His chin was slightly lifted as he replied, "I'll be going to my room. I must work on next week's sermon." He left the room without speaking to the men and Sarah watched him go, his back rigid.

"Thinks he's better'n the rest of us," Gordon Oberland muttered.

"Aw, he's not so bad," Walt interjected. "I think he was just hoping that after he spent all those years as a sky pilot us town folks might be easier to keep on the straight and narrow." He laughed. "Seems he might have been wrong."

Sarah looked so puzzled that Hank added, "The jacks call the preachers who travel around to the lumber camps 'sky pilots.'"

"We never had...." She caught herself before she went any farther.

The men looked at her politely and Gordon asked, "Yes? You never had what?"

"We never had sky pilots back home." She laughed lightly, "But then, we didn't have lumberjacks, either."

"And where's 'back home?'" Martin asked.

"Boston. I'm from Boston." It felt good to be so open about where she came from, but not wanting to answer any more questions she got to her feet and said, "If you'll excuse me, I'll say good-night. It's been a busy day."

"Are you sure you don't want to sit in?" Walt asked, hoping for the chance to spend an evening with a lovely and refined woman for the first time in as long as he could remember.

"Next time, perhaps," she said smiling. "Good night, Gentlemen."

CHAPTER 33

WHEN she got to the office on Monday morning Peter was waiting for her. "John wants to take a run out to one of the camps today and he wants us to go with him."

Her heart nearly stopped. "Which camp?" she asked, barely able to get the question out. *Please, God. Don't let it be Camp Seven!*

"Camp Seven," he said. "Our new clerk is having some problems. John wants to see if we can help him work them out before we have to let him go. I don't expect he needs too much help getting the hang of things." He frowned. "Nilsson's probably expecting too much from him. He's nothing but a slave driver and he goes through clerks like I go through pencils."

Sarah remembered the dislike he showed the day Thor helped her get her job, and wondered if Peter was being as unfairly critical of Thor as he seemed to think Thor was of the clerk.

"Besides," Peter said, "I think the main reason John wants to go out there it to get a look at how the crews are progressing. He likes to get out to the cuttings on a regular basis."

Camp Seven. My God! I'm going to Camp Seven. As it hit her, the blood drained from her face and Peter asked, "Are you okay? You don't look so good."

"I...I'm fine," she lied. How would he act when he saw her? Would the others recognize her? She was terrified of going and began to sort through her mind for reasons not to go but came up empty.

"You'll enjoy the ride out to the camp. You've probably never seen much of the surrounding country."

She followed him reluctantly outside to where John was already waiting with the carriage. *If you only knew,* she thought.

If she hadn't been so overwrought about going back to Camp Seven, she would indeed have enjoyed the ride. It was the first time she had been in a carriage since she left Boston. Her rides lately had been in wagons, and they lacked any kind of luxury. She felt like a rich lady, sitting in the back covered with a fur lap robe listening to the two men talk about production at the various Smitheson camps. They paid little attention to her, except to turn around now and then and ask if she was comfortable. She couldn't help wondering why they had bothered to invite her to join them, considering how they left her out of their conversation. She wondered if they would include her once they arrived at the camp.

It began to snow; soft feathery flakes that at first drifted gently down around them but soon were falling so heavily that at times she could barely see the road ahead of them.

"I sure hope we don't get snowed in," Peter said.

"We need the moisture. This winter is starting off much too dry," John said worriedly.

Snowed in! Sarah stiffened. The thought of staying overnight at Camp Seven terrified her. She didn't want to see Thor, and she wasn't ready to see her father again. Had he told Big Mary or anyone else who she really was? She thought not, but couldn't be sure.

It didn't take them nearly as long to get to camp as it had the first time she had made the journey. The two horses were able to make good time on the frozen roads, and they arrived well before lunch.

Sarah stared around her at the camp, fearful of getting out of the carriage but knowing she had to. As she stepped down onto the ground, Woody hurried toward them and she turned away from him pretending she was interested in something in the other direction.

Her heart began to hammer when she heard John speak to her. "Miss Stewart? This is Woody Olson." He slapped Woody on the back. "He used to be one of our best sawyers, and he's still a mighty handy fellow to have around."

"Howdy, Miss," Woody said, barely glancing at her. "I'll take care of the horses, John. Big Mary's got lunch ready."

Sarah wondered how Big Mary and Woody knew they were coming, and if Thor also knew. She followed the two men into the cook shack, her heart pounding.

"Boy oh boy, have I been waiting for this!" John Smitheson said, hurrying to the kitchen area, his limp barely visible, his cane tapping on the hard floor. "I swear, Big Mary, I'm tempted to hire on as a jack just so I can eat your cooking!"

"Oh, pshaw," Big Mary said with uncharacteristic modesty. "You're just saying that so's I'll keep on fixing your favorite whenever you honor us with a visit."

"Are you telling me you got hold of some venison liver?" he asked eagerly.

"You betcha. Soon's Red got back from town last week and said you were coming I knew you'd be hoping for liver. Thor and Jock went out yesterday and shot a nice, tender young doe."

Sarah had been standing in the shadows, not wanting Big Mary to get a good look at her. She felt a sudden ache of remembering as she watched Big Mary's helpers bustling around doing what she used to do. The bull cook was running back and forth from the kitchen to the door, loudly supervising the loading of the flaggins cart. All four of the long tables were set up, and she could plainly see how much more work had to be done during the season than during the summer when the crew was small by comparison.

Worrying about Big Mary seeing her, however, was not the worst of her problems. She heard the door open behind her and she turned and saw Thor coming through the door, his eyes carefully avoiding her as he walked directly to the kitchen to greet John and Peter. She felt a violent tug in her chest, almost as if someone had reached in and took hold of her heart. She wanted to run away, but at the same time she wanted to run into his arms. Both emotions were equally powerful, but she could do nothing but stand there staring at his powerful back. His silvery golden hair shone from the glow of a kerosene lantern hanging from the ceiling not far from where he stood and she ached to run her fingers through it.

She had barely managed to still the pounding of her heart when the men finished saying their hellos and John turned and looked across the room at her. "Come on in, Miss Stewart. Don't be shy. You remember Thor Nilsson, I'm sure."

He looked at Thor. "One of the best things you ever did was talking me into hiring this young lady. She's the best bookkeeper I've got."

He looked quickly at Peter Knox and said, "Except Peter, of course."

Peter didn't seem to notice the slight. "Yes. I'll have to admit you were right," he told Thor somewhat grudgingly, then added, "this time." His mouth was watering from the delicious aromas surrounding them, and he was unable to find fault with anything.

Sarah reluctantly walked over to the opening between the counters leading into the kitchen and Big Mary looked casually at her at first and then did a double take and stared at her hard.

"Is something wrong, Big Mary?" John asked. Then he answered his own question. "We decided that as long as our best cook was a woman, we'd give a woman a chance in the office." He tweaked Big Mary under the chin and then looked at Sarah, puzzled. "Do you two ladies know each other?"

"We've met," Big Mary said in a voice that sent a chill through Sarah.

"Let's eat," Thor said abruptly, taking John's arm and maneuvering him to a table.

Big Mary didn't say anything as she served the guests their lunch, completely ignoring Sarah. Sarah, for her part, could barely swallow her food.

The men carried on a conversation, something that never happened during meals at Camp Seven. Sarah figured it was because Thor, Woody and the camp clerk were the only ones who joined them to eat, and having guests was an occasion that warranted breaking the rules.

At one point John asked about Gray Wolf and Thor's eyes darted to Sarah and then quickly back to John and he said, "He's gone back to the Indians. I guess White Feather has softened some."

Sarah felt relief, but only a little. Her ordeal was far from over, and she knew it.

When they finished lunch John Smitheson looked at Peter and said, "You and Miss Stewart go on over to the clerk's shack and have a look at Elmer's records. See what you can do to straighten him out."

Elmer blushed and looked uncomfortable. He had barely looked at anyone during the meal and Sarah felt very sorry for him. She remembered all too well how hard it was to please his boss, but she could only imagine the humiliation of being criticized in front of all these people.

"I'll give you an hour, then we'll let Thor take us out to have a look at where the men are cutting. The Push and I have some things to go over." John turned to Sarah. "Have you ever seen anyone saw down a tree?"

"No, I haven't." It was true. There had never been any opportunity for her to watch the men cutting the timber. She had always been too busy doing her own work.

When Sarah, Elmer and Peter entered the clerk's shack Sarah felt another stab of emotion. The shelves were untidy and she longed to make them right again, the way they had been when she was there. They all sat down and Elmer opened his ledger, which was just as untidy as the shelves. They tried to explain some things to Elmer, but he simply looked at them vacantly. "Where's last summer's ledger?" Peter asked impatiently.

"I think it's back here," Elmer said as he jumped up and scurried behind the counter and pulled it from among the clutter and carried it back to the table.

Peter pulled it toward him and opened it, then pushed it over in front of Elmer. "This is the way it's supposed to be done. Don't you remember anything I showed you when you were in my office this summer?"

Sarah glanced at Elmer, who looked crestfallen, and said quickly, "Peter, why don't you go on back over to the cook shack and have some coffee and cookies. I can help Elmer with these ledgers. If there's something I can't figure out, I'll come and get you."

"Alright. I'm sure you can figure out what he's supposed to be doing just by looking at the summer ledger." He looked at Elmer, annoyed in the extreme. "It's right there for anyone to see if they've got a brain in their head."

"I'll bet you could talk Big Mary into some pie," Sarah said, knowing he probably couldn't resist the idea of more food, and wanting to get him out of the clerk's shack before Elmer expired from shame.

After he left, Elmer relaxed a little. "I'm trying," he told Sarah in a discouraged voice, "but I can't seem to get the hang of it."

She smiled understandingly at him. "Has anyone bothered to explain things to you since you got here? Being shown by Peter at Smitheson's can't have been very helpful. It all looks different when you're actually on your own."

"I know!" he said eagerly, happy to at last be understood. "The Push tried a little, but every time he comes in here to help me he gets all fired up for no apparent reason and storms out before I can get anything useful out of him."

She stood quickly and walked over behind the counter, her heart hammering. She had to struggle to control her voice. "Let me give you some suggestions about the wannigan," she said. Her back was to him and she began to move things around, putting them in their former places.

He stood up and came over and stood outside of the counter watching her, his hands in his pockets. "It don't matter none about the shelves." He said it as if he really believed it.

"It does, though. It'll make you feel like you have control over your territory. And it will give everyone else the same impression. If everything is in its proper place it's easier to know when you need to order more of something. Believe me, it makes things much simpler."

"Do you think so?" he asked, unconvinced. He wondered if the Push would be pleased with anything he did, no matter how well he did it.

"Try it. You'll see," she said. She made order on two of the shelves before she finally was able to breathe normally. Could it be that Thor stormed out of the clerk's shack because it made him think of her? If so, then why hadn't he come to town to see her again since that day?

She walked back over to the ledgers and sat down. He was still staring at the shelves. "I got to admit it does look better," he said. Then he came over and sat down and said, "I sure do appreciate you trying to help me. It gets mighty discouraging to try so hard and still never please the boss."

"I understand," she said sympathetically as she ran her hand over the pages of her old ledger. She felt embarrassed to be so proud of her own work, but she couldn't help seeing how much better her pages looked than his did. His pages were full of scribbles and messy erasures. She seldom had to erase anything. "I think perhaps you need to slow down. And try to be neater. Take the time to be careful. You'll make far fewer mistakes."

She didn't really believe what she was saying, because he made far too many mistakes to overlook, whether the numbers were neat or sloppy. But she sincerely felt sorry for him and wanted to help him. He was too skinny to be a lumberjack and his future looked grim if he didn't learn this job—and soon.

Her heart sank when she saw that he hadn't been doing running totals. She showed him how to do so on the men's individual log-count records so that at the end of the season he wouldn't have to go back and add the whole season's numbers again, except to proof them if he found an error in the camp totals. "This way you only have to spend a few minutes extra every day and it will save you hours and hours at the end."

She kept trying to convince him that neatness, as well as accuracy, was important. It hadn't occurred to him and no one had ever pointed it out to him. She had him enter the previous Saturday's production figures over again on a new page and he actually found that by slowing down and being more careful, he made fewer mistakes.

She was concerned because he was sloppy with his addition and he had a hard time understanding how important it was that the men's production totals matched the checkers' totals at the end of each day. "If they don't," she explained, "either someone is giving you wrong numbers of what he's cut, the checker is not being accurate, or your totals are wrong. You must repeatedly crosscheck. Otherwise there's no way for the Push to know if his production numbers are accurate. If they aren't, it's all on his shoulders. What you do is very important to him—as well as to the company."

He nodded, soaking up every word she said. No one had taken the time to help him—much less make him feel important. "I sure do appreciate all your help, Miss," he said shyly.

When the hour was up and she got up to go, she was concerned that her efforts might have been in vain, and that he didn't have it in him to do the work a clerk had to do. It had come automatically to her and she wished she could give him some of her natural ability with numbers.

"If you have any more trouble, come in with Red when he goes for supplies." For a moment she feared he might wonder how she knew so much about who did what at Camp Seven, but he didn't seem to notice. "I'm in the office every day and I'll be happy to help you." She shook his hand and left the clerk's shack.

Elmer went back and sat down, eagerly hunched over his ledger, the numbers having taken on a whole new meaning for him, and wondering how soon he could find an excuse to go to the mill and let her help him again.

When she stepped into the clearing she was relieved to see that it had stopped snowing and the sun was shining. They weren't going to have to stay overnight, at least. Maybe John would change his mind about going out to watch the cutting crews. She could only hope.

But her hopes were in vain, because just as she was about to enter the cook shack she heard John call to her from the stable. She turned and walked to where the three men were standing watching a man hitch the horses to the carriage. She breathed a sigh of relief that it wasn't Red Scanlon. This was a man she had never seen before.

"You can ride in back with Miss Stewart," John told Peter as he and Thor climbed into the front seat. As they drove John pointed out to her that the road was new, having been cleared the previous summer. He went on to tell her how many board feet of lumber they had gotten from the trees they had cut just to make the road. She didn't know how many board feet they had gotten, but she knew every inch of timber that had been cut down. She was the one who had entered it in the ledgers.

He talked the whole time as they drove, explaining things to her and pointing out the various types of trees. "The white pine is the king, though," he said, his voice filled with awe. "The place we're going has some of the biggest and best I've ever seen. I wish there were more of them, but they've been lumbering in this part of the state for decades and I don't know how much longer these old soldiers can last."

"In Sweden, each season we only cut an amount equal to the new growth," Thor said. "It would be good if we would use the same method."

She felt a sharp intake of breath at the word "Sweden," and immediately her thoughts went from trees to Annika and she felt an acute stab of jealousy.

John looked sideways at him and said, "How do the lumber companies make money doing that?"

She noticed Thor's back stiffen, and when he turned to look at John a muscle in his jaw twitched. "It is not so much the money they worry about. They worry about having some trees left. The way we are doing it, this clear cutting, there's nothing left but stumps and branches. Scrub trees take over and the pines don't have a chance." His voice was tense, but he was trying to remain calm. She knew him well enough, however, to sense his anger. She remembered having had just such a conversation with him once, and now she was surprised at how he agreed with her about the need to change the way the lumbermen operated.

Just then they reached the spot where one of the crews was cutting, and as soon as the horses stopped she heard the sound of voices. They got out of the carriage and walked about twenty yards into the woods. She looked around her, awed. The huge trunks of the giant trees rose skyward. *Like the columns of a mighty cathedral,* she thought. They rose up, tall and magnificent, to where their branches fanned out; creating darkness on the forest floor as the trees selfishly hoarded the light from the sun. The delicate needles shone like gems, reflecting moisture from the melting snow that had just fallen. It was soft under her feet where the ground was carpeted thickly with dead needles. Not enough snow had fallen yet to penetrate the thick over layer of pine branches. She felt suddenly calm, peaceful, at rest. She had been at Camp Seven the entire summer, but she had never felt the forest as she felt it now.

Just then she turned and saw two lumberjacks bend forward and begin sawing at the base of one of the largest of the trees. The men checked the angle of the saw and then the two-man saw bit into the base of the bark. They worked quickly, the muscles of their arms flexing, their motion rhythmic as they leaned together, one of them forward and one of them back, forward and back, forward and back, as yellow sawdust began to bleed from the cut in the wounded pine.

In a few short minutes they repositioned the saw in order to cut at an angle to the first cut. They withdrew the blade and one of the men kicked out the wedge they had formed. Then they stepped around to the opposite side of the tree and began cutting again. Another man came over and placed both hands on the tree above the men's heads and pushed against it as the two men kept up their rhythmic, deadly motion. She heard a loud crack and looked up at the top of the tree as it began to sway. She barely noticed as Peter took her arm and guided her away in the opposite direction from where the tree was about to fall. The two sawyers dropped their saw and pushed against the tree, helping the third man push it over. Then they stepped back and stood with the rest of them and watched as the doomed tree groaned and began to topple, gaining momentum as it fell with a great wrenching sound as branches high up tore against their neighbors. The tree toppled over with a crashing roar, sending up a great cloud of snow and dust and debris, and then lay still.

Sarah let out a gasp as she saw it lying there, a dead thing that had been—moments before—a thing of great majesty. She watched as the swampers moved in and worked from the lower end and up the long stem, lopping off the branches and leaving the felled tree looking even deader. The men weren't paying any attention to her because they were all busily moving toward the next victim. She turned and walked back to the carriage, climbed in and sat, head down, wishing she were somewhere far away from this place. She hated the men who cut the trees and she hated herself for having become a part of it.

"Well, what did you think?" John Smitheson asked when he and Peter finally came back to the carriage. She was thankful that Thor was not with them. He would stay in the woods to finish the day's work.

"It was...it was enlightening," she said, keeping her voice calm even though she wanted to scream.

He turned back to her, one eyebrow raised. "Enlightening?"

"Yes. Now the numbers will mean something to me. Up to now they were just black scratchings on white paper. They have taken on some color for me." She wanted to say that the color was blood red, but she did not. She had been so happy with her work. Now she wondered if it could ever again be the same. She leaned her head back against the seat of the carriage and closed her eyes, feeling as if it had been her own blood that had been shed.

Peter turned to look at her, sensing something was wrong. "Are you okay?" he asked with genuine concern.

She nodded, then said in a quiet voice, her eyes still closed, "Don't concern yourself about me. I'll be fine." How sad it was that this centuries-old forest would soon be gone, and in its place would be a ravaged landscape of stumps and slashings and scrub growth; and she would be among those who helped measure its demise in board feet.

She was relieved that they did not stop in camp again on their way back to town. She didn't want to face Big Mary and Woody again. She felt like such a traitor, having deserted Camp Seven without an explanation only to show up later as a Smitheson employee. A woman employee. And worst of all, someone who saw all of them as murderers who were destroying the majesty of the pine forest.

CHAPTER 34

BIG Mary spent the day fuming and waiting for Thor to return so she could confront him with her new knowledge. When Woody came in for his afternoon coffee she sat down across the table from him and blurted out, "Did you recognize her?" Strands of hair had come loose from her bun, and she reached up as she spoke, groping and poking at them in an attempt to get them back into their restraints.

He looked at her over the rim of his cup and saw how agitated she was. "Recognize who? Who in thunder are you talking about?"

"Her!" she cried, waving an arm in the air. "That female accountant. Didn't you notice anything about her?" She could barely hide her frustration that he could be so blind.

"I noticed she was mighty damn pretty. What else was I supposed to notice?"

She tossed both hands into the air and then brought them back down onto the table in tight fists, pounding them on the table for emphasis as she spoke. "It's Jesse Williams! Couldn't you see that, you idiot?"

His eyes narrowed as he looked at her, awareness slowly dawning. "Well I'll be damned! You know, I thought there was something awful familiar about her!"

"Is that all you got to say? Don't it make you madder'n hell how she comes waltzin' back in here like we're too dumb to catch on to her shenanigans? I knew it!" she said, slapping at the table for emphasis.

Woody eyed her carefully. "Shenanigans? I don't see why you're so riled up about this. She didn't hurt us none by pretending to be a boy—if that's what she did. Leastwise far as I can tell it didn't hurt nobody."

"That ain't the point!" Big Mary cried. "She's a cheat and a liar and I don't like playing the fool. Why, I was even worried about Nilsson getting too taken up with him...her!"

Woody took a bite out of a cookie, chewed it for a minute, then asked, "You gonna ask him?"

"You bet I am. As soon as he gets back here tonight I'm going to ask him if there was something going on the whole time he...she was here in camp." She got up and went back into the kitchen, all the while mumbling something under her breath.

Woody finished his coffee and got up, too. He carried his dishes to the sink and turned to face Big Mary. "Maybe we're wrong. Maybe she just *looks* like Jesse Williams."

"Hah!" she said, returning to the mountain of venison she was frying for the men for supper. She stopped long enough to jab the air in his direction with the meat fork. "That woman is trouble! There's gonna be hell to pay on account of that lying piece! You mark my words!"

It wasn't until after supper that she had a chance to confront Thor with her discovery. He was late getting to the cook shack and by the time he came in she and her crew were in the throes of feeding the men so she had to wait. "I've got to talk to you, Nilsson" she called to him from the kitchen as he sat down at the table. "As soon as you're done eating."

He wasn't surprised. He had known from the moment Sarah walked into the cook shack that day and Big Mary got a look at her that Big Mary would recognize her. It was uncanny. Just like White Feather seeing that Jesse Williams looked like Gray Wolf's mother. He had to allow that women had some kind of sixth sense that men lacked.

"Okay, let's have it," he said as he stood watching her scrape the giant black griddle. Wisps of her hair were flying in all directions with her movements and she looked wild and frantic. He, in contrast, stood calmly with his hands in his pockets, leaning with his shoulder against the doorframe that led into the back room.

"It's private," she whispered impatiently, nodding in the direction of the bull cook. She dropped the scraper onto the griddle and wiped her hands on her apron. "Let's go outside," she ordered, beckoning to him as she hurried toward the door. He followed her as she grabbed her coat and stepped out the back door. When they reached the woodpile behind the cook shack she motioned for him to sit on the log-splitting stump.

"I need to look at you when I talk," she said, as though speaking to a naughty child who was about to be scolded.

He sat down without protest, his legs crossed at the ankles and stretched out in front of him, his hands lightly gripping the sides of the stump. "Go on," he said, "let's have it."

"You're acting like you think you know what I've got to say," she said, feeling deflated by how calm he was.

"I do know."

"Why didn't you tell me?"

"I was sworn to secrecy."

"You tellin' me her swearing you to secrecy was more important than your loyalty to me, after all the years we've been together?" She emphasized her question by stamping one foot on the ground, both hands formed into fists that pumped at her sides in frustration.

"She wasn't the one who swore me to secrecy."

"Then who in hell did?"

He sat looking at her for a long time, sorting through the mixed emotions that filled his head and which lately never let him rest. She waited without speaking, too hurt and angry to speak further. When he finally spoke his voice was so soft she could barely hear him, so she stepped closer, cupping an ear. "I'm going to tell you something I promised not to tell anyone, and I'm doing it because I think you can keep your mouth shut."

She nodded and relaxed a little, then said, "You know I can if I have to."

"You have to. It's important to my friendship with Gray Wolf. If he knows I told someone it'll be the end for us."

"Gray Wolf? What has this mess got to do with Gray Wolf?"

"Her name is Sarah Stewart. She came here looking for her father in the timber, and I guess she figured the only way she could get work while she looked for him was to disguise herself as a boy." Sarah had never told him any of this, but he had put the pieces together.

"Why couldn't she be honest with me? I'd have hired her."

"No you wouldn't have. Besides, if you had, I'd have fired her before she got two feet inside the cook shack door and you know it."

She nodded, her shoulders dropping in acknowledgment. "Yeah, I guess you're right. But I still don't see what any of this has to do with Gray Wolf."

"Gray Wolf is her father."

She let out a gasp and stared at him. "No! You don't mean that!"

"I'm dead serious. But for some reason or other, she hasn't chosen to tell him who she is, and until she does, he wants it kept quiet that he already knows."

"How did you find out?" she asked, her head tipped to one side suspiciously.

"He carries a picture of his mother, and White Feather recognized Jesse and thought the spirits had sent him. Gray Wolf showed me the picture and I saw that it was the spitting image of a woman I met in Pine Crescent this past spring. She was even wearing the same brooch the woman in the picture wore. At least it looked like the same one."

Big Mary had fallen back several steps and was leaning against the cook shack. Even in the darkness he could see how shocked she was. "Is...is that the first time you knew?"

He nodded, surprised at how good it felt to talk to someone about Sarah. He wished she would open up and tell Gray Wolf who she was so he could be open about the way he felt about her. When she had arrived that day, he had all he could do to suppress his joy at seeing her. When they stood watching the tree fall he had been directly behind her, close enough to smell the scent of roses. He could barely restrain himself from reaching out and wrapping his arms around her.

"There's more you ain't telling me," Big Mary said, sensing where his thoughts had gone. "Was there.... I mean, did you...." She looked embarrassed. "There were times when I wondered if...."

He stood up and said, "Don't try to read any more into this than I have already told you."

She came over and stood looking up at him, her hands on his arms. "I'm happy you told me the truth. Now I don't have to hate her the way I was planning to."

"Hate her? Why would you hate her?"

"She's a liar. Remember how much you hate liars?"

Thor looked down at her, his brows drawn together in a deep frown. "I guess there's times when you've got to lie. I'm finding out that telling a few lies doesn't necessarily make you a liar."

She let go of his arms and started to go back inside, but then turned to him and said, "Damn! I already talked to Woody about this."

"Tell him you were mistaken," Thor said.

"I can't lie to Woody," she said firmly. "Not even for Gray Wolf."

"Then you'd better tell him the truth," Thor said.

"No. You tell him. It'll mean more coming from you and he'll be less apt to say anything to anyone."

"Don't you trust Woody to keep your secrets?" Thor challenged.

She paused, and then said, "So far we ain't had any. Secrets, that is. But you're right. I'll tell him. I guess maybe it's time he took me serious."

CHAPTER 35

FOR days she felt she never would get over the sense of destruction she had felt on her visit to Camp Seven. Often she would think about what Thor had said about how they did it in Sweden, measuring the cutting against the new growth. Did he really care, as he seemed to that day? He was, after all, part of the destruction, using the pine forests in America to earn money to return to his precious Sweden. Then she'd realize she was herself a part of it now, and her anger would fade, and in its place would be the sweet, low fluttering that began at the mere thought of his touch upon her.

Finally her busy days returned her to a sense of normalcy. Other than having to make an effort not to think about Thor, a near-impossible task, she again enjoyed her work. The memory of the fallen tree faded day by day, and she soon thought herself foolish for having been so overwrought by the mere cutting down of a tree. After all, how could they have built Pine Crescent—or any other midwestern city, for that matter—without cutting the trees? She longed for her feelings for him to die, or at least to fade, as her abhorrence over the tree cutting had. But rather than fade they seemed to intensify, and there was nothing for her to do but to live with the feelings.

The days passed and in the middle of a cold, snowy Saturday night in early December she awoke to a frantic knocking on her door. She threw on her wrapper as she called, "I'm coming."

When she opened the door Richard Vogel was standing there, his eyes wild and filled with fear. "Clemmie's asking for you. The baby's coming, and the doctor isn't there yet and...."

"The doctor? I didn't think the new doctor had arrived in town yet. Clemmie said...."

"He got here a few days ago, but he hasn't hung his shingle yet, so not many people know he's here. He wanted to get settled in before.... I'd better get back to Clemmie. Can you come?"

315

"Of course I can come. I'll be there as soon as I get some clothes on. Tell her I'll get there just as fast as I can."

When she got to the Vogel's apartment twenty minutes later Clemmie was in the throes of a severe contraction and her eyes were squeezed tightly shut, as if she could block out the pain if she could blind herself.

Sarah ordered Richard to get her a pan of warm water and a cloth and she leaned over the bed and took one of Clemmie's hands in both of her own. When Clemmie saw Sarah she relaxed a little. "Th...thank you for coming," she whispered hoarsely. "I didn't want to bother you in the middle of the night, but I didn't know who else...."

"It's okay, Love. Don't you worry about me. You just worry about yourself and your new baby. It'll all be over soon."

Richard returned carrying a basin of water and looking helpless.

"Set it down here on the bedside table," Sarah said, trying not to sound impatient.

Clemmie's pain had subsided, and Sarah slid a hand under her back. "This bed is soaking wet!" She put a hand to Clemmie's forehead. It was soaked with perspiration despite the coolness of the room.

"How long have you been having pains?" she asked Clemmie gently.

"I'm not sure," Clemmie said, her voice barely audible.

"Richard? How long?" Sarah asked.

"Since suppertime. When we sat down to eat she told me she thought it was time." He looked so scared that Sarah wanted to make him leave the room so he wouldn't alarm Clemmie. She decided the best thing to do was to get him busy doing something.

"Get some clean bedding so we can change these sheets," Sarah said firmly. Then to Clemmie, "Is it alright if I get you cleaned up? Or is the pain too bad?"

"N...no. It's stopped now. Sometimes...sometimes I don't have a pain for...for maybe twenty minutes. Then sometimes they come really often. Maybe every... every minute or two." She seemed to be more in control now, comforted by the presence of another woman.

Sarah managed to get Clemmie washed up and into a fresh nightgown, and then with Richard's help she changed the bedding, folding a heavy flannel sheet under Clemmie so she wouldn't have to change the whole bed again if Clemmie continued to perspire so heavily.

"What did you eat today?" Sarah asked, wondering if it was a good idea to eat when one was in labor, but knowing Clemmie needed strength. She had attended several births in Boston with Katie so it wasn't completely new to her. She wished Katie was here now, remembering how several of the neighbor ladies back in Boston, when they were ready to give birth, asked for Katie before they asked for the doctor.

Clemmie nodded. "I had some soup for supper. But I'm not hungry. Maybe a cup of tea?" She said it more to please Sarah than because she actually wanted tea.

Sarah gave Richard a stern look and he immediately left the room to do her bidding. Sarah looked at Clemmie and saw that she was having another contraction. This time it was longer and harder than any of them had been and before it was over Clemmie was again bathed in sweat. Sarah sponged her gently with a cool cloth, trying to soothe her.

When Richard came in with the tea she asked, "What about the doctor? When do you expect him?"

Richard looked guilty, as though it was his fault that the doctor hadn't arrived yet. "I thought he'd be here by now. He said he had to make one other call a few miles out of town. A sick child. He said first babies don't come real fast and that there'd be plenty of time."

"But when?" Sarah asked impatiently. "Didn't he give you a time?"

Clemmie was writhing in pain again and she put a fist into her mouth to keep from crying out. Sarah leaned closer and stroked her forehead and whispered, "Don't try to hold it in, Clemmie. You just go on and scream all you want to. There's no one to hear you except us."

Clemmie shook her head frantically back and forth, as if letting herself scream would mean she was giving up what little control she had over what was happening to her.

It was then that they heard a loud knocking on the door downstairs and a man's voice shouting. Richard ran out the door and she could hear his footsteps pounding on the stairs, followed by the sound of more footsteps hammering noisily back up the wooden stairs.

Clemmie arched upward in the bed and let out a cry and Sarah put her arms around her to keep her from falling out of bed. "It's going to be alright, Love. The doctor is...." She turned her head toward the door just as it opened and Richard hurried in, followed by a man in a dark suit carrying a small black bag.

"I'm sorry I was so late, Mrs. Vogel. The little boy was very sick. I got here as quickly as I could." The doctor hurried over to the bed and motioned Sarah aside so he could examine Clemmie. He barely looked at Sarah, who had backed away from the bed with a gasp, the back of her hand pressed against her mouth. It was Steven Caldwell, and he seemed not in the least surprised to see her.

Amid the flurry of the next hours, there wasn't time for Sarah to think about anything but Clemmie. It was an agonizing labor, and for a while they feared they would lose both Clemmie and the baby. But near dawn she finally delivered a husky little boy. After Steven looked him over carefully and pronounced him "fit as a fiddle," Sarah cleaned him up and dressed him in a flannel kimono, swaddled him in a blanket and brought him to Clemmie, who refused to rest until she held him to be sure he was really alright.

When Steven saw how efficiently Sarah handled the baby, he raised his eyebrows but didn't speak.

"You know very well Katie and I helped some of the neighbors with new babies," she said flatly, too exhausted to say more.

Richard was watching them, aware now that they knew each other, but too busy with his little family to care enough to ask for an explanation.

"Jesse," Clemmie said, as if something had just occurred to her.

Sarah turned around and looked at her. Was she delirious?

"I'm going to name him Jesse, after my very best friend," she said in a small, weak voice. "I want him to be strong and brave, just like that other Jesse." She smiled at Sarah and then closed her eyes, the baby lying quietly in her arms. They were both completely worn out.

Richard opened his mouth to protest, having already decided to name his son Richard. Sarah shook her head at him. She didn't say anything, but she didn't need to. Her eyes told him that after all Clemmie had been through to bring his son into the world she could damn well choose his name. Richard pulled a chair over next to the bed and sat down on it. He looked back over his shoulder and said, "Will you show the doctor out, Sarah?"

"Certainly. Do you want me to stay?"

"No. You've done enough. Her mother will be here on the first train. I wired her yesterday." He turned back to the bed, and then turned around again and said, "Thank you."

Sarah nodded and led Steven from the room.

"Would you like to stop at my place for some tea?" he asked when they were outside.

"What are you doing here?" she asked angrily, ignoring his invitation. The cold morning air was awakening her dull brain.

"I came because you were here," he said softly, well aware of how angry she must be with him—and deservedly so.

"Hmpf!" she said, tossing her head and walking on ahead of him.

"Wait!" he called, running to catch up to her and grabbing her arm to stop her.

She jerked her arm away. "You men are all alike! Always grabbing at me! Leave me alone!" With that, she turned and stormed away from him, leaving him to puzzle over what made her say a thing like that.

He stood watching her walk away from him in the dim morning light, for the first time realizing how much more beautiful she had become since he last saw her. Then he hurried along the boardwalk until he came to the building that was now his combination office and living quarters. It was right next to the millinery shop, and although it was far from luxurious, he knew he was going to be happy there. He was certain he would be happy anywhere Sarah was, and despite the information he had gathered about her being involved with a lumberjack named Thor—*Thor* of all things—he intended to win her back. After all, what kind of competition could some wild man named Thor possibly be?

The next day was difficult for Sarah. It was almost impossible to keep her thoughts on her ledgers. Not only was she physically exhausted from being up all night, but also she couldn't stop thinking about Steven being in Pine Crescent. She made up her mind that she needed to confront him, because he was apparently here to stay and she wouldn't be able to avoid him altogether. Pine Crescent was too small a place.

On her way home from Smitheson's that evening she stopped for a few minutes to see Clemmie and the baby. Clemmie's mother had arrived and had things well in hand. She was a small woman who moved quickly and efficiently, and when Sarah arrived she embraced her warmly and thanked her for being such a good friend to Clemmie. Sarah easily warmed to her.

"How are they doing?" Sarah asked.

"Just grand!" Mabel Tilletson replied with enthusiasm. "Isn't he just the cutest little button you ever saw?"

"He is that," Sarah said, smiling. "May I see them?"

"You go right on in. Clemmie's feeding him and she'll be delighted to have you visit." She frowned slightly. "She's still pretty weak."

"I won't stay but a few minutes," Sarah assured her. "I didn't get much sleep last night, myself. Although goodness knows I didn't have a night anything like Clemmie had."

Mabel was shaking her head slowly, a worried expression on her face. "And you can hope you never do. Most of us have an easier time than poor Clemmie seems to have had. I wish I had been here, but Richard insisted it wasn't necessary that I come until after the baby was born. I don't think Clemmie was cut out to have babes. Especially babes as big as Jesse. I was never able to have any more after Clemmie was born. She takes after me in the birthing department, and that's for sure!"

When she went into Clemmie's room, Clemmie was propped up on pillows with Jesse at her breast. She smiled when she saw Sarah and said, "I'm so glad you came. I wanted to thank you for being such a soldier last night."

"Me a soldier? Hah! *You* were the soldier."

"No, really, Sarah. I don't know what I'd have done without you. The doctor...." She thought for a moment and then said, "Richard seems to think you know Dr. Caldwell. Do you?"

Sarah sat down next to the bed and put a hand on the baby's head. It was soft and warm, and she felt a sudden stirring of emotion and wondered what it would be like to have a child. Thor's child. She quickly pushed the thought from her mind and said, "Yes, I know him." Then she looked directly into Clemmie's eyes and said, "It's Steven. You know, my Boston Steven."

"You...you mean the one who...the one who...?" Clemmie was aghast.

"Yes. That very one. Can you believe it? He says he came here because this is where I am."

Clemmie shook her head in disbelief. "Sarah, Sarah, Sarah! You have the most exciting life anyone could ever imagine! Having a doctor come chasing you across the country! Why, it's utterly amazing the way wonderful things happen to you."

Sarah wasn't sure she was serious. "You think this is wonderful?"

"Wh...why yes I do. Don't you?"

"Actually no. I think he has a colossal nerve coming here after what he did to me. In fact I intend to stop at his office when I leave here and tell him exactly that."

"But Sarah," Clemmie protested. "Think of it! You could be the doctor's wife and be an important lady in the community. And you wouldn't have to work so hard anymore."

The baby finished nursing on one side, and Sarah helped position him in Clemmie's other arm. When he was settled back down Sarah said, "I like to work. I like it far more than I would like sitting around being Mrs. Dr. Steven Caldwell, I can tell you."

Her thoughts went instantly to their furtive lovemaking in an upstairs bedroom at the Caldwell home and then to the unbridled passion in the livery stable.

Clemmie was watching her. "You love him, don't you." It wasn't a question, and when Sarah looked puzzled, she said, "Thor Nilsson. You love him."

"I'm not at all sure how I feel about Thor Nilsson," Sarah said, reddening. She stood up to go. "But I absolutely do know that I do not have the tiniest bit of interest in Steven Caldwell, and I'm going to tell him so. I don't want him hanging around Pine Crescent waiting for me to change my mind." Then she remembered that she didn't know where to find him. "Do you know where his office is?"

"He came by this morning and said he's living temporarily in the back of his office next to the millinery shop. He does seem like an awfully nice man, Sarah. Are you sure you don't want to at least give him a chance? After all, he did pull up stakes and come after you. Not many men would do that. I don't think you should be too hasty."

"I seem to remember you trying to convince me of the charms of our local hero. Have you changed your mind?" Sarah asked in a teasing voice.

"No. Not exactly. But beauty isn't everything. A doctor...."

Sarah laughed. "You're fickle, Clementine Vogel. I'll stop by tomorrow again after work."

"Will you stay for supper tomorrow? The doctor says I can't get up yet, but you could sit in here with me and we'll eat on trays like rich ladies. Mama is going to stay for a few weeks, and you'll love her chicken and dumplings."

"Okay, I'd love to have dinner with you." She kissed Clemmie's forehead and the baby's head and left the room.

Mabel also invited her to dinner the next night, and Sarah accepted, said good-bye, and hurried to find Steven Caldwell to straighten him out. When she arrived in front of his office she saw the sign above the door with his name on it. There was a light on so and she knocked firmly on the door. He called to her to come in, and when she entered the room found him unpacking a box of heavy books. He put down the one he was holding and came over to her and tried to take her hand, but she put it behind her back.

"I'm glad you came," he said. "I was afraid you might not want to see me again."

"I don't," she said flatly. "I only came to tell you it was a mistake for you to come here. I've managed to make a new life for myself and I'd just as soon forget about my old one."

"Forget? How could you possibly forget?" He took a step toward her as if to again take her hand and again she avoided his touch.

"It was easy," she said coldly. "All I had to do was find a few people who valued me for myself and not for the fortune they assumed I had."

He grimaced and turned away from her, put his hands in his pockets and stood staring at the books he had just arranged on a shelf behind his desk.

For a fleeting instant she almost felt sorry for him, but it passed quickly. "I can't force you to leave Pine Crescent, Steven. I can only try to make it clear to you that there's no longer anything between us. Do you understand what I'm saying?" Her voice was firm, and she was surprised at her own strength. She had worried that she would falter, and that he would use all of his many powers of persuasion to get her to change her mind.

He turned around and faced her, his voice surprisingly calm. "I don't blame you for feeling the way you do, Sarah. What I did was unforgivable. It didn't take me long to realize what a fool I had been. My life was nothing without you. I found out from Katie where you were and decided to come here. They need doctors in Pine Crescent. I can be useful. I won't have to be involved in all the phony social activity my father thinks is so important, and which I hate. Besides, I'd never be anything in Boston except my father's flunky. Out here I can be my own man."

Sarah opened her mouth to say something, but he held up a hand to stop her. "You don't have to say anything more, Sarah. I heard you the first time. But I'm staying. The West is big enough for both of us, and with time, maybe...." His voice trailed off.

Then he brightened suddenly and said, "We can be friends. That's all I ask. If it never becomes more, I can live with that. What do you say? Can we declare a truce? Can we just chalk it off to my having been shallow and brainless and insensitive and...."

"Enough. You've said enough." Then she shrugged and said, "I've done some pretty stupid things myself, actually. I guess I wouldn't want them to be held against me, either."

"Good!" he said, reaching out a hand but then pulling it quickly back. He didn't want to go too fast. "Then we can be friends?"

"Yes, I suppose so," she said, smiling for the first time. "Just so you don't go thinking it's any more than that."

"Don't worry," he assured her quickly. "I'm not going to assume anything. All I ask is that you be my friend and help me get used to this place." Then he grinned sheepishly.

She laughed. "I'll tell you one thing! You might get a bit bored. There's no opera house, you know." Why had she said that? It made her think immediately of Thor and of the time he had said those very words to her. She smiled to herself as she thought of that night. How different these two men were turning out to be.

"I must go," she said, turning toward the door and then turning back briefly as she opened it. "Welcome to the timber," she said, wondering if being a man and a doctor would clear a path for him through it, or if the timber would test him—as it had tested her.

CHAPTER 36

SHE sat looking out the window of her small office watching the snowflakes dance against the glass. It was Friday afternoon and Sunday was Christmas Eve. Little Jesse was being christened Sunday morning and the Vogels had planned a little get-together for that evening. They had invited Steven Caldwell to attend the church service with them and to come to their home that night. Sarah had begged Clemmie not to do that, but Richard and her mother insisted. Mr. Tilletson was visiting over Christmas and for some reason that was totally lost on Sarah, the Vogels and Clemmie's mother seemed to feel the need to invite an escort for Sarah. They reinforced their decision by agreeing among themselves that they wanted the new doctor to feel welcome. If he had to spend Christmas Eve alone in his rooms he would hate having settled in such an unfriendly town.

"I'm fine by myself," she protested when Clemmie said they planned to invite Steven to church as Sarah's escort.

"But Sarah, Dear. You know how people talk. If you're going to stand up in front of church as Jesse's Godmother people will whisper about you and Thor unless you give them something else to talk about. Having Dr. Caldwell there will shut them up."

"Shut them up? I doubt it. They'll probably buzz even louder because now I appear to be involved with *two* men instead of just one."

"You know as well as I do, that gossips have short attention spans and can only focus on one juicy tidbit at a time."

"Where in the world did you hear that?"

"I think I just made it up," Clemmie giggled. "But don't you think if you're seen with Dr. Caldwell everyone would treat you more respectfully? You said yourself that people on the street still talk about you behind their hands, as though you don't have the brains to know they're talking about you."

Sarah had thrown up her hands in resignation and said, "Invite him if you wish. It's all the same to me if I'm seen alone or with your Dr. Caldwell. You can't possibly know how little I care about what people think."

She stood up from her desk and walked to the window. She had half-expected Thor to come to see her after the incident in the stable and after her visit to Camp Seven. Oh, he had been angry and all of that, but surely after he calmed down he would want to see her again. She certainly wanted to see him. She didn't want to admit to herself that maybe their lovemaking had just been a wild impulse on his part, and that he was no more interested in her than he had once been in Lila—whom he had abandoned and left broken-hearted. She wanted to think that he had stopped seeing Lila because of her, but it was getting harder and harder to believe that. The more she thought about him, and the longer she waited for him to come to see her, the more convinced she was that the torch he carried for Annika burned brighter than anything else in his world.

"Miss Stewart?"

She turned quickly from the window to find John Smitheson standing in the doorway.

"I...I guess I was daydreaming," she said. It was nearly half an hour past her usual quitting time and she had no reason to feel badly about being caught staring out the window.

"Daydreaming?" He walked in and sat down across from her desk and motioned for her to sit down also. "From what I've been hearing around town, would I be correct to guess you're dreaming about our new doctor?"

"Lord no!" She said it so vehemently that his brows shot up in surprise.

"What else could a pretty thing like you be thinking about with such a dreamy look on your face?" He lifted his chin slightly and looked down the length of his nose at her, speculating.

Then he lowered his chin and said, "Ah, so our friend Nilsson isn't out of the picture after all." He was sorry the minute he mentioned Thor's name. He had heard the rumors, but had ignored them. Judging from the look on her face the rumors were true.

She stood up quickly. "I'm sorry, Mr. Smitheson. I'd best be getting on home."

She reached for the hook behind the door where her coat hung and he said hurriedly, "I'm sorry, Miss Stewart. That was none of my business. I didn't come in here to pry into your personal life."

She was holding her coat in her arms without putting it on, and she said, "What *did* you come into my office for, Sir? Is there something wrong?"

"Please," he said, motioning toward her chair. "Please sit down again. I need to talk to you for a moment."

She felt reluctant, but she hung her coat back up and sat down again, her hands folded on the top of her desk.

"I'm thinking of giving a wedding party for one of my old friends, and I don't feel comfortable asking my wife to become involved." He looked down at his hands resting on his thighs. "She has a difficult time with the jacks."

Sarah gave a wry little laugh. "I can certainly understand that."

"I can, too. But when it comes to planning refreshments, I'm pretty useless. I was wondering if you might be able to make some suggestions. You seem quite easy with the jacks who come in and out of here all the time. They treat you like a friend, and for a lady, well...."

"Why, thank you, Mr. Smitheson," she said with sugary sweetness, then added, "You don't need to butter me up. I'd be happy to help in any way that I can."

"Now listen here, Miss Stewart. I was not buttering you up. I meant every word I said. The men in the office have come to think very highly of you, as have I. I won't have you thinking I'm saying these things just to get you to do something for me."

He sounded so sincere that Sarah said, "I'm sorry, Sir. I didn't mean to...."

"Never mind that," he said, waving a hand in dismissal. "I'm having the party for a friend who's getting married the first Saturday in April—April seventh to be exact. I thought I'd do it right here in the office. There's enough space, I think. Hard to tell how many will show up, but MacKenna's pretty well-liked...."

Her heart lurched and she jumped up from her chair. "MacKenna? Doyle MacKenna?"

"Do you know him? Is something wrong?"

Struggling to regain her composure, she turned toward the window and took several deep breaths to steady herself.

"Miss Stewart? Are you alright?" he asked, alarmed by her behavior.

She turned her back to him and said shakily, "No...no. I...I guess I'm not feeling very well."

He stood up and said apologetically, "I'm sorry. Why don't we talk another time? You should go home now. Let me take you in my carriage."

"That's not necessary," she said. "You go on with what you were saying. Did you say Doyle MacKenna is getting married?"

"Yes. Yes I did. Do you know him?" He didn't seem quite satisfied that she was alright.

She nodded, straining with the effort to appear calm. "Please. Please go on."

He began again, now a bit hesitant. "As I was saying, we'll just have to try to make do with the space we've got. In early April the weather can either be miserable or balmy. We'll hope for the latter so people can spill outside."

As he talked she felt her heart sink. She had managed not to think about her father lately. Somehow she had successfully pushed him out of her mind because so much else had been happening. He was watching her intently, and she knew she had to say something. "Isn't he the man who's called Gray Wolf?"

John Smitheson smiled. He'd been thinking for a long time that there was some kind of connection between Gray Wolf and this woman. Maybe now he'd find out what it was.

"That's him, alright. The old buzzard's getting married." She seemed better now, so he decided to continue. "After all these years he's going to tie the knot. I've known Doyle for more than twelve years. He's a good man. Dependable. Saved my life once."

"He did?"

"He did. We were in Michigan, back before my father came to Minnesota looking for more timber. We were surveying a stand of timber MacKenna thought my father should buy. Back then I was just a snot-nosed kid doing whatever my father told me to do, and he told me to let MacKenna show me a particularly rich stand of white pine.

"I had climbed a tree to look over the timber. I should have let MacKenna do it, but I was full of piss and vinegar and thought I could do it just as well. He could climb a tree and survey a stand of timber that stretched as far as the eye could see and tell almost to the inch how much timber it would yield. I wasn't quite so smart—or quite so nimble. In fact I was pretty clumsy. I fell out of the damn tree and broke my left leg and my right ankle. And it was bad. I still can't figure out how I broke something on both limbs, but MacKenna said I landed on my feet. Like a cat. Except I wasn't as springy, I guess. But that wasn't the worst part. On the way down, a branch hooked into my side and made a nasty gash."

Sarah grimaced. "How far were you from a doctor?" Steven flashed into her mind, and she wondered if he would now be treating such injuries.

"Ten miles. That may not seem like much. He could have simply gone for help, but a storm was brewing and he didn't want to leave me alone. Plus, I was bleeding pretty badly. There I was, bleeding like a stuck pig and not able to take a step without screaming like a girl.... Sorry. I didn't mean...."

"It's okay."

"I'm bigger now than I was then," he said, patting his stomach. "But I was still a head taller than MacKenna, and a pretty heavy load." He laughed wryly and continued. "The man was strong as an ox. He fashioned a stretcher out of pine branches and dragged me ten miles through the woods."

Sarah said nothing. Here is one more person who admires and respects her father. Why didn't that make it easier for her to admit who she was? She didn't have an answer.

"When a man does something like that for you, you owe him," John said. "It seems like giving him some kind of a shindig is the civilized thing to do." He smiled and added, "Even more so now that he's decided to become a member of the civilized world. I guess a little party isn't too much to ask."

"He *asked* you to give him a party?"

"No! He'd never do that. I was up having a look at his place last week and...."

"His place?"

"Yup. He bought some land about fifteen miles northwest of here. He's been putting up a house and a barn, and come spring he intends to break ground for some crops. And he's already got two cows and a team of horses."

Sarah hesitated for a moment, not sure she wanted to know, but finally asked, "Is he marrying someone from Pine Crescent?"

"No. She's an Indian woman. Name's White Feather. Quite a beautiful woman. Her father's a chief.

"Didn't they have a baby just last year?" Her head was swimming from the effort of pretending she knew less than she knew.

"They did. Stillborn. She didn't want anything more to do with Gray Wolf after that. He never did explain the reason, but Gray Wolf said it had some-thing to do with her thinking they made bad medicine together. Anyway, they're back together again, and she's agreed that if things go alright—she wasn't sure she'd be able to live in a house—she'd marry him in the spring." He chuckled. "MacKenna says she calls it a White Man's foolishness to live in a house and get married in a church, but she's willing to give it a try."

"A church? The one here in Pine Crescent?"

"Yes Ma'am. Axel Wolff is going to marry them in the afternoon in what

MacKenna insists is going to be a small ceremony. Besides the two people standing up for them...."

"And who would that be?" she interrupted.

"That would be Thor Nilsson and Big Mary. He knows I'll be there, and some of the jacks. You couldn't keep some of them away unless you tied them to a tree. MacKenna doesn't think there'll be many, but I guess I don't know for sure. He doesn't think any of White Feather's people will show up. I guess the old chief—her father—is not too happy with what she's doing, even though he's a wise man and knows it's harder and harder to live the old way. He was particularly angry that she didn't mourn their first baby for a full year before deciding to get married. Anyway, I want whoever shows up to have someplace to congregate afterwards. Send the old fart—excuse me—send Gray Wolf off to his new life like a white man."

"Well I'll be damned," Sarah said under her breath.

"What did you say?"

"I said that sounds real nice." She stood up to go, feeling weak and awful.

He jumped up from his chair. "I shouldn't have kept you. You really don't look well."

"I...I'm fine. I just think I need some air."

"I'll get my coat and go hitch up the carriage and be ready in a minute."

She nodded. "Thank you," she said, unable to argue with him.

CHAPTER 37

THE next day she walked to church with Axel Wolff, and as they approached the front door she saw that Clemmie and Richard had already arrived. They were standing with her parents and Steven Caldwell greeting people as they walked past them into the church.

"I'd best hurry," said Pastor Wolff. "It looks like I'm one of the last people to arrive at my own church service." The strains of "Oh Come all Ye Faithful" poured from the front doors as they approached, and he tipped his hat to her and hurried into the church.

Steven stepped to her side and said, "Good morning. Merry Christmas. I've been looking forward to today."

She gave him a half-hearted smile and then concentrated on Clemmie and the baby. "Isn't it too cold to be standing out here? Shall we go inside?"

Clemmie said happily, "I'm sure he's warm enough. We wanted to show him off."

"I don't blame you one bit," Sarah said, tweaking the baby on the chin and pulling his blanket closer around his face.

As they walked into the church, Steven took Sarah's arm. There were too many people watching them for her to resist him. She let him escort her to the front pew, where she sat between him and Clemmie. She heard the sudden soft murmur of voices as they sat down and she knew everyone was talking about them. She wanted to be annoyed, but there was a part of her that felt a twinge of satisfaction at being escorted by the town's new doctor. She reminded herself that she didn't care what people thought, but the feeling persisted. She glanced sideways to look at him and he smiled at her. She had to admit to herself that he was quite handsome with his shining black hair and moustache and his elegant black suit and crisp white shirt. He should have looked out of place, but instead looked like somebody important who belonged exactly where he was. She understood how she could once have thought she loved him.

All at once she thought about Amelia and her aunt. What had happened to them? Did she want to ask him? No. She didn't even want to know. It seemed cold and uncaring, but they deserved nothing from her.

Pastor Wolff's voice rose and she looked up at him in the pulpit, trying to concentrate on the moment, but suddenly filled with thoughts of the livery stable. She gave a quick shake of her head, trying to deny both the memory and the feelings it evoked. As if he had been willed to distract her from such sinful thoughts in the house of God, little Jesse jerked his knees to his stomach and let out an unholy wail.

After the service the Vogels, Clemmie's parents and Steven and Sarah joined Pastor Wolff in the receiving line as people left the church. They cooed at little Jesse and fawned over Steven. Sarah shook hands and answered, yes, she was indeed a bookkeeper at Smitheson's, and smiled politely without answering when asked why such a pretty woman wanted to be a bookkeeper instead of a wife.

As they walked back to the Vogels' arm in arm, Steven asked, "Why indeed?"

She looked at him quizzically without slowing her steps.

"Why would such a pretty woman prefer working as a bookkeeper to being a wife?" His voice was teasing, but held an edge of seriousness.

"Does a woman have to be married just to satisfy everyone else? What if a woman does not wish to marry?"

"I remember a time when you did. Wish to marry, that is."

"That was a long time ago and I was a very different person." She didn't want to intentionally hurt him, but he had asked for it. "I didn't have any other way out of my Uncle's house. Now I'm in a place from which I don't feel the need to escape. I've gained the luxury of choice."

"Ouch!" he said, trying to make light of what she had just said, but feeling quite stricken by it.

"This is Clemmie and Richard's day and it's Christmas," she said, squeezing his arm almost affectionately, aware that she had been cruel. "Let's not spoil it for them. Let's just have a good time today and not dwell on the past. Alright?"

He nodded, smiling. He was quick to pull himself together. He was going to have to be more careful, or he would indeed lose her to the wild man from the timber. He had asked a few questions around town, and he was learning that this "wild man" had the respect and awe of most of the townspeople. Not only that, he had even heard one woman breathlessly relate the tale of Thor, Lila and "that lady accountant from over at Smitheson's." He could scarcely believe half of what she said—especially the part about Sarah calling Lila a "jack-jumping

Jezebel." But then, a lot was happening that he would never have expected could happen.

"Oh! I nearly forgot," Sarah said, interrupting his thoughts. "I need to pick up some packages I left in the hallway at Nell's." She smiled disarmingly and said, "You can help me carry them. Christmas you know. And I got Jesse the most darling little spoon for when he starts to eat real food. It even has a 'J' on the handle."

"Is it one of those where the handle makes a loop so he can hold it more easily?" he asked, in an effort to share her apparent enthusiasm.

"Yes," she said, smiling up at him mischievously. "Silver. Exactly like the one you had in your mouth when you were born."

"You're heartless," he said, letting go of her arm so he could open the front door of the boarding house for her. "Must I plead for mercy?"

She passed in front of him and into the hallway where they were greeted by Nell, who invited them into the parlor for tea and Christmas cookies with the other residents.

"Just tea," Sarah said, "Clemmie's mother is preparing lunch for us." She introduced Steven to everyone as they sipped tea, then they gathered her packages and left for the Vogels'.

"Perhaps I should take rooms at the boarding house," Steven said as they walked. "It seems pleasant and not as lonely as my current situation." She gave him such a cold look that he added quickly, "On second thought, I'd be a disturbance to everyone, coming and going at all hours as I do. Besides, I don't think the gossips in this town need any more fodder."

When she didn't say anything he continued. "Small towns are like that, I guess. They don't have anything better to do than talk about those who seem to be leading more exciting lives than they are."

She stopped walking so he stopped, too, looking at her over the bundles that filled his arms. "Did I say something wrong?"

"Out with it," she challenged.

He looked puzzled and said, "Out with what?"

"Quit dancing around what you've heard about me and ask me straight out what it is you want to know. Otherwise we're going to be tiptoeing around it every time we see each other."

He looked away from her and down the road, seemingly intent on something he couldn't see clearly. Finally, he turned to her and asked, "Are you seriously involved with this Nilsson fellow?"

She didn't answer right away but instead stood looking at him, her eyes scanning his face as if she was uncertain who he really was. Then she said, "It really is none of your business, but I'm going to tell you anyway. I would very much like to be seriously involved with him, but I don't think he's interested." She couldn't believe what she had just said, but somehow it felt right to say it.

"Is the man a fool?" He could only hope.

She shrugged her shoulders casually, but he could see that she was feeling anything but casual when she said, "He's in love with someone else. Someone from his homeland."

He wondered why her words were so reasoned when her face was in such turmoil. "Sarah, I...."

"For God's sake don't feel sorry for me! I'll deal with it." She stopped speaking and looked away. When she looked back at him she was again in control; her mouth set in a determined line. "I'm glad I told you. Now you know how I feel...why I can't...."

"Yes. I'm glad you told me. I heard...you know how people talk. I guess I needed to hear it from you." He wanted to say something else but instead said, "We should hurry. The Vogels are probably wondering if I picked you up and carried you off somewhere."

"Now who's being heartless?" she asked with a grimace.

"Sorry," he said sheepishly. "Are we even, now?"

"Not quite," she said with feigned hostility. She could see the humor of the situation. She wondered why she wasn't angrier with him than she was. After all, hadn't he once rejected her? Could it be that all she cared about was that his attentions satisfied the locals that she now had a respectable suitor? She had a fleeting sense of guilt that she was using him, and a moment of anger with herself that she was behaving as if she cared what the people of Pine Crescent thought about her. She quickly shrugged off both thoughts.

"Sarah, my dear," he said without looking at her, "there's something else I've been wanting to ask you."

"Good grief," she said, "what else is there?"

He cleared his throat and said, "I saw Katie you know."

"Yes, of course I know. You couldn't have found me otherwise, now could you?" She hesitated. "Is she alright?"

"She's fine. She told me the reason you came out here was to find your father."

It caught her off guard and she felt suddenly vulnerable, like he was attacking her from all directions. "Damn you, Steven! Stop interfering in my life." She hurried her steps so he had to run to catch up to her.

"I'm sorry, Sarah. Listen to me, please. I'm sorry. I won't pry any more, I promise." His voice was pleading.

She stopped walking and looked coldly at him. "Unless memory fails, you told me the other day that you were willing for us to be friends. We aren't going to be friends if you continue to behave like this. It's Christmas." Her voice was firm and her eyes were cool and steady on his. "I want to enjoy it. I don't want to have to spend the entire day with my guard up."

His shoulders fell and he looked away and said, "I think maybe I should make my excuses to the Vogels' and go back to my own place and leave you alone."

"For God's sake, Steven!" she snapped. "Stop acting like a spoiled child!"

He was grateful she hadn't agreed to let him go home. He wanted to be with her. He was going to have to get himself under control or he'd alienate her completely rather than winning her back. "You're absolutely right, Sarah. I'm being a fool. Forgive me and it won't happen again, I promise." He hurried on ahead, calling back over his shoulder, "Come on, slow poke, or Christmas will be over before we've had a chance to enjoy it!"

She was coolly courteous to him the rest of the day. She kept puzzling over why she had been able to so easily tell him of her feelings for Thor, but could not bear to talk to him about her father. She began to wonder if she wanted him to be jealous about Thor, but didn't want to share the pain she suffered about her father.

When she went into the dining room at the boarding house that evening for dinner, she felt distant and unsociable. The men seemed eager to talk to her, but she refused to allow herself to be drawn into a conversation. Usually she didn't mind the men and their flirting, because it was nice to have company sometimes; but tonight was different. Everything seemed to be getting too intense all of a sudden. Jonas Mickelson invited her to join them to play whist after dinner, but she thanked him and declined. She lied and said she had a headache, and she went to her room.

Her room was at the front of the boarding house, and from it she could see almost as far as Peterson's General Store. Beyond that the road curved and the rest of the town was out of her viewing range. She stood looking down the dark road, wondering why she felt so lonely and why she chose to remain alone with her loneliness. She did not, after all, still have to be alone. She had a respectable, attractive suitor, and she knew she should be flattered by Steven Caldwell's attentions. Hadn't he given up a life of luxury in Boston to come West to be with her? Instead of feeling good about all of that, it left her feeling even emptier. She kept making the same comparison she made the first time Thor touched her, and Steven always came up short.

Then, too, there was the matter of her father getting married. Why was that so troubling? Couldn't she accept that he had a right to happiness? At least he wasn't chasing one woman after the other, never feeling a commitment to anyone. He apparently cared enough for White Feather to bring her into his world and build a life with her among his own kind. He was no longer living like a savage. Didn't that matter? Couldn't she take some pleasure in that? It didn't seem so. No matter how hard she tried she could not get to an easy place with it. In fact she had already made up her mind that she would help John Smitheson with the party preparations, but would find an excuse not to attend the party.

She watched as a carriage came into view in the street below, and she recognized it as Steven's. He was heading in the direction of his office. She hurriedly stepped back from the window, not wanting him so see her standing in the window with her nose pressed against it, watching the world outside. It was just too pathetic.

She walked over to the bureau and picked up the empty snuff jar that sat in the middle of it. She had picked it out of the trash at Camp Seven the day before she left. She had tucked it into her tussock, the only tangible memento she had of her days as cookee and clerk. She reached up and swiped at a tear, and she went to the dry sink and splashed water from the pitcher into the bowl and washed her face. Then she stood up straight and looked into the mirror. "Stop feeling so sorry for yourself!" she said aloud. Then, as quickly as she had straightened, she slumped again.

"Thor," she whispered. If only she could be with him. She leaned on the washstand, her palms planted, elbows straight, and looked up again and into the mirror. "You stupid fool!" she said disgustedly, then turned abruptly and went to the door, paused for only a moment with her hand on the knob, took a deep breath and stepped with determination into the hall. There were people below in the parlor, laughing and alive, and she knew she had to become one of them or go mad.

CHAPTER 38

"HAS our Miss Stewart gone out?" Jonas Mickelson asked casually at breakfast on Christmas morning.

"I think she's still up in her room," Nell answered as she poured coffee into his cup.

Walter Cunningham, who had decided to remain in Pine Crescent to open some kind of a business—what kind he had not yet decided—and said, "I was hoping she'd be joining us for the day."

Everyone in the room looked at him with surprise and Horace Smith said, "Have you some particular interest in Miss Stewart? It's my understanding that she is...shall I say...that is...."

"I swear you men are worse gossips than any woman I know," Nell cut in, hoping to turn the conversation away from her only female resident. She didn't want to have to worry about romantic intrigues within her establishment, especially since there was already enough talk around town about Sarah Stewart and her two men.

Just then Sarah entered the room and said cheerily, "Good morning, everyone. Merry Christmas." She walked to the window and looked out at the large flakes drifting lazily down from a gray sky, softening the edges of the stark wooden buildings along the road.

"Are you planning to stay in today?" Horace asked. "Nell's got a real nice dinner planned and we were hoping you'd join us afterwards at cards."

Sarah groped for an acceptable excuse not to spend the day with them, but none came quickly to mind. "I'll be here all day, but I need to write some letters." She only had one person to write to, but no one needed to know that.

"Good!" Nell said cheerily. "Then I'll set a place for you at the dinner table."

Sarah sat down as Nell filled her cup and Effie brought her breakfast. "If I eat all this breakfast I won't have room for dinner," she said, staring at the plate of bacon, eggs and toast in front of her. She nibbled on a piece of toast and moved the food around on the plate, hoping no one would notice that she had no appetite.

"I already have the pies baking and I'm going to stuff the bird as soon as I'm done with breakfast." Nell was beaming as she contemplated the holiday feast. "As a special treat I got some oysters."

Jonas rubbed his hands together hungrily. "Oysters! How grand it is to live in such a time as this!"

There was a knock on the door and Nell set the coffeepot down, and wiping her hands on her apron went to answer it. Everyone's head was turned toward the door leading out to the entry hall, and several moments later Steven Caldwell stood in the dining room door with his hat in his hand. "I hope I'm not intruding upon your breakfast," he said, glancing around the room and letting his eyes rest on Sarah before they moved on again to the others.

"Not at all," Nell said. "Sit down and have some coffee. Have you had your breakfast?"

"Yes, as a matter of fact I have." He sniffed at the air. "It sure does smell good in here, though. Do I smell pumpkin pie, or is it just wishful thinking?"

Nell smiled broadly. "You sure do, Dr. Caldwell. Why don't you join us for dinner?"

Sarah stared at him, wondering about his presence at the boarding house so early on Christmas morning.

"Thank you very much, Mrs. Clark, but I'm taking the day and driving up to Hinckley. I was hoping Miss Stewart would honor me with her company."

Sarah had difficulty hiding her surprise. "I'm afraid I cannot," she said quickly. "I...I've already agreed to stay...."

"Nonsense!" Nell interrupted. "It would do you good to get away for the day. You work too hard." She smiled at Steven and it was easy to see she liked the idea of Sarah being with him. Perhaps it would quiet some of the rumors around town about Sarah and Thor Nilsson.

Sarah glanced around at the room, uncertain about what to do. Escape was offering itself in the form of Steven Caldwell.

He picked up quickly on her hesitancy. "It's Christmas Day and it's snowing and an outing is just what the doctor is ordering. What do you say? I need to make a quick visit to a patient who lives near Hinckley, and I thought it would be nice to have dinner up there."

She was watching him, looking for signs of anything other than friendliness and saw none. What harm could it do to spend the day with him? "Yes," she said, getting to her feet and pushing her chair back. "It sounds pleasant."

Steven had been sure she would refuse, and when she accepted he broke into a big smile.

"I'll get my things," she said.

He stood with his hat in his hand, wondering at his good fortune and telling himself he had better not move too fast. He would remain on his best, most casual behavior.

The air was crisp and refreshing, and Sarah settled back against the seat, the lap robe tucked around her for warmth. Steven seemed absorbed in driving the carriage, so she sat without speaking, letting her eyes wander from the horse's swaying backside to the snowflakes drifting thick and soft around them.

"It is beautiful," he finally said, breaking the silence. "I can't say I've cared much about the weather in Minnesota so far, but every now and then there comes a day that makes up for all the rest." They were past Smitheson's now and the road led northeast through cutover land. "It's too bad those magnificent pines have had to come down. This scrub growth is awful."

"It looks a lot better when it's covered with snow, don't you think?" She wasn't willing to rouse herself to anger over the loss of the forests on such a pleasant day. "Pine Crescent wouldn't be here if it weren't for the timber coming down."

Or Camp Seven, either, she thought to herself. She felt a slight pang of guilt at having accepted Steven's offer to spend the day with him and then ending up thinking about someone else. She immediately decided not to chastise herself. She had only promised him her company—not her every thought. It was Christmas and she was riding in an elegant carriage through the snowy day to a warm place for dinner and she intended to enjoy herself. She would think about whomever she pleased. She snuggled deeper into the warm lap robe, content.

He seemed to sense her contentment and he wisely chose to be still. There would be plenty of time for talk. He would be patient if it took weeks or even months to soften her resolve. Until then, he would be the very best kind of a friend. One who offered much and expected little.

They had driven for nearly fifteen minutes before Sarah broke the silence. "Who is the patient you are going to see?"

"His name is Oskar Wilhelmson. He lives with his daughter and son-in-law on a small farm just south of Hinckley. Nice man, but very weak. His heart is giving out."

"What do you hope to do for him today?"

"Not much I can do. I'd just like to check on him and see how things are going. I think his daughter feels relieved that someone is looking out for him."

"Aren't there any doctors closer? In Hinckley, I mean?"

"Certainly. It's just that I happened to be at his son's house treating a broken ankle a month or so ago. The son lives near Pine Crescent. The daughter and her husband were there helping with the chores." He smiled and said modestly, "I guess they liked me. She asked me to have a look at her father, and from then on I've been doing what I can." His smile faded and he looked sad for a moment. "It's hard not being able to really do anything for him. It's what I find hardest about doctoring. His life is ending and I'm powerless."

"Don't be so gloomy," she said. "I'm sure you've helped a lot. Just knowing someone cares enough to stop by on Christmas Day is more than most folks could expect."

The stop at Wilhelmson's didn't take long. At first they insisted that "the doctor and his lady" stay for dinner, but when Steven told them of their plans to go on to Hinckley, they accepted Steven's refusal and politely did not press the issue.

Sarah was pleased and surprised when they arrived at the restaurant. A large fireplace at one end of the room was festooned with pine boughs and red ribbons. A tall, gangly man took their coats and hung them in a small cloakroom, then led them to their table. The gaslights were turned low and candles burned on all the tables, giving the room an inviting glow. The room was fairly crowded and they were given a table in a corner, pleasantly out of the way. Steven ordered wine and they sipped it until their dinners came.

Their conversation was casual, mainly touching upon the differences between Pine Crescent and Boston, those differences so plentiful that it was easy to keep the conversation going. At one point Steven made the mistake of admitting that if it weren't for Sarah he would never have come to such a place. She stiffened visibly, and he knew he had gone into forbidden territory.

"But now that I'm here," he said quickly, trying to redeem himself, "wild horses couldn't drag me away. It's a fine place to practice medicine. Folks here are so undemanding and appreciative of whatever I do. Not like some of the snobs in Boston who demand more than is humanly possible. My father's patients seem to think it's their birthright to be pampered."

"Won't it be difficult to give so much attention to folks when your practice has grown?" she asked. "Won't you have to cut back some on the generous giving of your time?"

He shrugged. "Perhaps. But I don't see that happening for a long time." He was eager to change the subject. This day was not supposed to be about him and his practice. "And what about you? How do you like your job at the mill?"

And so it went throughout their dinner, and pretty much the same the whole way back to Pine Crescent. By the time he escorted her to her door early that evening she was feeling relaxed and comfortable. "Thank you so much, Steven. I truly enjoyed myself." She pulled her hand from the warmth of her muff and reached for his.

He took the proffered hand and touched it lightly to his lips. "The pleasure was all mine. We must do it again soon."

"Would you like to come in?" she asked, hoping he would not.

"No thank you," he said. "I need to get back to check on whether anyone is looking for me. Sickness doesn't take a holiday."

"Very well. Thank you again," she said smiling as she turned and went inside. He stood for a while outside the door, his hands pushed deep into his coat pockets. It was cold, but he felt very warm. He turned and jumped lightly from the boardwalk onto the road and then up into the carriage, feeling young and strong and happy and quite satisfied with himself and how the day had gone.

Sarah greeted the other residents, who were playing cards in the parlor, then excused herself and went to her room. She hummed as she tidied her room and then wrote a letter to Katie, telling her all about the recent events in her life. When she had finished she went to the window. It was still snowing lightly and an occasional wagon passed along the road on the way home from some Christmas celebration. She sighed deeply and turned from the window. She walked over to the bureau and picked up the snuff jar. She turned it in her hands, feeling the memories well up and fill her chest with an ache that washed away the memories of the pleasant day she had spent.

She went down the back stairs and slipped into the kitchen. Nell was wiping the stove and she turned and smiled when Sarah came in. "How about a cup of tea? Or maybe some coffee and a piece of pie?"

"Tea would be nice," she said, walking over and tossing the little snuff jar into the trash container next to the sink.

Nell looked at Sarah and then at the trash container and then back at Sarah. "Didn't Effie return the waste container to your room?"

"Yes, but I thought I'd bring this old piece of junk down here and throw it away as long as I was coming down anyway." If she threw it into her own waste container she'd be able to retrieve it, and what in the world was the point in keeping something that made her hurt every time she looked at it?

CHAPTER 39

THE camps in the pines were in full swing and the office at Smitheson Lumber Company was a constant buzz of activity. There was little time during the day for Sarah to think about anything but timber numbers. When evening came she either paid a visit to Clemmie and little Jesse or she watched the men play cards at the boarding house. Sometimes she even joined them in a game. Either way, watching or playing, she found the card games at least distracting.

Steven Caldwell became a regular visitor when he didn't have office hours, or when he didn't have an emergency that called him away to one of the surrounding farms. He was being easily absorbed into the little community, just as Sarah had suspected he would be. He was charming and he was a good doctor so he had no trouble endearing himself to his patients.

He easily won over the small community, but winning Sarah back was not so easy. She was as friendly to him as anyone could possibly be. Like a sister, he often thought with some dismay. He was beginning to doubt that he would ever be able to crack the shell she had placed securely around herself. He recognized that there was a shell because he had known her before events had hardened her. Sometimes when they were together she would stare off into space, not hearing the words he spoke. He could not blame her for protecting herself emotionally, but he was convinced it was not only what happened in Boston that had changed her.

Finally, on a mild winter evening in late January, unable to handle his frustration at her emotional distance, he began speaking gibberish to her. When he asked if she agreed with what he had just said she pulled herself back from wherever she was and said, "Why yes, of course I agree."

"I just told you there was a squirrel on your shoulder eating acorns from your hair."

She flushed slightly and looked down at her hands, which were folded tightly in her lap. "I...I'm sorry, Steven. I must have been thinking about something else."

"Something? More likely somebody," he snapped, not meaning to.

"And just what is that supposed to mean?" she retorted defensively.

"You know very well what it means," he said, springing to his feet, then just as quickly sitting back down.

They were at Nell's watching the men play poker. It was a Saturday night and Steven had tried to coax her out for a walk. She had insisted she was too tired to walk. He knew in his heart that the real reason she didn't want to walk with him was that she didn't want to be alone with him. "Come on, Sarah," he said. "Let's not argue. Let's take that walk."

Much to his surprise, she stood up and said, "I'll get my coat."

When they were outside on the boardwalk he pointed a finger first in one direction and then the other and asked, "You name it, my dear. You have but to lead and I will follow."

Again to his surprise, she said, "I think I'd like to go to the new saloon. I could use a little excitement."

"The new saloon? Are you serious?"

"Yes. It's right next to...."

"I know where it is. I thought you were joking about wanting to go there."

She tried to sound casual, but there was a slight catch in her voice. She was longing for the rough language of the jacks and the ribald hilarity of the bunkhouse. The saloon was the closest thing she could think of to capture some of what she suddenly missed so badly.

Steeling himself against the unpleasant idea of going into a saloon, which he thought inappropriate for the town physician, he threw his shoulders back in a show of enthusiasm, took her arm and said with false gaiety, "Very well, then. The saloon it is!"

The saloon was noisy and filled with people, but there were no ladies of the night present and Sarah was relieved that this truly was a saloon and not a brothel. Several of the people seated at the tables nodded a greeting to the couple as they sat down, and there were more than a few excited whispers behind hands raised discreetly to shield their words.

A waitress with fiery red hair and a spattering of freckles across her nose and cheeks came over to their table. "What can I get for you?" she asked, her eyes traveling over Sarah. The few women who came into the saloon were usually dressed in homespun, and she had never seen a woman with such beautiful hair. She unconsciously reached up and patted her own thin hair.

"What would you like, Sarah?" Steven asked.

"Whiskey," she said calmly, as though requesting a cup of tea. "Straight."

"Okay then," the waitress said with a slanted grin in Sarah's direction. "And you, Sir?" she asked, turning to him.

"I'll have a whiskey as well," he said, eyeing Sarah suspiciously. "And you can bring us each a tall glass of water."

Sarah was looking around the room trying to act casual, but her heart began to race when she noticed several tables with lumberjacks seated around them. None of them looked familiar, though, and she turned her attention back to Steven. "I see there are some lumberjacks here tonight," she said, trying to make innocent conversation while her heart settled itself. "It's warm for this time of year and the camps are slowing down."

"Is that right? And why would that be?" he asked, pretending he cared.

"They don't like it when they get too warm." She blushed, but went on. "They sweat and their clothes get wet. They much prefer it when it's really cold."

He inclined his head curiously and said, "You seem to know a lot about this kind of thing."

"I work for a lumber company. Remember?" Just then the waitress returned to their table with their drinks and Sarah picked up her whiskey, took a tiny sip, grimaced, and then set the glass down.

The room was again buzzing with talk and laughter, no one any longer paying any attention to them. "I've never been in here before," she said, trying to make conversation. "Have you?"

"Good grief, no! But if lively is what you wanted, we certainly found it."

He watched Sarah carefully as he sipped his whiskey. She seemed preoccupied. Although she obviously didn't like the taste of whiskey, and he couldn't imagine she enjoyed being in a room full of noisy people, she kept glancing around the room. She seemed inordinately curious about its inhabitants, most of them smoking and filling the air with a blue haze, and most of them well on their way to being drunk. He couldn't for the life of him figure out why she had wanted to come to this place.

A moment later he knew. She was staring across the room and his eyes followed hers to where two men sat at a small table on the far side of the room.

One of them had hair that shone golden in the light of the lantern above the table, and he knew he was finally looking at Thor Nilsson.

Steven felt a wave of anger stir in his gut and he pushed his glass away. He didn't need drink to fuel his displeasure. The look on her face was enough to do that. She pulled her eyes away from Thor and gulped down the rest of her whiskey. Then she looked over at him again, her eyes filled with a dewy softness that he had never seen before, and he felt a pang of jealousy so acute that it nearly took his breath away.

"I've had enough to drink," he said, his voice harsh and unpleasant, "and enough noise and smoke to last me into next year." He stood up and pushed his chair in and reached out to take her hand. "Let's go," he said, in a tone that made her open her eyes wide and stare at him, the dewiness gone.

"I don't think so," she said in a quiet, but firm voice. "We just got here."

He was standing and looking across the room at Thor Nilsson, no longer pretending he didn't know exactly what was going on. He pulled his eyes back to Sarah and said cruelly, "I'm leaving. If you want to be with him, be my guest."

"What are you talking about?" she asked, trying to sound innocent.

By this time the people at the surrounding tables had stopped talking and were watching them. She noticed they were attracting attention and she reached up and tugged at his coat sleeve and whispered, "Sit down. Can't you see that everyone is staring at us?"

He sat back down on his chair and leaned toward her, his face gray with anger. "You dragged me into this place so you could look for this Nilsson character, and...."

A shadow fell over the table and they looked up to see Thor standing over them. The lantern hanging from the ceiling behind him flickered and went out. "You are the new doctor in town, I understand," Thor said, addressing Steven in a steady voice. He nodded briefly at Sarah and said politely, "Evening, Miss." Then he looked at Steven again and said, "Nilsson's my name. Thor Nilsson. I work for Smitheson. Welcome to Pine Crescent."

Steven stood up slowly and took Thor's proffered hand. "My name is Steven Caldwell. *Doctor* Steven Caldwell," he said, angry with himself for bragging like a small boy in a schoolyard trying to establish himself at the top of the pecking order. "And this is Sarah Stewart," he added, knowing it was unnecessary.

Her brain was telling her that it was all terribly civilized, but her hand darted out to Steven's half-empty whiskey glass and she raised it to her lips and swallowed it, nearly choking in the process.

"We've met," Thor said, looking with interest at her hand, which still clutched the empty glass. His eyes moved slowly upward until they rested squarely on hers. "Careful with that stuff. You best keep your wits about you. You never can tell when you might get mired in some deep mud." Then he turned and walked out the door, leaving Sarah and Steven and everyone else in the saloon staring after him.

After several long, tension-filled moments, Steven looked at Sarah and asked, in a voice hard enough to cut through glass, "Are you satisfied? *Now* may we leave?"

She looked sharply up at him, clearly annoyed. "Satisfied? What ever in the world are you talking about?"

"Cut the crap, Sarah! You know damn well you dragged me in here hoping to see him."

She sat back in her chair and met his angry look with one that was even angrier. "That's a lie!" she retorted, lying.

He glanced quickly around, aware that they were still the center of attention. "Keep your voice down. You're making a scene."

"A scene?" she cried, loud enough to be heard above the noise. "*This*, my dear fellow, is a scene!" With that, she stood and picked up one of the glasses filled with water and threw it into his face, then turned and stormed out the door.

Sputtering and swiping at his face with both hands, he looked around and smiled foolishly. When he had finally regained his composure, he straightened his lapels with what dignity he could muster and said aloud to the gaping onlookers, "Just a little lovers' quarrel." Then he calmly placed a dollar on the table and walked out of the saloon.

She started to go home, but halfway there she changed her mind and turned around and went to Clemmie's. Richard was in his office downstairs doing some paper work and little Jesse was asleep. Clemmie was pleased to see her and she put on the pot for tea and they sat at the kitchen table.

"I'm so furious with them both that I don't know what to do!"

"I can see how upset you are, Sarah. Tell me what happened."

She explained the events of the previous hour and Clemmie listened intently without interrupting. She got up to pour the tea into their cups and when she sat down again she said, "It's not very hard to figure out that Steven is jealous."

"I know! That's the part that makes me so furious! I didn't ask him to come here. I haven't given him the slightest reason to think I'm still interested in him. He keeps saying he just wants to be my friend, and then he acts like...like a jealous lover!"

"Don't misunderstand what I'm going to say, Sarah. I know you well enough to believe you when you say you aren't interested in him. But men sometimes have a hard time hearing what we say to them. They like to interpret our words in a way that suits them. When you do things that encourage them, well...."

"Encourage him? What in the world have I done to encourage him? I've merely been civil to him, the way I would be to anyone who...who...."

"I think that's the crux of it. It's nearly impossible to know how to behave in this situation. Maybe you need to draw a firm, clear line and *never* see him."

Sarah made a circle on the table with the bottom of her cup, then looked innocently at Clemmie. "You mean like when you asked him to come to Jesse's christening as my escort?"

"I deserved that. But yes, I guess that's what I mean. Like the trip to Hinckley on Christmas Day and his visits to the boarding house. Everything you do with him. You may have to stop all of it. It may be the only way you can make it clear to him that it's over between you."

Sarah groaned. "I thought I already did that!"

"Apparently not. And what about tonight? Did you ask him to take you to the saloon because you wanted to be with him?"

"Of course not!" Sarah insisted vehemently. Then, after a short pause, she said, "In the end, we both knew I was using him and why I really wanted to go to the saloon."

"Maybe he finally got the message. It sounds to me like maybe he did. From what you told me, he was pretty upset."

"Upset, yes. But without hope for us? I'm not so sure. I'll lay odds he'd forgive me in a minute if I asked him to." She stood up and paced around the room waving her arms as she spoke. "That's one of the things I find so...so disgusting! Why does he take this from me? Doesn't he have any backbone?"

"That's not fair, Sarah."

"Fair? Who said anything about fairness?" Then she stopped pacing and looked questioningly at Clemmie. "Why isn't it fair?"

"You said yourself that he admitted he had been less than a gentleman back in Boston, and that he wanted to make amends. I think he's letting you treat him badly because he thinks he deserves it. Once you get it out of your system, he figures he'll have a chance. I'm sure Steven Caldwell has plenty of backbone. I don't think he'd put up with this kind of treatment in any other circumstance."

Sarah walked over and sat back down. "You're too kind to him, Clemmie."

Clemmie shrugged. "I'm just telling you how I feel about what's going on. And I think he'll continue to put up with your treating him badly until the time comes when you make it perfectly clear that you are once and for all done with him."

To Clemmie's surprise, because it was so uncharacteristic of Sarah to behave like that, she watched as Sarah put her arms on the table and put her head down into them and muttered, "Fool, fool, fool!"

"Who are you calling a fool?"

Sarah sat up and looked at Clemmie. "Me. I'm the fool."

"Alright. Out with it. We've gone round and round with this Steven business, but something tells me there's a whole lot more going on." She paused, uncertain about how far she dared venture into such dangerous territory. Making up her mind, she barreled ahead. "It's Thor. He's the reason you're so upset."

Sarah stared helplessly at her, her mouth halfway open to protest, but her head refusing to let her continue the pretense. "Yes!" she groaned. "I've tried so hard not to let myself care about him."

"But why? Why can't you just let go and...and love him?"

"It sounds so simple," Sarah said, her voice filled with anguish. "And maybe it would be simple if I didn't know what I know about him."

"And that is?" Clemmie's head was tipped to one side, her eyes soft and full of sympathy.

"Sweden! Sweden and that yellow-haired female who was too stupid to know what she had. I hate her...him...."

"You're blaming a woman in Sweden for what Thor is doing. Does that make any sense?"

Sarah groaned and said, "Of course it doesn't make any sense. Whoever heard of love making sense?"

Clemmie sat back in her chair. "And it wouldn't make any sense for you to let yourself love him if he's going to leave you and go back to Sweden. That's it, isn't it?"

"Yes, yes, yes, yes! Of course that's it. How can I stand it if...? What if I come to depend upon him to be there and he...? How can I ever trust that he'll care enough about me to...?" She was unable to complete any of her thoughts, and her frustration showed itself in tears that began to run down her cheeks.

Clemmie reached across the table and covered both of Sarah's hands with her own. "And what about Doyle MacKenna?"

Sarah pulled one hand away and swiped at her tears with her sleeve. "Doyle MacKenna? What has my father got to do with any of this?"

Clemmie squeezed Sarah's hand for emphasis as she spoke. "I think it has everything to do with this, my dear. I think you're afraid to let yourself care about any man because the one man in the world you should have been able to depend upon was not there when you needed him. How were you supposed to learn to trust? Who ever gave you any reason to trust? Your father? Steven? Your uncle? Uncles? And now when you find someone you could care about he's got one foot in America and the other one in Sweden. No wonder you don't trust men. Your world has been filled with nothing but...nothing but...terrible and disgusting cads!"

Sarah leaned back in her chair, surprised by Clemmie's vehemence, and Clemmie stopped talking, surprised by her own brash interference in Sarah's life. Neither of them spoke for several long moments. Then Sarah stood up wordlessly and walked to the window and stared out. There was no sound outside and the only sound inside was the ticking of the clock on the hutch next to the wall.

Clemmie got up and went to her and put her arms around her waist from behind and rested her chin on Sarah's shoulder. "I'm sorry, Sarah. I've wanted to say that for such a long time. I didn't mean to hurt you. It's just that...."

"It's okay, Clemmie. You're right. I know you are. I just haven't wanted to admit it to myself. I keep trying to be this...this pillar of strength."

"And you are, Sarah! You're very strong. But there are times when we have to admit to ourselves that we need other people. We deserve people who care about us."

Sarah folded her own arms over Clemmie's, and they stood like that for a long time.

Finally, they pulled apart and Clemmie said, "How about some more tea?"

Sarah nodded and went to the table and sat down again, her face pinched with thought. "I'm going to figure out what it is I want to do about him. About my father, I mean." She looked up at Clemmie, who was watching her intently. "I have to. Maybe if I do that, I can get on with my life."

"Does that mean you'd be willing to risk telling him who you are? Even though it might mean that he doesn't care?" Clemmie was hoping to force Sarah to look squarely at the issues she was going to have to confront.

Sarah nodded slowly. "Yes. After all, what's the worst thing that can happen? Maybe he'll laugh and say, 'How do I know you're my daughter? Just because I was one of the men who slept with your whore of a mother doesn't make me your father. Go away and leave me alone so I can be happy with my *real* family.'"

A sob broke through her last words, and Clemmie walked over and put her hand on Sarah's shoulder, kneading it gently. "That's right, Sarah. That's the absolute worst thing that could happen. Could you live with that?"

Sarah nodded, her lips trembling. "I've already been living with it. In my heart I guess I've convinced myself that that is exactly what he'll do."

"If he does," Clemmie said, almost in a whisper, "he could not possibly be your father."

"But he is! I know he is!"

"That's right. And you can't know how he'll react when you tell him, but I believe he's an honorable man and will not disappoint you."

Sarah turned her head and looked up at Clemmie, her eyes wide and almost hopeful. "Do you really think so?"

Clemmie nodded, "I know what kind of a person you are, and like my father always says, 'the apple does not fall far from the tree.'"

CHAPTER 40

STEVEN spent the following week in what could best be described as an impotent rage. At first his rage was directed at Sarah, but it soon shifted to the wild man who didn't appear wild at all. Thor Nilsson appeared to be cool, in control, and worst of all, dangerously attractive. It wasn't hard to understand how Sarah could have feelings for such a man. But Nilsson hadn't appeared in the least interested in Sarah. Could it be that he didn't reciprocate Sarah's feelings? Was he really planning to go back to Sweden, the way Sarah had said he was going to? And if so, didn't that leave Sarah in Pine Crescent—alone? Steven didn't even care if she came to him on the rebound. He had to redeem himself, quickly. He had to be ready when the wild man went away.

As far as Sarah was concerned after the incident in the saloon, she knew Steven had lied to her and that clearly he had no intention of being simply a friend. He had acted like a jealous boor. Clemmie was right. She had to make Steven understand, once and for all, that she was not interested in him.

She had trouble, however, whenever she let herself remember how brazenly she had used Steven to take her to the saloon where she might see Thor. What kind of person was she becoming? She was even hoping for a chance to go to Camp Seven again just to be near him, however casually. This after what had happened between them and he seemed not the least affected by it! Had she completely lost her morals?

Another troubling thing was that she was feeling a growing annoyance at how everyone who had anything to do with Smitheson Lumber Company was always fussing over Gray Wolf, and now were all wrapped up in his wedding plans. What would they think of him if they knew he had a family that hadn't mattered in the least to him? She thought bitterly about confronting him where there were plenty of other people around to finally see him for what he really was.

She was walking home from work one evening, her head spinning with confusion, when almost without realizing it her steps took her to Steven's office door. This at least was one thing she wasn't confused about. She knocked several times before he answered. He looked tired and downcast but brightened at the sight of her.

"Oh, it's you," he said, quickly running his fingers through his hair.

"Yes it's me," she said, pushing past him into the room.

"Come in," he said.

She ignored his sarcasm and turned to face him squarely. "We need to talk," she said.

He motioned toward the chair that sat in front of his desk. "Won't you sit down? I'd offer you some refreshment, but I'm afraid I don't keep any food in here and...."

"I don't want to sit down and I don't need any refreshment."

He folded his arms across his chest, unconsciously readying himself to shut out what she was about to say.

Her chin jutted forward and her voice rose. "I want to get something straight between us. Nobody twisted your arm and made you come out west to live in a run-down building in the wilderness without...without food in the cupboard. You have no one to blame but yourself."

He flinched and his folded arms tightened against his chest.

"Furthermore," she continued, "when I said I forgave you for what you did to me in Boston, I lied! I do not forgive you! It was unforgivable! I deserved far better from a man who was supposed to love me!" Now that she had begun to open up she couldn't stop. "When it first happened, I thought you had broken my heart, but I was wrong. You actually did me a favor. Do you know why?"

He shook his head dumbly, wishing he could stop her words.

"You did me a favor because you made me see that I deserve much better than you. I deserve someone who will value me for what I am and not for what I have. Clearly you did not. And just because you came out here to find me and make it right doesn't mean I have to accept you back into my life. I do not! I am rejecting you, Steven Caldwell, just the way you rejected me." She had raised up on her tiptoes, the better to meet him eye to eye, her hands on her hips, her anger making her words come out mixed with little spatters of spittle.

He needed to say something, but "Okay" was all he could manage to get out.

"Okay what?" she demanded.

"I accept your rejection," he said simply, dropping his arms and then turning his palms up as if to ask what else he could possibly do but accept.

"Good! Because I am done with you and your phony friendship. As far as I'm concerned you can stay in Pine Crescent or you can go back to Boston. It's all the same to me." She turned to go and he took a quick step toward her and reached for her arm. "Don't you dare touch me," she said, jerking her arm away.

"Sarah, listen to me, please," he said, knowing he couldn't just let her walk away like this.

"No! I've heard far too much from you already. Leave me alone! I mean it!"

He watched helplessly as she stormed out the door, unable to think of anything to say or do that would stop her.

Hurrying home, she wondered why she didn't feel better about what she had just done. Was she taking everything out of Steven? Was her anger and frustration with both Thor and her father burning such a hole inside her that she had to take it out on someone? She didn't know. All she knew was that she had done it and now she was finished with Steven once and for all.

CHAPTER 41

JOHN Smitheson suggested that they have Big Mary and her crew prepare the food and bring it into town the morning of the wedding. "We'll drive out one of these nights to talk about it with her. Would that be possible?" he asked.

Sarah hesitated, not wanting to get into close contact with Big Mary again, but her heart fluttering at the thought of seeing Thor.

Not waiting for an answer, he said, "How about tomorrow? I'll tell Maggie I won't be home until late."

When they walked into the cook shack the following night, Sarah's heart was pounding so hard she feared everyone in the room could hear it. The men had just sat down for supper, and they nodded respectfully to the big boss and to Sarah and continued eating.

"I didn't know you were coming," Big Mary said, "or I'd have planned to have some venison liver for you."

"Whatever you're having smells plenty good enough. You got room for two more?"

"We always have room for you, Sir," she said as she motioned to one of her helpers. "Set two more places for our company."

When the men finished eating and left the cook shack Thor remained seated, his arms folded across his chest. "You got something on your mind, John?" he asked, his eyes avoiding Sarah.

"Actually, I wanted to talk to Big Mary about Gray Wolf's shindig."

Thor's eyes darted quickly to Sarah, but mention of Gray Wolf didn't seem to faze her.

Sarah caught his glance and looked at him for a brief moment and then looked quickly away again, pretending to be interested in what Big Mary was doing in the kitchen. Sarah had no way to know whether she recognized her, but if she did, she was putting on a good act.

"Come on in here and sit down," John called to Big Mary.

She turned her head to look at him and started to say something, thought better of it, then came to the table and sat down, smiling far too sweetly at Sarah. She might be able to accept the reasons for Sarah's subterfuge, but she didn't have to like being duped.

"By the way," John said, turning to Thor. "How's Elmer doing with the books?"

"He's been doing fine, but he's not here right now," Thor answered. "Won't be back for a month."

"What do you mean? This is the busiest time of the year."

"In exchange for his agreement to stay on after the season and work for the summer, I gave him some time off to go home and spend some time with his family."

"What's wrong with you?" John said angrily. "We never hire a clerk during the summer."

Thor's eyes darted to Sarah and then back to John. "It'll be different this time. I won't be here, and a new foreman won't be able to keep the books. He'll have all he can do to run the camp. The men can be hard on a new foreman...."

"Wait a minute," John interrupted. "What the hell are you talking about? What new foreman?"

Sarah's pulse began to race and she stood up quickly and went into the kitchen, pretending she wanted a glass of water. The men ignored her, but Big Mary's eyes narrowed as they followed her movements.

"I was going to come in to tell you, but I've been pretty busy. I'll be leaving as soon as the season ends."

The room had grown silent, and when Sarah returned to the table John was staring dumbly at Thor and Thor's eyes were on the table, one finger tracing a worn spot on the oilcloth.

Big Mary sat perfectly still, eyes focused on a hat hanging on a hook at the far end of the room.

John stood up and began pacing around the room, his limp exaggerated, stopping now and then to touch something; a corner of a table, the edge of a counter, his own hair. When he spoke, his voice was steady, belying the agitation of his movements.

"Well then. It's a good thing I came out here when I did. It'll take some time to find another man."

"Why not Jock Lehtinnen," Thor asked, obviously having already decided to suggest him.

John thought for a moment then said, "I'll think about it. Have him come in and talk to me after you've made up your mind."

"I have. I have made up my mind," Thor said, turning to look at Big Mary who had just made a guffawing sound deep in her throat.

"What? What's the matter with you?" he growled at her.

Her eyes were steady on him now, her jaw squared, looking at him as though she had been betrayed but saying nothing. Once more he was leaving camp and hadn't told her. Her eyes shifted to Sarah as if to shift the blame to her.

Sarah and Thor were staring at each other. It was out in the open now. He was leaving and that was that.

John's words forced their attention to him and away from each other. They had not heard what he was saying until he said, "You can't go a month during the season without a clerk. Summertime is one thing, but.... What were you thinking when you sent Elmer away?"

"I can handle it myself," Thor said stubbornly. "It's only a month."

John laughed wryly. "Like hell you can. This is the busiest time of the year. It was during the summer when you ran into trouble the last time, and if it hadn't been for that boy who took over the clerk's job—what was his name?—you'd have been sunk!"

"Jesse," Big Mary shot at him, glaring for an instant at Sarah then back at John. "His name was Jesse and he saved Nilsson's ass alright. Too bad he ain't around anymore. If it hadn't been for him getting lucky with *my cookee*," Big Mary said, "he would've stumbled through the summer like the damn fool he is." Big Mary's bottled up frustration was spilling over into the room. "That whole cookee-clerk business was the craziest thing I ever saw happen in a camp and I've seen a lot of crazy crap!"

Thor's eyes were scanning the walls and Sarah's eyes were on the floor. Big Mary had no idea how crazy it had actually become.

John held up both palms and said, "Whoa Mary. Let's not get all fired up over this thing. We'll work it out without any heads rolling."

He turned to Sarah and said, "You can come out on the weekends until Elmer gets back. From what he told Peter after you helped him, you know as much about it as he does. And I know you'll get it done a lot faster. Two days a week ought to do it easily."

Sarah let out a small choking sound and everyone looked at her, except Thor who was also about to choke.

"Why, I..." was all she could manage to stammer.

"I'll take that as a yes," John said with finality. "I will, of course, pay you extra for your efforts. I'll expect you to keep up your work at the office so we don't fall behind, but I consider this to be very important."

He turned to look at Thor, who appeared to be about to burst. "You okay about this?"

"Yaw, but I don't think...."

John interrupted him and said, "Seeing as how you don't intend to continue working with Smitheson, I know you'll let me make this decision for you. I know it will cause you some inconvenience, but you'll just have to put up with it."

He looked at Big Mary, who had settled into a giant sulk. He knew she held an unusually important place in the goings on at Camp Seven. "And you? Do you have a problem with this?"

Big Mary looked at Sarah as she spoke. "Don't you worry none. You ain't putting me out, you can be sure of that."

All this was almost too much for Sarah. Not only the idea of coming back to Camp Seven to work, but that Thor was leaving. Before she had time to realize what she was doing, she turned to him and asked, "What made you decide to leave so suddenly?" She couldn't believe she had the temerity to confront him.

"It's not sudden," John answered for him, barely glancing at Thor. "He's been telling me he's leaving for five years and he's still here. This time probably won't be any different."

"You had better believe me," Thor said, getting up and heading for the door. "And if I had known I was going to have a female in my camp, I'd have left sooner."

"Hmpff," Big Mary finally said into the sudden silence. "And what does that make me?" She felt her anger stirring again. She wanted to tell Sarah to stay the hell away from Camp Seven, but instead looked at John and asked, "And where is she supposed to sleep? Or do you expect me to give up my cabin and bunk in with the men, seeing as how I ain't a female?"

John cleared his throat and said to Big Mary, "She can sleep in the clerk's shack."

"No she can't," Big Mary retorted.

"And why not? The clerk will be gone," he said.

"Because Nilsson sleeps there," she said stubbornly.

John gave her a black look. "He can bunk with the rest of the men. I've made my decision, and that's final. Now let's get on with this wedding food." Then suddenly he said, "Shit!" and pounded the table with his fist. He looked from Sarah to Big Mary and said, "Excuse me, ladies, but this whole business about Nilsson thinking he's leaving is a colossal nuisance!"

Half an hour later, having finally discussed the food for Gray Wolf's wedding party, they went to climb into the carriage for the ride back to Pine Crescent. Sarah stood for a moment and listened to a familiar sound coming from behind the cook shack. Through the nighttime stillness she heard the crack of an axe striking wood, over and over and over again.

CHAPTER 42

JOHN Smitheson arranged for Sarah to drive one of his carriages to Camp Seven after she assured him that she could handle it. When she arrived on the following Saturday morning one of the kitchen helpers, a scrawny boy named Jack, came out to take care of the horse while Sarah went directly into the clerk's shack and went to work. She knew exactly what to do with the scraps of paper that had accumulated between the pages of the ledger, and she felt a familiar pleasure as she translated Thor's scribbles.

Sometime past noon, as she still sat bent over the ledger, the door opened and Jack came in carrying a plate of food covered with a white cloth. "It's past lunchtime and Big Mary says you gotta eat."

"Why, thank you," Sarah said, for the first time looking up at the clock on the wall. "Good grief! I completely lost track of the time." She stood up and stretched, but was immediately aware of the boy's admiring stare. She straightened quickly and took the plate from him. "Thank Big Mary for me. I'll bring the plate to the cook shack when I'm finished."

"No need," he said quickly. "I'm happy to come get it."

She smiled at him reassuringly, realizing for the first time how young he was. He couldn't be more than fourteen years old. "That would be nice."

He grinned happily, blushing, and then turned and ran from the clerk's shack. She smiled to herself, wondering why he made her feel so old. If only she could confide in Big Mary. It would make everything so much easier for her in camp. But there was no way she could do that. Ever since she had first come back to camp with John Smitheson, she suspected Big Mary knew who she really was; but for some reason everyone was pretending Sarah Stewart was Sarah Stewart and Jesse Williams was Jesse Williams.

That evening when she went to the cook shack for supper, a place had been set for her across from where Thor usually sat. Whether Big Mary liked it or not, Thor reminded her that Sarah had been sent by their boss and would be treated well. That didn't apparently mean, however, that he had to show up for supper.

He didn't. She could hear the sound of someone chopping wood out back, and she knew where he had gone instead. She tried not to notice his absence, and was amused and distracted by the way the men kept stealing surreptitious glances at her.

Once when she came over to the table with a plate of meat, Big Mary sniffed the air and said, "I can't understand what stinks so bad in here. One of you jacks must've fallen into the grease bucket."

Several of the men blushed, and several others cleared their throats nervously. They had washed up and combed their hair for supper hoping to attract the attention of "that pretty gal from the office."

She couldn't help smiling, but knew she shouldn't talk at the table. She did, however, whisper to the man sitting next to her, "I think everyone looks awfully nice."

He blushed uncontrollably and muttered something under his breath that sounded like, "Aw gee, Ma'am," but she couldn't tell for sure.

After supper she declined Woody's polite invitation to come to the bunk-house to listen to the music. When she got outside, she listened but heard no sound from the direction of the woodpile. She wondered if he had gone to join the others at the bunkhouse. She thought perhaps he had gone into the sauna, but when she looked in that direction no smoke came from its chimney.

She went to the clerk's shack and worked by lamplight for several hours and then she spent some time making order on the shelves. Finally, around ten o'clock, she went to bed without having laid eyes on Thor.

He was, however, at the table the next morning for breakfast. He might as well not have been, because he ignored her completely, never once looking up from his food and leaving the cook shack as soon as he was finished.

She worked for about an hour after breakfast and then went into the cook shack and asked Jack to hitch up her carriage. "You done, already?" Big Mary asked, a touch of grudging respect in her voice. She may have harbored an intense distaste for Sarah's lies, but she couldn't deny what a good worker she was.

"Yes I am," Sarah answered. "I'll see you next Saturday."

She went out into the clearing, which was alive with the activity of men doing their laundry, sharpening their saws and axes and having their hair cut. She could tell they were watching her whenever she wasn't looking, and Jack stood holding the horse's reins longer than he needed to.

Red Scanlon happened to be going into the stable and he called to the boy, "Let go of the horse, you damned idiot."

Jack blushed and handed her the reins and she drove out of camp, wondering how Thor had managed to ignore her so completely. As she drove back to town, a sick feeling grew in the pit of her stomach. Did he feel nothing for her?

Finally, during supper on the last Saturday night she was to be in camp, he came to eat with them. The other three weekends he had been at breakfast only twice, but never at supper. There was something different about him, but she couldn't figure out what it was until he looked at her for the first time since she had come back to camp to do the absent clerk's work. His eyes were so filled with emotion that she had to look away, fearful the others in the room would notice. No one seemed to, but it left her shaken and confused and she forced herself not to look at him again. When he finished eating, he stood up and left the cook shack without speaking. The rest of the men went to the bunkhouse and when Big Mary and her helpers finished their work, they all went there, too.

Sarah stepped out of the clerk's shack several times that evening to listen to the sounds coming across the clearing. She could not hear the sound of an axe, and she wondered if Thor was with the men and if she should go there. After all, it was her last night in camp and it would only be sociable of her. Instead, she went inside and tried to work, but she couldn't concentrate because she kept remembering the way Thor had looked at her.

After nearly an hour, unable to get anything done, she went outside and stood looking up at the star-filled sky. It was cold, and she leaned back against the log wall of the cook shack and hugged herself for warmth. She was going to go inside when she saw a shadow approach from the main road. She sunk further back against the wall so as not to be seen. As the shadow approached she saw that it was Thor, walking slowly with his head down and his hands in his pockets.

When he entered the clearing, he stopped walking and looked over at the clerk's shack. She was glad she had hidden in the shadows, but she thought foolishly that he might be able to hear her heart pounding. He stood like that for a long time and she began to worry that he might come to the clerk's shack and find her skulking outside. Instead, he turned and headed for the stable, where several minutes later she saw lamplight seeping through the cracks in the stable loft.

Then she remembered that he never slept in the bunkhouse, and if she was sleeping in the clerk's shack, he probably slept in the stable loft. She glanced around the empty clearing and then hurried into the stable. It took several minutes for her eyes to grow accustomed to the darkness. She could hear the horses munching and shifting about, and could feel the warmth of the stable from all the animal bodies. She looked around and spotted the ladder, then climbed to the loft.

He turned abruptly when he heard her, his arms halfway out of his jacket. "Go away! Leave me alone!"

There was fear in his voice and she stepped backwards down one rung in the ladder. "Thor, please. I only want to talk to you."

He finished taking off his jacket and hung it angrily on a nail on the wall and then turned to face her. "Talk?" He made a disparaging sound deep in his throat. "Talk is a waste of time."

She climbed the rest of the way up the ladder and stood looking at him, feeling foolish to have come. But she was here now and there was no sense turning back. "You've been avoiding me. I want you to tell me why." Her question surprised her nearly as much as it surprised him.

His eyebrows lifted and he asked, "What makes you think I've been avoiding you?" He sat down abruptly in the hay, his knees raised and his forearms resting across them. "You give yourself too much credit. I have work to do. I was working. Walking. Oh, what the hell!" His face was tormented. "What do you want from me? Why can't you leave me alone?"

"Leave *you* alone? You're the one who won't leave *me* alone!" she retorted, her angry tone matching his and making her feel foolish for having come, and for saying something so obviously untrue. Something she only *wished* was true.

They glared at each other for a long, tension-filled moment. Finally, his shoulders fell and he lowered his head and pushed his fingers into his hair. He began mumbling words in Swedish, and she crossed the loft and fell onto her knees in front of him.

"Don't you see?" she said softly, remembering how he had looked at her at supper. "Don't you understand how...how it is between us?"

He stopped mumbling and raised his head to look at her and knew there was no place to hide any longer. "What does it matter? You don't understand what it would mean if...." He stopped speaking and raised his hands and placed his palms on either side of her face and looked probingly into her eyes. He couldn't explain about Gray Wolf, but maybe if he tried to explain about going home....

"Since I was a young boy on my way to this country...." He stopped, trying to make sense of it. "I have worked my heart out so that I could return home. You are the only thing that has ever gotten in my way."

She nodded as she covered his hands with her own. "There is not enough wood to cut or enough miles to walk for you to escape from what we feel," she said, barely loud enough for him to hear.

"Yaw," he whispered. "Yaw."

They sat like that, neither of them speaking, until finally he could bear it no longer and he let out a helpless sigh and pulled her tight against him and buried his face into her hair, murmuring the strange-sounding words of his native tongue, which she could not understand but understood nonetheless.

She felt warm and safe, if only for now. She knew at last that he cared for her, but she had no expectations. He would stay—or he would go—but for now, she was in his arms.

Thor felt the power she wielded that could destroy his dream; as well as destroy his friendship with the man who had been his best friend almost as long as the dream had lived within him. Despite what Gray Wolf had said to him that Sunday evening back behind the cook shack, he knew in his heart that Gray Wolf was a long way from accepting him making love to his daughter.

But in the end, nothing or no one outside of the stable loft meant anything. They were together, and the force of it transcended logic and good sense.

It was early morning when she finally left him, and the sound of music coming from the bunkhouse had grown still. She stole furtively back to the clerk's shack and lay in her bunk for only moments before she fell asleep.

She awoke to someone pounding on her door. "Who is it?" she called sleepily.

"It's me, Jack. Big Mary says you're not going to get breakfast if you don't hurry."

"I'm coming," she called, jumping up.

She arranged her hair and clothing as best she could; given the beating they had taken in the hay the night before. When she arrived in the cook shack no one seemed to notice she looked any the worse for wear.

Thor was not at breakfast, nor chopping wood, and she didn't see him before she left. She wondered what it meant that he was still avoiding her after what had happened; but it was probably for the best. They would not have been able to keep their eyes off of each other if he had been at the table.

She drove back to town, content, the memory of their lovemaking still sweet and warm on her flesh.

CHAPTER 43

HE ran a finger along the inside of his collar. "Damned thing itches," Gray Wolf told Thor. They were standing outside of the church waiting for the minister to arrive. White Feather and Big Mary were inside, sitting quietly in one of the front pews. White Feather was dressed in her white buckskins and Big Mary wore a black satin dress with a white lace collar, her hair in its usual tight bun, but uncharacteristically neat.

"That's what you get for deciding to get married," Thor said. "I didn't think I'd see the day."

"Well, you're seeing it, but I'm paying a price I didn't expect to have to pay."

Thor didn't understand. "A price? You mean besides being tied down?"

"Being tied down doesn't bother me anymore. In fact the thought of being settled in my own place pleases me greatly." His gray eyes grew dark as he spoke. "I have to tell the girl."

Thor's heart began to race and he asked, trying to mask his feelings, "Girl? What girl?"

"Sarah. Who do you think? I have to tell her I know who she is. And I have to do it today."

Thor felt uneasy. "Why? Why now all of a sudden? Isn't getting married enough for one day?"

"You'd sure think so!" Gray Wolf admitted. "It's White Feather. She said she wouldn't go through with the wedding unless I promised to make a clean breast of it with the girl."

Thor's palms began to sweat, and he rubbed them onto his pants. "Maybe you should just leave her alone."

"I can't do that. White Feather thinks it's wrong. Besides, it's time Sarah's life got easier. It can't be easy pretending all the time. Maybe she'll finally be able to quit working like a man and settle down with that new doctor in town and be a respectable wife."

Thor felt the angry flush rising up his neck. He had the feeling that he was being betrayed, and that Gray Wolf had been searching for an excuse to tell Thor to leave his daughter alone.

"What makes you think that's what she wants?" he asked through tight lips.

"What do you know about it? Think for once in your life. He's a doctor. She could settle down and be a respectable member of the community and shut down all the gossip about...about...you."

Thor felt dangerously close to coming out with the truth. "I know a lot more about what she wants than you do. It might not be the doctor she's interested in. Did you ever think of that?"

"Yeah," Gray Wolf said, "I think about it all the time. The one conclusion I keep coming to is that she deserves someone with some stability, not...."

"Stability?" It was too much for him. "How do you know this doctor is stable? You barely know the man, and you've known me for ten years."

Thor's eyes were so full of rage Gray Wolf thought he might hit him. He didn't need a broken jaw on his wedding day. "Calm down!" Gray Wolf said, taking a step backwards. Then he sighed deeply, seemingly resigning himself to something. "Don't you see? That's the reason. I do know you. For ten years, every time something happens that you don't like, you threaten to go back to Sweden and finish what you started back there. Now you're finally doing it. I always knew you'd get on a boat home quicker than a load of logs on a wet ice road if things didn't happen to suit you. How stable is that?" He tossed his arms into the air. "I can't believe we're even having this conversation."

Thor hated having it thrown in his face even if it was true. "You're a fine one to talk about having this kind of a conversation," he growled. "If you hadn't turned tail and run from Boston like a scared rabbit...if you had had an ounce of backbone she wouldn't be out here in the timber getting roughed up by a passel of no-accounts!"

Just then, the minister came into view, waving as he came toward them. "Good morning!" he called jovially.

Gray Wolf gave Thor one last look of warning and then walked to meet Axel Wolff, leaving Thor standing alone, confused and shaken. He could still change his mind and not leave to go home, couldn't he? Who could stop him? Then, as he always did when he couldn't accept some other emotion, he settled into a silent, black fury.

***

Sarah had been unable to sleep the night before the wedding. She had resolved to tell her father who she was, but her resolve to humiliate him had softened. She was too happy to hurt anyone. It was true that she had not seen Thor since that night in the stable loft, but she knew the camp had been too busy for him to get away. She would see him today, and how could she doubt his feelings for her? Somewhere in the back of her brain she was beginning to believe he would be staying in Minnesota. How could he not want to be with her?

She took special care getting dressed and fixing her hair and hurried to the office to prepare for the big day. At ten o'clock, Woody arrived with two kitchen helpers. Red Scanlon drove the wagon and helped unload the kettles of food and the bread, rolls, cakes and pies.

"Big Mary's with Thor over at the church," Woody told her, chuckling. "She was nervous as a kitten and all dressed up fit to kill."

"It's a big day for everyone," Sarah said, busily arranging platters of food on the long table they had set up on one side of the room. People started to arrive shortly after noon, and by the time the wedding was over and the wedding party arrived the party had already started. The only thing that had been served thus far was beer because Sarah had covered the food with white cloths so that people wouldn't start to eat until Gray Wolf and White Feather arrived. Everyone shouted a greeting when they came into the room. A moment later Sarah saw Thor come in and she wondered why he refused to look at her, but was too busy to worry about it right then.

"A toast!" John Smitheson called above the noise. The room grew quiet and everyone strained to see John through the crowd. Seeing the difficulty, he got carefully up onto a chair so people could see him. "A toast to the bride and groom." Everyone clapped their hands and cheered with approval. When the room had grown quiet again, John looked at Gray Wolf, who was standing with his arm protectively around White Feather's waist. "May your lives together be long and happy and prosperous!"

Again, cheers from everyone.

"And may all your children look like their mother instead of their father!"

With that last, the room filled with raucous laughter and cries of, "You tell 'em, Boss!" and "Amen to that!"

Big Mary pushed her way through the crowd to where Sarah stood and said, "What do you say we let these folks eat?" Sarah nodded and the two women set about uncovering the food. Gray Wolf and White Feather led the way along the long table. White Feather, strikingly beautiful in her white buckskins, spoke little. None of White Feather's family had come and Sarah wondered at that, but did not say anything to anyone about it. She was too busy waiting for the moment when she could get her father aside to talk to him, and she wanted to focus on what was between the two of them and no one else.

To her surprise, Steven showed up around two o'clock. She was curious about who might have invited him, but short of being rude, she casually ignored him. She had made it clear that she wanted nothing to do with him and she was not going to lead him on in any way. Every now and then she'd feel him watching her, but she carefully avoided looking at him.

She also often caught Thor watching her from somewhere in the room, but he never made an effort to cross the room to speak to her. She tried not to think about it and kept herself busy. Besides, right now she was too nervous and apprehensive about what she was going to say to Gray Wolf to think about Thor.

The moment to speak to her father came late in the afternoon when people were done eating and were milling around talking to each other, most of them half drunk. She noticed that Gray Wolf held a glass but seldom drank from it. Just when she had gotten up enough nerve to approach him, to her surprise he caught her eye from across the room and motioned to her to come into her office.

Nervously, she crossed the room looking around for Thor. She saw him near the bulletin board talking to Red Scanlon. When he saw her, he turned away. Really puzzled now, she entered her office. Her father closed the door and stood looking at her carefully. "I wanted to thank you for all you've done." He nodded toward the other room. "John tells me you've worked hard to make it all happen. I'm guessing it was not easy for you."

He looked very different today from the other times she had seen him. He wore a dark brown suit and a white shirt and his silver hair shone. He had cut it, and the skin showed white in contrast to the rest of his tan, weathered skin, making him look somehow vulnerable. She couldn't help thinking how handsome he was, and she felt a strange and unexpected surge of pride.

"I was happy to do it," she said, then realized what he had just said, "Why do you think it was hard for me, Sir? I had plenty of help." He was studying her carefully and it unnerved her, her resolve to tell him who she really was dissolving as they stood there.

He slowly reached into his pocket and took out a small package. He looked at it for a long moment, as if not quite sure he wanted to do what he was about to do, but then stretched out his hand for her to take it.

"You...you didn't have to do that," she said, putting both hands behind her and taking a step backwards.

"Take it," he said. "Please. I want you to have it."

She stared at the package and then at him. "You don't have to do this," she said again.

He reached out and pulled her arm from behind her and placed the little package into her hand. "Open it," he said, his eyes searching her face.

She did as he bid, nervously unwrapping the small picture frame and staring at the woman in the picture. At first she couldn't focus because she was so taken aback, and because she feared she was not going to be able to say what she wanted to say to him. But as she looked at the picture she grew slowly aware that she was looking at...at herself!

"What...where...." She looked at him in astonishment. "Where did you get this?" She looked at the picture and back at him and then back at the picture. "It looks like...like me! But it can't be!" She raised one hand and clutched at her brooch. "She's wearing my brooch!"

He shook his head, slowly. "No, my dear. You're wearing *her* brooch. It's my mother," he said gently. "Your grandmother. It's how I knew who you were." He gave a small, nervous laugh. "Actually, it was White Feather who recognized the striking resemblance between you—Jesse—and my mother. Part of the reason she agreed to this marriage was that I promised to be honest with you."

Her throat tightened and she couldn't speak. She turned away from him and faced the window behind her desk. So that was it. If it weren't for White Feather making it a condition of their marriage he would have let her go on making a complete fool of herself. She could have gone on pretending she was someone she wasn't until hell froze over as far as he was concerned. Clemmie was wrong. He was a cad, just like the rest of them.

She spun around to face him, and then held out the picture to him. "Keep it. I don't want it."

When he refused to take it, she placed it sharply onto the desk and headed for the door. He stopped her by taking hold of her arm, his face flushed. "Don't go. We need to talk. Your mother. How is your mother?"

She stopped dead in her tracks, and then turned looked at him, her eyes filled with quiet rage. "My mother?" She gave a cold laugh. "I never knew her.

I was told both of you had died in a fire. You weren't dead at all. You were merely...gone."

"Sarah. Please."

"Thor knew, too, didn't he?" she said through tight lips, ignoring his question about her mother, awareness dawning on her about Thor's behavior and the reasons for it.

He nodded. "I made him promise not to tell you. I wanted to give you a chance to...." His eyes were filled with remorse, but she didn't care.

She started again for the door, and again he reached out to stop her but this time thought better of it. With her hand on the knob, she turned back to him. "You asked about my mother. She was gone, too, but at least she saw that I was cared for."

He winced, and then said, "Gone? Where did she go? How...?"

"How was I cared for, do you mean?" Again she laughed coldly. "I lived with my aunt and uncle. He thought he was doing me a favor letting me live with him and giving me his name. In truth, he did me no favors."

"Oh Christ," he groaned. "William Stewart! That bastard was never any good...."

"You're right," she said, smiling with her lips but not her eyes. "He really *was* a no-good bastard. There are many of those, aren't there? But William Stewart is dead, and good riddance."

His thoughts were racing ahead of her words. "Lorna. Where did she go? Why didn't she take you with her? Why...?

"Why? I guess because she didn't think it was fitting to keep a child in a whorehouse. But you needn't worry about her. She's dead, too. And you might as well be." He looked stricken, and she wished she felt more pleased about it. She pulled the door open and fled from the room.

She stood in the crowded room for a moment, her mind racing. *The Indian camp.* She knew as surely as she breathed that that was when it had happened. It all made sense now. Gray Wolf telling her his real name. White Feather treating her like an honored guest. Thor enraged and almost leaving her behind because he was going to have to pretend he didn't know who she was. He had known not only that she was a woman; he knew she was Gray Wolf's daughter. She was boiling mad. They had made a fool of her. They had both known who she was and why she had come to the timber and they let her suffer through months of torment.

As quickly as the anger had come, it was washed away by a wave of humiliation so strong that it made her weak in the knees. It was her own fault for having been dishonest. They had known who she was, but they couldn't have known why she had chosen to disguise her identity. They might, in fact, have been completely confused by her behavior. They could well have been waiting for her to make the first move. She pushed those thoughts from her mind. She wasn't going to take responsibility for him...them. Her father only told her who he was because otherwise White Feather wouldn't have him.

And as far as Thor was concerned.... The thought of him made the color rise to her face. He had cared more about keeping his friend's secret than about being honest with her. What did that say about what she meant to him? She felt a sick wave of embarrassment. She couldn't blame him for what had happened between them. She had practically thrown herself at him.

Her eyes darted around the room like a drowning woman looking for something to grab onto. She saw Steven and pushed through the crowd to him. "Take me home," she said. "I need to get out of here."

He was talking to one of the lumberjacks about an old injury the man had suffered falling from a tree. He had no idea why she had this strong urge to escape a party that had seemed to go very well for her, but quickly saw the opportunity it presented.

"Excuse me," he said to the man as he took Sarah's arm and they made their way toward the door.

As he hurried to get his rig she stood waiting, and to her horror saw Thor standing several yards away talking to Big Mary. He looked at her and then at Steven's rig pulling up and then back again at her. Sarah turned away and refused to look at him again.

At the same time, the door opened and Gray Wolf stumbled out of the building. "Sarah! Please! We've got to talk!" he called to her desperately.

"I have nothing more to say to you," she called back over her shoulder loud enough so Thor could hear, then hurried to where Steven waited for her to get into the buggy.

"What's going on?" Big Mary asked, her eyes darting from Gray Wolf to Thor to Sarah and then back around again.

Thor was already piecing together a twisted scenario of what was happening. He had stayed away from Sarah the entire day, giving Gray Wolf time to settle the business between them. And what had he gotten in return from his friend?

He had obviously convinced her that the doctor was the right man for her. He let the anger take him deeper into a jealous rage such as he had never felt—not even when Annika told him she would not marry him.

He was too angry to think straight and to wonder why, if she was letting her father tell her which man was worthy of her, she was storming away from both the man her father had spoken against and the man who had spoken.

"Take me home," Sarah said to Steven, ignoring Thor and not wanting to try to understand the expression on his face. She glanced once at her father and at White Feather, who had also come outside. Gray Wolf's face was ashen and when White Feather tried to put a reassuring hand on his arm he pushed it away.

After they were seated in the carriage and they were driving away Steven turned his head toward her and said, "Do you want to tell me what happened, my love?" He sensed power and he reached over and stroked her arm.

She grabbed his hand and jerked it away, her eyes ablaze, all of her pent-up feelings finally coming to the surface, pouring out of her. "Don't touch me!" she screamed. "And don't call me your love! I am neither your love nor anyone else's! Take me home!"

She was too overwrought to at first realize that they were going in the wrong direction. Instead of turning down the road to the boarding house he continued straight on past the train depot going south. "Where do you think you're going?" she cried. "I told you to take me home!"

He looked sideways at her, his eyes filled with concern. "It's okay, Sarah. I'll take you home soon. Right now I think it would be best if we ride for a while so you can calm down."

"I don't want to calm down!" she shouted, trying to grab the reins from him.

"Whoa," he called to the horse, stopping the carriage and turning toward her. "I'm talking to you now, not as a friend but as a doctor. You need to calm down. Do you want to tell me what happened?"

"It's none of your business," she cried, her eyes frantic and her voice pitched too high. "I want you to take me ho...." All at once the strength of her anger drained out of her. Her shoulders fell and she dropped back against the seat and broke into piteous sobs.

He did not try to touch her or to comfort her in any way. He merely sat quietly, the reins loose in his hands, and waited. After what seemed like hours, but was really only minutes, her sobbing stopped and she closed her eyes, her head resting against the seat.

"Do you want to ride a little while?" he asked quietly. "I won't try to make you talk."

She nodded slowly without looking at him.

It began to grow dark, the sun hanging below the trees, the shadows growing long. It had been a warm, sunny day, but the evening air was growing cold as the sun descended. She shivered and pulled the lap robe up around her shoulders. Finally, after nearly an hour, he turned the carriage and headed back toward town. Neither of them spoke until he pulled up in front of the boarding house.

"Do you want to talk?"

She shook her head quickly, a tear once more finding its way down her cheek.

"Are you alright?" he asked.

She nodded, again without speaking, and got down from the carriage. He didn't make a move to help her, knowing the best thing he could do for her now was not to touch her. She walked to the door and before going inside, turned and said, "Thank you, Doctor."

CHAPTER 44

SHE slept fitfully that night and awoke Sunday morning with a throbbing headache. She refused breakfast but drank several cups of strong coffee. The men joked about her having partied too much the day before, but she gave them a look that put a quick end to their teasing.

She walked to church and found Clemmie sitting alone in a middle pew. She slid in beside her and asked, "Where are your menfolks?"

"Jesse has the sniffles so Richard stayed home with him. I didn't want to risk not seeing you this morning. How was the wedding?"

"I'll explain later. Shhh," she whispered, putting a finger to her lips as Pastor Wolff cleared his throat from the pulpit and began to speak.

When the service was over they walked together back to the depot and Sarah told her what had happened. "Spend the day with us today. I don't think you should be alone right now."

"Thanks for the invitation. I won't argue with you. I don't think I could tolerate the men today and I surely don't need to spend the day staring at the walls in my room."

The baby was asleep and Richard was glad for an excuse to go downstairs and get back to work. "Trains keep on running no matter what," he said. "They don't give a hoot what people might have on their minds, and it looks to me like you two have plenty on yours."

Sarah stood looking out the kitchen window while Clemmie made tea. "You should eat something," Clemmie said. "I've got some Boston brown bread left over from supper last night. How about if I butter a nice thick slice for you."

Sarah grimaced. "I don't think I can face anything remotely connected to Boston this morning. Besides, you know how I lose my appetite whenever...." She didn't finish her sentence. Whenever her mind was in turmoil she had trouble eating, but this felt different. She dismissed the thought and merely smiled apologetically at Clemmie.

She sat down and sipped the hot tea, then looked over the rim of her cup and said, "I wish I wasn't so confused."

"Confused? You mean about your father?"

Sarah nodded. "He made it perfectly clear to me that he wants to talk to me, and yet...." Her voice trailed off.

"Sounds like it to me," Clemmie agreed. "I guess I'm confused, too. I mean.... I don't really understand why you won't talk to him. Isn't that why you came West?"

"Yes, of course."

"Then tell me why you won't."

"After all these years you'd think he'd be curious. He knew who I was and he ignored me."

"So what if he ignored you for a while? He finally did try to talk to you, and what did you do? You ran off like a frightened chicken."

"I wasn't frightened! I was angry. He only tried to talk to me because White Feather forced him to." She pushed away from the table and went to stand in front of the stove with her arms folded across her chest. "It makes me angry just thinking about it.

"Sarah, Sarah, Sarah," Clemmie said shaking her head. "Sometimes I think when it comes to your father you twist everything so you can look at him in the very worst possible light."

"I do not!"

"You do, too! There's your father, begging to talk to you and all you can think about is that White Feather told him to do it. If he didn't want to do it he could have refused."

"Then she wouldn't have married him," Sarah said stubbornly.

Clemmie got up from the table with a look of mild disgust. "Oh alright. Go ahead and feel any way you want to about it. You will anyway."

Sarah grew silent, fearing Clemmie was probably right. Finally she said, "You must think I'm an idiot."

"I don't think that at all. What I think is that you're feeling sorry for yourself."

Sarah's eyes flashed angrily. "What did you say?"

"I said you're feeling sorry for yourself. You came out here to find your father. You found him. You've dragged your feet long enough. It may not have turned out exactly the way you wanted it to, but we can't always control how and when things happen. God works in mysterious ways. It does no earthly good for us to rail against life because it takes a direction we don't like."

Clemmie stopped speaking and Sarah looked down at the tablecloth and waited. When Clemmie continued her voice was gentler. "I don't mean to sound harsh. It's just that if you keep up this way you'll never be happy. If your father wants to square things with you why can't you let him? Stop fighting it."

After several minutes Sarah looked at her, her eyes full of misery. "I'm afraid."

"Afraid? Afraid of what?"

Sarah was staring at her hands, turning them over and examining first the backs of them and then the palms. Then she looked back at Clemmie. "I'm afraid of hearing the truth. I'm afraid he's going to tell me he barely knew my mother, and what he did know about her he didn't like. When he found out she was pregnant he wasn't at all sure the baby was his and he wasn't about to get saddled with a woman he didn't care for—to say nothing of a brat he wasn't even sure was his. So he left."

Clemmie was sitting back in her chair, her mouth agape. When she could finally gather herself together enough to speak, she said, "Whew! You don't sound confused to me. You sound like you know exactly what to expect. How clairvoyant you are!"

Sarah shrugged sheepishly, but said nothing.

"We've already talked about this, Sarah. We agreed you might not like to hear what he has to say. I've said it before and I'll say it again. Your father cannot be as awful as you think he is and still be your father."

"Now who's being clairvoyant?"

"You're so stubborn!" Clemmie said, her frustration apparent in the set of her jaw. "I don't want to talk about this anymore. The next time you mention your father to me, I want it to be *after you have talked to him.*"

Sarah remained stubbornly silent for a long minute, then finally nodded reluctantly.

"Good," Clemmie said. "Now that we have that little matter settled, what about the other man in your life?"

"What other man?"

"Come on, Sarah. You know who I mean."

Sarah looked downcast. "I don't want to talk about him."

"Well then. It looks like we're going to have to talk about *me.*"

"I'm sorry, Clemmie! I didn't mean to be so selfish."

Clemmie laughed. "I was only joking. Everything in my life right now is... well, a bit boring, compared to yours."

"Are you feeling sorry for yourself because you're bored?" Sarah asked mischievously.

Just then, they heard Jesse cry in the other room, and as Clemmie rose to go to him she said, "Stay for dinner. I'm going to roast a chicken and you can help me stuff it. I'm such a lousy cook."

"What makes you think I'm any better?"

"You used to be a cook's helper. That should count for something."

***

On the following Friday morning she arrived at work and found her father waiting for her. He was wearing denim coveralls and a denim shirt, and with his short hair he hardly looked like the man she had first met. When she avoided his eyes and looked at his hair, he ran a hand through it and said, "Farmers don't have long hair."

She looked around the room and then back at him. "Is White Feather with you?" Her voice was cool, distant, and she tried not to think of Clemmie's admonishment.

"She's at home," he said, his voice steady. "I wanted to talk to you alone."

She took off her coat as she walked into her office. He followed her, watching as she hung her coat and then went over and stood looking out the window, her back to him.

She heard the door close and turned, thinking he had left. He had not. He was standing in front of it, his hands at his sides in tight fists.

"I have work to do," she said, hating herself for the way she was acting but powerless to stop.

"John knows I'm coming. You can take the day off if you need to. We can go somewhere else or we can stay here. It doesn't matter to me where we talk, but we *are* going to talk."

She started to protest but the expression on his face told her it would be no use. She sat down and motioned for him to sit down too and said, her voice still cool, "Talk then."

He sat across from her, his eyes filled with stubborn determination. "I wasn't going to do this but I can't stop thinking about what you said the day of my wedding. You said some awful things and I can't just sweep them under the rug and ignore them."

She gave a scornful laugh. "My experience so far is that you ignore things quite easily. Did White Feather send you again?" She had a strange sense of being above herself in the room, as if the cruel words were coming from someone else. "You really needn't have bothered to come. I know how busy you must be, what with a new wife and a brand new farm and...."

"Dammit! Stop it!" he said, jumping up from his chair and slamming a fist on her desk. His rage was palpable, and the force of it made her flinch and push herself away from him and against the back of her chair.

"This is between you and me, Sarah," he said as he sat back down, making an effort to steady himself. "It has nothing to do with White Feather. It's about what happened nearly twenty years ago. Whether you like it or not I'm not leaving until we get this out in the open."

They stared at each other until Sarah stood and broke the uncomfortable silence. "Would you like some coffee? The men always make coffee first thing and I can get you some."

"I'll have some if you will," he said with some relief, rubbing the damp palms of his hands along the sides of his pant legs.

She returned with two cups of coffee and pushed the door shut with her foot. She set one of them on the desk in front of him then went around the desk and sat down holding her cup without drinking from it, her eyes squarely on his.

"Why did you go?" she blurted, her voice quavering. She banged her cup down violently onto the desk and it splashed over onto the blotter. She ignored it. "Why did you leave us?" She leaned toward him across the desk. "How could you do that? How could you just go away and leave her to...."

"Sarah, I...." He was searching for words to say that might ease the anguish he saw on her face. He said simply, "I loved your mother."

"Then why...?"

He didn't let her finish. "I loved her and she loved me, but whenever we tried to set a date to get married we'd run up against the same arguments."

"Arguments? What kind of arguments?" she asked scornfully.

He sighed deeply, remembering. "She was a stubborn woman, your mother. I wanted to go West and she wanted to stay in Boston. I guess when it comes down to it, it was that simple."

She turned away and stared out the window for a long moment. Then she looked back at him and asked quietly. "Couldn't you have at least waited until I was born? Didn't you worry about what might happen to me?"

His eyebrows drew together and he said, "Do you think I left knowing...do you think I got on a train and rode away from a woman I loved who was carrying my child? My God!" he said with a groan. "No wonder you don't want to have anything to do with me! Christ! What an asshole you must think I am!"

She was staring at him, not sure whether to trust him. "You didn't know?" she asked in a small voice.

"No I did not," he said, his voice firm and his eyes steady as he met her gaze. "If I had known, I'd have forced her to marry me and come West."

He sat thinking for a moment then smiled a wry, knowing smile. "She knew it, too. That's the reason she never told me." He leaned back in his chair and folded his arms over his chest as he looked down at the floor shaking his head. For the first time he realized what must have happened. When he looked up again, his expression was pained. "You told me she couldn't keep you with her because...."

She didn't let him finish. "I never knew anything about her. Not until the night I overheard my aunt and uncle talking about her. The night my uncle shot himself."

He grimaced. "What else have you had to go through because of what we did?" He leaned forward, letting his elbows rest on the desk, his head in his hands, his face down so she couldn't see his expression. He sat silently for a long while as if deep in thought. Finally he sat up, leaned back and said resignedly, "Tell me. Tell me all of it."

He listened intently as she told him about life with her aunt and uncle, and of the lies she had been told about her parents' death. Her voice was surprisingly calm as she told him what she had overheard and about how Amelia cruelly told her the story of her real beginnings. She even told him about how Steven had rejected her, carefully avoiding any reference to the behavior that might tell him she was just like her mother.

When she seemed to have run out of words, he said, "My God! You must hate both of us!"

She shrugged, the gesture belying the hurt so visible on her face.

"I can't take away all those years you suffered on our account. I wish I could, but I can't."

She nodded but said nothing.

"You have a lot of guts, Sarah," he said. "You've been through more than anyone should ever have to go through and none of it was your fault. I wouldn't blame you if you never forgave me." He could see that she was trying hard not to cry, but he continued anyway. "The one glimmer of hope I have for us to be father and daughter is that you came all this way looking for me and once you found me you stayed. You wouldn't have done it if you had given up completely on me. I want to believe you held out hope that I wasn't...wasn't....." His words hung in the air.

Her eyes were moist, and she spoke with difficulty. "I didn't tell you who I was because...I was afraid you'd tell me...."

"You were afraid I'd tell you I didn't care then and I don't care now. That's it, isn't it." It wasn't a question.

She nodded, the tears now running down her cheeks and her words pouring out along with them. "When I saw how much you cared when your baby d...died, I hated you because you never cared enough about me to stay and see that.... You cared more about your new family than you cared about me and my...my mother!" She began to sob uncontrollably, the pent-up hurt releasing itself in a torrent. She put her head down on the desk and gave herself up to it.

She felt his hands on her shoulders. "Hush, Child. Hush now. Don't cry. It's okay. I'm here and I'm not going away. Shhh." He gently squeezed her shoulders, kneading softly with his hands as he spoke words of comfort to her. He felt the tension locked in her young shoulders and stayed where he was. "I'm so sorry, Sarah," he whispered hoarsely. "I'm so very, very sorry for all of it."

She didn't say anything, but nodded almost imperceptibly. Then she reached up and put a hand on one of his. They stayed like that for a long time.

Finally he cleared his throat and walked to the window and stood looking out. Then he turned to her and said, "I'm going to leave now but I'd like to come back sometime soon."

She closed her eyes and then opened them, nodding. She could see that he, too, had had enough for one day. She went into the other room with him and they both saw Jock Lehtinnen standing at the far end of the room talking to Peter Knox and John. When they saw Sarah and Gray Wolf, John nodded and motioned for them to come over.

The men shook hands with Gray Wolf and smiled knowingly at Sarah. It wasn't hard to see that everyone knew what was going on. Sarah felt the need to clear the air, so she said, "What brings you to town, Jock? I thought you'd be home by now."

"'Afraid not," he said. "It looks like you'll be seeing my ugly face around here all summer."

"That will surely disappoint your boys," she said, not caring that Jesse had been the one he talked to about his family.

He seemed not to notice. "They'll get over it," he said.

"Speaking of families," Peter said, looking at Sarah and then at Gray Wolf. "We sure were surprised to find out about...that is, I mean...that was a swell trick you pulled on everybody out at Camp Seven."

"Shut up, you idiot," John said angrily.

Sarah raised a hand in protest. "It's okay." She said, smiling sideways at her father. "After all, how many women get a chance to be the character in a lumber-jack story?"

The men all laughed at that and Jock said, "It's the truth. It's all the men can talk about."

"I was always good with numbers in school. She takes after her old man," Gray Wolf said proudly.

She was caught off guard by how good his words made her feel and she blushed.

"I'd better get going," he said, putting his arm around her shoulders and giving her a squeeze. "I've kept her away from her work long enough."

After he had gone she turned to Jock and said, "So tell me why you're working this summer instead of going home to your farm."

As soon as the words were out of her mouth she knew. "He's gone, isn't he?"

Jock nodded. "He left three days ago."

"If you and Elmer need any help with the books let me know," she said, nearly choking on the words. She hurried into her office and closed the door. She did not cry. She had cried enough for one day—for a lifetime, actually. She sat down at her desk and opened her ledger, but the numbers blurred. "It's all too much," she whispered. "It's just simply all too much."

CHAPTER 45

HE came to see her often after that, and during those visits she gradually learned something about his relationship with her mother. He told her about boat rides in the park, the opera, fine restaurants, and about all the things they were able to do because their parents were well-to-do. He also told her that the reason he had been so eager to go West was to get away from his father and his brother.

"I can understand your wanting to get away from your brother," she said, remembering how Duncan MacKenna had behaved toward her. She told him about her visit to his brother's church.

"I'm not surprised," he said shaking his head sadly. "Sounds like he hasn't changed much." He paused then said, "My family wasn't all bad, though. I loved my mother and my grandfather. They were the only people I missed after I left Boston—except your mother."

"What about *her* parents? My other grandparents. Couldn't they have helped my mother so she wouldn't have had to...had to...?"

"Lorna was always a handful for them. She was close to her sister, but I doubt she could ever have asked her parents for help. She did things her own way and she was awfully proud. Too proud to go to her parents with what she would consider a mistake she had made."

"I vaguely remember seeing them when I was a child. They fussed over my cousin, Amelia, but showed no interest in me. I remember feeling invisible. It's the first time I can remember hating Amelia."

He shook his head sadly and murmured to himself, "They took their disapproval out on an innocent child."

A sad, wry smile turned up one corner of her mouth. "Too bad they died before they found out what a rat Lettie's husband was. If they had, they could have ignored Amelia, too, and then I might not have hated her so much." She seemed to think better of what she had just said. "No. That's not right. She made me hate her all by herself."

He tipped his head back and looked up at the ceiling, as if he could find the answer to some of life's riddles written there. Then he let out a long breath, looked squarely at her and said, "It's done. They can't hurt you anymore. Hating people who can't hurt you anymore is a big waste of time and it only breeds bitterness."

"I don't hate them anymore," she said, "and I don't think I'm bitter except...."

His eyebrows went up, the scar over his eye clearly visible in the late-morning light from the window. "Except?"

"How could she do what she did?" She tried to keep her voice steady but her lips quivered.

He sighed and leaned forward; his hands folded loosely, his forearms resting on his knees. He suddenly felt very tired. He would not destroy the image he had tried to give her of her mother. "I'm going to give this my best shot, Sarah, but you need to understand that I can only guess."

She nodded and said softly, "That's all I ask. You're the only one who can even try to explain her to me."

"She chose to keep me out of it," he began. "That meant she had to provide for you, and she never did anything halfway. She must have decided it was the only way she could make up to you for what she had taken from you."

"That doesn't make any sense," Sarah said softly, not arguing but simply trying hard to understand. "She left me with Aunt Lettie and a pack of lies. I never even saw a picture of her. I'll never know what my own mother looked like."

"She was very beautiful, I can tell you that. She had soft golden-red hair, and her eyes were the color of the ocean on a calm day. Her skin, well...." He smiled, lost for a moment in remembering.

"Then I look nothing like her," Sarah said, convinced no one would ever call *her* beautiful.

"No. No you don't. You already know you look enough like my mother to be her twin." He reached into his pocket and pulled out the picture and looked searchingly at it and then tried to hand it to her. "I still want you to have it."

She shook her head. "No. You keep it. I know how much it means to you." She touched her brooch. "I have this."

He put the picture back into his pocket. "Someday this, too, will be yours," he told her. "I only wish I had a picture of your mother to give you."

"Oh, so do I," she said. "I don't know what she looked like and I don't know...." She paused; not sure she wanted to ask the next question, but asked it anyway. "I still don't see how...how she could...could do what she did."

He didn't answer right away, mainly because he didn't understand it either. "She was a good person, Sarah, but she never did anything halfway. If she was going to take care of a child by herself I know she'd want to give you every advantage. The way she chose to do it still baffles me, but if it hadn't been for your uncle doing what he did, you'd be a very rich young lady."

"But...."

"It was the price she chose to pay, but it wouldn't have kept her from being ashamed. What she did made her ashamed. It simply had to. I'm sure it's the reason she never tried to see you." He paused, his eyes soft, sad. "I believe she did what she thought she had to do. She thought it was the right thing for you, but she gave up her own decency in the process. More than that, she gave up her own child."

Sarah did not speak. She sat, her hands folded on her desk, staring somewhere beyond the room and beyond the two of them. Finally, she met his eyes and said, "You may be right, but you may also be wrong. She might simply have been...." She stopped, drained.

He nodded, and then lowered his eyes to the floor. He had done his best. He could do no more.

***

After that, on the days her father came to see her she would work late to make up for the time they spent together, although John Smitheson kept insisting there was no need for her to do so. "I owe your father my life, so giving up my bookkeeper for a few hours is little enough in repayment."

One morning early in May he came into her office flushed with excitement. "Come outside. I've got something for you."

He saw her confusion. "It's a present for your eighteenth birthday."

"My eighteenth birthday was last winter." She remembered all too well that it had come and gone without anyone knowing. It was supposed to have been the day she received her inheritance and her freedom. So much for should-have-beens.

"Then it's not any too soon for you to get your present." He took her arm and led her outside and pointed to a bay mare hitched to a two-person carriage.

She let out a small cry and ran down the steps and stroked the mare's forelock as she looked back over her shoulder at him. "Mine? Is she really mine?"

He stood watching her, pleased by the happiness on her face. He approached the horse and patted her on the flank. "She's very gentle. She'll give you no trouble. I've made arrangements with Ezekial over at the livery stable to board her and take care of her for you."

"I can't believe it," she said, feeling suddenly flustered. She stared at the ground, and then, as if making her mind up about something she looked at him and said simply, "Thank you, Father."

"There's a catch." She eyed him suspiciously and he quickly added, "You need to give me a ride back to the farm." Before she had a chance to protest he said, "John knows already. He said it's okay for you to leave."

As they drove to the farm she kept thanking him over and over again until he was forced to say, "Enough. You've thanked me enough. It's the first gift I've ever given you and God knows it's little enough."

"It's not little," she insisted, turning to look at him. "It means an awful lot to me." She thought for a moment then said, "It's not just Katie Girl...."

"Katie Girl?"

"Yes. I'm going to call her Katie Girl. It's not just Katie Girl and the rig. It's.... Well, it's...it's just that no one ever gave me anything really nice before."

"I'd say it's high time," he said smiling fondly at her.

When they arrived at the farm it was late morning. White Feather heard them coming and was standing on the front steps waiting for them. Sarah tried not to stare at her middle, which had grown thick.

Gray Wolf followed her gaze and said, "The baby's due early in September."

Sarah pushed down a stab of jealousy, feeling petty and ungrateful. "That's really nice," she managed to say.

White Feather opened the door and said, "Come in and I will show you the house." Sarah followed her inside while Gray Wolf took Katie Girl to the barn.

The house was bigger than Sarah had expected it to be. There was a small pantry at one end of the kitchen in which they kept the foodstuffs that didn't go into the root cellar. Dishes and cooking utensils were also kept there, along with the household linens.

The kitchen had a large stove, and at one end of the room there was a fireplace. A large kettle hung over the fire. White Feather went over and stirred its contents. "My husband knows it is easier for me to cook over a fire. It is hard to change my ways," she said, glancing suspiciously at the stove. "I am trying."

"Gray Wolf likes to drink milk," White Feather said with a small grimace as she went to the window and pointed out at the well. He puts it into a bucket and lowers it down where it is cool. The butter, too." She grimaced again. "He says I will get used to white man's food, but I am not so sure."

Just then Gray Wolf came into the house and heard her remark about white man's food. He laughed and walked over and put his arm around her shoulder and looked at Sarah. "I keep telling her she can eat whatever she likes." He sniffed the air. "Ah! Rabbit stew! You hungry, Sarah?"

"Starved!" she lied. In fact the smell was making her quite ill, but she forced herself to appear enthusiastic as she helped White Feather set the table.

"After lunch I'll show you around outside," Gray Wolf told her as he heaped her plate with the stew.

She looked down at the food and suddenly felt gorge rising in her throat. She pushed her chair back and ran outside. She managed to get as far as the privy before she vomited on the ground in front of the door. She leaned her head against the door clutching her stomach, rivulets of perspiration running down between her breasts.

She felt a hand on her shoulder and without thinking, tried to shrug it off. "I'm fine," she insisted without much force.

White Feather ignored her protests and took her arm. "Come inside and lie down," she said firmly. Sarah, too weak to protest, allowed White Feather to lead her into the house and into the bedroom. She was thankful that Gray Wolf had somehow managed to disappear.

"Rabbit stew is not white man's food," White Feather told her softly. "I am sorry the smell of it made you ill."

Sarah lifted her head from the pillow, thought better of it, let her head fall back again and closed her eyes. "You must forgive me. It smelled awfully good, but I...."

"Rest now," White Feather interrupted. "Later I will make you some tea."

She dozed off, and when she awoke she heard Gray Wolf and White Feather speaking in low voices. She sat up and lowered her feet carefully to the floor. After a few minutes she got up and went into the other room. "I'm terribly sorry," she said as she looked first at her father and then at White Feather. "I'm sure you'll never invite me back. At least not for dinner." She was trying to make light of it, but she felt awful about what had happened.

As if nothing whatever had happened, Gray Wolf got up and went to the stove. "How about some tea? Then we'll go outside and see the rest of the farm."

"I don't care for anything," Sarah said, "but I want to see the rest of the farm."

"First the tea," White Feather insisted as she poured it into a cup and handed it to Sarah. "There are some herbs in there that will make you feel better."

It smelled different from anything she had ever smelled, but she sipped it and found it quite soothing.

"Sit," White Feather ordered as she pulled a chair out from the table. "There is plenty of time to see the farm."

She drank all of the tea because they were both sitting at the table watching her. When she was finished her father slapped his knees with his hands and stood up and said, "Let's go."

The barn stood west of the house, back and away from the lake. Two cows grazed in the barnyard, along with a team of Percherons and Katie Girl. When they went inside the smells assaulted her and she had to lean against one of the stanchions. He reached for her and she waved him off. "I'm not ill. I was just remembering...." Trying to pull herself together, she ran out into the open air.

He was watching her anxiously, not wanting to meddle but mightily curious about what it was she was remembering. "Are you sure you're okay?"

She nodded as she breathed air into her lungs. She was afraid he was going to think she was a real mess if she didn't perk up. Frantic for something to say to change the subject she remembered that he had told her he picked up Katie Girl and the rig that morning at the livery stable.

"How did you get to town this morning, Father?"

"Woody Olson gave me a ride," he answered, relieved to be talking about something outside of themselves.

"Woody? What was he doing around here? Isn't he still working at Camp Seven?"

"Yes, but he's been here looking at some land. He's got a crazy notion he wants to buy a farm." He laughed at what he had just said. "Pot's calling the kettle black!" She laughed with him, both of them grateful for the air having cleared.

They walked down the long slope in front of the house to the lakeshore and he picked up a rock and skipped it over the water. "Makes me feel young again, being by the water. My grandfather used to take me to the ocean." He stared off into the distance and for an instant could almost see his grandfather walking toward him.

He turned to look at Sarah. "I'm happy you're here." Without waiting for any kind of reply he added, "I've been remembering them. My mother, I mean, and my grandfather. Lorna, too. Without you they'd have stayed in the past, lost to me."

"Surely you must have thought about them during all this time."

His eyes were filled with regret, but only for a moment. "I always tried not to. I didn't like the sadness. Now it seems I can think about them without...now that you're here.... I only wish your mother could know that it wasn't all a waste. It meant something after all. It meant you."

She turned away so he couldn't see her face. She still felt weak and a little queasy and his words made her want to cry. "I'd better get back to town. It's getting late."

"Sure thing. I'll get Katie Girl hitched up."

As she drove home she thought about all that had happened that day. Despite her reaction to seeing White Feather again with child and her getting sick from the rabbit stew, they had made her feel welcome. She remembered her father's kind words, realizing at the same time how much independence his gift had given her.

Then a small voice somewhere deep inside spoke to her, disturbing her reverie. *It was not the rabbit stew.*

CHAPTER 46

I T was June when she knew for sure. She had suspected the possibility for quite a while, but kept denying it to herself. What was she going to do? What in the world had she gotten herself into? She had walked headlong—eyes wide open—into a mess the likes of which even she hadn't known before. She thought about going to Hinckley to a doctor so she could be absolutely sure. She even considered going to Steven, but she was too ashamed. Besides, neither of those actions would have done anything except confirm that she did indeed have a very large problem.

She drove to her father's farm on a Saturday, arriving at lunchtime. White Feather insisted that she eat with them and although she wasn't in the least bit hungry, she nibbled at the fried fish and the homemade bread. When they finished eating, she asked her father if she could talk to him alone.

They walked outside and sat down on the hill above the lake. The air was warm and would have been pleasant had it not smelled of smoke. "Where is it coming from?" she asked worriedly.

He looked up at the sky as if by doing so he could glean the source of the smoke. "Hard to say. It's almost always like this lately. We need rain—bad! It hasn't rained at all since the beginning of May." He turned toward her, his face questioning. He already knew her well enough to know something was bothering her.

"What's wrong, Sarah?"

"I have something to tell you," she said, her eyes focused on the water, "and it's pretty awful."

"Whatever it is," he said soothingly, "you can tell me."

"I'm with child."

She said it so matter-of-factly that he wondered if he had heard right. When she didn't say more he remained silent, letting her words settle into his brain, trying with all of his strength not to judge her. After all, who was he to judge anyone?

"What about the father?" he finally managed to ask.

"He's gone. History seems to be repeating itself."

"Gone?"

She nodded but still did not look at him.

He knew right away. "It's Thor."

"Yes. But he doesn't know," she said with surprising calm. "That's what I mean about history repeating itself."

He sat for a long time staring down at the lake. A mallard duck kept ducking its head into the water looking for fish and coming up empty.

He suddenly remembered the day of the wedding and how Thor had tried to tell him about his feelings for Sarah, and how he wouldn't let him. "I told him to leave you alone. He tried to tell me...Oh God," he groaned. "It's my fault he's gone!" He stood up, clearly agitated.

She looked up at him. "Tell me. What did he try to tell you?"

"I'm so sorry, Sarah! If only I'd known. I was spouting off about how I wanted you to be happy and how it would be good if you married the doctor and he was so mad he nearly hit me. He asked me how I could be so sure of what you wanted."

Despite everything, she felt a wave of joy. "Do you think....?" She couldn't say the words, but he seemed to understand without her saying them.

"Yes," he said, turning to look at her, his eyes intense. "He was crazy with it. He didn't know what to do about you." He paused, thinking, then said, "He shouldn't have listened to me. He should have...."

She held up her hand to stop his words. She couldn't bear to hear any more. It was enough simply to know that he hadn't made love to her and walked away without another thought. She turned from him and wandered down to the shore. As soon as she moved in that direction the mallard took off into the air.

He came and stood beside her, his hands pushed deep into his pockets. "I don't know if you can ever forgive all the things you have to forgive me for."

She looked at him briefly then looked back at the water as she spoke. "We all make mistakes. Maybe this one is not so bad."

"How can it not be bad?" he asked.

"I wouldn't want him to stay with me if he loved someone else more than he loved me, or if he wasn't sure," she said reasonably. "I wouldn't want him to always regret not going back to Sweden." She shook her head. "No. I wouldn't want that."

"I'm going to write to him," Gray Wolf said, his mind already made up.

"No!" she said sharply, and then added more softly, "No. Promise me you won't do that." Her eyes pleaded with him.

His shoulders sank and he breathed a deep sigh. "Ah yes," he said. "History does indeed repeat itself." Then he said, his voice firm, "I will promise on one condition."

"What? What condition?"

"That you'll come here and live with us. We'll be a family. The five of us."

She stared at him, looking for signs that he was only saying it because he felt guilty. He clearly was not, because his face was too filled with emotion for her not to believe his sincerity.

She nodded, tears stinging her eyes.

"It'll be okay, Sarah." He put his arms around her and she let him hold her close for a long time. "You'll see. It'll be just fine," he whispered.

They walked back to the cabin where White Feather sat outside on a chair shelling peas into a kettle. She smiled when she saw them and looked from one to the other without speaking.

"Sarah has agreed to come and live with us," he said without further explanation.

White Feather nodded, as if she had known all along. "It is good," was all she said.

***

"I'm going to quit my job and go live with my father." They were sitting on the train platform on a Sunday afternoon in late June, little Jesse in a basket at their feet. The air was hot and still and the baby was fretful.

"I think he's teething," Clemmie said quietly, letting Sarah's words settle in.

When Sarah said nothing more, Clemmie turned to her and said, "Is there something wrong? Aren't things going well at the mill?"

Sarah laughed wryly. Her work always seemed to be the one thing that never went badly. Everything else seemed about to topple over on her at the most inconvenient times. "Things at the mill are fine. It's just that...I think maybe I just want to get to know my father better."

Clemmie picked Jesse up from the basket and tried to soothe him. "It's okay, sweetie. I know it's too hot. Hush now and be a good boy."

A train whistle sounded and in the distance they heard the rumble of a train and before long saw it coming around the bend, black smoke billowing from it's smoke stack. "Phew," Clemmie said, grimacing. "I'm getting real sick of smelling smoke all the time. Either it's the trains or the fires. It seems like it's never going to end." She put Jesse back into the basket and picked it up. "Let's go inside. It's hot, but at least the windows are closed and it won't stink of smoke."

When they got inside it was almost unbearably hot with the windows closed, so Clemmie sighed and opened them. "I guess there's no escaping the smoke. It's better to breathe smoke than not to be able to breathe at all." Then she said hopefully, "Maybe it will be less smoky at the farm."

Sarah knew Clemmie was trying not to make a fuss over her leaving Pine Crescent. They would miss seeing each other almost every day. Sarah wanted to explain her reasons, but she simply could not. "It's smoky there, too."

Clemmie went to put Jesse down for a nap in his room and when she returned Sarah was putting a kettle on for tea. "I hope you don't mind. I wanted some tea."

Clemmie flapped a wrist and said, "Help yourself. I think it's too hot for tea, but you go ahead." She fell onto a kitchen chair looking downcast.

Sarah went to her and put her hands on her shoulders. "I'll miss you, too, but we'll still see each other."

Clemmie looked up at her, her eyes filled with the unconcealed hope that she could convince Sarah to stay if she could find out what was wrong. "Is it because of Steven? I know he's been bothering you a lot lately, wanting to see you socially and all. Is it getting too hard to deal with him?"

Sarah shook her head. "It's not that. Steven means well enough. He thinks I'm lonely now that...now that...." She stopped speaking. She missed Thor something awful, and knew it was going to hurt for a very long time. Now she also had to deal with the sadness of having to leave Clemmie, and she'd surely miss Nell and the men at the boarding house. They had become her friends.

When the tea was ready Sarah poured herself a cup and asked, "Are you sure you don't want some?"

Clemmie shook her head, her face so filled with sadness that Sarah couldn't help herself. She had to tell her the truth so she would understand. Clemmie had been her good and true friend, and she deserved honesty.

"I'm going to have Thor Nilsson's baby," she said, her voice so steady she hardly believed her own calm.

Clemmie's mouth fell open and she blinked several times. Then she went to Sarah and took the cup from her hand and set it on the stove. Then she put her arms around Sarah and held her without speaking. Before long both women were crying softly. After what seemed like an eternity, Clemmie pulled away and said, "You poor baby. I wish you had told me sooner. You can stay here with us. You don't need to leave Pine Crescent at all."

"Nonsense!" Sarah said. "I won't even consider such a thing."

"Why not?" Clemmie asked. "You always say you don't care what people think." She thought for a moment and then asked, "Does he know?"

"No. No, he doesn't know."

"You need to write to him! Tell him!"

"No!" She said it so sharply that Clemmie took a step back.

"But why ever not? I don't understand."

"He needed to go home. It's for the best. If he had stayed because.... I don't want to spend my whole life wondering if my husband married me only because he had to."

"Oh, Sarah! How can you say that? You know he loves you. Otherwise you wouldn't have...." She didn't finish.

"I'd like to think that's true," Sarah agreed. "I hate for anyone to think of me as a fallen woman. Like my mother."

"You said you don't care what people think. Have you changed your mind?"

"It hasn't so much to do with what people think as it has to do with...with the baby. I don't want it to grow up and not have a family, the way I did. My father will be like a father to this baby, and there's White Feather and their baby and, well...."

"Does Steven know?" Clemmie interrupted.

"My God! Of course not!"

"Why not? He obviously loves you. Let him marry you and be the baby's father."

"Clemmie! How can you say such a thing?"

"It's a wonderful idea." Her eyes went to Sarah's middle. "You aren't showing a bit. You wouldn't even have to tell him."

Sarah bit her lip and looked perplexed for a moment and then she started to laugh. "Why Clementine Vogel! You are a real vixen! Do you mean to tell me you would stand by and let me dupe our good doctor?"

Clemmie was thoughtful for a moment. Then, looking quite serious, she said, "I would. I most certainly would."

Sarah looked at her friend for a long minute, and then said, "I couldn't possibly do that, and you know it."

Sarah retrieved her cup of tea and they sat down at the table across from each other. Silence filled the hot room. There wasn't a lot more either of them could say.

CHAPTER 47

GRAY Wolf built a large room onto the back of the house for Sarah and the baby. She did more than her share of work around the farm, partly because she felt better when she was busy, and partly because White Feather was accustomed to living the Indian way and was struggling to have to learn so many new things. She was grateful for the help Sarah was able to give her, and the two women came to laugh often over mistakes they made.

"You surely planted a lot of vegetables," Sarah remarked one day as the two of them pulled weeds from between the rows in the garden.

"Yes," White Feather agreed with a sardonic smile. "It would be good if I knew what they all were."

Sarah laughed and said, "We'll know what they are when they're ready to eat."

The garden was growing far better than the crops in the field. Gray Wolf had already managed to clear several acres and had planted some corn and some wheat. The dry conditions that had begun in May continued, and he feared they would lose all that he had planted except the garden. He used the horses and the wagon to tote buckets of water up the hill from the lake to water the vegetable garden. His hope was that they would be able to put enough supplies into the root cellar to feed them during the winter without having to buy everything in town.

One day in early July as Gray Wolf and Sarah worked in the garden, Sarah brought up the problem of not knowing how to preserve food. "I'm willing to help, but I don't know much about canning. Katie did a small amount, but I never learned how to do it myself."

Gray Wolf straightened and leaned on his hoe, his face serious. "Speaking of the canning, there's someone who will be able to help us. I have something to tell you and I hope you'll be as pleased about it as I am."

"Why wouldn't I be pleased with something that pleases you?" she asked as

403

she got to her feet and arched her back to relieve the stiffness she felt whenever she pulled weeds on her hands and knees.

"We have new neighbors, and they're going to be stopping by one of these days. They're going to help with the canning in exchange for some of our garden crops."

"Good," she said. "We can use the help. And besides, it's going to be nice to have someone nearby to visit." The expression on her face showed, however, that she was not as pleased as her words made it sound.

Gray Wolf understood why. She seemed happy most of the time, but she had begun to draw into herself. She refused to go to town with him to see Clemmie, and she grew stonily silent when he suggested she see Dr. Caldwell about the baby.

"I've been wanting to tell you, but I was waiting for a good time. I guess this is as good as any. Big Mary and Woody Olson went to Duluth and got married."

"Why didn't they tell anyone?" Sarah asked, knowing she had no right to feel hurt and left out but feeling hurt and left out anyway.

"They hadn't planned to marry. Woody told me it just kind of happened. Anyway, they've bought some acreage on the eastern edge of our land."

She didn't say anything, but he watched the mix of emotions playing across her face, and the shame that seemed to finally settle there. No matter how hard he tried he couldn't get her to accept that she was human, and that falling in love and acting upon it was perfectly normal.

"How long have you known?" she asked finally.

"About a month. I stopped at Camp Seven one day on my way back from town. Big Mary told me she wasn't getting any younger and was thinking about maybe accepting Woody's proposal because she'd probably never get a better one."

"I thought she was happy at Camp Seven."

"She was. As long as Thor was the foreman. She was used to him and his ways, and she had a hard time accepting Jock. Seems he can be pretty temperamental."

"As if Thor can't...couldn't," she said.

"The Devil you know is better than the Devil you don't, my grandfather always used to say."

Sarah shrugged her shoulders and said, "She hates me, you know."

"Don't be silly. She doesn't hate you. Actually she thinks quite a lot of you. Says she never had a harder worker." He paused, as if what he was going to say would be better left unsaid. "She says it took somebody special to trouble Thor Nilsson the way you did."

"Hah!" Sarah said bitterly. "I may have troubled him, but I surely ended up with most of the trouble." She stopped speaking, her face suddenly contorted with the hurt that seemed lately to linger just beneath the surface. As the child growing within her became harder to deny, her true feelings were also becoming harder to deny.

He let the hoe fall to the ground and awkwardly put his arms around her. "You underestimate yourself, Child. He just couldn't seem to get rid of that crazy damn notion about going back home to get even with that Swede woman. Then when I gave him all that trouble about...." He stopped. They had been over all that and there was no use digging it up again. "Anyway, Big Mary knows as well as I do that he didn't go easy."

She felt the tears start. She was so tired of the sadness. She tried instead to focus on the kindness in her father's words. "Thank you," she said. "Thank you for saying that."

***

As White Feather's due date approached it became harder for her to help with the chores. She was due in September, and had not been feeling well. Gray Wolf and Sarah both watched over her and made her rest often, aware of what had happened to their first baby.

Sarah felt physically well after the first few months and was able to work hard most of the time. She even learned to milk the two cows. When her father worried that she might be working too hard she assured him that it was the best medicine for her. White Feather's fragility gave Sarah something to worry about besides her own circumstances.

CHAPTER 48

THE first morning Big Mary and Woody came to begin the canning, Sarah was nervous. It didn't last long, however. The minute she got down from the wagon in front of the cabin Big Mary walked up to her and put her arms around her. When she released her, her eyes were wet. "I've missed you. In fact the real reason I quit Camp Seven was that I could never find another cookee as good as you."

Woody jumped down and hobbled quickly around the wagon and stood next to Big Mary. "Yup. She did nothing but complain after you left. Never forgave the Push for taking you away from her to clerk for him, either."

Sarah, her own eyes wet, felt intense relief.

"So what's ready to be put up?" Big Mary asked eagerly, in a hurry to change the subject.

White Feather, who stood quietly watching the reunion, said, "I am a stupid wife. I do not understand some of this food."

"Oh pshaw," Big Mary said dismissively. "If they tossed me out into the wilderness I'd starve to death and need you to come and save my sorry ass. It so happens that you're the one who got tossed into a wilderness and it's me who's here to help. Ain't that right, Woody?"

Woody grinned happily. "Can't wait for some of them fresh garden vegetables."

"How about some apple pie? I've baked two pies and you can taste them and tell me how I've done," Sarah offered modestly. The pie was quite good and Sarah got more honest praise than she had expected.

After they finished their pie, the men went to pull stumps from the area Gray Wolf was now clearing and the women went to the garden. "My, oh my," Big Mary said admiringly. "This garden is as neat as a pin and as healthy as can be."

White Feather smiled proudly and said, "It's water from the lake that makes things grow."

"And growing they are," Big Mary agreed. She bent down and picked a pea pod, broke it open and tasted the peas. "Mmmm. Sweet as candy. These are more than ready. Let's get busy."

They filled their aprons with pea pods and then sat in front of the cabin shelling them. By the end of the day they had a good supply of canned peas and a promise from Big Mary to return every few days so they could work on whatever was ready. Over the next weeks they would fill the shelves on both farms with jars of peas, corn, green beans, tomatoes and pickles. The root vegetables would wait until later in the year to be harvested.

For supper that first night, as they ate new potatoes, fresh peas and roast pheasant—along with more apple pie—Big Mary said, "Sure wish we could get enough berries to put by. I've been in the woods and can find hardly a single berry that's not dried up like a raisin."

"I've got my taster all set for some chokecherry wine," Woody said.

"Next year," Gray Wolf said. "There's always next year."

***

Early the next morning when Sarah went to the barn to milk the cows, her father had already begun and was singing.

Oh, you'll take the high road, and I'll take the low road, and I'll be in Scotland afore ye; but me and my true love will never meet again on the bonnie bonnie banks of Lock Lomon'.

She smiled wonderingly. "I've never heard you sing before."

He laughed and said, "My grandfather used to sing all the time. I can still hear his voice." Then he continued, louder than before.

"'Twas there that we parted in yon shady glen,
On the steep, steep side o' Ben Lomon'
Where in purple hue the highland hills we view
An' the moon comin' oot in the gloamin'.

"It's awful, I know, but it makes me feel good," he said smiling up at her.

"It's not awful. It's nice."

"You're just trying to make an old man feel good."

"You're not old and I am not. Besides, why shouldn't I if I can." She felt herself blush. "You and White Feather have been awfully good to me. It can't be easy having a permanent guest."

"A guest?" He stood up, the milk pail in one hand and the three-legged stool in the other. "You're not a guest! You're my daughter! I don't want to ever hear you call yourself a guest. Do you hear me?"

She nodded, chastened.

"You've got to get over this idea that you've done something wrong and that you don't deserve anything good to come out of it. You've done nothing wrong except fall in love with someone who was too stupid to know he was in love, too."

He was always trying to reassure her about Thor's feelings, and she wished she didn't need him to keep doing it. But she did. "You're probably all wrong about how he felt," she argued weakly.

"I've known that boy for a long time, and now I know you. He couldn't possibly spend as much time with you as he did without having strong feelings for you. The first time he brought you to the Indian camp it was plain as the nose on his face that his feelings for you were strong even before he knew you were a woman."

"Hah!" she said. "Those strong feelings don't have to be love, though."

He set down the pail and the milking stool and put both hands on her upper arms. He looked sternly at her and said, "I want to kick his ass for leaving, but I don't doubt for a minute that if he knew about this he'd hightail it back here so fast...."

"No! You're not to write to him! You promised!"

"Aw, don't you go worrying your pretty head. I'm not going to interfere with your wishes. Besides," he added, "I like having you here with us and I'm not ready to give you up."

***

That night they were sitting in front of the fireplace after supper, White Feather sewing colored beads onto a pair of tiny moccasins in the dim light, and Sarah rocking idly, content. Her father's voice filled the dark spaces of the room and she felt warm and comforted. She wasn't even disturbed when he began to speak of the early years when Thor first came to the timber. For the first time since she had come to live at the farm he began to talk about his earlier years in the timber, and she closed her eyes and listened.

Her father would glance over at her now and then. He sensed that she was ready now to hear him talk about the man she still loved. Once she was able to hear about him—and perhaps talk about him—she would grow easier with her loss. He knew all too well that one does, after all, live through pain and finally put it to rest.

"They were good, those early days in the timber. How well I remember the stillness, just before dawn when the woods were dark, the branches of the white pine blocking out the starlight. We always walked together—Thor and me—out of camp and into the pines. It was always a pleasure to work with that boy, even before he really knew what he was doing. He was always eager to do more than his share." He wanted to add, "Just as you are, Sarah," but he didn't.

She seemed content to listen, eyes closed, rocking slowly, her hands folded across her rounded stomach. He talked for a long time, until the fire burned away to ashes. At last, he sighed and reached over and patted White Feather's knee.

She smiled a wistful smile and said, "I miss the forests around the big lake. And my family. I miss my family."

Sarah opened her eyes and looked at White Feather. She had never heard a word of complaint from her before. "Why don't you and Father go for a visit to see them?" she asked.

White Feather shook her head sadly. "No. If they want to see me, they will come."

Sarah looked at her father, not understanding. "The old chief is not happy with his daughter for marrying a white man and taking on the white man's ways."

White Feather silently continued her beading. Sarah wanted to say something, but couldn't think of any words that would comfort her, so she said, "I'd like to learn to sew beads like you, White Feather."

White Feather looked up from her work. "I will teach you. We will make moccasins for your little one, too." Then she put one hand on her stomach and looked at Gray Wolf. She had grown very large, and the child moved within her, making her uncomfortable. She put down her work and got slowly to her feet. "I need to go outside," she said softly.

Gray Wolf stood and looked at Sarah. "You ready to go out, too?" He had grown accustomed to the two women needing to use the privy several times in the evening or during the night, and lately he never let them go alone.

"Two birds with one stone?" Sarah asked in a teasing voice as she got up to follow them out the door.

"Sure could use some rain," he told Sarah as they stood together outside the privy waiting for White Feather. The stars were barely visible in the hazy sky.

"It's bad, isn't it?" Sarah asked worriedly.

He nodded and ran his fingers through his hair. "Yup. It's bad. I've never seen so much smoke. There's always smoke in the timber, but it's been constant all summer. I'll be glad when the fall rains come."

Sarah slept badly that night. She kept hearing her father's words about Thor—and about the smoke.

***

On a Saturday night in early August, Gray Wolf hitched the wagon and they rode the short distance to the Olson's farm so the two women didn't have to walk. Their cabin was smaller than the Mackenna's, but the barn was about the same size; and in addition, they had a chicken coop, a team of horses and a cow, two pigs and a goat, a dozen laying hens and a rooster.

"You've got quite a start already," Gray Wolf said as he patted Woody on the back.

Woody looked around his small spread proudly. "Not bad for an old man with a wooden leg, wouldn't you say?"

"Don't forget you've got one of them there helpmates that's second to none," Big Mary teased, although she was clearly proud of her husband and the farm.

"My brother and his two boys came up from the city and spent two weeks helping with the buildings," Woody said. "I can't hardly take all the credit. Even with that extra-special helpmate I got me."

"Why don't you two women come inside while I see to our supper," Big Mary said. "If you men are going to smoke them damn pipes, sit outside." Almost as an afterthought, Big Mary looked at Sarah and said, "I've got a surprise for you. We've got more company coming."

Oh no, Sarah thought to herself. *Who in the world was she going to have to see?*

It was White Feather who asked, "Who is coming? Is it someone I know?"

Big Mary lifted a kettle cover and stirred something with a large spoon. "You know John Smitheson, but you don't know Clementine Vogel."

Sarah gasped. "Clemmie's coming? Really?" She could hardly believe it. She didn't think Richard would allow her to come within miles of her wayward friend.

"Yup. John's bringing her out in his carriage. Seems Mr. Vogel can't leave the station."

Sarah could hardly contain her pleasure. "Oh! It will be so nice to see her. I hope she brings little Jesse."

Big Mary turned to look at her. "You should be real proud, having a friend who named her little boy after you."

Sarah reddened. "Clemmie's been a good friend," was all she could manage to say.

When Clemmie and John Smitheson arrived, John greeted the women and then went outside to sit with the men while they smoked their pipes.
Clemmie and Sarah were so happy to see each other they could hardly stop talking. Sarah was disappointed that she had left Jesse at home with Richard. "You'll see him as soon as we get back," Clemmie told her.

"Are you going somewhere?" Sarah asked.

"Jesse and I are going to stay with my parents for the rest of the summer. I just can't stand this smoke any longer. I was so happy when Mr. and Mrs. Olson stopped by and asked me to come for a visit before I go. She said you and your father and stepmother were coming, too. I could hardly wait to see you. You look wonderful! This farm life must agree with you."

"I do like it. It's so peaceful. Oh, don't think it isn't a lot of work. But then, I like to work."

"If you like to work so much," Big Mary said as she pointed a large spoon in Sarah's direction. "How's about you get the table set? She sounded stern, but Sarah understood Big Mary well enough to know that behind her seemingly harsh words lay sincere affection.

Sarah felt contentment she hadn't known in a long time, but her good feelings were tainted by something she overheard later in the evening. She had gone outside to use the privy, and upon her return she passed under the open window and heard her father say something, his voice raised.

"Hush up," Big Mary commanded. "Do you want her to hear us arguing about this?"

She heard her father answer, "No, but I promised."

"You told me you promised you wouldn't write to him. You didn't say nothing about me doing it. It just ain't right him not knowing."

"Okay, okay," he said.

Sarah stood very still outside, her heart pounding inside her chest. Part of her was enraged that Big Mary had interfered, but another part of her felt an overwhelming urge to see Thor and be with him again. She leaned against the house, her eyes closed, and smelled again the dusty, sweet hay upon which they had made love. Then the baby stirred, almost as if to remind her that she dare not think about it too much or it would make her crazy.

Later, on the short ride home, she wanted to talk to her father about what Big Mary had done. Instead, she remained silent, listening to the clatter of the wagon wheels and the voices of her father and White Feather as they made idle conversation about the weather and their visit to the Olson's. There was a time not long ago when Sarah would have suspected that her father wanted Thor to know so he'd come home and they could be rid of her. Now she knew better. He only wanted her to be happy, and she could see how he could be relieved that someone had done what he had promised he would not do.

As for Sarah, she was not such a fool as to think that a letter from Big Mary would bring Thor back to her. Big Mary would have surely told him that she was living happily with her father, and that knowledge would satisfy any concerns he might have for her well being, and that of the child she carried.   Besides, he probably had himself convinced the baby was Steven's—if the way he looked at her and Steven the day of her father's wedding was any indication. She imagined him married by now to Annika's beautiful sister, Gretchen, having accomplished both his desire for revenge and his desire to be married to a woman with golden hair. He was gone from her forever, and she had to accept it.

Cruelly, however, he would come to her in her dreams and remind her of what it was like to be with him, and how it felt when he made love to her.

CHAPTER 49

S HE awoke before dawn on the morning of September first, unsure of what had awakened her. Then she heard White Feather's groans in the next bedroom and she knew. She got up and dressed quickly and went into the other room.

Gray Wolf was gulping down a cup of coffee and a piece of bread, his eyes wild and full of fear. "I didn't want to wake you, but I've got to go for the doctor."

"You should have gotten me up right away. How long has she been in labor?"

"Not long, but it's already pretty intense." Then he put into words what they were both thinking. "I can't help thinking about the last time."

"I know," she said, putting a reassuring hand on his arm. "Go. I'll take care of her until you get back."

She could see how worried he was about leaving her alone with White Feather.

"I've been through this before," she told him with more confidence than she really felt. "Back in Boston Katie and I attended quite a few births, and I was with Clemmie when little Jesse was born."

He kissed her lightly on the forehead and gave her a little squeeze. "Take care of yourself, too," he said and was out the door.

She followed him and watched while he harnessed the team.

"Too bad Big Mary and Woody have gone to St. Paul to visit his brother," Gray Wolf said. He wondered if he should tell her about the real reason for their visit to the Cities, but he decided not to. She already had far too much to deal with today.

Katie Girl whinnied in the barnyard, almost as if to say she wanted to go, too. Sarah seldom rode alone any longer and when they went somewhere Gray Wolf always chose to take the big team because they were so much faster.

"Please don't worry so much. We'll be okay until you get back."

"Sarah, I...." He put one foot up onto the buckboard, then set it back down again and turned back to face her. "There's something I need to say to you. It's about this new baby. I want you to understand that you were and are my first child."

"I know that, but there isn't time right now to...."

He ignored her protest and went on. "I don't want you to think you're less important to me than this baby will be."

"I know! Go!"

"If she's able to rest, do the milking. If not, the cows are going to have to suffer." He climbed up onto the seat, slapped the reins and yelled, "Giddyap!"

She nodded and waved to him until he was out of sight. Then she went into the house and closed the door and stood with her back pressed against it, her eyes shut. *Oh God! Can I really do this?*

The sound of White Feather's cry brought her up sharply, and she ran into the bedroom. White Feather was writhing in pain. "I'm sorry I took so long," Sarah said as she went to the bed.

White Feather's eyes were pinched shut. "Gray Wolf. Where is he?"

"He's gone to get the doctor, but I'm here with you now. What can I do to help you?"

White Feather shook her head frantically, as if to deny that she needed help. Nonetheless, when the pain eased, she relaxed and let Sarah bathe her with cool water from a basin that Gray Wolf had put on the table beside the bed. Sarah saw the pair of scissors and the length of string coiled neatly next to them. The two objects filled her with fear and she prayed silently that she would have no need of them before the doctor arrived.

White Feather's pains came and went at sporadic intervals for several hours, then stopped. After nearly half an hour with nothing happening, Sarah said, "I need to milk the cows. If you need me before I'm finished, call as loudly as you can. I'll hurry."

White Feather nodded but did not answer. She had a far away look in her eyes that troubled Sarah, but there wasn't time to think about it.

When she finished milking the two cows, she stood outside for a few minutes. She put both hands on the small of her back and arched backward, hoping she could stretch out some of the soreness. When she looked up, she felt a sharp stab of fear. She had never seen such a strange color in the sky.

She hurried into the house and ate a piece of bread. She knew she had to keep up her strength, but as usual, her stress took away her appetite. She made some broth for White Feather, but when she took it in to her White Feather had fallen asleep. She went quietly into the other room and sat down in the rocking chair and tried to relax…but couldn't. She felt an uneasiness she could not define and it was impossible for her to sit still.

She got up and went back outside and looked down the long hill to the lake. The wind was blowing gently from the southwest, carrying with it a cloud of blue-gray smoke. As she watched, the sun shone through for a moment, bathing the land in a pale yellow light that looked as if it was coming through a diffusing filter.

The cows and Katie Girl were moving about restlessly inside the enclosure next to the barn as if they knew something ominous was about to happen. She told herself not to be worried. After all, fires had burned all summer and there had been no real danger. Her father had told her the smoke came from stumps that smoldered to life under certain weather conditions, but burned themselves out without doing any harm except to smoke up the air. The rains would come, and then the hot, smoky summer would be over.

She thought she heard a cry and she hurried back inside. White Feather was bathed in perspiration and her face was contorted with pain. "Father will be back soon with the doctor," Sarah said, with far more certainty than she felt. When the pain subsided she wiped White Feather's face with the cool cloth. White Feather said something, but her voice was so weak Sarah couldn't make out what she was saying. She leaned closer so that her ear was next to White Feather's mouth.

"Call the boy Matthew," White Feather whispered in a raspy voice.

"Hush now. You need to relax. There'll be plenty of time to choose a name for your baby. You can decide later. Besides, it might be a girl." She tried to make her voice light, but she felt something akin to terror and she struggled not to show what she was feeling.

Then White Feather grabbed Sarah's arm with more strength than Sarah believed she possessed. Her eyes were filled with fierce determination. "It is another boy," she said, "but this time he will live. I am the one who will die."

"Don't talk like that!" Sarah said, pulling her arm away so she could take White Feather's hands. "You're going to be fine. Father will be back soon and…."

White Feather shook her head and her eyes bore into Sarah's like burning coals. "The spirits do not like what I have done. I should not have left my people." She was engulfed in a wave of pain and she cried out and pulled her hands from Sarah's and reached above and behind her to grab the bed posts. She raised up, her back arched, and let out a long scream. To Sarah's horror, White Feather's scream rose to a crescendo and slowly merged with the cries of a baby. She tore the covers back and saw the writhing, wet creature that lay, arms flailing, screaming as if protesting the indignity of his birth.

Without thinking, her motions automatic, Sarah tied the cord and cut it. Then she picked the baby up and cradled his slippery body against her while she searched the room for something to wrap him in. She found the linens White Feather had prepared for the arrival of her baby and wrapped him in a blanket and carried him back to the bed.

White Feather lay so still that Sarah feared she might be dead. "White Feather?" she pleaded. "Are you awake? Here's little Matthew. Here's your beautiful boy." The baby had stopped wailing and he seemed to be looking up at Sarah as if taking her measure, but then his eyes lost their focus and he closed them.

White Feather held up one hand weakly, beckoning to Sarah to put the baby beside her. Sarah tucked the baby in beside his mother, her eyes fixed in horror on the pool of blood seeping slowly outward around White Feather on the bed.

"Oh, my God!" she cried, unable to keep the alarm from her voice. She grabbed a towel and placed it between White Feather's legs, hoping to staunch the bleeding while she searched for more towels. She ran into the other room and grabbed a stack of linens from the pantry shelf. By the time she got back to the bedroom the towel she had used was already soaked with blood.

Just then she heard a roar that sounded like thunder. She ran from the room and went to the door and looked out, hoping to see rain. There was none. There was nothing but a deathly silence, and in the distance, a huge black cloud, billowing and swirling madly through the trees, reached to the heavens and blocked out the daylight.

Running as fast as she could, she went inside and grabbed Matthew. "We've got to get to the root cellar! Try to sit up and I'll be right back for you!"

Grabbing a kerosene lantern from the kitchen table, she ran with Matthew to the root cellar, deposited the lantern on a shelf, then laid the baby onto a pile of burlap bags and then rushed back to the house.

White Feather had managed to get to a sitting position and blood was dripping onto the floor. "I don't think I can walk," she said with a great effort.

"You must! Lean on me!" She struggled until she got White Feather to her feet, and then half carrying her, half dragging her, somehow got her outside.

White Feather stopped moving, and Sarah shouted, "We can't stop! There isn't time!"

White Feather was looking up at the sky, her eyes transfixed. "They are coming for me," she said in a voice that was eerily calm.

"Yes! Father is coming with the doctor! But we must hurry!"

"No. The Great Spirit is coming for me. Look!" She pointed across the water at the huge, whirling black cloud.

"Be still! We've no time to think about spirits! Come on! We've got to get to the root cellar!" She no longer had time to be gentle, and with a strength she didn't know she had managed to get the other woman to the root cellar and down the three steps into the dank, earthy place where she knew they'd be safe. She positioned some of the burlap bags against the dirt wall at the back of the cellar and helped ease White Feather to the ground in a sitting position with her back against the wall.

Matthew had begun to cry and Sarah picked him up. "He's hungry. Let me help you." Without ceremony she pulled open the front of White Feather's nightgown and placed the infant into his mother's arms so she could nurse him. He eagerly took the breast and Sarah sighed with relief. She knew that babies often had trouble figuring out how to get milk from their mothers and she said a silent prayer of thanks that this baby appeared to have the instincts he needed so badly right now.

Somewhat relieved, she ran up the steps and stood outside looking around. Then she felt a sharp stabbing pain in the small of her back. "Not now. Oh please, God! Not now!"

It had grown eerily still, but in the distance she heard what she thought were horses and a wagon. Without thinking she began to run toward the sound and she saw her father returning. He was standing up in the wagon whipping the horses with the reins. And he was alone!

She ran to him and he jumped down without securing the horses. "It's a fire! A big one! I got halfway to Pine Crescent and had to turn back. It's coming this way. Where's White Feather?"

"In the root cellar. She had the baby. It's a boy." She felt a wave of relief. She wasn't in charge any longer.

He grabbed her arm and pulled her after him down into the root cellar. "Good God, it's dark in here!" he said.

Sarah quickly lit the lantern and held it for him as he got down on his knees in front of White Feather and the baby. "Are you alright?" he asked, terror in his voice.

White Feather nodded, but said nothing.

He kissed her softly and caressed her hair, then kissed the baby's head. "The ground is so hard," he said helplessly, turning to look up at Sarah. "You take the baby and I'll pick her up so we can put some of those burlap bags under her." He handed the baby to Sarah and reached down to lift White Feather, but then stood looking at his hands. They were covered in blood. He looked at Sarah and then at White Feather.

"Do not worry, Husband. It is time for the Great Spirit to take me," White Feather said, as if welcoming her departure from this life into the next.

Just then they heard a loud roar and Gray Wolf grabbed the lantern from Sarah and set it back on the shelf and ran outside. She placed the baby back in White Feather's arms and followed him outside.

They both stared with alarm across the lake at the black, billowing cloud. "It's getting close!" Gray Wolf shouted. "The animals! I'm going to take them into the lake!"

He ran to the wagon, untied the horses and tried to pull them with him toward the barn. They were rearing up and whinnying in terror, and he ran back into the root cellar, grabbed several burlap bags, then took them and covered the horses' heads so they couldn't see. It calmed them down somewhat, and he was able to pull them along to the enclosure where the cows stood bellowing and Katie Girl whinnied and pawed at the ground. Then he slapped wildly at the cows' behinds and pushed them down the hill toward the water, along with Katie Girl and the two big horses.

Sarah stood helplessly watching him, the pain in her back moving now around to her groin, making her hunch over in pain, her arms wrapped around her stomach.

"Go back inside!" he shouted.

"Leave the animals!" she screamed, standing upright with an extreme effort. "Leave the animals! Father! Please!"

She looked across the lake and watched with terror as the black cloud began spewing red bolts of flame. "Father! Oh God! No! No!" she screamed. She was standing just outside the open door, and the force of the explosion that consumed Doyle MacKenna and his animals knocked her backwards down the stairs and onto the floor of the root cellar.

CHAPTER 50

SHE had no way of knowing how long she had been lying there, but when she awoke she could still hear the roar of the fire outside. Struggling to sit up, she felt dizzy and reached up and felt the large bump on the back of her head. Then a stabbing pain in her lower back made her cry out.

White Feather lay stretched out on the steps, as if she had crawled up and closed the door. Sarah went to her to try to help her get into a more comfortable position.

"White Feather? Wake up." She put her hand on White Feather's shoulder and shook her...none too gently. When she didn't respond, Sarah raised her voice, frantic. "Wake up! Please wake up!" But White Feather did not respond and would not respond ever again. "No! No! Don't let this happen! Please, God! No!"

She had no choice but to drag White Feather away from the steps so she could get outside. But when she touched the door, it was hot. She backed down the stairs and put her head down and bit her lip. She was determined not to cry. There was nothing she could do to help White Feather and nothing she could do to help her father.

Matthew began to cry and she started toward him, but the pain grabbed her again and she sank onto the floor on her knees, clutching her stomach. The baby was coming, and there was nothing she could do about that, either. She lost all track of time, slipping in and out of consciousness as the pains came and went. Somehow she managed to crawl onto the burlap sacks to try to comfort Matthew in her lucid moments, but he finally became exhausted and slept.

After what she thought must have been hours, the pains became unbearable and she knew it was getting close. "It's too soon for this baby to come," she muttered weakly. She began shivering, although it was hot in the cellar. Then she felt an irresistible urge to push, and a moment later her baby was born. She was so weak she could barely move but she managed to reach down and pull the tiny infant up and onto her stomach. She remembered vaguely thinking she had to find a way to tie the cord, but then she slipped into unconsciousness.

She awoke to hear Matthew crying, but her own tiny girl did not move nor cry…nor breathe. She tied the cord and cleaned herself as best she could, all the while trying not to think about her dead stepmother lying on the dirt floor. She wanted to move her into a more comfortable position, but knew she could not. She swaddled her dead baby into one of the burlap bags and laid her on White Feather's breast, covering them both with several more of the burlap bags. It was difficult to see, because the lantern was running out of kerosene and the flame had dimmed, and because tears filled her eyes and blurred her vision. But she saw enough to know that the baby had a fuzz of golden-red hair.

Her chest hurt from her sobs, and her head throbbed violently. She tried once more to open the door, but it was still too hot. Finally, heartsick and resolved that she could do nothing but wait, she picked up Matthew and sat down with her back against the wall with him in her arms. She watched as the lantern flame flickered and went out. "It's just the two of us now," she whispered, her voice hoarse. "All we have is each other." She smoothed her hand over his silky black hair and when he nuzzled her she took him to her breast. "All we have is each other," she repeated, soothed by the closeness of his small, warm body. Then the pain in her head forced her to cry out and Matthew stopped suckling and let out a wail and she felt the darkness close in upon them.

***

Much later, in her delirium she saw the door open and filling the doorway with his large bulk stood Thor. There were people behind him, but the light from the door blinded her so she couldn't see who they were. They followed Thor down the steps and she imagined that she heard gasps. Thor came toward her and took Matthew from her, handing him to someone. She tried to cry out, to resist him taking Matthew from her, but no sound came from her lips. He picked her up and carried her out into the sunlight, holding her tight against him, and she dreamed that he was muttering to her in that strange language she could not understand.

In another dream she lay in a strange bed and Steven Caldwell was leaning over her, his fingers probing the soreness at the back of her head. He straightened and turned toward someone standing in the doorway. "She's still unconscious. I don't know if it was the fall or the shock. There's nothing we can do but wait."

Then she slept again.

Steven went into the other room and Thor followed him reluctantly, glancing with a worried expression over his shoulder as he closed the door. "You came back to a real mess," Steven said to Thor. "It's a good thing Big Mary wrote to you."

Anger flashed in Thor's eyes and he said, "That is not why I came back."

"I thought...."

"They arranged to pick me up in the Cities so they could bring back supplies, but they are not the *reason* I came back," he said angrily. "It's a damn good thing they did, or they would have been here and they, too...." He couldn't finish.

"Don't get the wrong idea here," Steven said holding up raised palms in a defensive gesture. "It's none of my business why you came back. I'm just glad for Sarah's sake that you did."

"A helluva lot of good it did," Thor mumbled, the anger gone and a look of extreme self-loathing taking its place.

As if to change the uncomfortable subject, Steven turned to Big Mary and said, "I brought some clothes for Sarah and the baby from the relief supplies. I'll bring them in before I leave." He shook his head in disbelief. "I can't believe how the people around here have responded. It restores my faith in us."

"Us?" Big Mary asked, her head on one side.

"Us. Folks. You know, humans. There've been times lately when I've wondered." He looked at Thor. "I'm not leaving myself out. I've behaved pretty badly toward...." He stopped, aware that he was getting into an area where he didn't need to go. It was over between him and Sarah and had been for a long time. No sense opening old wounds. The new ones were bad enough.

Woody was sitting in the rocking chair holding Matthew and Thor walked over and took Matthew from him. He cradled the baby in the crook of his arm and stroked his silky black hair. "He's got his mother's hair and skin, but I can't tell who he looks like." He looked across the room to where Big Mary stood watching them. "I was hoping he'd look like Gray Wolf."

Big Mary gave Thor a penetrating look, then frowning said, "Won't bring him back. Nothing will." She came over and ran a finger over the baby's cheek as her eyes challenged Thor, as if to say his friend was gone and he had to accept it.

Woody stood up and took the baby from Thor and went to put him in his cradle in their bedroom. When he came back into the room he said, "Let's get it over with."

Big Mary said, "You men go along. I'll stay here with Sarah and the baby."

"You sure?" Woody asked as he put a hand on her shoulder and squeezed it gently.

She nodded. "I'll say my prayers here. Alone. I don't need to watch those poor souls get buried. I've seen enough." She looked at Steven. "Don't you think you better get on back to town. There must be folks needing you."

Thor seemed to revive from some far away place and he looked at Steven. "We appreciate all you've done." The words seemed to come with difficulty.

Steven looked back at him and said, "She's a dear friend, and I'd like to think of myself as your friend, too."

Thor stared at the other man for a long time, then nodded briefly and turned to open the door. Then he stopped and looked back at Steven and asked, "Do you think we should be doing this without...without her." He nodded toward the closed door of the bedroom.

"Got to." Woody said, taking it upon himself to say what no one else wanted to think about. "The heat...." He didn't want to finish.

"There's no way to know if...." Steven paused, then began again. "There's just no way to know when she'll come out of it. I don't think we can wait."

Thor grimaced and walked out the door, his back rigid, his eyes avoiding contact with anyone.

The three men had worked for two days clearing away the MacKenna homestead. Nothing remained but bits of broken and charred objects, most of which could barely be identified. Thor had searched frantically for something, but would not say what it was. When he finally found what remained of a small oval picture frame, he had picked it up and stood frozen with it in his hand.

"What is it?" Steven asked, making his way through the pile of debris to look at the thing in Thor's hand. The frame was twisted and the glass had been shattered. Nothing remained of the picture that it had held except a small scrap of what looked like a face. He couldn't tell if it was the face of a man or a woman. Thor didn't answer, but had slipped the frame into his pocket.

When they had finished clearing away the rubble that had been Doyle MacKenna's farm and had buried the animals, they had dug three graves on top of a rise at the edge of the MacKenna property. Woody had built a wooden fence around them, and he had also built three coffins.

Now, when it was time to put the body of the baby into the small box, Thor angrily waved the other two men aside. Since that moment when he saw his dead child, he had fought to control himself, but now his big hands shook uncontrollably as he held her against him for the last time. Shaking, his face tear-stained, he placed her inside the small coffin and closed the lid with a soft thud and began to hammer it shut, hammering furiously until Woody took the hammer from him.

After White Feather and the charred remains of Doyle MacKenna were placed into their coffins, Thor reached into his pocket and took out the picture frame and put it next to Doyle's body. Then he raised his eyes and looked first at Woody and then at Steven and said, "It was his mother. Sarah's grandmother. He'd want to have it with him."

The three men carried the coffins through an opening in the fence, lowered them into the ground and began shoveling the dirt over them. They did not speak, and when they were finished they remained helplessly silent. They all knew someone should say something but none of them was able to do it.

It was Woody who broke the silence. He began to sing a hymn. As he sang, the notes of the hymn carried upward into the morning sky, strangely fitting in the stillness around them. Thor and Steven stood, their hands folded and their heads bowed, letting the words Woody sang say what they could not. When he finished singing they stood silent again. There were no words that could express the horror and the pain of what they had been through. So none of them tried.

Finally Woody turned and went back to the wagon. He had fashioned three wooden crosses and he carried them back to where Thor and Steven still stood. "These'll do until we can get something better. I carved names on two of them, but...." He carefully pushed them into the soft earth then stood holding the third one as he looked at Thor.

Thor stared at the object in Woody's hand as if it was something he could not quite understand. Then awareness seemed to dawn on him and his eyes met Woody's and he said, "Catherine. It's my mother's name." He looked at Steven, his eyes searching the other man's face for validation of so weighty a decision.

Steven nodded. "It's a beautiful name." Then, seeing it wasn't what Thor needed to hear, he added, "I know Sarah would approve."

Thor seemed to relax a little, and he watched as Woody put the cross on the third grave.

"I'll carve the name later," Woody said as he stood and surveyed his grim handiwork.

Steven looked up at the sky, clear and blue as it had not been for months. "It's good that the smoke is gone."

Thor nodded, then turned and started to walk away.

"Ain't you riding back to the house with us?" Woody called worriedly after him.

Thor shook his head without turning.

Steven and Woody watched him go, and then got into the wagon and drove silently back to the Olson house.

CHAPTER 51

SHE sat bolt upright and screamed and someone rushed into the room. "Hush now. It's alright. You're safe."

She slowly became aware of her surroundings. The bright morning sun was streaming in the window and Big Mary was standing next to the bed. Through the open door she heard men's voices.

"Wh...where am I?" she asked, her voice raspy and weak.

"You're at my house," Big Mary said, sitting down on the side of the bed and taking her hand. "You and your little brother are both here."

"My father...is he...."

Big Mary shook her head slowly and her eyes told Sarah what she couldn't find the heart to put into words.

Sarah closed her eyes, trying to fight the image of flames. "It was so awful! A great black cloud came and then it started shooting fire, and then.... He didn't have time...the animals...he was trying to save the animals instead of himself!"

"Hush, Child," Big Mary soothed. "Try not to think about it. You're safe and so is your little brother."

"Matthew. His name is Matthew. It's what White Feather wanted him to be called. She told me so, before.... I wanted to help her, but I must have fallen, and I...."

"We know his name. You kept calling out for him. But you mustn't think about that now. You're both alive and that's what matters."

"Where is he?"

"He's in the other room sleeping. We've been giving him cow's milk thinned down with water and sweetened a little with maple syrup and he takes it like it was his mother's milk."

Sarah instinctively touched her breasts. They were swollen and sore, but so were her head and the rest of her body. A wave of intense sadness swept over her as she remembered all that had happened and tears slid down her cheeks. "I couldn't help them," she sobbed, "and then...and then my baby...."

Big Mary couldn't speak, the horror of it welling up inside of her. All she could do was put her arms around Sarah and let her cry.

When Sarah finally stopped crying she asked, "How long.... How long have I been here?"

"It's Wednesday. We found you Sunday morning."

Through her tears Sarah saw Thor standing in the doorway. So none of it had been a dream. He came into the room and Big Mary got up to leave.

"I'll be in the other room if you need me," she said.

Thor came over to the bed and stood looking down at her. He wanted to say something to ease the pain he saw so clearly on her face. "Sarah, I...."

She looked at him for a long moment, and then slowly turned her head away. He said nothing as he left the room, closing the door so quietly she wasn't sure he had actually gone. She lay very still, thinking how vulnerable he looked. Not at all like the powerful, angry man he had been when he went away.

But somehow she didn't care. Images of the fire again swam before her eyes, and she relived the last minutes before the fire claimed her father's life. She felt again that awful moment when she knew White Feather was dead, and when she knew her own baby, too, was dead. She wept, unable to erase the nightmarish pictures that played over and over again in her mind. At times she thought about Thor, but whenever she did she forced him from her mind.

She knew why he had come back and it made her miserable. One evening, when they thought she was asleep, she had heard Big Mary and Woody talking about it.

"Sometimes I wonder if I did the right thing," Big Mary said in a voice filled with self-doubt.

"Don't do no good beating yourself up for doing what you thought was the right thing."

Big Mary sighed. "I know. I thought.... Well, you know. Seeing as how any fool could see she still loved the man."

"And the ignorant galoot sure as hell loved her," Woody said. "He was just too damned stubborn to admit it—even to himself."

Big Mary sighed again. "I guess what's done is done, and if he don't like what's happening he can always go back to Sweden."

Sarah buried her head in her pillow, not wanting to remember any more. Big Mary had written and told him about her pregnancy and he had come back. Had she been so convincing that he had no choice but to return? She hated thinking about it, and when the ugly thoughts assaulted her they were soon swept away by the even-uglier memories of the day of the fire.

As the days passed Sarah's strength slowly returned, but Big Mary and Woody worried about the sadness that seemed to dominate her every waking moment. The only one who could bring a smile to her face was Matthew. He never cried when she held him. He seemed to save his most winning behavior for his sister. It was almost as if he knew that he was her lifeline. But when he was asleep the sadness would come over her like a living thing that possessed her. Sometimes she would go outside and sit on the step in the early morning hours when she couldn't sleep. Her eyes would scan the trees at the edge of the clearing in which the house stood, trying not to think about what lay beyond them and out of sight.

One evening as they sat in front of the fire, Sarah suddenly looked down at her dress. She seemed bewildered as she ran her hands over the fabric of the unfamiliar garment she was wearing. It had been nearly two weeks, and she had never once noticed that the clothes she put on were not her own. Panicked, her eyes met Big Mary's.

Big Mary sat across from her in the rocking chair and she smiled reassuringly, relieved that Sarah at last seemed to be regaining a sense of the present.

Sarah read the message in Big Mary's eyes and her shoulders sagged and she said, "Everything is gone, isn't it." It was not a question.

Big Mary went to the other room and returned moments later and handed her her brooch. "You were wearing this like you always do. The rest...."

Sarah clutched the brooch and Woody said softly, "Steven brought clothes from town. Lots of good folks gave things to help out."

Sarah stared at him. A mixture of emotions played on her face, and then she said, "Thank you both for all you've done for me. And for Matthew."

Big Mary closed her eyes and then opened them again, unable to stop the tears. "I thank the Lord every day for the privilege of caring for the two of you."

***

On a cool morning in late September, Sarah stood by the fence watching Woody milk the cow. She looked up at the bright sky and a sense of longing came over her. She turned and began to walk toward her father's land, her feet propelling her almost against her will. When she got over the last rise and the MacKenna property came into view she stood silently gazing around her. The trees were gone and nothing remained of the buildings except carefully raked rectangles of earth. Surrounding them were charred earth and stumps of burned trees poking grotesquely out of the blackened ground.

She hesitated for a moment, then turned and walked to the lake, to the spot where she had last seen her father. She felt a hurt in her chest that clutched at her like a cruel hand and she let out a cry of anguish. She sank to the ground, her head lowered and her hands scratching violently at the charred ground, as if by digging hard enough she could destroy the very earth and wipe out the memories that refused to stop assaulting her.

She heard footsteps and turned to see Thor standing behind her. He reached out a hand to help her up, but she shook her head violently at him and scrambled to her feet. "Wh...what are you doing here?" she asked angrily.

He took out his handkerchief to wipe away the sooty tears that smeared her face, but she pushed his hand away. "Don't touch me," she said through clenched teeth.

It was too much for him and he reached out and put his hands firmly on her upper arms. "Listen to me, Sarah! You can't go on like this. Big Mary says...."

"Hah!" she scoffed. "It seems Big Mary does a lot of talking—and writing—that she shouldn't do."

His brows drew together in a puzzled frown and he started to say something, but seemed to change his mind about what to say. "We need to talk, Sarah. I've been waiting until you felt better. I know you've been through hell and I didn't want to...."

"Hell? And how would you know what I've been through?"

She started walking away but he grabbed her arm and stopped her. "Don't do this. You can't shut me out like this."

She gave a strange, almost hysterical laugh and he pulled her against him and held her despite her struggle against him. She tried to pull away so she could pound on his chest with her fists, but he was too strong for her, and she finally gave in and let him hold her. She didn't want to respond to him but something deep within her that was out of her control yearned for his touch, and she fell against him and let the tears come. They just stood there, his cheek against her hair and her face buried in the crook of his neck. He smelled of the outdoors, and of pine. The rest of the forest could burn to the ground, but she knew in her heart that, to her, he would always smell of the pines.

It was a long time before he relaxed his hold on her and she was able to pull away and swipe at her tears with the back of her hand. "I'm so tired of crying," she said, almost to herself rather than to him. Then suddenly she stared up at him, seeming to realize for the first time where she was and who she was with.

As if he read her mind, he said, "I stop by every time I go back to Pine Crescent."

She looked at him vaguely and he said, "I told Woody and Big Mary not to tell you. I wanted to tell you myself. I bought some land, but I'm not there much yet."

She kept looking at him, unable to manage a coherent thought.

"I've been spending most of my time in Pine Crescent...or rather what's left of it."

"Pine Crescent was...was burned, too?"

He nodded. "There's so much to be done. People's homes have burned and they have no place to stay. They need shelter and food and I'm trying to do what I can to help." He shrugged helplessly, as if to say no one could possibly do enough. "John Smitheson headed up a crew of men to bury the dead and we put up some tents. We finally began putting up some buildings the other day."

She tried to fathom what he was telling her. Woody and Big Mary had told her nothing, and she knew they had been trying to protect her from the truth.

"Gone? Pine Crescent is gone?" she asked dumbly. Then she frantically grabbed his sleeve. "What about Clemmie and Jesse? Tell me! What happened to Clemmie and Jesse?"

"I...I don't know."

Her hands clutched at him. "You're lying to me! She's dead, isn't she? She's dead and you aren't telling me!"

He took hold of her shoulders and shook her. "Stop it! I said I don't know and it's the truth! There were some survivors but no one is sure who.... We can't be sure."

He looked very weary and she realized that he, too, had been through much. Her shoulders fell and the fight went out of her. "You'd better go. You have better things to do than spend the morning with a crazy woman."

"Don't say that!" he said, almost as if he had to deny her craziness to both of them.

"I need to get back," she said weakly. "Big Mary and Woody will be worried."

"Let me give you a ride," he said. "My wagon's up the hill." He hesitated then said, "It's up next to the cemetery. That's why I stopped. I go there whenever I can and this morning I saw you down here and...."

Her face had grown deathly white and he was afraid she might faint. She had not yet considered where they might be buried and she started to back away from him, her eyes dark with terror. Then she turned and started to run in the direction of the Olson's farm, stumbling as she went, and he stood dumbly and watched her go...his legs turned to helpless rubber.

As she approached the house Big Mary came running toward her just as she collapsed.

"Woody! Come here, dammit! Where are you? Woody!"

Woody came hobbling out of the barn. "What? What's wrong?" Then he saw Big Mary leaning over Sarah's prone figure.

She came to slowly, and they were able to get her into the house. She kept apologizing for being so much trouble, and Big Mary, true to character, scolded her for going off for a walk before she was well enough to be up and around. "Least you coulda done is tell us where you were going," Big Mary said accusingly, trying to sound angry but failing miserably to hide the relief in her voice.

Three days passed before Sarah had the strength to raise the issue of their new neighbor with them. "You didn't tell me Thor Nilsson bought land nearby." They were having dinner, and Matthew was asleep on Woody's lap.

"How do you know about that?" Big Mary asked.

"I saw him the other day. The day I went walking. He was on his way to Pine Crescent to help. You didn't tell me about Pine Crescent, either. What else haven't you told me?"

They looked nervously at each other, and then Woody said apologetically, "We didn't want to upset you with any of this."

"Upset me? I'm a grown woman! Don't you think I have enough gumption to face the truth? I'm sick of being treated like a baby! And besides, I don't care in the least where Thor Nilsson lives!"

The baby stirred and opened his eyes in surprise, then made sucking movements with his mouth and settled back into sleep.

"I want to see where they're buried," she said, her voice still loud and angry. "I have a right to know!" She stood up and pushed her chair violently away. She looked at Big Mary and suddenly her face crumbled and she began to cry.

Big Mary stood up quickly and put an arm around her shoulder and made her sit in the rocking chair. She looked at Woody and motioned to him to bring

Matthew over, and he handed the baby to Sarah. She clung to him and buried her face in his hair, crying softly so as not to wake him.

Big Mary quietly cleared away the remains of supper and after nearly an hour she took Matthew and put him into his bed. Sarah didn't resist, but instead sat rocking and staring straight ahead.

"I think it's time," Big Mary told Woody.

"You sure?" he asked, plainly disturbed by the idea.

"Yup. Sometimes a dose of reality is necessary." She took Sarah's hand and said, "Come along. We're going to the cemetery."

Sarah looked at her in horror and shrank back in her chair. "No! I can't!" she whimpered, regretting her earlier pretense at bravery.

"Stop it!" Big Mary commanded, taking her by the shoulders and shaking her. "Stop it! Enough! They're at peace, but you're not. It's time you come to grips with it. Your father would expect you to go on living, dammit, and so do I. I don't give two hoots in hell what you do about Thor Nilsson, but I care a whole bunch about how you handle the rest of it. Now get up off that chair and get yourself up to the cemetery and say the prayers you ain't said yet!"

Her words and actions surprised Big Mary as much as they surprised the other two people in the room; but the impact they had on Sarah was astonishing.

She blinked twice at Big Mary, then stood up, smoothed the front of her dress and then her hair. "Yes Ma'am," she said in a clear voice. "Are you ready?"

"Been ready for days. Just waiting for you." Big Mary turned to Woody. "Hitch up the wagon for us, then stay here with Matthew. We'll be back shortly."

"Do you have a Bible?" Sarah asked.

Big Mary nodded and hurried into the bedroom and came out carrying a worn black volume.

They rode without speaking. It was growing dark, but the white fence stood silhouetted against the sky as they approached the top of the hill. Sarah got down from the wagon and walked steadily and firmly without pausing, opened the gate and stepped inside. She looked back over her shoulder at Big Mary, who looked worried.

"I'm okay," Sarah said as she knelt at the first grave and traced her father's name on the cross with her finger, then rose and did the same at White Feather's grave. When she got to the third grave, she saw the name "Catherine" carved in it and she again looked back over her shoulder at Big Mary, her eyes questioning.

"It's Thor's mother's name," she said so softly Sarah could barely hear her. "You were...he didn't know...."

"It's okay," she said. "It's a fine name. She has his mother's name and my mother's hair."

She stood up then, and stepped back to where Big Mary stood transfixed, watching her anxiously. Sarah reached out a hand and touched Big Mary's shoulder. "I'm okay now," she said.

Then she calmly opened the Bible, flipped some pages, found what she wanted and started to read aloud, "The Lord is my shepherd, I shall not want...."

CHAPTER 52

IN early October as the days grew cool, Sarah felt life returning to her. She had not lost control of her emotions since that night Big Mary shocked her back to herself. She began to take regular trips to the little cemetery, and she began helping with the chores and the cooking.

Thor had not stopped by again and she was sure he had given up all hope of her speaking to him again. His name never came up and she knew Big Mary and Woody were purposely avoiding mention of him. She also knew, however, that she would have to see him sooner or later, and she might as well get it over with.

"I'd like to go to Pine Crescent. Will you take me tomorrow?" she asked Woody one night at supper.

He looked nervously at Big Mary before answering. She nodded to him, so he said, "Okay. If you think you're up to it."

They left early the next morning. It felt good to be in the wagon going somewhere. She hadn't seen anything beyond her father's land since the fire. She knew the fire had been extensive, although the Olson farm and everything west of it had been spared. Even so, she wasn't prepared for what she saw. As they passed over the rise beyond the MacKenna land, she could see that the trees were gone as far as the eye could see. "It's all gone," she murmured as she gazed around at the waste.

He nodded. "Yup. Pretty soon there'll be farms all over this territory. Only good thing to come out of that damned inferno is that the land got cleared fast. Pull the stumps and plant. That's all they'll need to do."

"You sound sorry."

"Nope. Ain't sorry about the farms coming. Only thing I'm sorry about is that my land still needs to be cleared." He grinned at her. "But what else has an old man got to do?"

"You can plant on my father's land," she told him.

She thought for a moment, then said, "I suppose it's our land, now. Matthew's and mine." She had the sense of slowly waking from a long sleep. There were so

435

many things she had not thought about. "You can plant on our land. That way Matthew and I won't feel so beholden to you and Big Mary."

"Don't talk foolish. You ain't in no way beholden."

"Yes I am," she said firmly. "You and Big Mary have been everything to me and Matthew. I'll never forget all you've done."

Woody was watching her face, the reins loose in his hands. The road was blackened from the fire but still passable and the horses seemed to know where they were going. He looked at her for a long time, then said, "You're family to us. Always will be."

She reached over and put her hand on his knee and squeezed it. "You make it possible for me to live without my father, Woody." He turned away and coughed and for a long time neither of them spoke.

Then Sarah asked, "What about Camp Seven?" She dreaded his answer.

"Camp Seven wasn't burned, thank the Good Lord."

She sighed deeply with relief. "Then all the men from there are okay?"

"Far's I know. Leastwise them that was in camp or west of it."

She had needed that piece of good news and she smiled as she looked around her. The sky was clear and bright, the air cool on her face. For the first time since the fire it felt good to be alive. The Olson farm had been west of the fire, and so had Camp Seven; there was still happiness to be found despite all that had been lost.

When they finally neared Pine Crescent they could not recognize the place that had so recently been a growing town. Nothing remained of the railroad tracks except twisted metal and burned railroad ties. "My God!" Sarah exclaimed. "The trains can't even run!" As they crossed what was left of the tracks Sarah stared around her. Nothing remained. No trees, no houses, no church, no train depot. Nothing. Except scattered helter skelter around the area between where the depot and Smitheson's once stood, were dozens of small tents. The beginnings of wooden structures lined the road that had led through town. In the center of it all stood a crude shanty with men milling around outside of it.

They parked the wagon and tethered the horses, then walked to the shanty. It was a cook shanty, and a cook whom Woody recognized from one of the Smitheson camps, two bull cooks from another camp, and three women were preparing food.

"Smells just like a lumber camp," Woody observed, sniffing.

Potatoes, beans, salt pork and beef, bread, gallons of coffee and tea were all being prepared in huge wash boilers. Sarah stared at the women as Woody talked with the cook, who was explaining that they were preparing the food for the men who had come to town volunteering to help with the cleanup and the rebuilding.

Sarah paid no attention to what he was saying. She was too busy staring at the women. She didn't recognize one of them, but she knew the other two. One of them was a big woman with hair the color of ginger and she knew immediately that it was Ginger from the hotel. One of the other women lifted her apron to wipe the sweat from her forehead. Her golden hair was piled on top of her head in a bun that was coming apart, leaving strands of hair dangling around her pretty face. Lila felt Sarah's stare and turned to look at her. For a moment she appeared ruffled, but she quickly regained her composure and nodded an unsmiling greeting and went back to her labors.

Sarah told Woody she was going to walk around the camp and she went outside and stood for a moment to catch her breath and to calm herself. Along the outer edge of the camp was a fence surrounding a makeshift corral, and men were herding cows, horses and oxen into it.

"We've rounded up the strays," a man told her. "They need to be fed or they'll die. There's no grass out there."

As she was passing between two of the tents a man stepped out of one of them, and she stood face to face with Steven Caldwell. "Sarah! What are you doing here? Should you be walking around so soon?"

She waved a hand dismissively and said, "It's about time! I've been a good-for-nothing fool for far too long. But what are *you* doing here?"

"Trying to help as best I can. I've set up a hospital of sorts in this tent," he said, motioning to the tent from which he had just emerged.

Sarah's eyes scanned the surrounding "village." "Who are all these men? I hardly see anyone I recognize."

"They've come from all over the area to help. They set up these army militia tents so they'd have someplace to stay. Most of the women and all of the children have been taken to neighboring towns until there are places for them to come home to. We finally got some lumber, but I can't wait for the trains to start running again. They tell us it'll be only another week of so." He took her arm and beckoned toward the shanty. "Come with me and we'll talk. I need to get something to eat. I haven't had a bite since dawn. Are you hungry?"

She shook her head. "I'll wait out here for you." She sat down on one of the many bales of straw that were scattered in front of the cook shanty. Several men who were sitting and eating nodded to her and she nodded back but didn't speak. When Steven came out and sat down next to her, she was aware for the first time that he looked older. There were lines at the corners of his eyes and his dark hair was graying at the temples.

"Have you been getting any rest?" she asked him.

"As a matter of fact, no," he said as he scooped beans into his mouth. "And until these folks came," he motioned with his fork toward the cook shanty, "I was barely eating anything. God, It's been awful. I've run out of words to say to people who've lost everything they own—along with family members. I treated a man this morning who cut himself with an ax while he was trying to help clear stumps. The poor man lost his wife, his three sons and his daughter. Yet he's here helping others who've lost much less. Lawson's far more brave than I could ever be." He shook his head in disbelief.

"Lawson? Sam Lawson?"

He nodded and her face registered shocked surprise. "Oh no! I met those people the first time I went to Camp Seven. Sally—Mrs. Lawson was expecting. She must have had that little girl she wanted so badly! How awful!"

She watched him as he ate, wondering how it was that a man like him could come to a place like this and remain after all that had happened. "Are you going to stay, Steven?"

Her question surprised him. "Stay? I…I never even considered anything else. Where…where would I go?"

"Home, of course. Back to Boston. Surely you must want to be back in civilization again. Think of it. You could be in a place where people die quietly in their beds, not out here where… ." She made a sweeping gesture, "out here where God only knows in what horrible way anyone is going to die."

He looked at her as if she had spoken blasphemy, then said resolutely, "I'm staying. I'm not a religious man, but I believe I survived all of this in order to be of help. I intend to stay and help however I can. Maybe before I die this will have become a place where people die in their beds the same as they do in Boston."

"Perhaps," she said, not feeling much hope.

He finished eating and set his plate on the ground. He looked at her, his eyes serious. "How's your little brother?"

"Matthew? He's fine. He's already smiling."

"Do you…" He hesitated. "Do you feel any resentment toward him?"

"Resentment? What on earth are you talking about?"

"I...I only ask because...well...."

"Why are you asking me such a question?"

He looked away from her as if he was embarrassed about what he was about to say. "Matthew lived, and your own baby didn't. And your father...."

"Oh, Steven," she cried. "How could I resent him? He's the only family I have left!"

"I'm sorry I asked." He waved an arm to encompass their surroundings. "All this has made me a little nuts."

Something occurred to her, and she looked probingly at him. "Steven?"

"Hmmm?" He was staring straight ahead and seemed to be far away.

"Steven. Look at me."

He did as she asked, a quizzical look on his face.

"Will I be able to...can I have more children?"

His brows drew together and he stared at her, then understood what she had taken from his question about Matthew. He reached over and took her hand and said, "Yes. Of course you can."

Her face registered relief, but then uncertainty. "Are you telling me the truth?"

"Yes, absolutely. I'd never lie to you about something like this.

"Why...why do you think...why did I...."

Her question hung in the air until he finally said, "It's hard to say, Sarah. We'll never know for sure." He looked at her, his eyes filled with sympathy, but also with a longing she didn't want to recognize. He looked away as he spoke. "What with the fall you took and the physical and emotional strain of that day, it's really not a surprise."

"It was pretty awful, but as time has passed I realize how lucky I was to have the time I did with my father. And I know he didn't suffer. It happened so fast...."

She looked up at the sky, her eyes distant. "It looks like rain." Then she smiled at him, a smile filled with sadness. "It's alright Steven. I'm not looking for reasons. My baby died before she lived and I have to accept it, along with the rest. I'm grateful for what I have. Woody and Big Mary have been like parents to me. They've given us a home and made a life for Matthew and me. I have to put the sad, hurtful things in the past."

"I don't want you to grow bitter about all this."

"Bitter?" She remembered her father warning her against being bitter. Now Steven seemed worried about that same thing. "No, Steven. I won't be adding bitterness to my list of woes. And besides, my father would have expected me to take care of my brother."

They sat silently for a while, each with thoughts they could not or would not share. Finally she asked what she had been dreading to ask. "Have you heard any news of...of the Vogels?"

"I should have told you, but there's been so much going on."

"What? What have you heard? She's dead! Oh God, she's dead!"

He put an arm around her shoulders and said, "No. She's not. Didn't she tell you before she left? She was going to take Jesse and visit her parents until the smoke cleared." Then he dropped his arm, fearing he had overstepped his bounds.

"Of course!" she said, as though she hadn't even noticed that he had touched her. "I plumb forgot!" Then her face clouded. "But Richard stayed in Pine Crescent. What about Richard?"

Steven shook his head sadly. "He stayed at the telegraph, trying to warn the surrounding towns about the fire, and...."

"Oh no!" she said, her hands squeezed together over her heart. "Not Richard! Oh, poor Clemmie! I must write to her!"

"Actually," he said, "I got a letter from her."

"You did?" She sounded surprised.

"Yes. Can you imagine? They deliver the mail to us in this godforsaken place! Even now, when none of us has an address. The United States mail is a wondrous thing."

"What does she say? She must be heartbroken!"

"I'm sure she is, but she's terribly worried. She had no idea who survived. She asked first about you. She's frantic. She doesn't know what happened to any of us. I need to write to her, but I've been so busy I haven't had the time. I'm glad you asked about her. It reminded me that I can't let another day go by without answering her letter."

"I'll write, too," Sarah said. "I have so much to tell her."

Steven grew silent, and Sarah felt the tension building in him. There was something else he wanted to tell her. She could feel it. "What is it, Steven? You have some other news. What aren't you telling me?"

He turned toward her, his eyes tired and sad. "It's about Lettie."

"Lettie? What about my aunt?"

"She's dead."

"Dead? What do you mean, dead? How? How did she die?"

"Amelia wrote to me and...."

Sarah interrupted with a derisive laugh. "Dear cousin Amelia! And how is the sweet thing?"

"Sarah! Don't behave like this. It scares me."

"I'm sorry," she said, regaining control. "Tell me what happened."

"After Amelia left she seemed to lose her will to live."

"Amelia left? Where did she go?"

"Her uncle arranged a marriage to some old geezer and she...."

Sarah started to laugh. It was the first time she had laughed since the fire and she suddenly felt ashamed. She put her hand over her mouth and looked guiltily at Steven, who was struggling to keep his own laughter from breaking free.

"The old guy had a lot of money and she settled down in his big mansion and began jumping into bed with the gardener, the old man's son from his first marriage, and whoever else she could lure into her clutches."

"Amelia wrote and told you this?" she asked, incredulous.

"No. I'm getting ahead of myself. She wrote and told me about her mother's death. The rest of it I got from my father, who writes and keeps me up on all the gossip."

She looked at him suspiciously. "How long have you known about my cousin and her...her escapades?"

"Months."

"And you chose to tell me today? Why today?"

"I thought I had to tell you about your aunt and it helped explain why she... why she stopped wanting to live." He reached down and absently drew a stick man in the dirt with one finger. Then he looked back at her. "I'm always amazed when I see how people can decide they want to die and then...then up and die. As if there wasn't enough death."

She put her hand on his arm. "It's been difficult for you, hasn't it Steven?"

He smiled wanly at her. "Not so bad. Not nearly as bad as it has been for a lot of these folks."

"I'm sorry about Aunt Lettie. She did the best she could, poor thing."

"Do you remember that day in your uncle's rose garden?" Steven asked suddenly.

She stared at him. "Why are you asking me such a thing?"

"It just occurred to me that it was really a case of Amelia...of the pot calling the kettle black. I'll never get over being such a fool and listening to her."

She slipped a hand into his and held it for a long time as they both stared off into space. Finally she said, in a voice filled with quiet understanding. "It's okay, Steven. In light of all that's happened, it doesn't seem so important anymore. Besides, you're here and you're my friend and it means a lot to me."

He turned to her, his eyes filled with emotions she dared not name. "I'm supposed to be the wise doctor," he said, "and here you are taking care of *me*."

Just then two men approached Steven. One of them looked at Sarah apologetically and said, "Excuse us, Miss. We don't mean to interrupt, but...."

"What is it?" Steven asked, getting to his feet.

One of the men held out his hand and Sarah grimaced. It looked as though it had been burned, but it was hard to tell because it was so red and swollen. "You've got a bad infection. Let's get you over to my tent so we can treat you before you lose that hand."

With barely a nod to Sarah he led the men off toward his tent. Almost as an afterthought, he turned and called back to her. "I'm sorry. Are you going to be around for a while?"

"Don't worry about me," she called to him. "I'll see you before I leave. And Steven...."

He stopped and turned to look at her.

"Have you seen Thor? Thor Nilsson?"

"He's around here somewhere." Then he turned and walked away, his shoulders slumped with fatigue—and something else.

***

She looked around for Woody and found him talking to a group of men and went and stood next to him. "You doing okay?" he asked worriedly.

"I'm fine."

"You sure?"

"Honestly, Woody. You're like an old mother hen."

"If I don't bring you home in good shape Big Mary will have my head," he said, not without some seriousness.

"Have you seen Thor?" she asked innocently.

He turned quickly to stare at her, as if he hadn't heard right. When he saw that she was serious, he said, "No, but someone said he's with Smitheson seeing to some lumber that's being delivered by horse and buggy because the trains ain't able to get here yet."

"I think I'll just wander around for a while," she told him.

"Fine. I want to talk to some of the men over on the north end of town." He laughed and said, "I called this a town. Don't that just beat all?"

"It'll be a town soon," she said as she walked away waving a hand at him. "I'll see you a bit later on."

They stayed around for several more hours, and between listening to groups of people talking, and seeing Steven twice more, she learned about the horror that had been the fire. Everyone remembered seeing it coming as a massive black cloud of smoke, just as she had first seen it. It billowed black and wild, stretching into the sky and blotting out everything, and then began tossing out great bolts of flame. She shuddered when anyone described it, remembering the last time she had seen her father, the flames approaching toward him with a thunderous, hungry roar. The fire had swept through the region like a hurricane, feeding on the dry slashings and the underbrush, consuming most everything in its path. It had burned an area more than nine hundred square miles, and had only stopped when it reached the marshes and cutover land along the Wisconsin border.

The residents of Pine Crescent did have a warning, albeit a short one; but they had grown complacent because they had smelled smoke for months and few believed a fire could actually be so deadly. The only survivors had been those who had taken the warning seriously and had gotten onto a train going north or had luckily been out of town that day.

Steven was one of those who had been out of town. He had been treating a patient twenty miles west of town. Ginger, Lila and another of Ginger's girls had been in St. Paul shopping for new clothes for the girls who worked for Ginger. The Smitheson mill had been completely destroyed, but John Smitheson and Peter Knox had not been at the mill that day. They were at a camp far out of town that had not been in the path of the fire.

She was unbelievably happy that Camp Seven hadn't burned. Red Scanlon, however, had been in town for supplies with Paddy Roark and they were both killed. She could hardly bear the thought of those two carefree men being burned to death in the very timber they had worked so hard to cut down. Most of the dead had been buried in a mass grave, and she thanked God that her own family was buried on the MacKenna land.

Early in the afternoon, it began to rain. "Time for us to get back home," Woody told her.

"I need to say good-bye to Steven," she said. "Then I'll be along."

"I'll be in the cook shanty having coffee. Come there when you're ready."

She was walking between the tents, dodging the puddles that were quickly springing up, when she looked up and saw four men walking toward her; they were John Smitheson, Peter Knox, a man she did not know, and Thor Nilsson.

John was limping badly. When he saw her, his face lit up and he said, "I'll be damned! If you aren't a sight for sore eyes! Tell me you're okay. I'm so all-fired sick of seeing dead people, that I could...." Then he stopped, realizing what he had just said. He took her hand and kissed it, contrite. "I'm sorry, Sarah. That was unbelievably thoughtless of me. I...."

"It's good to see you, Mr. Smitheson. You don't need to apologize to me. I know you, too, have been through hell."

He looked helplessly at her and opened his mouth to say something, but then closed it again. He looked at Thor and said, "We'll meet you at the cook shanty when you're...." He didn't finish his sentence, but instead gave Sarah a small bow and beckoned to the other two men to follow him.

Sarah and Thor stood looking at each other wordlessly. Then Thor said, "What are you doing here? You should be resting."

"I've had enough rest. I can't lie around for the rest of my life. I wanted to know what's going on." She felt uneasy and for some reason apologetic. "I've been useless! Look at this place," she said, looking around her. "It won't ever be the same. Nothing will ever be the same. And I've done nothing to help!"

The mere sight of him had released something in her, and she had to fight the urge to reach for him. But she was determined to steel herself and not fall apart again. She looked up at him, wanting to say something that didn't sound gloomy and self-pitying, but then she suddenly realized how awful he looked.

"Are you okay?" she asked. "You look exhausted."

He took off his cap and ran his fingers through his hair. "I guess I am. It's been...." He didn't finish his sentence but instead turned and walked a short distance and went into one of the tents, closing the flap behind him, never once turning to look at her.

CHAPTER 53

SHE stood staring after him, unsure of what to do, then knew that she must go to him—for both their sakes. She opened the tent flap and stepped inside. There were two cots along either side of the tent with only a small space between them. He was sitting with his elbows on his knees and his head in his hands.

"Thor, I...."

He looked up and saw her standing there and quickly got to his feet. "I need to get back to work," he said jerkily.

"No!" she said, then more softly, "Not yet. We need to talk." She had no idea what she was going to say to him but knew it was time for them to talk straight to each other.

He sat back down as suddenly as he had stood, watching her, wary.

She walked over and sat down on the cot across from him, so close their knees nearly touched. "I've been acting badly since...." She gave a derisive little laugh. "If it hadn't been for Big Mary, I'd still be curled up in bed like a helpless baby."

"You don't need to make any excuses after all you've been through."

"I haven't been through any more than a whole lot of people around here. You know that better than I do, because you've been here helping people. I've helped no one. All I've done is lie about feeling sorry for myself."

He opened his mouth and she motioned for him to be still. "I'm alive, and life is for the living. I can't go on dwelling on what happened."

It was easy to see that he wasn't so sure she really felt this way. "There hasn't been enough time for you to...to get over all this." He made a sweeping gesture with his arm, and then dropped it helplessly.

"You must think I'm trying to deny how I feel. I'm not. I had nearly an entire summer with my father. It was a gift I thought I'd never have, but I had it. White Feather was like a sister to me. I won't ever forget the time we spent together, but they're gone. I hope to a better place."

"But...."

"I know, I know. I'll grieve for them as long as I live." She reached up and touched her brooch. It had always been reassuring and familiar, but was even more so now. She did not speak of their dead baby, but they both felt the words that were not said. Tears sprang to her eyes and she brushed them away with the back of her hand.

"Big Mary told me that my father would expect more of me than—than what I've been these past weeks. She was right."

"I have...I have no words," he managed to say.

She nodded, her eyes closed against the hurt so visible on his face. Then she opened them again and said, "You've lost as much as I have. Your friends. Men you've known and worked with and cared about." Then, softly, "She was your child, too."

They were silent then, not either of them able to look squarely at the other. She got to her feet and walked to the tent opening and lifted the flap. "It's starting to rain. There'll be mud." She turned to look at him. "Do you remember?"

He nodded and came to stand beside her as they both looked out at the rain. Finally she said, "I'm so sorry. I'm so sorry about everything." She put a hand on his arm. "You've done all you can do, and now it is time for you to take care of your own needs. Go home, Thor. Go back to Sweden and forget all of this. Save yourself. From us."

The shock on his face made her take a small step backwards. "Save myself? Go back to Sweden? What are you talking about? I already went back to Sweden and now I'm home. Why in hell would I go back to Sweden?"

"I...I'm sorry. I thought...."

He was glaring at her, angry now. "You thought? What did you think? Do you think I don't know what I'm doing? Do you think I am going to keep on running back and forth across oceans because I don't know what I'm doing?" He threw his hands in the air in despair and went back and sat angrily down on the cot, his head again in his hands mumbling what she assumed were cuss words in his native tongue.

She went and sat down next to him and put her hand on his shoulder and tried to make him look at her. "Of course not. It's just that.... Well, it's just that I know Big Mary wrote to you and told you to come back to Minnesota because...." She stopped.

He lifted his head and looked at her then, his eyes searching her face. "Yaw. Yaw, she wrote to me and told me...."

"And you came home and I am so grateful you cared enough to do the right thing, but now...."

"The right thing?" He looked totally confused.

"I know how responsible you are, and I know that when you learned that I was, well, you know."

"Responsible? Of course I am responsible. What kind of a no-good bastard would I be not to want to take care of you and our child? Do you think I'm worthless as well as stupid and shiftless? Is that what you think?" His anger was escalating, and somehow it made it all easier for her. She understood him best when he was in a state of barely suppressed rage.

"No! I don't think any of those things about you. It's just that after all those years of wanting to go back home and...and do whatever it was you wanted to do for so long.... After all that time and finally getting there and then having to leave again because...." Now it was her turn to throw her hands into the air. "Oh hell! You know what I mean."

He was silent then, his eyes searching her face for she knew not what. After nearly a minute he said with surprising calm. "So that is it. That is what you think." He got to his feet and started pacing back and forth in the small space between the cots, seemingly deep in thought. Then he got down on his knees and reached under one of them and pulled out his rucksack, dug around until he found what he wanted, tossed several items onto the cot and stuffed the rucksack back under it.

Then he sat down across from her, sighed with resignation and began to speak. "I am going to tell you about my journey to Sweden, and the reasons why I returned home," he said with great calm, "and you are going to listen to me without speaking for once."

She nodded weakly and he began, "When I left Minnesota I wanted nothing but to get away from you. I wanted to go back to Sweden to do what I had promised myself for more than ten years I would do. The first thing I did when I got back there was to see my family. My father and mother are on the farm with one of my brothers. They have grown old, and it hurt me to see them so changed." He looked down at the ground for a long time, and when he finally raised his head to look at her his eyes were full of sorrow. "I will never see them again."

"It must have been more than they could bear, seeing you leave again."

"It is my turn to talk."

She closed her mouth and bit her lower lip.

He was speaking very carefully, as if he wanted her to hear every word. "I knew I had to see Annika."

She felt a sharp stab of jealousy and wanted to ask about her beautiful sister, but she bit her lip again and said nothing.

As if reading her thoughts, he said. "I also saw Gretchen. It is hard not to see everyone in such a small village. Gretchen has been married to a man from a neighboring village for five years and has five children—all girls. Annika's husband, Olaf Hanson, died of consumption a year ago. He and Annika had no children."

Her heart was racing, and she felt slightly dizzy, but she could not stop her words. "Is Annika still beautiful?"

Her question confounded him. "What does it matter if she is beautiful? What has it to do with anything?"

"I just thought...I always thought...."

He seemed to consider his next words very carefully. "Everyone says she is as beautiful as ever, but I could no longer see it."

She waited, silent. His hands were clasped loosely between his knees, and he looked down at them, almost as if he didn't recognize them as his own. She wanted to ask him a question but was afraid of the answer, so she sat without speaking, waiting.

"She was waiting for me to come home," he said. "She visited often with my parents and they told her that whenever I wrote to them, I promised that I would be coming home soon."

Sarah sat quietly watching his face. He seemed so calm. He had had a chance to finally marry the woman he had dreamed about for ten years and he had to leave her and his beloved homeland behind because he felt responsible for her. And he had come home to this horror. All because of her.

"Big Mary was wrong to do what she did," Sarah said, the words painful to say but needing to be said.

"You are not listening to me," he said. He reached over and picked up the two things he had taken from his rucksack, and as he did he said, "When I saw her again.... When I saw Annika again, I felt nothing. Not anger. Not love. Nothing. I had been longing for a woman who is cold and selfish, and fighting against my feelings for a woman who is worth more than ten of her.

"It was then that I realized I had spent more than a decade wanting revenge on someone who had actually done me a favor. If she hadn't rejected me I'd never have come to America. And if I hadn't come to America, I would never have found…." He hesitated, then said, "You."

She felt slightly dizzy. Was he trying to mollify her? Well, it wouldn't work. He had a right to his own happiness. "Thor, I…."

He held up a palm to stop her words. "Quiet. You must be quiet now." He paused, then said, "I know I made a mistake, leaving the way I did. I know that if I had stayed things would have been different."

"Different? Surely you aren't blaming yourself for what happened!"

"Not the fire. I am not God. But if I had been here things would have been different, that's all I'm saying. Maybe…." He stopped then, knowing how futile those thoughts could be. He needed to confront what was within his power to confront. "I walked away from you and I don't blame you for hating me for that. But it is time to tell you what I should have told you months ago."

He saw her confusion, and he quickly went on, his eyes on hers, intense. "Remember that first night? When you wouldn't leave the saloon and I feared for your safety?"

"You did?"

"I did. A beautiful woman alone in a town filled with wild men! Can't you see why I wanted you safe?" He seemed to be remembering something. "The longest day I live, I will never forget the way your hair smelled of roses." He went on, unable to stop the flow of words now that they had begun. "When you came to my camp pretending…. Even before I knew you were a woman I was already going out of my mind over you."

"Thor, please…."

He held up his hand again. "Don't interrupt. I need to say these things. I wanted to shoot myself because I cared about a boy. A boy! Can you understand how that felt? Can you understand how crazy that made me?"

She was staring at him, listening, struck dumb by his words.

"Those times we were together were so powerful I couldn't admit it to myself. I kept trying to deny my feelings because I thought what I wanted was in Sweden. I was wrong. I know that now and I want you to know it." He started to say something, then seemed to think better of it and stopped.

He started to speak and stopped again, then finally said, "Gray Wolf wanted you to marry the doctor. I used it as another excuse to leave. I'm ashamed of that. I should have stood my ground like a man. I did not."

She sat silently looking at the firm clean lines of his face, the startling blue of his eyes, dark with intensity. She reached over and put a hand on the side of his face. "Thank you," she whispered. "Thank you for telling me all of that." Then she shyly took her hand away and folded both hands safely back into her lap.

"I can see you do not believe me," he said with a wry laugh. "But I can prove to you that I came back because I wanted to and not because Big Mary told me I must."

She eyed him suspiciously as he handed the documents to her. At first they were nothing but a blur because she was unable to focus. Then, slowly, she saw what they were. One of them was the letter from Big Mary, postmarked July 20th. The second was a receipt for the purchase of a ticket for passage on a ship to America. It was dated July 10th. She kept looking at the two documents, first one and then the other, not understanding what they meant.

"Big Mary mailed her letter to me ten days after I bought my ticket."

She looked at him, uncertain still. "Was this the only letter?"

"Yaw. It was the only letter."

She stared at the two documents, their message as clear as her thoughts were jumbled.

He reached over and lifted her chin so she was forced to look at him. "If you hate me and can never forgive me, I will understand. But at least you know the truth."

"Oh Thor," she said weakly. "I don't hate you. I've never hated you. I never could." She closed her eyes against the tears that burned against her eyelids. "I hate these damnable tears!"

But she couldn't seem to stop herself from the terrible compulsion not to believe him.

He wiped away her tears with his thumbs, and began to speak again, the words pouring out of him in an unfamiliar torrent.

"It wasn't until I saw Annika again that I knew what you meant to me. How I felt about you. How I always felt about you. When you were the Mud Lady and when you were Jesse Williams and when you were Sarah Stewart. I loved you then and I love you now, and I will always love you. Everything I care about is here. *This* is my home. I will never leave again, even if it means watching you marry the doctor and raise *his* children. I will be your friend if I can be nothing else. But I will not go away." It may well have been the longest string of words he had ever uttered, and when he was finished he took a long, deep breath.

She looked up at the roof of the tent. It had begun to rain harder, and she heard the raindrops spattering above them. Then she turned to him, her eyes wet. "I have loved you for a very long time. I, too, should have fought for us."

He sighed wearily. "Between me and Gray Wolf I am afraid it would have been a very big fight."

She nodded and reached up to touch his face. "Do you think we can begin again?" She felt a sharp stab of guilt. Dare she feel this happiness after all that had happened?

"Yaw. Yaw." He stood up and pulled her to her feet, wrapped his arms around her and held her with a gentleness she didn't know he possessed. "Yaw. It will be so," he whispered softly into her hair.

They stood together for a long time letting all the pain of being apart, and all the pain of their unspeakable loss, begin at last to heal.

Finally, after many minutes, she kissed him softly and pulled away from him. "I must go. I wish I did not have to leave you," she said softly, "but Woody will be worried."

He walked to the opening in the tent and raised the flap. The rain had slowed, but the charred earth had already begun to turn into black mud. He picked her up and strode out of the tent toward the cook shanty as though she weighed nothing; just as he had done that night so long ago.

"I'm able to walk, you know," she said.

"And I am able to carry you," he whispered into her hair.

When they reached the cook shanty he stepped inside and his eyes searched until he saw Woody. He motioned with his chin to him and Woody hobbled over looking worried because Sarah hadn't arrived under her own power. Everyone in the tent was watching, including Lila, who seemed to have lost her ability to stand and had sunk weakly onto a bench.

"Get the wagon and take Sarah home. She must rest now."

Woody gulped and nodded. "Yeah, Boss."

"I'm not your boss!" Thor corrected.

"Yes Sir," Woody said, hobbling out of the tent.

"You're acting like his boss," Sarah murmured softly into his ear, inhaling the scent of him. It did not surprise her that he still smelled of the pine forest.

"Old habits die hard," he replied.

She looked around the shanty at all the people who were watching them. Some of them had remained after the fire, and some of them were people who had come to help; but all of them were working to rebuild the town. Pine Crescent would rise again from the corpses of the burned timber, and in that she saw a glimmer of hope for the future.

She tightened her arms around Thor's neck and kissed him firmly on the mouth for everyone to see. She *really was* Thor Nilsson's woman, and now she knew it. He had done all he could do, both with words and with actions, to make it clear to her. At long last she was ready to accept the truth of it.

He carried her out to where Woody was just pulling up with the wagon. He lifted her easily up onto the seat, kissed her gently on the forehead and said to Woody, "Keep her safe until I get home."

He smiled at Sarah and said, "Soon. I will be home soon."

Woody grinned at Thor as he flicked the reins, and they rode away from the small cluster of tents. Sarah had come to Pine Crescent in sadness, and he was bringing her home as a happy woman; and because of that, he knew she would be greeted by perhaps even a happier one.

Sarah twisted around in the seat and watched Thor until she could no longer make him out through the rain and the fading light. Then she turned and folded her hands in her lap, truly content for the first time in many months. Pine Crescent was being rebuilt. Much of the white pine was gone, but the land would heal—just as the people would. And in the western sky a small break appeared in the clouds.